CAPITAL CITY

CAPITAL CITY

THE URBAN GRIOT

www.urbanbooks.net

Urban Books
1199 Straight Path
West Babylon, NY 11704

ISBN- 13: 978-1-60162-134-4
ISBN- 10: 1-60162-134-5

First Printing (Urban Books) December 2008
Printed in the United States of America

10 9 8 7 6 5 4 3 2 1

This is a work of fiction. Any references or similarities to actual events, real people, living, or dead, or to real locales are intended to give the novel a sense of reality. Any similarity in other names, characters, places, and incidents is entirely coincidental.

Distributed by Kensington Publishing Corp.
Submit Wholesale Orders to:
Kensington Publishing Corp.
C/O Penguin Group (USA) Inc.
Attention: Order Processing
405 Murray Hill Parkway
East Rutherford, NJ 07073-2316
Phone: 1-800-526-0275
Fax: 1-800-227-9604

They walk in circles
hungry
dancing to the white man's tunes
scrambling
to get a piece of the action.

But once the music stops
the playtime is over.
—POW!
Six feet under.
Who's up next?

Musical Chairs

In the tradition
of Iceberg Slim, Donald Goines, and Chester Himes.

For the hardcore stories
of Claude Brown, Eldridge Cleaver, and Malcolm X.

And in honor of the masters;
Ralph Ellison, James Baldwin, and Richard Wright.

I dedicate this book to the brothers from
New York to L.A., Detroit to Houston, and Jamaica to
Africa.

CAPITAL CITY

CHAPTER 1

Butterman

Steve is dying to jump into my car.

"Come on, Butterman, gi'me a ride home."

"I'm not goin'nat way, Joe."

"Where you goin'?"

"I'm 'bout to go up UDC."

He smiles through crooked-ass yellow teeth. "What, 'chu got a pretty bitch up there, you'n?"

"Naw."

"Well, yo, you know niggas gon' be gettin' paid wit' Christmas comin' up and all."

Steve looks serious now, and he's talking my language: business.

"Yeah, I'm gon' set us up for two ounces t'night. Matter of fact, tell Rudy to beep me if you see 'im."

"Yeah, I just seen'nat nigga up U Street a couple of minutes ago. You might be able t' ride up there and catch 'im."

"Aw'ight, well, let me get out'a here then. I'll catch you later on."

Steve is out here shaking like he's cold as shit. But I don't have time to drive him home. He need to buy a better coat instead of wearing that cheap, plastic-looking, black nylon jacket he got on. I mean, I pay these niggas enough money to buy some nice gear; they just blow it on stupid shit all the time.

I'm riding up Fourteenth Street Northwest. I'm about to turn west. Then I'll head north up Connecticut Avenue to get to UDC before Wes gets out of school at two o'clock.

"YO, DA FUCKIN' LIGHT IS GREEN!" I shout. I hate that shit. People get to the light and start daydreaming. Stupid-ass white girl.

TLC on the radio. They kicking it. I'd bang all of them; just let me meet them. I got game for all the girls, *including* famous singers. Mary J. Blige can get some of this too.

I luck up and get a parking spot right out in front of the school. That's good timing; they're just getting out now. I jump out and stand in front of my car, waiting.

Here comes this girl Brenda. She's smoothly brown-skinned with long-ass hair running halfway down her back, and a phat-ass body—phat to death! But I banged her already and her shit wasn't all that good.

"Ay, Butterman."

I smile. "What's up, girl?"

"Nothin'. Who you up here for?"

She all excited and shit. I should give some girl name just to fuck with her, but I'm not gon' do that; she might mess up my play with her girlfriend Latrell. I booked Latrell at the Ritz last Sunday night. She a light-skinned girl with her own money. She goes to American University, and she's bad as shit!

"I'm out here to check on my boy Wes. You know 'im, right?" I ask Brenda.

She looks back toward the school. "Yeah, he must still be in'nat building."

"Yeah, well, that's what I'm up here for."

"Oh," Brenda says. She acts like she's disappointed. I guess she's wishing I could have came up here to see her.

"Aw'ight, I'll catch'chu," I tell her. She cock-blocking now, and it's all kinds of pretty girls coming up out of this school.

"Oh, okay den. Call me, all right."

"Yeah, aw'ight." *Jus' get da hell out'a here!* I'm thinking. Damn, I hate when girls just sit around you with nothing to say!

She walks toward the Van Ness Metro station.

Yeah, here comes Wes! He's wearing this dark blue trench coat, probably a London Fog. But Joe needs to stop dressing like an old-ass man and buy some hip gear. For real!

"YO, WES, what's up? Come here, man."

I walk over to him. He frowns at me like I'm sweating him. Fuck it, I am. I know this nigga needs some money. He needs to stop fronting.

"What's going on?" he asks me.

"Stop lookin' all down an' shit, man. Christmas is right around the corna."

"Yeah, just another day for Mr. Charlie to collect black peoples' checks."

"Look, man, you not in school now, so stop pushin' that political shit."

His eyes follow this sexy-looking tan-skinned girl walking across the street. She's probably going into Taco Bell. She a cute little something, wearing a three-quarter-length tan leather coat, like mine. But my joint got the cowboy tassels hanging down from the sleeves and on the back. Wes got good taste though.

"You want me to call her for you, man?" I ask him with a smile.

Wes breaks out of his trance. "Hunh? Oh, no."

"You starin' at her like you wanna eat her shit, you'n."

I laugh to try and lighten him up.

"Yeah, she's probably more your type anyway," he says.

"What'chu mean by dat?"

"She probably wants it fast and glamorous, like this car you have."

He looks at my white Mitsubishi 3000 GT. I just got the shit a month ago. I was out in Alexandria, Virginia, when these bammas shot up my white 300 Z Turbo, thinking I was somebody else because I had tinted windows. That was it for me! Too many guys in trouble got Zs.

"That's why I'm tryin' ta bring you in, Wes. When you start makin' money wit' me, you can *pick* the girls you want. For real!"

Wes frowns. "Yup, right before I go to jail."

I shake my head and get serious. "Look, man, I'm gon' have you jus' dealin' wit' da money. You ain't gon' be sellin'. I need you to be like, my banker. 'Cause I'm 'bout ta cut a lot'a niggas loose."

Wes finally smiles. "Look, J, I don't think we're in a movie here, so it's not as easy as you make it sound. Okay?"

I smile and shake my head again. He amazes me. Anybody else would be dying to be down, but you can't trust most of them. That's why I'm trying to cut a lot of these runners loose now.

"You got my beeper number, right?" I ask him.

"It's on my dresser at home. And you better get a move on."

He points behind me, where a meter maid is eying my car.

"Oh shit!" I yell. "Yo, I'm 'bout to move now."

"Okay," she says, grinning in her blue uniform and

hat. D.C. Parking Authority ain't no joke! These parking ticketers act like they get extra paychecks for writing tickets.

Wes is heading for the Metro. That's all right. He's gonna be down soon, I'm telling you. I got everything all mapped out. All I have to do is make a few more thousand and make that connection in New York.

I'm gon' fuck Max's head up. He thinks he the only one that got slammin'-ass ounces in D.C. I'm gonna go up to New York, buy a quarter-kilo and blow you'n out of the water. For real! He carrying me now, talking that trash he talk. But wait when I make my move. He'll see. I'm gon' have it going on.

I'm heading back to Georgia Avenue now. I got all kinds of stuff to do today. First I have to get my hair cut; then I have to get fitted at this tuxedo place for my cousin's wedding next week; and I have to touch base with Max for those two ounces—damn, I hate dealing with that loser. And then I have to talk to my runners before I fly to stay with my girl in Atlanta this weekend.

Damn, I almost forgot! I have to pick up Keisha and Little Red to see my boy Red at Lorton today. Red got four years for beating down this dude from Baltimore; dude thought Red was a punk. Man, Red beat down many niggas back in the day. He big as a linebacker for the Redskins now.

Tub? Man, that was my straight nigga. He went down when we had a shoot-out with some crew from Southwest last year. DeShawn shot two of their boys. But nobody seen him since. You'n just up and disappeared on us. And John-John? Aw, man, that nigga got strung out on drugs and fell in love. He got this girl pregnant and shit. He was always girlin' anyway. He didn't have the stomach for this drug game. Joe was always acting paranoid. So me? I have to start the shit all over again. And by the time Red get out, we gonna have a cartel. But first, I have to get rid of these stupid-ass runners. These niggas don't know their face from their ass.

I walk inside my favorite barbershop on Georgia Ave.

"Hey, it's the man named Butter!" shouts Georgie, the head barber. Georgie been cutting heads for *years*. He's always telling us about it.

"Yeah, it's him, the man wit' all the women," I holler back.

I take a seat in the small cushioned chair and grab a *Jet* magazine. It's about four of us waiting and only three barbers cutting heads today.

"Yo, where Gene at?" I ask Georgie. Georgie has thick gray hair and a tanned complexion. His skin shines like shit. More than mine!

"That young'un don't wanna make no money," he says. "You young'uns t'day just don't value how much hard work can do for you. Why, me and my brother Isaac used to be hustlin' all up and down this avenue: washin' cars, carrying groceries for old ladies and everything else you could do to make a buck." He smiles at me while cutting this older guy's head. "You know that's why they call me Georgie, right?"

"Yeah." *I done heard the shit a million times before,* I think to myself. But I wonder if Georgie sold any drugs. He probably did. Everybody has to put in some illegal time before they can really house shit, you know. That's how all them rich-ass white people got theirs.

"Yeah, I just don't know about us black people t'day," Georgie says. He shakes his head to the middle-aged brown-skinned man wearing a business suit and tie in his chair.

Georgie is still talking that old-timer shit: "I mean, wit' all the skills these young'uns have, and the educational opportunities and everything, I just don't see what their problem is."

"They need money and they're tired of being poor," I instigate, just to get Georgie started.

He stops and turns off his clippers, looking at me. "Let me tell you somethin', son: all the money in the world can't make a sick man healthy unless he knows *how* he's sick. And if he don't *know* he's sick, then the money gon' kill 'im jus' like the drugs, jus' like the whiskey and these scandalous and dirty women."

Niggas start lunchin' when Georgie says "scandalous and dirty women." But he still got his mouth running while cutting dude's head.

"Have you ever heard the dumb-man's joke about the Martian that came to earth?" he asks me.

I smile. "Naw."

Shit is about to get good now. I love these damn "dumb-man's jokes" he talks about. That's that old-timer shit, when niggas ain't have no money to go to the movies. They just sat back and told crazy-ass stories.

The barbershop is quiet as hell now. We all waiting to hear this dumb-man's joke.

"Well, a green Martian came to earth and met a black man, a white man, an' a Korean. And he said to all three of them, 'Which one of you is the smartest?' The black man scratched his head and said, 'Well, I don't know.' The white man looked him in the eye and said, 'Whoever has studied the hardest.' And the Korean bowed and said, 'The man who has progressed today more than he has progressed yesterday and less than he will progress tomorrow.' Then the Martian asked, 'If I could give you anything in this world that you want, what would that thing be?' The black man jumped up and down and said, 'I want all the money in the world.' The white man said,

'Love and happiness.' And the Korean said, 'If such a thing could be achieved on this earth, then I would ask to live forever healthy.' So the white man was given a beautiful wife who cooked, cleaned and had the best—excuse my French—pussy in the world. The Korean lived to see Judgment Day. And the greedy nigga was rich for about five years before he spent up all his money. Then he went back to the Martian for another wish. And the Martian said, 'I gave you what you asked for the first time. But I'm a fair man, so what would you like to have now?' And the black man looked down at his feet and then looked the Martian in the eye and scratched his head. 'Well, I think I would like to have some brains this time. 'Cause da good Lawd knows I'm *ti'ed* of bein' stupid.' "

Niggas start laughing like hell. Georgie stops cutting until dude in the chair gets back to normal. I knew this shit would happen. That's why I led Georgie on like I did. That old-timer shit is a trip.

It's a quarter to four. I got a fresh, high-rounded, temple-tape cut. Now I'm rushing over to Keisha's house to get her and Little Red to head to Lorton. When I get to her house on Fifth Street Northwest, she and Little Red are waiting on the patio outside in the cold.

"Why you got him out in the cold like this?" I ask her, jumping out to open the door for them.

" 'Cause you thirty minutes late and I was ti'ed of waitin' in'na house," she says. Keisha always had that damn mouth of hers. I don't see how Red was able to put up with her all these damn years.

Keisha's dark-skinned with that shiny skin like Georgie. Little Red is brown, browner than Red but lighter than her. He don't have rusty brown hair like Red either. We just call him Little Red because he's Red's son.

"Now you know we gotta rush up dere befo' Lorton visitin' hours is ova wit', you'n."

This girl never could talk too damn well, to me. But fuck it, it's Red's girl.

"I know that shit," I tell her.

"Wail, you bes' ack like you wanna get to it den."

I shake my head and turn on my radio. Babyface and Toni Braxton are on.

"Naw, Joe. I'on wanna listen t' dat," Keisha says, pulling out a tape. "Dis Junk Yard."

"Ruff It Off?" I ask her.

She smiles. "Yay'ah."

We head for I-95 South with this big-butt girl bouncing in my new car to this Junk Yard single: "Ruff it off! Ruff, ruff, ruff it off!"

"Yo, do you have ta act all crazy in my shit?" I ask her.

She looks at me and rolls her eyes. "Joe, I mean, 'nis ride is like dat 'n all, but ain't nobody gon' hurt'cha damn car."

I shake my head and keep driving. Little Red is in the back seat, chilling.

"Li'l Red? You cool back there, shaw'?"

He don't even answer me. He nods his head and smiles.

"Li'l Red a cool nigga," I say to his mother.

She looks at me like I said something wrong. "My son is not a nigga, okay?"

I start laughing. "Girl, you know what I mean."

"No I don't. And I'm ti'ed of all y'all bammas callin' people nigga dis and nigga dat."

"Oh, like *you* speak proper English."

"I ain't say nothin' 'bout propa English. What I'm sayin', Joe, is I don't want nobody callin' *my* son a nigga. He is not a nigga. My son is a li'l human bein'. A *black* human bein'. And I want him t' be proud of himself and not a nigga."

She has a point, so I don't say nothing else about it on our ride to Lorton. Maybe I should stop saying "nigga." But I mean, once you get used to saying it, it's like a habit.

We get to Lorton and give our names and I.D. at the sign-in table. Red comes out to the visiting table looking healthy as shit and built like a Mack truck.

He salutes me, pumping his fists, "Y-o-o-o, nigga!"

I smile at Keisha, then look back to Red. But Keisha jumps in before I can say anything.

"Mitchell, why mus' y'all always use that word 'nigga'?"

" 'Cause, he my nigga," Red answers.

I laugh like shit.

"That's not funny, Butterman. I don't see what's so funny, *Jeffrey*."

Keisha looks mad as shit. She even used my real name.

Red says, "Yo, cool out. Aw'ight?"

"No, I ain't gon' fuckin' cool out. *Y'all* need t' *cool out* wit' all dat nigga shit."

Red shakes his head. I know what he's thinking: *Yo, why couldn't you leave this damn girl home and jus' bring my son up here ta see me?* We smile at our hidden message.

Keisha stands abruptly. "Well, I have to go t' *da women's room*, not the *niggas' room*."

Red shakes his head and grins. "She trippin', man. So what's up?" he asks me seriously, playing with his cool-ass son.

"I'm still tryin' t' pull all the strings together," I tell him. Honestly I don't know, because that nigga Wes is acting like a girl afraid of dick.

"So what's up wit'cha banker boy?" Red asks me.

I smile, thinking that Red knows me well. "Man, you'n actin' like he don't want no money, Joe."

Red's nostrils flare like a dragon; it's the look he gives niggas before he kicks somebody's ass. "Well, fuck that nigga, man! Is it anybody else you can trust wit' da money?"

"Naw, man, that's why I'm sweatin'nis nigga. I mean, he got that brotherly love that I was tellin' you about."

Red looks frustrated. "Man, fuck dat *'brotherly love'* shit you keep stressin'! Niggas ain't got no love, man. It's all a money thing now."

"What about us?" I ask. I almost sound like a girl, an innocent virgin again. But the shit came out my mouth, so I can't take it back.

"We *is* brothers, nigga! We is brothers!" Red looks strongly at his son. "And he ya nephew. You hear me? He ya nephew."

We quiet down and talk small talk when Keisha comes back to the table. And when it's time to leave, Red looks at me and says, "Yo, make sure you put some flowers on Tub's grave next Wednesday. That nigga would'a been twenty-four."

We get back to the District by seven-thirty. I drop Keisha and Little Red off and beep Max at a pay phone. He calls me back five minutes later.

"Who dis?"

"It's B."

Max laughs over the receiver. "Oh, what's up, Butter-bitch?"

See, that's why I hate this nigga! "Yo, man, I need two by Tuesday. I'll give you eighteen hundred for 'em."

"Eighteen hundred? What'chall niggas think I'm stupid? I know it's Christmas time, punk. I want a grand apiece like usual."

"Man, you crazy! I heard you been cuttin' that nine-hundred deal for other niggas."

"Look, man, take it or buy some weak shit from some-body else. I hear Leon got some powder this week."

Leon gave his runners some fucked-up 'caine that peo-ple were getting sick off of. Nobody fucks with him like that no more.

"Yeah, whatever, man."

Max laughs and hangs up. I see how he's trying to play things though; he's gon' try to ride out the holiday season. Niggas get just like the white man, sooner or later. For real! That's why I have to get with that New York connection: them niggas that Bink know.

I rush back to my plush-ass apartment in Silver Spring and check my answering machine for my girl's phone call.

"Yes, it's me, and I can see that you're not *home*, but I'm still horny, so I'm gon' go out and buy me some dick t'night."

BEEP!

She trippin'. I'm gon' tear that ass to pieces when I get down there tonight. It's a quarter after eight now, so I just missed her call by fifteen minutes.

I start to grab my bags. Then the phone rings.

"Hello."

"Guess who, baby?"

"Janet Jackson."

"Janet Jackson?"

"Oh, oh, oh, it's you, baby. What's up?"

She sucks her teeth. "Yeah, aw'ight. I got'cha Janet Jackson."

"Yeah, and I got your go-out-and-buy-me-some-dick shit, too."

She laughs. "So you got your plane ticket and every-thing?"

"Yeah. Did you get us a hotel room?"

"Yeah."

I shake my head and smile. "I still can't believe they don't let'chall have male guests at Spelman."

"Baby, this is an old-fashioned school based on principles."

I laugh. "Then how you get in there?"

"Funny. 'Cause I was smart; that's how."

"If they knew how nasty you are, they would expel you."

"Are you complaining?" she asks seductively.

I smile. "Naw."

"Oh, 'cause I'm only nasty with you, sweetie."

Yo, my dick is hard as a rock. We gonna fuck something fierce tonight.

"Well, I'm on my way, aw'ight."

"All right; I'm doin' leg exercises for you, baby."

She laughs because she know that her nasty mouth is turning me on. But don't get the wrong idea about my girl; she's sweet as hell and fun to be with. She's dark-brown-skinned with beautiful model features and an hourglass body. Young'uns were sweating her like shit when she went to La Reine Catholic School for girls in Suitland. But she was on *my* Jimmy. People say it was because I was light-skinned with curly hair and money. I mean, I don't really care, because the way I figure, a girl has to like you for some reason. Some girls like niggas because they're athletes, you know?

I beep a couple of my runners on an outside pay phone and tell them to finish selling what they got and hold the money until I get back Monday morning. I wouldn't usually tell them no shit like that, but I only have about three hundred dollars left on the street from this week, so it wouldn't be too much of a loss. But I swear, I'm getting tired of these dumb-ass bammas losing money and claiming robbery. That's why I'm about to cut some of these runners loose and start selling ounces.

I park my car in the garage for the weekend. I call a cab to take me to the Silver Spring Metro station. I'm on my way to Atlanta to be with my sweetheart. And yo, I love Toya to death! I'd die for that girl. And she'd die for me.

Shank

Stick-up kids is out t' tax.

Nice & Smooth, sampled by Gang Starr: "Just To Get A Rep." But I ain't out to get no rep; I need some money to pay my rent. I'm not trying to be homeless. Fuck that shit! Somebody's getting robbed tonight, and I know just the motherfuckers: some bamma-ass hustlers.

It's some niggas that hustle up near Ninth Street Northwest. They just started getting paid, so I know they don't have no major fire power yet. And I got my .38 for their asses. I throw on my black leather jacket and my black knit hat and grab my shades. It should be an 82 bus coming down Rhode Island Avenue any minute now.

Shit! The bus is taking all day. I might as well start walking down.

My mom probably thinking I'm gonna lose the lease on my apartment. I got news for her ass. I'm keeping this crib. Fuck being homeless! I'm not KRS-1, and it's already too many homeless motherfuckers in D.C.—the nation's capital and shit!

All the bus stops have that *Bodyguard* movie poster. I mean, it was an all right movie, but they only talking all that shit about it because Whitney Houston is starring in her first film. I still can't believe she married Bobby Brown. I wonder if she got some good ass.

Here comes the bus now. I put my shades on before I get on. I don't like people staring at me on the buses, so I try to stay incognito.

"I do what the hell I wanna do, got'dammit! You don't tell me what I can and can't do! I'm a MAN!"

These crazy niggas be trippin' on the buses. This bum is out his fucking mind, talking to himself.

"Do I tell you what to do? No. So don't tell me a FUCKIN' thing!"

I get off the bus at Eighth and Rhode Island Northeast. I have to walk under the Metro bridge and catch a G bus to Northwest. It's about nine-thirty. And it's Friday night, so I know them young'uns are out there.

This old lady looks scared as hell when I walk past her. She's coming out of McDonald's and she probably thinks I'm out to rob her since I'm dressed in all black with shades on at nighttime. I can't blame her for being cautious. But I ain't the type to rob old ladies and shit like that. You go to jail for that shit, eventually. I only rob motherfuckers in the game: drug dealers, other thieves and addicts.

This shit is more dangerous because these niggas will shoot as fast as I will. But I don't feel that you should bring regular people into this shit. You know what I'm saying? They work hard and honestly for their money. But if I don't have nobody else to rob . . . I don't know. I just don't know.

I'm waiting for the G bus on Fourth Street now. This bus is taking all day. Or I guess I should say night. But who gives a fuck? I'm out of school now anyway. Niggas thought I wasn't gon' graduate. But Anacostia was easy. All you had to do was show up and do a little bit of homework. Them motherfuckers who failed or dropped out didn't wanna do nothing.

Ever since I was an infant I knew I was different. Paid no attention to my moms when she rifted.

Yeah, that's my nigga Redman. He from Jersey too. But

I think Redman say he from Newark. That's where all them hardcore, New York-type Jersey niggas are from. Naughty By Nature from East Orange. My cousin Peanut used to hang back there. He had this bad-ass redbone bitch up that joint he used to stay with. And Queen Latifah from Jersey; The Lords of the Underground and The Poor Righteous Teachers are from around my old way in Trenton. They ain't came out with no new records yet. *You, black man! Tell the real story!* Man, they were like dat!

I'm just standing out here reminiscing. Here comes the bus now, and it's a good thing it came, because these young'uns about to get killed, staring at me like they hard. I'd fuck them punk-ass bammas up. They better find themselves some toys to play with. Like Rakim said, "I ain't no joke!"

I get off the G bus at Rhode Island and Georgia Avenues Northwest, and walk into the 7-Eleven. I buy an apple juice and down the shit. Now let me stroll around here and take care of business.

Oh my God! I don't believe this shit. These motherfuckers out here gambling inside of an alley. How easy can you make a stick-up? I knew these young'uns were bammas. Like Ice T says, "I ain't new ta dis."

I ease up on these niggas and put my back to the wall so I can see everything.

I take my shades off so these niggas can see my eyes. You know if you got a motherfucker by watching his eyes flicker. And mine stay steady as steel.

"What's up, what's up?" I ask with a smile.

I got my trey-eight pointed at this first dude wearing a green bomber jacket.

"Yo, man," he says. He got his mouth wide open like he about to piss on himself.

"Back da fuck up off the money!" I yell. I'm staring at

these motherfuckers like I could kill them with my eyeballs. I stay glued to the wall. And if anybody comes running around this corner trying to be a hero, they gonna make the *Washington Post*.

"Line'na fuck up and empty y'all pockets!" They do it, like pussies. "Now throw the money in'na pile!" I tell them. "You, in the green bomber, pick that shit up and give it to me."

He reaches out his hand with the fumbled money in his grasp.

I frown at him. "Motherfucka, make that shit neat. 'Cause I don't want no money fallin' out my hands."

He straightens out the bills. I look past him to the fifth nigga, standing in the back of the line. Joe looks edgy, like he got a gun.

"Yo, you'n in'na back? Get'cha ass up here!"

He walks to the front, shaking like shit. I got my .38 pointed at his heart.

"You packin', ma-fucka? Is you packin'?"

"Yo, man—"

"Shut da hell up and get'cha hands in'na air." He does the shit. And he can't look me in the eyes. He's a bitch with a gun. "Where da fuck is it at?"

"In my belt, man, please."

I put my .38 muzzle to his stomach and pull his gun out with my left hand. He got a .22; a piece of shit. I knew these niggas were bammas when I checked them last week. But I didn't think it was gonna be *this* easy.

"Anybody else got a gun?" I ask, staring.

They shake their heads. "Naw."

"Anybody want revenge?" Nobody says nothing. "Aw'ight, well, if anybody wants to know, motherfuckin' Shank did it. And if they got beef, then look my name up in'na fuckin' Yellow Pages under K, for killas." I stick the

.22 inside my pants pocket and speed off with my trey-eight inside my jacket.

Them young'uns had seven hundred and fifty-two dollars. That ain't bad for a three-minute hit.

I wonder who they working for. Whoever it is, they didn't teach them much of shit. You never gamble when you supposed to be making money. You never walk your whole crew into an alley either. And you always keep a gun someplace where you can pull that shit in a flash. I mean, that nigga *did* have the gun ready, but he was a bitch. Then again, if he would have missed . . . *It's curtains, Mugsy! Curtains!*

I'm laughing at the shit now. Punk-ass motherfuckers.

I call up to the Howard Towers Plaza to see if my pretty bitch is there. I let the phone ring five times and her answering machine comes on. Fuck it, I hang up. I'll catch her tomorrow. I should call back and tell her to stay her ass in the house tomorrow so I can get some pussy when I want it. But fuck it, let me head back home.

I get back in the crib in time to catch the last couple of minutes of *Def Comedy Jam*. Martin Lawrence a funny motherfucker. Here comes Russell Simmons.

That nigga dresses plain as hell. Man, if I had the kind of money he got, I'd wear nothing but dope shit. I'd dress like my man Bink. That motherfucker got gear.

This TV I bought from Benny is working good. Then again, it better, because I gave that motherfucker a hundred dollars for it. That's all in the code of the game; I don't rob other niggas when they got straight-up merchandise for sale. It's just like a thieves' creed. But some people go by their own rules. Them niggas end up dead or in jail.

Me? I just need enough money to get hip to some other game. Maybe I should go in with Benny and them. They warehouse their stolen shit. But you know, the cops might raid them after a while. It just don't seem too stable.

I need to hook up with some kind of racket where I can get some steady cash. I should ask that nigga Bink if I could get in with them. But I don't know. Bink keeps his game pretty tight. That's my boy though!

Damn, I'm tired. I might as well throw a tape in my box and nod out.

I put in Showbiz & A.G. Them niggas came off!:

The Giant is great! So step back. I know you were told, black, about the Soul Clap.

Wes

Another day, another struggle. But without a struggle there is no victory.

I finally get up out of bed to take a shower after just watching my clock for the last half-hour. My mother is due to call me any minute. There goes the phone now and I'm drenched.

I dash to my bedroom with shower water dripping all over my rug.

"Hello."

"Yeah, Raymond, now you make sure you set up everything and you talk to the fat white man named Eddie at the entrance to find out where all my stuff is. And remember that you don't have to get the full price for everything that you sell. You can make bargains where you see fit. And hang in there until at least six o'clock, because a lot of times the crowds come in late. Okay?"

"Okay, Mom."

"All right then, I'll talk to you tonight or either tomorrow morning."

My mother hangs up. I lay softly across my bed, naked. I'm wishing I had a beautiful black woman naked with me. Oh, how I would caress her and kiss her and cuddle her until she couldn't take it any longer. Then she'd say, "Raymond, I'm yours. Take me. I love you dearly."

My penis sits erect at even the thought of any romantic encounter. And although I have a dedicated girlfriend, I still have wet dreams at night. I can't seem to help it. My lust is strong.

I get dressed and look outside to see how the weather is. It looks windy. WKYS radio says it's going to be forty degrees.

I lock my apartment door and head to the Fort Totten Metro station. I get there and buy a rail pass to wait for the train. A lovely brown-skinned sister is waiting with me. She looks to be about my age and glowing with confidence.

"Hi," I say cheerfully.

"Hi," she responds, uninterested.

She wears gold loop earrings and a long purple coat that shines like it's waterproof.

"Is that coat waterproof?" I ask her.

She looks at me confusingly. "No. Why you ask me that?"

I smile. "Well, it sort of has that glazed appearance that waterproof things have."

She smirks. "Well, *no*, it's not waterproof," she repeats, shaking her head.

Was it something that I said, or is she simply overreacting? Or maybe I need to douse my contact lenses in more solution. No, it can't be that. I see just fine.

The train comes and the brown sister with the waxed purple coat walks to the next car. I doubt if she's trying to avoid me, but it's still irritating.

I sit down adjacent to an older brother in the seats to my left. It's early Saturday morning so the train is nearly empty.

"Hi you doin', brotherman?" he asks me.

"I'm hanging on a string, trying to pull myself in," I respond.

He laughs. "So whadda ya think about Bill Clinton as president?"

"Well, I don't honestly think he cares much about my generation, especially after he dissed Sister Souljah and Jesse Jackson."

"Unh-hunh. But what about him being able to get us more jobs and things?"

"It depends on what 'us' you're referring to. Because if you mean politically conservative blacks, whatever that means, yeah, he'll probably get *them* further employment. But if you're talking about the masses of disenfranchised blacks, then no, I don't think he'll do anything."

The brother nods his head. "Well, at least we got a Democrat in office, 'cause I swear, them damn Republicans were reversing the entire country. I mean, Reagan and Bush have just taken back everything that we gained over the past thirty years."

"Oh yeah. Like what?" I challenge. I'm starting to get one of those vibes that tells me this brother is one of those who just blows hot air. He probably didn't even bother to vote.

"You know, like civil rights and stuff," he says, grinning.

"What particular things are you referring to?"

"Well, a lot of things."

"Like what?"

He laughs, probably feeling uncomfortable. I bet he thought he could just blow some wind my way and had no idea that I happen to be a political science major. I'm about to graduate in one more semester.

"You puttin' me on the spot, ain't'cha?" he asks, chuckling to himself.

"Well, you know, what I've found is that many American citizens, white and black, have become professional complainers. At the same time, they have not even the slightest idea of how politics work, nor do they participate in voting. Like for example: Did you vote for Bill Clinton last month?"

He laughs again. "Naw, li'l brother. You got me there. What are you, a student of politics or something?" he asks me embarrassingly.

"Yeah, I'm about to graduate next term from the UDC."

He smiles broadly. "Unh-hunh. So I'm sitting here with a damn political expert, running my damn mouth off and got caught."

"I wouldn't call myself an expert, but I would say that I know more about the political process than ninety percent of Americans." *And more than ninety-nine percent of blacks*, I'm thinking.

"I bet you do," he say, chuckling some more. "So, could you ever see yourself running for some type of office, young brother?"

"Well, eventually, I might have to."

I stand up at my stop: Judiciary Square.

"Keep up the good work, young brother."

I smile at him, nod and step off the train.

I walk to Seventh and Pennsylvania Avenue Northwest, through the clean and empty downtown streets to wait for a 36 bus. It arrives in less than five minutes. We pass the Capitol building. It amazes me that it just sits there in stone-throwing distance while all the blacks who complain about this country's system pay no attention to this building—as if it doesn't really exist. I tell you, it's amazing!

I arrive at the African Market Festival on Pennsylvania Avenue Southeast, by eleven a.m. and talk to the white man—who, ironically, manages the predominantly black flea market. Washington, D.C., is seventy percent black, but you wouldn't know it from the local business community. The heavy-set white man collects everything for me as I set up my mother's table. I have off from my telemarketing job today, so I offered to take over my mother's stand while she goes to Baltimore for a Coalition of Black Women meeting. They'll probably discuss the elected officials like Senator Carol Moseley-Braun from Illinois; Maxine Waters, the congresswoman from California; Sharon Pratt Kelly, the mayor here in D.C.; and some other black women leaders abroad.

There will be more black congresspeople in office when President-elect Bill Clinton takes over in January, 1993, than there has ever been in history. I have to do some research to see if that includes the Reconstruction Era of the 1870s. But all these new Blacks in office won't change anything. The gap between them and the masses is too wide. My knowledge base is expanding past the grasp of my fellow generation right now. And that scares me, because I'll be another brother that can't affect present situations; I'll be too mentally distant.

"Hi you doin'?" asks a round-bellied and gray-haired brother. He's setting up at the table across from me.

"I'm all right," I say, forcing myself to smile. I don't really feel friendly yet. I really wanted to remain home and dream about making love to a black woman who likes to have sex three times more than my present girlfriend does. Sex can be used as an excellent stress releaser, you know.

"So you're Charlene's son?" he asks me, now extending his hand.

I shake it politely and say, "Yeah, that's me."

"Well, I see you don't have red hair or freckles like she does," he responds amusingly.

"Nope, I take after my father."

He sorrows up. "Yeah, I heard about that deal in Germany," he says. "But that's just how this country'll do us. I remember when Vietnam was trying to draft my son." He shakes his head fiercely. "No way, Jose. I sent my son down South, and when they went for him down there, I told him to come back home. And when they came back again, I sent him to my brother's home in Memphis, Tennessee."

I laugh. He's starting to lighten me up.

"What's your name?" I ask him.

"Tony. And yours is Raymond, right?"

"Yeah, I guess my mother talks all about me graduating from college this spring."

"She won't stop one minute," he says jokingly. He tosses his hand on my shoulder. "But it's always good to see our young men doing the right thing, you know. It gives an old guy like me some hope for the future."

"You don't look that old to me."

He smiles. "Thanks, young fella. That's from healthy living." He laughs and walks back to his table. I guess when you keep that energy and enthusiasm like he has, you're bound to stay young.

By one o'clock, packs of customers finally come to my mother's table.

"You sellin' T-shirts, you'n?" asks a tan-skinned girl about thirteen with braided hair.

"Yeah, which one do you like?" I ask her.

"Do you have that shirt: 'IT'S A D.C. THANG'?"

I look through my mother's box of shirts, but I don't remember seeing any like that when I hung up the samples.

"Nope, I think we have just the ones that are displayed."

"Oh," she says, eyeing the many books spread out across the table. "Dag, you'n, what kinda names is dese?"

"African names."

She looks me in my face for an explanation. "Are dey from Africa?"

"No, Molefi Kete Asante is in Philadelphia, Jawanza Kunjufu and Haki Madhubuti are both in Chicago, and Amiri Baraka is in New Jersey."

"Oh." She smiles at me as if she has nothing else to do. She lingers about the table, picking up and putting down various African-American books. "Why dey got African names like dat, Joe?"

"Because some blacks in America believe in going back to the roots of our civilization, which is Africa."

She shakes her braided head. "I ain't from Africa; I'm from Sowfeese, D.C.," she responds with serious pride, meaning "Southeast."

I smile. "You'll understand in a few more years when you mature."

She frowns at me. "Are you tryin'na say I ain't mature?"

"No, I'm sorry, I didn't mean it exactly that way. I meant it more in a cultural and historical sense."

She peers at me as if she's trying to figure out my angle. "You tryin' t' get smart wit' me, ain't'chu?" She's smiling now, like we're playing some kind of guessing game and she's just figured it out.

"No, I'm not," I tell her, chuckling at her accusation.

She starts to walk away. "Aw'ight, man, but I know you was."

Maybe she's right. I seem to be losing tolerance for the ignorant. And that's bad, because then I'll end up like those "uppity" blacks who slander the masses.

Three boys hurry to my table next. "Yo, you'n, you got dat T-shirt wit' da .45 gun on it?" one asks. They range in height and colors from dark brown to reddish brown to yellow. I'm reddish brown myself.

"No, we don't sell those type of shirts," I tell them.

"Oh."

They look disappointed. They've probably been looking everywhere for these shirts.

"Why do you guys want shirts like that?" I ask them curiously.

"I'on know, you'n, dey jus' like dat," the lightest one says. He's also the shortest.

The taller, darkest one steps forward and picks up Terry McMillan's novel, *Waiting To Exhale*. "My mom has this book, Joe," he says to the others.

"Yeah, my sister has it too," says the one who's my complexion.

"Do they have any other books?" I ask. *Stupid question*, I'm thinking. *Of course they do.*

"I'on know," the tall, dark one answers.

"Do you guys play sports or anything?"

They start to snicker. "You sound like a white boy, you'n," says the one who's my complexion.

They laugh. Then the first light-skinned boy adds, "I know, Joe. He talk like he a teacha or somethin'."

The darkest one asks me with a smile, "Are you a teacha?"

"No, but I should be one," I respond. "And the first thing I'd teach you all is that we don't have to be 'a white boy' to speak *English*. Not 'proper English', but *English*, period."

"Whatever, you'n," says the one who's my complexion.

They dash away as quickly as they came.

Tony walks back over to my table, smiling, and grips my shoulder. "Give 'em some time, Ray. Give 'em some time."

I've only sold eighty-three dollars in merchandise. It simply isn't that many people here today.

By now it's five o'clock, and I'm a little tired of coaxing black customers into buying while explaining *why* we should support each other. It's ridiculous! I mean, we seem to support everybody else, but I guess *black* merchandisers don't have the right goods.

I pack up my mother's things and get ready to leave, feeling exhausted. Tony walks over to me once more. "It takes many full moons before a man can become a wolf," he says, winking his right eye at me. "You hang in there and you'll end up runnin' down all the prey."

I look at him confusingly, not because I don't understand what he's telling me, but because of the way he puts it.

He looks at me and laughs. "Patience, young fella; patience is a virtue."

"Well, we must be the most patient people in the world, because it seems like we've been waiting forever," I say with a loose tongue.

Tony looks at me sternly. "The key word in your sentence is *seems*, because a lot of people can't even see when they're on the right path." He walks away briefly, leaving me to ponder, but then he walks right back. He talks to me in a lowered tone: "Man, I'm so tired of black folks blaming everything on 'the man' that it makes me sick. Now I'm not sayin' that the pig ain't dirty; he's most definitely dirty. But you, me, and any other black man or woman on this earth make ourselves what we're gonna be in life, not 'the man.' You hear what I'm sayin' to ya, son? It's gon' be you and not 'the man.'"

I get home by six-thirty and throw myself across the bed again. I know my mother told me to hang in there until six, but I couldn't stand it. It's hard as hell to hang in there with black people. I mean, this is really a full-time job with no paid vacations.

I call my C&P phone mail service for messages.

"Hey, Wes, this is Marshall. We goin' to the movies about seven to see *A Few Good Men*, so call us back if you goin'. And oh yeah, did you see *The Distinguished Gentleman* yet? I mean, it was all right, but I'd tell people to wait for the tape to come out."

Typical, I'm thinking. *We always want to wait for black things. Black culture is always secondary.* There are all kinds of stupid white movies, but I guess we just don't pay that much attention to critiquing them as much as we do our own.

"Wes, this is Sybil. I've been meaning to talk to you about our relationship for weeks now, and well, I never really could slow you down enough to tell you. I really think that we are drifting apart as a couple, and I think it's best that we part ways for a while to gather our real emotions. Please don't be angry with me, but I had to do this. And don't call me back for at least a week, because we really need to think first."

Now this is really a trip. As conscious and as positive as I claim to be, I'd rather be the one to drop her. I guess the male ego overrides everything, or at least that's how I feel right now.

Damn! I guess life's a bitch and then you die. But hell, maybe I should try to at least die happy. Can I have that: just a little bit of happiness? Please, God.

Wow, I'm going crazy, asking for favors! But isn't that what everybody does when they're in a bind: ask for favors? Shucks, now I need a new girlfriend!

I turn on my stereo and that "Rump Shaker" song is on. They must play it about ten times a day now:

All I wanna do iza zoom, zoom, zoom in'na boom, boom.

Ridiculous! Stupid! And more stupid! But that's us, unfortunately.

CHAPTER 2

Wes

"You hear about the *Malcolm X* movie? asks Marshall, running in out of the cold.

I'm sitting inside the lounge area in building 38 at UDC, awaiting my final exam for the semester. We break for winter vacation through the Christmas and New Year holiday season this week. And more importantly, Kwanzaa, the seven-day African-American tradition started in 1966 by revolutionary activist Maulana Ron Karenga in California is coming up.

"No, what about it?" I ask Marshall, looking down at my notes.

"Yo, they said that movie theaters were giving the wrong tickets and saying that it was sold out, when it wasn't."

I look up at Marshall, who's light brown and wearing thin-rimmed gold glasses. He's standing medium height and wearing a dark brown leather coat. I remember that I *did* hear about the *Malcolm X* dispute.

"And yo, they said that they were selling tickets to *Home Alone II* to people who wanted to see *Malcolm*," he continues. He shakes his head in disgust. "Man, I tell you, the white man won't let a nigga up."

"I don't see why people were thinking it would be portrayed like he really was, anyway," I comment. "I mean, it just seems to me that a lot of people would rather see Malcolm's gangster/pimp years than his revolutionary years."

Marshall shakes his head violently. "Naw, man, you wrong. Dead wrong! I mean, yeah, you might be right that a lot of people are into that, but there are way more of us inspired by him."

Up comes Derrick: dark brown, solidly built and wearing a dark blue down coat.

"What's up?" he asks with a smile as other students swing around him on their way to classes.

I point to my notes. "This is up. This last damn test," I tell him.

Derrick and Marshall shake hands and exchange smiles. I remain seated, hoping they will allow me to get back to cramming.

"Dallas!" Derrick yells at Marshall. "Dallas all the way!"

"You crazy, boy! San Francisco and Steve Young is *too* strong!"

"Naw, buddy. Nobody can stop Emmitt Smith. That boy is *bad!*"

"Okay, we'll see in the playoffs."

I raise my head. "None of us are Redskin fans?" I ask.

They both look at me confused. "*Redskin fans?* Naw, man, that's them white people coming in from Maryland and Virginia," Derrick says, slapping consenting hands with Marshall.

"I know, 'cause that boy Rypien is a bum and always was a bum; nigga gon' try t' hold out for more money."

"I didn't know white boys could be niggas," I comment, facing Marshall.

Marshall looks at Derrick and grins. "Everybody in America are niggas except the ones who control the money. You know that, Wes; you're the political science major, right?"

Derrick laughs. "That about sums it up."

"Well, look, gang, I'd love to sit here and bullshit, but I have a test coming up," I announce.

Derrick smiles. "You knew that last week and last night, but now you act like it just snuck up and grabbed you."

"It did," I lie jokingly.

"All right then, man," he says, walking off.

Marshall stays and sits down beside me on the small cushioned couch. "Yo, boss, I heard you and Sybil stopped kickin' it."

I face him, looking baffled and turning away from my notes. "How you know this?"

"Shaunta told me."

"Well, how does Shaunta know?"

He frowns at me. "Come on, man, you know they best friends."

"Why does Shaunta have to tell *you* this?"

"I mean, it wasn't like she just came out of the blue and said, 'Oh, by the way, Sybil and Wes aren't talkin' anymore.' It was more like Sybil was having problems trying to keep her life in order, which, of course, would include something about you."

I grimace. "Hell, everybody has problems. I mean, she's trying to act as if she's the only cotton picker on the plantation."

Marshall smiles, getting up to leave. "Whatever, man. That's between you and her."

"You mean it *was* between me and her."

I get back to my work only to be interrupted by Candice.

"Oh my God! I'm so happy I saw you, Wes! Are you ready for this test today?"

"No, but I'm trying to get ready," I say. I'm trying my hardest not to seem like I'm staring at her.

She squeezes beside me in the spot that Marshall just held and leans into me to read my notes. "Oh shit! That's notes for an essay?"

"Yeah."

"Damn, Joe! I hate them essays!" she yells convincingly into my ear. Her perfume is driving me wild. I could just imagine myself in between her firm, cream-colored legs as her painted nails trickle down my back with her sweet, cherry-colored lips kissing my neck.

"That's the majority of the test," I respond to her, feeling a hard-on rising.

Candice sighs strongly. Her dark eyes twinkle as she hypnotizes me: "You gon' help me out, Wes?"

I want to say, "If you go out with me or introduce me to one of your girlfriends." But I don't. I don't have the heart.

"Yeah, I can probably help you," I tell her instead.

She squeezes me like I'm her child and kisses my cheek. "Great! So what is your essay about?"

I grin with much enthusiasm as I explain: "How to educate the masses on the importance of the black vote, using the historical markers of the Reconstruction Era in the South, voting drives during the civil rights era and the Black Panther Party programs of the late sixties and early seventies."

Candice shakes her pretty, finger-waved head and smiles deliciously. "Damn! You know ya shit, Joe!"

I must say, the final wasn't as difficult as I thought it would be. I helped Candice to summarize a general essay on how women can promote political awareness to their kids by being active in local politics. And my essay? It was excellent! Although I think six pages was a bit much.

I'm taking the bus today instead of the Metro so I can stop in the Adams Morgan area and pick up a new book to read during this commercialized holiday called Christmas. News reports say that Christmas, ironically, is the most dangerous time of the year. Both Muslim and Afri-centric followers fast during the holiday season.

I enter Yawa Books & Gifts, say "Hi" and check the shelves. But I know what I want already: the third Easy Rawlins detective novel, *White Butterfly*, by Walter Mosley. Mosley is one of the top African-American writers today, and male. It seems the black women novelists have been getting most of the press.

I pay for the hardback copy, toss it into my leather bookbag and head out for work. By now it's after three o'clock, which means the loud-mouthed school students are going to flood the buses.

Here they come now, rumbling down the bus' aisles.

"Y-O-O, JOE! What Miss Wallace give you on'nat test?"

"Aw, you'n, 'nat bitch gay'me a D an' shit!"

"Ahh. I got a C, shaw'. I passed all her tests."

More black teens flood onto the bus. A bunch of girls board.

"Get'cha black, dirty ass off me, boy! You play too fuckin' much!" shouts a heavy-set, light-skinned girl with one of those hard-curled hairstyles.

A senior black woman looks at me and shakes her head. She's probably thinking, *Lawd have mercy on these here young'uns. Dey mowfs is da most terrible things on this here green earth.*

"Shut da fuck up, you ol' Miss-Piggy-lookin' bitch!" the boy responds to the girl.

"HA HA HA HA HA!" the other youths howl.

"What, boy? Dat's why ya black ass gotta wear fluorescent headbands at night so dat people can see yo' black behind!"

"HA HA HA HA HA!"

"Ay, you'n, she betta shut up before I go home and get my Ginsu knives and make a Thanksgiving dinner out her fat ass!"

"HA HA HA HA HA!"

I'm chuckling myself by now.

"Boy, you need to go back to Somalia wit'cha fam'ly, wit'cha skinny-ass self."

"Oh, you'n, she called'ju a Somalian," a lighter-skinned, lanky boy instigates.

"What? Yo, Joe, that fat bitch could feed er'rybody ova dere. Dey need'a drop her out'a plane ova dere an' shit."

A slim, brown-skinned girl tries to get up for her stop.

" 'Scu'me," she says, meaning *excuse me.*

The boy beside her wearing a black skull cap doesn't let her pass.

"I said, *Excuse me,*" she pronounces. But still he ignores her until she forces her way past him.

He then shoves her out into the aisle. "Go 'head, you dirty bitch. Dat's why you burnin'."

"Whatever," she says, walking down the bus' exit steps.

The boy jumps up and tries to spit on her as she steps off the bus. He just misses her. I look at him sternly as he re-takes his seat, but he doesn't acknowledge me.

"I hate that bitch!" he says to his giggling friends. "That girl always be tellin' on somebody." He recognizes my reprimanding stare. He turns and whispers to his friends, but he's loud enough for me to overhear him: "Fuck is Joe starin' at, you'n?"

Hearing him, I turn away. I figure there's no sense in getting involved with an insane youth who may shoot me. I have better things to do.

The bus gets quieter as I approach my stop. I can hear the same boys snickering about me as I get up to transfer busses:

"Ol' pointy-shoe-wearin' bamma."

"He he he," they giggle as the ring leader continues:

"Ol' biscuit-head, Inspector-Gadget-lookin' mutha-fucka."

I feel like punching my fist through his evil-looking brown face. But of course, I'm not going to. I just shake my head and get off the bus, glad to have made it through another one of these embarrassing encounters. These are the types of encounters that make me want to scream, "Fuck the youth!" But I don't, because I still have faith in black people. That fool on the bus represents only a *small* number of our youngsters.

Butterman

It's Tuesday, a week before Christmas, and I have to pay this nigga Max two thousand dollars for two ounces of cocaine. That's highway robbery, but he has the best shit in D.C. and I don't have time to check these other niggas' product out. I figure I can flip at least thirty-five hundred dollars by this weekend if these workers act right. I'll get another two ounces and flip that for another thirty-five, and then turn around and do it one more time before New Year's.

I should have ten grand by January, '93. Then I'm gonna buy a quarter-kilo from them niggas that Bink is down with up in New York. But first I have to cut some of these runners loose, so I call a meeting together at our spot.

I roll up and hop out of my thirty-thousand-dollar car. Buying this damn ride made me take a short. But fuck it! This car is sweet as hell!

All six of these niggas are looking like lost kids waiting for Daddy to come home with the groceries. This shit is pitiful.

"Yo, man, 'ney been askin' for da new shit, B. What's up wit' it, Joe?" Steve asks me, still wearing that cheap-ass black jacket.

"It's comin', nigga, damn! Now let's sit over here and game-plan." I walk to some steps near our meeting spot and take a seat. These niggas huddle around me like I'm Joe Montana.

"Aw'ight, here's the deal," I start off. "I'm 'bout to speed up the pace and do some new things, but the money has t' stay tight, and y'all be fuckin' up. I can't have that shit." I look specifically at Bean, a long, tan-skinned, slinky-looking nigga. He been fucking up constantly.

"I mean, I had an emergency wit' my fam'ly, man, and—"

"What? Man this my money you dealin' wit'!" I say to that weak-ass game he's kicking. "I don't wanna hear shit about no emergencies unless you tell *me* first."

You have to be hard with these dumb-ass bammas or they'll try to play you every time.

"Whatever, man," he says, trying to shake it off.

I get back to my plan. I'm gon' have to cut Bean loose; him and Kevy. Kevy too young and might mess his whole life up. I don't want that kind of shit on my conscience. Young'un is pretty cool.

"Anyway, we gon' flip—" I stop in mid sentence. *Hell am I doin'?* I'm thinking. I can't let all these niggas know! "Yo, Bean and Kevy, let's take a ride."

I open my car doors and look back to Steve, Rudy, Otis, and Fred. "Yo, I'll be back in a few." Bean and Kevy hop in looking puzzled.

I ride down Georgia Avenue not saying anything. Bean is sitting up front with me and Kevy is in the back.

"So, what's up, man?" Bean finally asks me.

I glance at this fat-ass young'un walking up Georgia past all the store fronts to my left. These young'uns be packing some fat asses.

"I'm gon' have ta let'chu go, man. Biz'ness is gettin' too important. It's a new year comin' in," I tell Bean. I continue to watch the road, staring out at the car ahead of me.

Bean sits quiet and Kevy hasn't said anything yet. I guess he's waiting for our regular private discussions. I've been like a big brother to him, but I can't afford having him work for me no more. The shit is getting too risky.

"So dat's how you gon' do me, man?" Bean asks at a red light. He's staring at me like he wants to do something, but he know what time it is. I'd get his ass killed in a heartbeat.

I keep staring out the front window. "I ain't got no choice, you'n."

Bean nods his head, pissed off. "Oh yeah? Well, yo, let me da fuck out den!" I pull over to the curb and let him out. He jumps out and slams my door. "Watch'cha back, nigga!"

"Yo, get up here up front," I say to Kevy. I'm not worried about Bean; he ain't nothing to be worried about.

Kevy sits up front with his blue jeans hanging off his ass and a black bandanna tied around his tapered bush, like most of these young'uns is playing. He's brown-skinned with a pretty-boy face, wearing a thick, black coat.

"You gon' cut me loose too, you'n?"

Shit, Joe looking all depressed, like I'm a girl telling him he can't have no ass.

"When you need money or somethin', you just let me know, aw'ight?" I tell him, avoiding his question.

He nods and looks away from me out the window to his right. "What I do wrong, Butterman?"

He's still looking out the window, not trying to face me.

"Look, Joe, you fifteen years old, and you should be doin' other-type shit, you'n. I mean, when I was ya age, me and my boys was goin' t' da go-go's and shit like that, bookin' girls."

"I thought we was cool, man."

"You'n, we is cool."

"Naw, Joe, you tryin'na cut me short."

He's facing me now with anger in his eyes. Damn, I guess I'm selling him out.

"Look here, shaw', you don't really know how this shit is, man. It ain't always about tryin' to look out for every-body; it's about gettin' money. Now if you got caught or shot at or any other dumb stuff, I'd feel responsible for that shit. I'm not like these niggas that be havin' kids runnin' round sellin' caps and shit like that. My plan is about gettin' as much money as I can so I can move on to some other-type shit. For real!"

"Aw, dat's game, you'n," he says in almost a whisper. "Yo, let me out right here so I can get me somethin' ta eat."

I pull up in front of Wendy's. "You need any money?" I ask him.

He looks at me surprised. "How much you gon' gi'me?"

"I got twenty dollars."

He frowns, probably thinking, *That ain't shit!* That's all he gon' get right now. I have to buy them two ounces from Max today. Then I have a phone bill to pay, and I have to pay that tuxedo place when I pick up that suit for my cousin's wedding for Saturday. That nigga asked me to be in his wedding with his boys: all college-type dudes.

I give Kevy the twenty out of my coat pocket, make a U-turn and head back up Georgia Ave.

Damn! All these stores on the avenue seem like they're closing down. I mean, it's still a lot of businesses on Georgia Ave., but it ain't like it used to be when I was little. I remember me, Red, Tub, John-John and DeShawn used to ride our bikes all over this ave. And I got my first piece of ass down here by this cute girl that lived on New Hampshire. It was during that first year when I started hanging with them young'uns.

We were riding our bikes past her house when she came down the steps, looking pretty as hell. Tub fucked around and ran into me from staring at her.

"Damn, Tub!" I shouted. I was embarrassed because she saw us looking like bammas.

"Aw, shut up before I take you back t' da store and exchange you for marg'rin."

Red said, "Yo, Butterman, she starin' at you, shawdy!"

"No she's not," I said. I was afraid to even look at her. I wasn't really cool yet. But I'd learn.

"Yes she is," Red insisted. "Ain't she, y'all?"

"Yeah, and she look pretty like shit, man," John-John said, almost as light as me with regular kinky-type hair.

I took a glance at her. She looked like one of my long, wavy-haired cousins from down South Carolina. But she was darker with that tanned Hawaiian look.

I was shocked! I ain't know what the hell to do!

Red pushed me off my Huffy. "Go talk to her, young'un."

I looked up at her waiting on her steps and whispered back to him, "What do I say to her?"

Tub busted out laughing. "Aw, dat boy don't know what to do wit' no girl, shaw'. He prob'bly don't even know where ta put his dick at."

"Come here," I heard a mousy voice say.

"Oh shit, shawdy, she told you to come!" DeShawn said all loud, looking like Buckwheat in need of a haircut.

This girl just laughed at us. I was having a nervous fit by then, and my face was turning all pink. I could even feel the blood rushing.

"Hi," I said.

"How old are you?" she asked me immediately.

I was stuck for a minute. I knew she looked older than us. Then Red yelled, "He's fourteen," lying like shit.

She sucked her teeth. "You ain't fourteen. Are you?"

Shit, I ain't even gon' lie! I was damn near ready to tell her the truth: that I was twelve. This girl had me hypnotized. But then Red came to the rescue.

"How you gon' tell me how old my cousin is?"

"Oh, I didn't know," she said, backing down. Red always got respect from people like that.

"Now is you gon' give him your phone number and stuff?" he asked her.

She looked at me and grinned. "If he want it."

I damn near choked on air. But I got Shaneeka's phone number and shit. And me and Red snuck back down there like three days later to hook up with her and one of her girlfriends. We didn't want them other niggas to know because all they would do is cock-block.

Red was in the other room, making a bunch of squeaking noises on the bed with Shaneeka's girlfriend. I was trying out kisses with Shaneeka. We were all over her girlfriend's house and we were hurrying up before her girlfriend's mother would get back home from shopping.

"No, not like that," Shaneeka was telling me.

I tried to kiss her again.

"No, forget it," she said. She was frustrated that I didn't know what I was doing. Then she started pulling her shorts down. I saw this fuzzy-ass hair pop out from inside of her panties. I ain't even gon' lie! If little niggas could have heart attacks, I would have been dead.

"What are you doing?" I whispered, shocked at her.

She grabbed my little dick and started pulling at my shorts button. "Come on, do it to me."

She took down my shit and put it in herself. Then she started squirming around in circles. I got into it and started squirming back.

After a while she started grabbing my ass into her. "Harder, boy. Harder."

I did the shit. Then Red came in the room with the other girl and started laughing at us.

"Come on, y'all. Y'all gotta hurry up 'cause my mom is prob'bly on her way," Red's girl said.

Shaneeka shoved me off of her right when it was starting to feel good. "Okay, come on," she said. She re-buttoned my shorts as if I was her son.

Me and Red ran back outside and pulled our bikes out from some bushes to ride home and brag.

"Ay, Butterman, guess what?" Red asked me, pedaling back up Georgia.

"What?" I said, trying to keep up with him.

"'Dem girls was teenagers!"

"They were?"

"Yeah, that girl I had was fifteen and she said Shaneeka is fourteen, going on fifteen."

"You don't think they lying?" I asked. We had lied about our ages.

Red smiled. "Yeah, you right. Dey might be lyin'."

But that was years ago. I ain't afraid of *no* pussy now, except for them trick hoes. I don't fuck with them. I mean, I just figure it's too many bad-ass girls I can holler at without having to deal with no tricks. That crazy shit is for ugly-ass bammas. Not me.

I get back to our hustling spot and tell my runners the deal on the new 'caine before riding to pick it up from Max. I take Steve with me. Steve is silly, but he has more sense than them other niggas.

We ride down North Capitol Street, heading for Max's setup in Northeast.

Steve pops a tape in my sound system. "This a Rare Essence P.A. tape, you'n. They was playin' at the Pavilion when you went to stay wit'cha girl last week."

"Yeah," I respond blandly, thinking about some other shit.

"Yeah, Joe, an'na bitches was in'nere. Matter a fact, that girl Tamisha was askin' 'bout'chu, you'n."

"Fuck that girl, man! She keep sweatin' me, and I told her I got a girlfriend already. I hate when girls try ta break you up with your girl just t' get with them."

"I know, 'cause them-type bitches ain't no good no way. They'll leave *you* for the next ma-fucka."

I smile, making an illegal left turn onto Florida Avenue. "Yeah, well, I ain't gotta worry about no girls leavin' me. I knocked Tamisha already anyway."

Steve laughs. "You did, hunh, Joe? I guess you don't worry then, as pretty as you is. I mean, if I was a girl, you'n, I'd prob'ly give you some pussy too."

We laugh like shit as we roll up on Max's runners.

"Yo, get Max!" one yells toward the alleyway.

Max strolls out grinning, carrying money in his hands. Them niggas probably back there shooting craps—as cold as it is.

"So, what's up? You know what the deal is, right?" he asks me, leaning past Steve in the passenger seat. Max leans his heavy body into my window, looking in with his goatee and brown face.

I turn the Rare Essence tape down. "Yeah, we can do that."

"So you got the cash on you?"

I frown at him. "You got the shit on *you?*"

"Man, what I look like, a fuckin' walkin' drugstore t' you? Now you know if you got the money, we do biz'ness. But if not, then ride ya yellow ass back around here when you get paid."

His young'uns are standing outside my car, laughing and shit. I never had to go through no cheesy shit like this when Red was rolling with me. I'm gonna have to get with a new muscle man, you know, somebody that can scare the hell out of a nigga.

"This a nice-ass ride, Joe," says one of Max's boys. This short, sneaky-looking brown nigga look like he might try anything, like he don't respect me. That's one of the main disadvantages of being light-skinned and pretty: most people think they can play you.

I ignore his ugly ass. "Yo, Max, let's go ahead and make that transaction in another half when I beep you, unless you got it now." These niggas are starting to make me jumpy without my crew. When me, Red, Tub and DeShawn were running things, we were housing shit. But now I'm out here all by myself.

Max nods. "Yo, come on around back."

I look to Steve, signaling if he has the .25 automatic I gave him. He nods and gets out of the car ahead of me.

"Aw'ight." I jump out with Steve and walk into the alley. I'm feeling edgy as shit right now, but Steve *will* shoot, so it's cool.

"Yo, get this nigga two ounces, man," Max tells one of his boys.

I have to give it to you'n, he always did have a large crew. It must be about ten of his boys around here. And I bet everybody on this block is scared to say anything to them.

We make the exchange. Me and Steve hustle back to the car and hop in. This sneaky-looking young'un is still eying my ride.

"Yo, you know that nigga, you'n?" I ask Steve inside the car.

"Yeah, dat's Squirrel. He ain't shit."

Squirrel is the perfect name for 'im, I'm thinking. *He looks like a damn rodent.*

Steve says, "Yo, man, if you don't mind me sayin' it, we gon' have ta get some new trigga-happy niggas with Red in jail and shit, 'cause Max is startin'na carry you." He shakes his head and grimaces at me. "That nigga trippin', you'n."

"Yeah, I was just thinkin' the same thing myself," I tell him.

We ride through H Street Northeast. We jet back up North Capitol. I give the first ounce to Steve to cook up and break down into 8-balls (one-eighth of an ounce) and measure off some twenties (twenty-dollar bags). I keep the second ounce and take it with me to the crib. If they sell the first ounce by Thursday, then we in good shape.

I get home and walk into my bedroom to check my answering machine:

"Hi, J, this is Latrell. I'm going back home to West Virginia Thursday, so I'm calling you to ask if you want to hang out with me before I leave.

"It's about, umm, seven-thirty. Call me back when you get in. Okay?"

BEEP!

Damn, that's the only message I got all day! Well, fuck it, let me call this girl back. She might be down to give me some pussy later on. That shit would relax my nerves right about now. I could use the comfort of knocking some ass.

I look through my jackets to see where I had her phone number. I find it in my blue Karl Kani jacket.

"Yeah, is this Latrell?"

"Hi, *Butterman.*" She laughs. "Why they call you that?"

I hate when people ask stupid-ass questions. I mean, this girl knows what I look like. She's asking me this shit just for a conversation piece.

" 'Cause I make love like butter, slippin' in an' out," I say, just to bullshit her. I don't give a fuck! I already got a girl, and I ain't in the mood for no small talk.

"Oh, you do, do you? Well, I wouldn't know about that."

"Are you goin' out tonight?" I ask her, cutting through the preliminaries.

"I'on know. Why?"

"You want me to come over there?"

"Well, if you want to."

"Yeah, I wanna see you."

"Okay, you know how ta get over here?"

"Yeah, American University, right? I been up there before, many times."

"Oh, you have?"

Now she's sounding like I'm a whore. And I am, but that's not why I was up at American.

"Yeah, dey used to have the summer basketball leagues up there."

"Oh. Well, yeah, you can come."

She gives me her dorm and room number. I grab a few Trojans and head out the door. WPGC is playing "The

Rebirth of Slick" on my car radio. That's a slammin'-ass jam: *I'm cool like dat. I'm phat like dat.* And that other shit they talk about. I don't really understand nothing they say, but the music is cool.

I get over to American University and park my car in their campus parking lot. And yo, as soon as I get out of my car it's some fat-ass light-skinned girl eying me with big, bubbly eyes.

"What'chu wanna meet me, girl?" I ask her.

She stops and smiles. "I know you. Don't they call you Butterman?"

"Yeah, but come here." I meet her halfway in the parking lot. She looks all right, you know, just something to bang when you don't have nothing better to do. But Latrell looks way better than her. "So what they call *you*?" I ask her.

"My name is Shawn," she tells me.

"Oh yeah? I had a boy name *De*-Shawn before he disappeared on us a few years ago."

She laughs. "You don't go here, do you?"

"Naw, I used to go to Duke, like five years ago, before I quit."

"Why?"

I hunch my shoulders. "College ain't for er'rybody. Anyway, what's your phone number?"

She gives it to me before I break out. I doubt if I call her though; she don't look good enough. I keeps nothing but star, model-looking girls.

I get to Latrell's dorm. She's waiting for me downstairs in the lobby. She must want this dick *bad!*

"What's up? I ain't know you was gon' be down here waiting for me."

"Yeah, because sometimes they act funny at the front desk and I ain't want you to have to go through that." She smiles. "You know how racism is."

I smile back at her. "Yeah, I know."

Latrell's a pretty, caramel-skinned chick with short, curly hair and luscious brown lips. She walks in front of me to the stairway door. Her body looks like it's gonna be some good ass. For real! I'm gonna enjoy it.

We walk into her room. She has pictures of herself everywhere.

I grin at her. "You jus' in love with yaself, hunh?"

She laughs. "I figure if you're gonna put pictures up, they might as well be of you and your family."

I sit on her neatly-made bed. "What if I don't feel like goin' back home tonight?" I ask her. I still don't give a fuck! So if she tries to front on me, then fuck her. I mean, I love my girl, but if other girls want to give me some ass . . . I'm taking it.

She smiles at me like she know we gon' be banging. "I guess I could let you stay over."

"Oh, well, I might as well take my boots off and chill."

I pull off my Timberlands and stretch out across her bed.

She grins at me and walks over to her television sitting on her dresser, and turns it on.

"You get cable in here?" I ask her.

"No."

"Well, shit, ain't nothin' on TV. I mean, you might as well throw on the radio."

She smiles and turns off the TV and clicks the radio on. When she gets close enough to me, I lean up and squeeze her hips. She looks me in my eyes and moves closer to me. Now I *know* I'm about to knock it.

"You have some pretty eyes," she tells me.

"I do?"

"Yes, you do." She leans against me on the bed.

"Well, you got some pretty lips," I tell her.

"How pretty?"

Her lips touch mine, so I'm going for the bomb. "This pretty." I kiss her real good and she works the tongue action.

Man, turn out the lights; this shit is about to get X–rated. For real!

I'm sitting here now after putting this girl to sleep. I ripped her ass up! It was good as hell, too. No joke! I had her biting my shoulder and all kinds of kinky shit. And then I got a beep on my pager.

Fuck it, she 'sleep, so ain't no sense in me asking her if I can make a phone call.

"Yo, it's B," I answer.

"It's Steve. Yo, man, that muthafucka Bean went crazy and came up here shootin' up shit! He ain't get none of the stuff, you'n, but da cops came and cleared out the area. Now we gotta chill for a while."

"Aw'ight, man, I'm 'bout t' be out in a few." I hang up, pissed.

Shit! This game is getting hectic. I need me a motherfucking hit-man! These niggas out here won't let me *rest*! I can't even get me some *ass* in peace! Now that's fucked up!

Shank

I'm on a Greyhound bus heading for Trenton, New Jersey, to stay through the holidays with my cousins. I haven't seen them in a year. I usually visit, you know, like six, seven times a year, but this year I was fighting back and forth with my Mom to give me some fucking money. She kept talking that job shit all the time. That drugged-out motherfucker she still supporting ain't got no damn job.

But she want me to go get one. I mean, I can see myself now, in some bamma-ass McDonald's uniform, asking a motherfucker, "Can I take your order?" Naw, fuck that shit! That's dumb shit!

I always wondered why I never stayed in Jersey once I found out how to catch the bus back to Trenton. I don't know; it seems like I liked being called Shank and having people scared of me. Back in Trenton, I'm just Cool-ass Nell. My cousins ain't afraid of me or nothing. You know what I'm saying? But niggas in D.C. that don't really know me . . . I'm terrorizing them motherfuckers.

It's peaceful on this bus. It ain't even no people talking or nothing. I can chill with this kind of shit, you know, with nothing on your mind but time. Yup, that's the only thing I'm worried about is when we gon' pull up in Trenton. But I always have to transfer in Philly for the new New Jersey Transit line. Sometimes I chill in The Gallery in downtown Philadelphia. And yo, some *down-ass bitches* be up in there!

I remember this one bitch booked *me*. In Philly, they call it "cracked on," like you opening a safe or some shit.

Yeah, well, this fat-assed light-skinned girl said, "Unt, unt, unh. I just love myself some pitch-black mens." It was like two years ago in the summertime.

I kicked that shit right back to her: "Yeah, I love me some fat-ass women, too."

She laughed like shit and said, "Well, what's your name?"

"Cool-ass Nell," I told her, throwing a toothpick in my mouth. I used to *keep* toothpicks. I don't know why and shit. I guess it just gave me something to do to look cool.

Anyway, this girl gave me her number. I got with her one time in North Philly and laid my pipe to her ass. But I didn't fuck with her too much after that. I never had no long-term bitches. You know what I'm saying? Fuck that falling in love shit! But the thing that trips me out is that light-skinned bitches stayed on my dick more than any other girls. I got this redbone girl that go to Howard University now. "Redbone," that's what my cousins call light-skinned girls. And yo, no bullshit; this Howard girl I got looks just like Sade without the freckles. She has a long-ass, shiny forehead and everything. I booked her ass at Kilimanjaro's when I was chilling with that nigga Bink.

You can holler at any bitch when you rolling with Bink. *That* motherfucker be having some bitches!

Damn, I'm starting to get bored now. It seems like this Christmas-Eve ride is taking longer than it usually takes.

This little girl sitting across from me on the right has a Walkman on, bobbing her head. It's probably TLC or Mary J. Blige. Them bitches are popular as shit right now.

I could use a Walkman. I got all them tapes back at my crib and no Walkman. But I got the shit in my head:

Yo, tell me how Finesse was back in the days as a little kid, you know.

Hey, Look at Shorty: Lord Finesse. That's a funny motherfucker! Boy can rhyme his ass off, though; I can't even front. That boy got skills: *Return of the Funky Man.* His first album, *Funky Technician,* was rocking too. Nigga had a bunch of old, black gangster beats from the '70s with DJ Premiere producing.

I say, People, people. Come on and check it now. You see the mike in my hand, now watch me wreck it now.

Guru and DJ Premiere. Gang Starr: *I'm The Man.* That's my shit! I got all their tapes. Them niggas are slammin'.

BOOM! BAM! Here comes The Shank, the man, grippin' steel in his right hand; I got a plan to smash suckas like the Hulk. And I ain't gotta be Jack the Ripper for muthafuckas to get stalked. Go out and buy your own body chalk. 'Cause ya dealin' wit' a killa that won't balk, nigga. And when I got a mike I'm suspect to pull the fuckin' trigga.

So for you punk MCs that can't understand, translation: it's best you be a Runningman. Or transform into an Autobot. 'Cause The Shank is scopin' suckas and killin' 'em on the fuckin' spot.

You betta die now instead of later. 'Cause when ya jet out, I'll hunt'cha ass down like a Terminator.

Don't even fiend or dream of wreckin' my scene. 'Cause like a late-night bitch, you'll get stripped clean.

I leave challengers butt-naked when I wreck it. So if you bought'cha wack-ass tape, don't even sweat it. 'Cause suckas battle me and run out of their luck. You'll get'cha ass kicked, then I'll tell Scotty ta beam ya up.

I'm seekin' battles and out for pay. But fuck the fame; you weak-ass niggas know my damn name. Say MC Shan, then add a motherfuckin' K.

Yeah, that's *my* rhyme! All I need is a record deal. I got skills like Positive K, to pay the bills while giving niggas thrills and chills down their spines as my rhymes blow their motherfucking minds.

I'm finally pulling up into Trenton after transferring buses in Philly. It's about six-thirty and dark already. I yell at a cab and get him to ride up Broad Street to my old 'hood in North Trenton.

Ain't nothing changed; it's still the same crazy-ass-looking poverty, rat-maze public housing and sky-high project buildings. But when you're used to something, it's your home. You know what I'm saying?

I grab my bags, hop out of the cab and walk the familiar path to my Aunt Pam's crib.

"Nel-l-l-l. What's up, nigga? My mom said you was gon' be here. I thought she was fakin' the game an' shit, man."

My older cousin Oz is shaking me around and all, you know, that rough, macho shit. He lost a lot of weight since I saw him last. I wonder if he fucking with the pipe. It would be fucked up if he is.

"Come on, man, damn. Let me get in'na house," I tell him, smiling and shaking him off me.

He throws his big hands up in my face. "What; what'chu got? You ain't got nuttin' for these guns, ock."

He's jabbing at me with lefts and rights, but I don't feel like fucking around with him. I put my bags down and walk toward that good-smelling food coming from inside the kitchen.

"Hey, Darnell!" My favorite aunt hugs me and steps back. "Well, ain't you the most handsome young black man."

She always calls me handsome. She ain't never had no problem with that colorstruck shit. And I appreciate that, because a lot of niggas in D.C. are colorstruck like a motherfucker. Niggas hate jet black in that Washington–Maryland–Virginia area. But you know, you still have people who love shiny black young'uns. But not my mom. I think she's always had a problem with being black. That's why she left Trenton to be with that crazy light-skinned nigga Julius.

Now I have a twelve-year-old, light-skinned sister. She looks like me and my mom in the eyes though. We all get it from my sharp, hawk-eyed grandmother.

Young'uns are sweating my little sister already, just waiting for her to start fucking. Shit! I figure I'm gon' have to break a lot of necks.

"You know your cousin Emil got sent to New Castle for car theft in Philadelphia," Aunt Pam says. I don't know if she's telling me or asking me, but I didn't know about it.

"He did?"

"Unh-hunh. The boy was hard-headed; just *had* to hang out with the wrong crowd."

She gets back to fixing that good-smelling Christmas-Eve dinner. Oz comes in and leans over with a spoon and sneaks a taste of the chicken stew.

"Dammit, Ozzie! What I tell you about that? Now, move!"

Oz laughs and heads back to the living room.

"William gets out of the Youth Detention Center for this coming weekend," my aunt tells me, still preoccupied with cooking. She still has a nice shape, youthful appearance and a good attitude. I figure Aunt Pam has to be at least forty-five.

"Where Cal at?" I ask as I walk out from the kitchen.

"Oh, dat boy upstairs prob'bly readin' them ol' comic books of his. But it's a good thing that you and him ain't never been in no trouble. Hell, maybe you two will go on and do something good with y'all selves. And oh yeah, Darnell?" She calls before I make it to the steps leading upstairs.

I walk back to the kitchen while Aunt Pam waits for me. She whispers, "Look, I got two hundred dollars for you when you go back. You hear me? But don't let Ozzie know, 'cause he done messed around and let himself get hooked on them damn drugs."

I nod my head and head upstairs to check out Cal, my big, brown, Baby-Huey-looking cousin. This boy's into comic books, art, Kung Fu movies and all kinds of other stuff.

"Nel-l-l-l. Bet, we can go to the movies t'night t' see *Tresspass*. Ice T *and* Ice Cube in it." He stands up from drawing a comic hero sketch and shakes my hand.

I grin at him. "You still inta drawin' shit, hunh?"

"Yup, 'cause it's this new black line of comics coming out called Milestone. DC Comics been advertisin' it. And yo, I'm gon' get mine next."

"Oh yeah?" I sit on his bed, filled with comic books and hip-hop magazines. I pick up a copy of *The Source*.

"That's the issue that sums up the events of '92," Cal says. "Ice T messed it up for a lot of hardcore raps because of that "Cop Killer" song."

"Man, 'nat "Cop Killer" shit wasn't rap! That was like some rock and roll–type shit."

"Yeah, you right. They always blamin' controversy on rap." He smiles at me all of a sudden. Cal always smiles when he starts asking me about cultural shit. We always had a lot of things in common. Now he's always trying to say that I'm more like him than what I try to be.

"You still buy comic books, man?"

"Naw," I lie to him. He's trying to cut me a short, and I ain't going for it. I don't care if I *do* read comic books. So the fuck what? That don't make me more like him.

Cal's still smiling at me, but I'm as hard as Superman, and that shit he stressing ain't no Kryptonite.

"Did you see *Malcolm X*?" he asks me.

"Yeah."

"*South Central?*"

"Yup."

"*Candyman?*"

"Yeah, that was da shit!" I make my voice deep and hoarse like in the movie: " 'Cannn-dy-mannnn. Cannn-dy-mannnn."

"'Dat ma-fucka wasn't no joke, you'n! But dey could've made that movie better than that. I mean, that ol' legend shit was better than the movie was."

"I know," Cal says, smiling again. This nigga always gets me talking more than what I usually do. But fuck it, ain't nobody know. I mean, this motherfucker's my cousin!

"Did you see *Unforgiven*?" he asks me.

"Yeah, but I don't see what the big deal is wit' dis one.

I mean, Clint Eastwood shoots the muthafuckas up, collects the money and leaves, jus' like in all the rest of his movies. But Morgan Freeman went out like a bitch. He gon' talk all that shit and then get scared to shoot and gets his ass kicked."

Cal cracks the hell up.

I keep talking: "Yeah, Joe, he always be playin' them Uncle-Tom roles any fuckin' way. *Driving Miss Daisy.* Fuck Miss Daisy! I'd drive that old, white bitch t' hell!"

Cal falls out on the floor. Yo, this boy is crying! Now, I mean, that shit I said ain't *that* damn funny. But that's how Cal is; he'll laugh and have a good time while everybody else too busy trying to be gangster cool. You know what I'm saying? That's why I love this nigga. I mean, I can really have a good time with him.

After a while, me and Cal go to the movies and watch *Tresspass.* These two white firemen drive down to East St. Louis to find some lost fucking treasure in some old-ass building. They end up meeting Ice T and Ice Cube and some other thug niggas trying to kill this other motherfucker for shooting their homeboy. Them actors that played in *South Central* is in it. And it's this silly-ass bum that ends up with all the gold and shit after everybody goes crazy trying to get the treasure for themselves.

"You know what the irony of that movie was, Nell?" Cal asks me as we head back to the crib.

"Yeah, greed leads to destruction . . . the honest man is the righteous man . . . and the poor will inherit the riches of the the earth."

Cal bear-hugs me with tears in his eyes. "I love you, man! I mean, you know, you understand shit like I do. And yo, don't it come easy. It's like you don't even have ta think about it, it just comes to you."

I shake him off of me. "Yo, man, cool da fuck out. It's bitches out here. Dey might think we faggots."

"Aw, man, nix dem girls. They ain't about nothin' but hairdos."

"Yeah, but dey pussy is good, boy. When'na last time you had some ass?"

"Aw, man, I had some ass last week."

"Yeah, sure ya right."

"I did. I did."

"No da hell you didn't! Dreams ain't included, mafucka."

Cal laughs like shit as we jump on the bus. "Yo, but when we get home, Nell, I wanna show you this poem I wrote about art, because we on that same creative wavelength, man, I'm tellin' you."

I shake my head, smiling. I'm thinking, *This nigga lettin' nem comic books go to his head.*

We get back to the crib and go up into Cal's messy-ass comic-book room. He digs through some notebooks with graffiti scribbled all over them.

"Here it is!"

Yo, this nigga's excited as hell.

He starts to flip the pages. Then he stops to read. "The Artist Question," he says. He's sitting up on his bed all proud-looking. He looks like he's just been asked to give a speech at his high school graduation:

"What is art . . . to the poor man, but his life, his soul and his aspirations? What is art . . . to the rich man, but dollars, prestige and conversation? Some say art . . . is personal, introverted and self-consumed. But what is art . . . when no one sees it, hears it, feels it, or is shocked to life, by its heavy inspiration?"

Cal looks at me hard as shit. Seriously! "Look, man, I'm gon' be an artist. I already am. All I gotta do is get the right connections.

"Now you can be a gangsta if you want, but that life

don't never last long. Especially for niggas. But art? Man, that shit lasts forever."

"Yeah, but even artists need money, muthafucka. You gon' be out on'na street corna wit' a damn paintbrush in ya hand, paintin' muthafuckas' faces and shit."

We laugh like shit. But damn! That poem was pretty tough. I think my cousin Cal is serious. What do you know?

CHAPTER 3

Shank

Four hundred and fifty-two people were killed in Washington, D.C., in 1992. Damn! But like 2,000 are killed in New York every year. But you know, New York got like 12 million motherfuckers living there.

It's Friday, January 8, 1993, and the whole country is talking about this ass-kissing President Bill Clinton. I mean, I never trusted nobody that goes out of their way for shit that don't seem all that valuable. Now, ain't no other president ever cared about black people. But this white nigga shows up on Georgia Avenue and visits a couple McDonald's—fucking up traffic with his jogging and shit—and niggas all of a sudden think he's Jesus Christ.

I know who da fuck Jesus is!: "A Rage In Harlem," sampled by Da Lench Mob.

I'm getting off the B6 bus in Chinatown. But that's fucked up, because what happened to Niggatown? D.C. supposed to be seventy-five percent black, and we ain't got no Niggatown. I should call up comedian Paul Mooney and say, "Yo, D.C. ain't got no Niggatown, black. What's up wit' dat?" He'd probably say some shit like "Well, that's because they got rid of your real, cocaine-sniffin' field nigga—Marion Barry—and replaced him with a female house nigga that don't like the word 'nigga.' Matter fact, if Sharon Pratt Kelly stays in office too long, you might end up with a High Yellatown."

I'm laughing to myself. Paul Mooney a funny motherfucker. He supposed to have a tape coming out called *Race*.

"Transfer, brotherman?" this limping, light-brown nigga asks me.

"Naw, I'm usin' it."

"Oh, okay, main man. You take care now."

Bums are always down here asking for money. Fuck *that* shit! I'd rob a million motherfuckers before I end up asking people for spare change.

I head to Ninth and F Streets to see what kind of new gear I can buy. I want some black Boss jeans and one of those rust-colored Carhartt coats like them construction niggas wear.

"You got any change on you, brotherman?" a dark, bummy dude asks me. He has gray hair, but he don't look that old, just fucking dirty.

"Naw, Joe, I need my damn change."

He giggles with a missing tooth. "Unh-hunh, yeah, I know what'chu mean. You have a nice day, young brother."

You know, it's amazing how cordial these niggas are when they're bumming for some money. That's probably the only time they call somebody "brother."

I walk into this Asian-owned store and bells go off. I feel like a damn cow.

Here comes this Asian bitch rushing up to me now. "Cin I he'p you?"

"Naw, I'm just lookin'."

I walk past the bitch and look around. They got all this bright, colorful-looking disco shit. Only bammas buy dumb shit like this. I look at a couple pairs of their jeans, but they're no Boss jeans.

"Y'all got any Boss jeans?" I ask her.

She frowns. "Wha' you say?"

"Boss jeans? Do y'all have any Boss jeans?"

She looks back to dude at the front counter. He's probably her husband. He shakes his head. "No, no. No Boz jeans."

I leave. Motherfucker can't even say "Boss." "Boz jeans" and shit. Them Asians are trippin'.

I walk into another shop, two stores down. I don't know what race these people are: East Indians, Italians, Jews, one of them motherfuckers. They all look the same to me. You know, they got that dark-ass white skin with dark hair and dark eyes.

"We have sales on these jeans here," this dark-haired, creamy-looking white dude says to me. I wasn't even looking at these corny-ass jeans. They always put this bamma stuff on sale.

"Naw, I'm lookin' for Boss jeans."

"Boss jeans? They back here, brotherman," this tall black dude hollers from the back of the store. These creamy-looking guys always got some niggas working for them, even in New York, Jersey and Philly.

I walk to the back with black dude and check out some size thirty-two waists. I flip over the price tag and it says forty dollars. Damn! I forget I bought my last pair of Boss jeans hot, for twenty.

"We got some Calvins and Karl Kanis over here."

Black dude leads me to the other side of the store. Karl Kanis ain't no damn cheaper. And I don't want no Calvins.

"How much are them Karl Kani T-shirts?" I ask him.

"These right here?" black dude says, pointing to them.

What da fuck this nigga think I'm talkin' 'bout? I hate when people ask stupid-ass questions. I think a lot of people do it out of habit.

"Yeah," I tell him.

"Oh, they twenty dollars."

"Can I get two for thirty?"

"Oh, I'on know, brother." He looks back toward the front of the store to them creamy-looking white niggas. "Hey, Alim, he wants two of these for thirty."

Alim? These niggas must be Arabs then.

"We can't give you that price," Alim says to me.

I shake my head. "I only got thirty dollars, man, and I want the jeans. I mean, this the last of my Christmas money."

Black dude smiles. "Yeah, I know what you mean; that Christmas money blows in'na wind."

Alim looks at me like he knows I'm lying, but fuck it. Either he gives me my price, or I ain't buying shit.

"Okay, gi'me thirty dollars." He says the shit like he's mad.

I dig in my jeans, making sure only a twenty and a ten come out. I always set my money up with alternating bills just for occasions like these.

Alim looks at me funny as I give him the money.

"We can't do this again. Only this time," he tells me, stuffing my clothes in a plastic bag.

Yeah, whatever. Fuck dude! I mean, that's what business is about: negotiations and shit. These motherfuckers always want you to pay *their* prices.

I walk around downtown and snatch a bag of corn

chips off the side of a food stand. If he catches me, fuck it, I'll pay for it. But if not . . .

Well, ain't nobody stop me, so I guess the shit is free.

This big, mean-looking, tan-skinned dude looks at me at the corner like he wants some drama. This motherfucker better step before I stick my four-inch blade in his ass and rip his intestines out. They'll have to put his ass back together again like the *Re-Animator*. And thinking about movies, I have to check out *Hoffa* and *Sniper*. It's a whole bunch of other stupid movies coming out. *Aliens 3*; I'm most definitely going to check that shit out. Dude from *Roc*, Charles Dutton, is gonna be in it.

I wonder if I should go check out a couple movies now . . . Fuck it, I might as well. I ain't doing nothing else today.

I go down into the Metro and jump on the Red Line train to ride all the way up to Bethesda. I like going to the movies up there. I can see as many flicks as I want. All you have to do is pay for one ticket and go from one movie to the next. But you can't do that shit at Union Station. Them niggas that work there will sweat you for your ticket stubs.

I don't like them motherfuckers working up there at Union Station. I remember I was about to kill one of them. This punk gon' try to say that I didn't pay to get in.

"Hey, excuse me, do you have a ticket stub?" this skinny, faggot-sounding nigga asked me.

I looked at him like he was crazy. "Yeah, I got a fuckin' stub!"

"Can I see it, please?"

"For what?"

"Because I didn't see you show it to anyone."

I frowned and went to take a seat, ignoring him. Joe followed me!

"Excuse me, if you're not going to show me your ticket stub, then I'm sorry, but you're gonna have to be escorted out."

Yo, I couldn't believe that faggot-sounding dude said that dumb shit to me! So I challenged his ass.

I put my arm out for him to try to "escort me out."

"Go 'head and grab me so I can kill you," I told him. I gave him a no-bullshit stare. And you know it, that bitch-ass nigga got the fuck out my face! I was gonna stick my knife in his ass.

So I sits down in peace and chills. Then, like, four ushers in them faggot-ass blue-and-maroon uniforms came marching down the aisle like they were the fucking police.

"Is this him?" the oldest-looking dude asked.

"Yeah," the faggot said.

I just took out my stub and showed it to them. Then the older dude looked to that faggot-sounding nigga. "He has a stub," he said.

"Can I see it?" faggot dude asked me.

I put the stub back in my pocket and said, "Why can't I watch a movie in peace? Is it because I'm black like you, you'n, and you don't respect me? I bet if I was a white boy you would'na said nothing to me."

That shit worked like a charm. The older guy started walking back up the aisle, followed by the rest of them niggas. But that's why I hate Union Station; they act like they got million-dollar jobs. Peasant-ass motherfuckers!

I get back to the crib by eight o'clock after seeing *Hoffa*. That movie was long, but it was like a flashback movie. They could've did a better job, but fuck it. I guess they got their point across; Hoffa was running with the Italian Mafia and they might have gotten his ass.

Italians got shit like I got it; niggas are afraid to snitch on me. But I ain't never have to kill nobody yet. I mean, niggas don't ever get me to that point. But these young'uns are getting crazier and crazier. I might have to kill one of these motherfuckers before it's over with.

I need to hook up with Bink. I know I can find his ass up Georgia Avenue tonight at the Ibex. And if I don't catch him up there, I'll catch him at the East Side tomorrow night. Bink always at a party.

I roll out to the Ibex around ten. I get up there around eleven. And bingo, my main man is outside wearing a purple leather coat, blue jeans with brown leather in the front, Timberland boots, and a purple velvet Kangol hat—the puffy kind.

"H-a-a-a-y, my nigga Shank." We shake hands and grin at each other. "Where you been at, man? You been hidin' out an' shit?"

"Naw, man, takin' care a biz'ness."

"Hey, well, we all doin'nat."

"Yeah, that's what I wanted to talk to you about." I step to the side of the crowd.

"Yo, Bink, come here for a second, man," one of Bink's boys calls.

"Hold on, man. I'm hollerin' at my boy Shank." Bink steps off to the side with me. "So what's up, man?"

I look into his face. Nigga got smooth-ass skin like mine. He just a little lighter than me. Under his hat you can see that he has a fresh haircut. This boy *stays* geared.

"Man, I need some dough on the regular. You know what I'm sayin'?" I tell him.

Bink pulls out a knot from inside of his purple leather coat and peels out a hundred-dollar bill. "Here, nigga. Now don't ever say that I don't love you." He gives me one of those arm-to-chest hugs that all the cool niggas are doing now after watching that Pete Rock and CL Smooth video, "Straighten It Out."

I slide the hundred-dollar bill in my pocket. "Yeah, this on time, man. But I'm sayin' I need to be *in* wit' somebody, you know?"

Bink nods his head and squints his eyes, like he's on. "I'ma tell you what I'm gon' do for you, right." He tosses his arm around my shoulder and walks me around the corner.

"Yo, Bink, where you goin', man?" one of his boys shouts at us.

"I be da fuck back, man! Damn! This my boy right here, Joe." Bink shakes his head and smiles. "It fucks wit' a nigga when he too popular sometimes, you know? Anyway, like I was tryin'na tell you, man; you ever heard of Butterman?"

I nod. "Yeah, he used to swing wit' Red and Tub before their shit went under."

Bink nods back to me. "Yeah, that's him. That light-skin ma-fucka so pretty, if he was a bitch, he'd be my top whore."

We laugh like shit. This nigga Bink be lunchin'.

"Anyway, Shank, Butterman is havin' problems because Red was his real respect. Now wit' Red up in Lorton . . ." Bink shakes his head and smiles. "You see what I'm gettin' at, right?"

"Yeah, da muthafucka need a trigga-man."

"Exactly."

"YO, BINK!"

"YO, hold da hell up, now, shit!" Bink looks at me and shakes his head again. "Man, you see what I gotta go through, Shank? These niggas act like bitches wit' hot pussies sometimes, man, I'm tellin' you."

Bink gives me Butterman's beeper number and I step

off. It ain't no sense in me paying to go inside Ibex. He the only reason I was up here in the first place. Just seeing this nigga with a trail of women makes me want some pussy. And where Bink goes, the bitches ain't far behind. You know? Some niggas are just cool like that.

I ride the 70 bus down Georgia Avenue and get off at that Wonder Bread Plaza shit. I walk up to a telephone at the Howard Towers Plaza-East and call my redbone honey.

Her answering service comes on: "Hi, this is Carlette. I'm sorry I'm not in right now, but please leave a message and I'll return your call promptly."

I hang the phone up and step.

Damn, man! Nights like this make me wanna go down on Fourteenth Street and buy a hooker. I mean, I need some ass. I'm thinking about going back up to the Ibex to get with Bink again. That motherfucker can get the ugliest niggas some pussy. And I'm not saying that I'm ugly. I ain't never been ugly. I just don't talk to too many bitches, you know? They don't love you no damn way. But fuck that! That's a long-ass hike back up Georgia Ave.

I head back to the crib and chill. Damn, I missed the *Def Comedy Jam* show again! But that's cool. I'm gon' beep this motherfucker Butterman tomorrow and get on his payroll. This one-man-show shit ain't paying bills like I want it to. I'm gon' have to get in good with you'n. You know what I'm saying? Butterman!

These girls don't know me from Jack, but yet I feel like The Mack.

Yeah, that's my boy Phife from A Tribe Called Quest: *Like Butter.*

I wonder when them niggas gon' drop their new album. Their shit is always slammin': *I left my wallet in El Segundo. I left my wallet in El Segundo. I left my wallet in El Segundo . . . Come on, let's go.*

Butterman

Yeah, there goes Bink now, wearing a *purple* coat! Get the hell out of here! Only a nigga like Bink can get away with wearing some shit like that. That's a cool-ass nigga. I knew I would catch him up at the Ibex tonight.

I roll my 3000 up to the curb and blow my horn. I roll down the passenger-side window so he can see me.

Bink leans inside my 3000. "H-a-a-a-y, baby, I just gave my man your number, 'bout an hour ago." He checks out my car. "Yo, dis a smooth ride, B."

"Yeah, it's aw'ight. But yo, I wanna talk to you about somethin' else, man."

Bink leans back and nods. "Oh yeah? Well, hold up den, 'cause I wanna ride in'nis new shit'chu got." He walks over to talk to his crew.

"Ay, Butterman? Why you ain't been callin' me, Joe? I mean, what's up wit' dat shit? I thought we had somethin' goin'."

She's wearing some tight-ass, off-white stretch pants and a short black leather jacket, looking good enough to eat and leaning against my open window. But fuck her!

"Ay, Tamisha, don't fuck wit' me t'night, aw'ight?"

Bink hops in on the passenger side.

"Don't fuck wit'chu t'night? Aw, naw, Joe, why you tryin'na carry me like dat? What; my pussy wasn't good enough for you?"

Bink says, "Damn, well, if it ain't good enough for him, I'll take some."

She sees him, but she doesn't smile at his humor. "Oh, hi, Bink." She looks at me again, like she's trying to figure out what else to say. Her hair has some fresh curls in it. I guess she just got it done today. And yo, the girl looks *good*. She's light-skinned with bright eyes and silky brown hair. But no girl got shit on my baby Toya. That's my heart!

Tamisha looks at me depressed-like. "Butterman, if you get time, come by and see me, okay?"

"Aw'ight."

"I'm serious."

"Look, I said aw'ight."

She sucks her teeth and huffs, like a spoiled high-school girl with a tantrum. "Aw'ight now, 'member you tol' me." She walks away from the car, switching her tight ass.

Bink shakes his head with a grin. "Got'damn, B! *Did* she have some good pussy?"

"Yeah, it's aw'ight. But she loud as shit."

"Oh yeah? I like 'em loud. It makes me feel I'm gettin'na job done. You know?"

We laugh like shit as I make a right turn and head down Georgia.

"Yeah, let's go down'na Ritz; we might meet some new whores," Bink says.

I put on The Pharcyde. Bink takes out a bag of weed and a cigar and starts filling up a blunt.

"Yo, you just got this tape?" he asks me. "These the ma-fuckas, man. I like my man DJ Quik from out da West Coast, too. *Way II Funky* is bumpin'."

"Yeah, so what boy you gi' my number to?" I ask him, cutting through the small talk.

"Oh, my man Shank; he a cool nigga from back in my high-school days at Anacostia."

"Is he hard enough to be respected?"

Bink frowns at me, carefully sealing the blunt. "Nigga, is you crazy? That ma-fucka a top-line killa. He jus' need some dough on'na regular, so he tryin' t' get put down. And he my boy and everything, but I already got enough niggas on my payroll.

"I ain't no ATM out here, you know?"

"Oh yeah? What he look like?"

"Li'l shorter than me, dark, slick, and smooth as hell. Boy wear black everyday, damn-near."

"A lot of niggas know 'im?"

"Man, shit, I'm surprised you don't."

Bink takes his first hit on the blunt. We roll slow around the Ritz on Ninth and E Streets, downtown Northwest, checking out the scenes.

Bink squints his eyes as he starts to feel it. "You see all these ma-fuckas peepin'nis ride, B? They prob'bly thinkin', 'Hey, look, it's *Speed Racer!*' an' shit."

We laugh as I catch a jones myself. "Yo, pass that weed, shaw'." I pinch it, take a hit and start choking. "Damn, this shit is strong!"

"What'chu think it was, nigga?" Bink even giggles cool. "Man, I only get the good shit. But damn, ma-fucka, I'm gon' have ta roll another one the way you killin' it."

"Yeah, you see I'm in'na car wit'chu. I'on see why you didn't roll two up in the first place."

He smiles and fills up another one. "Cool. *'Take two and pass. Take two and pass. Take two and pass, so da blunt will last'.*"

We laugh like shit, *feeling it* while Bink is in here trippin' off of that Gang Starr song.

"So when Red gettin' out'a Lorton?" he asks me.

"He got four years. He'll prob'bly get paroled after two."

Bink frowns. "He got four years for beatin' *one* ma-fucka?"

"Naw, man, Red was already on probation. He had a record longer than my dick."

We start lunchin' off of this strong-ass weed.

Bink says, "Nigga, you ain't got no long dick. Er'rybody know dat dark-skinned ma-fuckas got the real black Johnsons. But I gotta give it to you, B, you the only nigga I know that might get more pussy than I get. Besides that nigga Spoon; Spoon be havin' car loads."

I nod my head, saying, "Man, I gotta get up on'nat New York connection you got. Fuck these girls; they ain't goin' nowhere."

Bink nods back. "Yeah, well, why ain't you tell me in'na first place?"

"You know, I thought, like, maybe you wanted to keep your hook-ups t' yourself."

Bink smiles slyly. "You know, it's funny how our true intentions come out under the influence of some weed an' shit."

We laugh again.

Bink says, "Naw, man, I ain't tryin'na hog up no connections. I can shoot up New York next week and set'chu straight. They got some good blow up New York, baby. I *keeps* my ma-fuckin' customers."

I giggle. "Shit, we sittin' out here talkin' 'bout addicts and drugs like we got an official biz'ness."

"Yeah, we do. I mean, if black people don't buy shit else, they'll buy weed, smack, caps and motherfuckin' beer."

"You ain't lyin', Bink."

"And den all these activists be talkin' all'at shit about us: 'STOP THE DRUG DEALERS: STOP THE VIOLENCE ' Man! Dey need t' be stoppin'nis white man from doin' all the shit he be doin'."

"I know."

Bink nods. "Yeah, an'na only reason niggas is gettin' shot up in'nis biz'ness is because we all greedy as shit now, you know. And I can't really blame a ma-fucka 'cause niggas been poor for so long. It's like wakin' up in the mornin' and sayin', 'Damn, am I supposed to be poor all my life?' You know what I'm sayin', B? 'Cause that's the reality of it."

I nod my head and finish off the weed. I lean back into my car's smooth leather interior, still listening to Bink.

"I mean, my pop tol' me when I was a li'l ma-fucka. He said, 'Boy, it's gon' be a lot of people who criticize how you choose to make a livin', but until they can give you a job that pays the bills; fuck 'em!' "

I drive Bink back up to the Ibex at two-thirty before his crew rolls out from the party. It was some deep shit he was talking about. I agree with that nigga on some points, but I never been poor. I always had money. In fact, I didn't have to be in this drug game. I could've taken the "honest route," whatever the hell that is. I mean, you're always taking advantage of someone to make a bunch of money in America.

I walk in my apartment bedroom and look at all my girl's pictures; they smother my walls and all my dressers. Damn, I love this girl! I pick up her graduation picture and look into her face. She has perfect deep brown skin, and I love that shit! I mean, it feels so good to roll up next to a dark and beautiful woman. It really feels like I'm black when I'm making love to her. I can't lie; I've always felt a bit confused about how black I am.

I remember that big turning point in my life before I started hanging out with Red and them. My family was riding down South in my pop's dark blue Lincoln to visit relatives in South Carolina. It was a Saturday in the summertime and we all had dress clothes on because my father was always into appearances.

"A man's appearance means more than words sometimes, Junior," my father was saying as we rode down I-95 South. We had suits and ties on, and my mom and sisters were wearing dresses. The air-conditioner was on and all, but I still didn't see why we had to wear suits on the damn freeway!

We made a stop to get some gas. Me and my father went to use the bathroom around the corner of this rusty-ass-looking gas station. When we came out, my father accidentally bumped into this hillbilly-looking white man wearing a dirty white T-shirt. He had a pack of cigarettes rolled up in his sleeve. Yo, no lie, this dirty white man looked like something right out of *The Dukes of Hazzard.*

He said, "Hey, aren't you gonna say, 'Excuse me,' nigger?"

My father glanced at him and said the shit. Then he added, "And I'm not your nigger."

"You a nigger if I say you are, boy."

Then his dingy white girlfriend came pulling his arm. That only seemed to make him more persistent on dissin' my pop.

"No, now girl, these niggers come through here lookin' all dressy an' gon' treat us here like shit."

That white nigga mugged my father in his face and tried to spit on him. I was looking up to my father like, "Kick his ass, dad! Kick his ass!" But I ain't say nothing because I thought it would have been a natural response.

Man, my punk-ass father grabbed my arm and hustled me back to the car like ain't nothing happen. We jumped back into the car. My mother could tell that something had happened. My father was acting like a zombie and driving like a damn wild man.

"What's wrong, Jeffrey?" she asked him.

"Damn racist pigs," he mumbled.

"Who?"

"I just don't want to talk about it, Mariam! I just don't want to talk about it."

After that shit, you could take me to all the rich black events in the world, and I'll still look at black people as nothing but niggas. I mean, we just get our asses kicked constantly; then we want to complain about how we act toward each other. We don't even say nothing to the white man, but we'll talk all the shit in the world to each other. So fuck it! Fuck college! Fuck jobs! Fuck that rich black shit! And fuck everything!

I look at my girl's picture again. I'm wishing she was here with me. It's damn near three o'clock in the morning, but I'm gon' call her up anyway.

"Hel-lo," she answers sleepily.

"Hey, baby, it's me."

"Unh, why you callin' so late? I called you, like, twelve o'clock. You wasn't home."

"I know, but I love you, girl. I love you t' death. I mean, I feel like flyin' down'nere to see you t'night."

"Hmm, are you okay? Did you bump your head or somethin'?"

The weed did fuck me up a bit, but I know what I'm saying. "Naw, I'm aw'ight. I just needed to talk to you before I went to sleep. I mean, you know, I wish you wasn't all into that independent, workin' shit. You didn't even come up here to see your family or nothin' over the holidays. That ain't right, Toya. Why you doin' me and your mom like this?"

She gives me a long sigh. "Do we have to argue about this again, J? I mean, I'm too damn tired for this."

"I don't see why you can't just go to Maryland—"

"For the same reason that you dropped out of Duke," she says, cutting me off.

I should have never told her about that. But it's done now. I mean, I tell all girls that I at least went to college. I don't want them to associate me with all these other dumb niggas that haven't even set foot on a college campus. Plus, as anti-white as I seem, going to Duke for a year is still like a status symbol to me for all these college girls that I meet.

"Look, J, I'm tired. Okay? Now, I love you too, but can you call me in the mornin', please?"

"Yeah, girl, I mean, I just needed to talk to you."

"Why, are you feeling that left-out shit again? I told you, Jeffrey, all black people feel alienated in some way. It's not just light-skinned people and it's not just you. Now, I can't keep babyin' you."

"Babyin' me?"

"Jeffrey, stop! Now, I'll talk to you in the morn—"

I hang up on her. Shit, the weed did it! I call her right back.

She says, "What is wrong with you, Jeffrey?"

"Baby, I—"

"You can't keep doin' this to me. I can't take this shit, man. God!"

"I know, girl, but—"

"It's no buts to it. I love you and I'm gonna always love you, but you have to learn to love yourself and I can't do that for you."

"I know—"

"Well, you gotta cool out and appreciate all the things that you do have, Jeffrey. I mean, a lot of guys would love to be you. Okay? Please! Now, call me in the morning."

"Aw'ight," I tell her.

"I love you," she says.

"I love you too." I hang up and fall on my back across my bed. I'm glad Bink let me have the rest of the weed. I'm gon' smoke this shit up! Nobody knows how I feel but me. No-fucking-body!

Wes

"The death toll is already up to twelve, and it's only been nine days into the new year," Marshall says. He's sitting on the floor in front of his 19-inch color television set. Walt, Derrick and I are over to watch the NFL play-offs on a Saturday afternoon.

All I'm thinking about is love. Love conquers all, but I don't have a new girlfriend yet. I haven't talked to Sybil since she broke off with me. I've tried, but I think she's screening my phone calls and won't return my messages.

"You seen them advertisements for Khallid Muhammad coming to end the silence from The Nation of Islam on the *Malcolm X* movie?" Derrick asks me.

"What?" I ask. I wasn't paying close attention.

"Khallid Muhammad s'posed to be coming back to D.C. to talk about Malcolm X, the movie and his split from The Nation of Islam next month."

"Oh yeah, I heard about that."

Walt stretches his long, basketball-playing legs and gets up to grab a soda out of Marshall's refrigerator.

"Ay, Walt, man, don't drink up all my sodas like you did last time!" Marshall shouts into his kitchen.

"Aw, man, that was after we had just finished runnin' ball."

"I'on care. I'm just lettin' you know ahead of time."

"So what do you think about Clinton sending troops to Somalia?" Derrick asks me.

"It's about time," Walt answers. "Them people been starvin' for the longest over dere."

I look at Walt with a grimace. "Stick to playing basket-ball, would you?"

"Oh, what'chu tryin'na say; I don't know much about politics?"

"Yo, if y'all gon' argue t'day, y'all can go outside in the cold," Marshall tells us.

"I think most of the issues we end up arguing about are always too complicated for us to understand," I tell Derrick, who lounges beside me on Marshall's couch.

"Like how?" he asks me.

"Like, the United States gave the so-called rebels in Somalia the weapons to begin with, but a lot of us don't know that."

"Yeah, just like they gave Saddam Hussein weapons *and* money," Walt tacks on. He smiles as if he's proven me wrong about him not knowing anything about politics. "See, I keeps up on the news, boy." He sits back down onto the smaller couch to our right.

"Yo, they still talking about what that white lady said about them black baseball players," Marshall says, still paying attention to the television.

"Oh, that's Marge Schott. She called them 'million-dollar niggers,'" Derrick responds.

Marshall laughs. "That shit sounds funny to me. I wouldn't care, as long as I had a million-dollar paycheck."

"I wouldn't either," Walt says with a smile.

"Ay, Wes, you seem too quiet today, man. That's why I keep messin' with you," Derrick says with concern on his face.

"I'm just not too talkative today. That's all."

"Boy havin' girl problems," Marshall instigates.

"Now, why you gonna bring that up?" I ask him, feeling agitated. We always feel hurt when we're lonely.

"Aw, man, everybody has girl problems at some time or another," Marshall retorts. "Wes, you need to stop girlin'."

"I wouldn't say anything to you if you were having girl problems."

"So, that's you."

"Well, that's my point; I'm a better person than you are."

"He's a better person than I am. You hear that, Derrick? Now, just before Sybil broke up with him, he was tellin' me that she wasn't all that," Marshall reveals.

"You said that?" Derrick asks me, grinning.

"I mean, she aw'ight, but I can see where he's comin' from," says Walt. " 'Cause she don't have *no* body."

Everyone laughs but me.

"Now, Walt, all the girls that you talk to are overweight and loud-acting," I respond.

We all laugh, including Walt.

"So, I ain't complainin'. I'm workin' on'nis girl now. And yo, she phat t' death!"

"Who you talkin' 'bout? Judy?" Marshall asks him.

"Yeah, now tell 'em. Ain't Judy dope?"

Marshall smirks. "No, she ain't all that."

Derrick and I laugh.

"What?" Walt retorts. "Aw, man, you crazy! She like dat."

"Whatever, man," Marshall says, chuckling.

"Yo, we should go to Kilimanjaro's tonight," Derrick suggests.

"Naw, the Roxy," Marshall retorts.

"What'chu think, Wes?" Derrick asks me.

"Aw, that nigga don't care where we go. He just want a new girlfriend," Walt says, being rewarded by more laughter.

"Funny, Walt. Real funny," I tell him.

By ten o'clock we're all ready to go to Roxy's. Marshall drives me home so I can change my shirt and pants and put in my contact lenses.

We all walk into my Northeast apartment.

"Man, this place is small. I'd go crazy livin' in'nis li'l shit," Walt says.

"Yeah, as soon as you move out of your mom's house," I retort.

"Ut-oh, he's callin' you a mommy's boy, Walt. You gon'

let him get away with that?" Marshall says, instigating again.

"Aw, man, why move out on free food, free rent and free use of a telephone for this-type shit?"

I smile. "Well, when you work for a telemarketing firm, this is all you can afford," I respond.

"I thought you make up to eleven dollars an hour doin' that shit," Walt says.

I pick out my outfit and start to iron it. "No, that's just what they put in the newspapers. You have to be a pro on sales to get that kind of hourly wage."

"So what do y'all sell?" Derrick asks from my bathroom, taking a leak.

"Aw, man, a lot of things. I don't even feel like going into it. We get, like, new things to sell every week."

"Yeah? So y'all damn near like a telephone catalog, hunh?" Walt asks me.

Marshall laughs. "Telephone catalog? That shit sounds funny, you'n."

I smile. "Yeah, I guess you could say something like that."

"You gon' wear a yellow shirt, man?" Derrick walks into my room asking.

I look at him confused. "Yeah, what's wrong with that?"

"Yo, I got a yellow shirt like that back at the crib," Walt adds.

"Yellow shirts are see-through, 'cause you can see your undershirts through 'em," Derricks tells us.

"Aw, dis silly nigga worried about somebody seeing his damn undershirt. What'chu got stains under your arms, Joe? Buy some new ones then," Walt says.

"Oh, let's not talk about stains, Walt, with your ring-around-the-collar ass."

Marshall laughs *real* hard and loudly.

"Fuck you laughin' at, Marshall?" Walt challenges. "What about them bamma-ass jeans you got on? Nigga wearing jeans with pleats in 'em."

"So, what's wrong with that?"

"They look like girly jeans, that's what."

We all laugh but Marshall.

"Now, that don't even make no sense. He ain't never seen no girls wearin' no jeans like these."

"They might start wearin' 'em after they see you in 'em t'night. They might wanna borrow them joints."

We laugh out of the door.

"Oh yeah, Wes, bring that Digable Planets tape you got," Marshall reminds me.

"They out already?" Derrick asks as I run back inside.

"Naw, Wes just got the single," Marshall answers.

We get to the Roxy and Marshall rides around several corners in the Dupont Circle area trying to find a parking spot.

"Damn! It's a lot of niggas out here t'night," Walt says.

"Yeah, that's them Howard students coming back to school," Derrick says.

"You know, as much as we be around them Howard girls, I ain't been able to get with one," Walt tells us.

"I had one. But that girl got on my damn nerves. She was just tryin' to use me for my car," Marshall says.

"Use you for your car? Aw, man, this piece a shit," Walt retorts.

Even Marshall laughs.

"It gets you around though. And she always wanted me to take her to malls and shit like that so she could shop. But outside of that, she acted like she was too busy for me."

"Man, I got some boys that tell me some of them Howard girls is freaks. You just gotta know which ones to talk to," Walt says.

"Well, I don't want no freaks," I comment to him.

"Aw, nigga, ya lonely ass'll take anything," Walt says. After finding a parking spot, we hop out of the car and walk back toward Roxy's.

"Yeah, some of them Howard girls are cool," Derrick says. "My cousin Jerry went with a Howard girl for a long-ass time."

"Why they break up?" I ask him.

"I'on know, man. It was somethin' my cousin did."

"Yeah, but your cousin is light-skinned," Marshall comments.

"You light-skinned too, nigga," a darker-skinned Walt says.

"Yeah, but I don't have the hair, nor the money."

"What does being light-skinned have to do with anything?" I ask innocently enough. Really, I just want to see what kind of discussion comes from it.

"Man, you crazy! This whole damn D.C. area is colorstuck," Marshall responds.

Derrick nods in agreement. "I know, 'cause when I was in New York last summer, the guys who had the most game got the girls."

"That's the same way it is down here; game and money," Walt retorts. "I think y'all niggas just makin' excuses because y'all ain't got no game." Then he adds with a laugh, "And no money."

"No, girls down here are definitely more into light-skinned guys than they are up in New York," Derricks persists.

Walt frowns. "Yeah, whatever, man. Guys are more into that light-skinned shit than girls are. And I know more dark-skinned guys that got more girls than all the light-skinned niggas you know."

"What about that boy Spoon?" Marshall asks.

Walt looks shocked. "Oh, now, I'on know *nobody* that

got more girls than Spoon. But that nigga jus' in wit' all them go-go bands."

"Yeah, he drive a baby-blue Beamer, too," Derrick adds.

"That's just one nigga," Walt says back to Marshall.

"Aw'ight, what about that boy Butterman?" Marshall asks next. Now *I'm* shocked to attention. I didn't know Marshall knew Butterman.

"Oh, now, *he* got some honeys too. But did you ever see his girl?" Walt asks with stars in his eyes. "Yo, you'n, that girl is bad as hell! She look like a straight-up model."

"Yeah, she is like dat," Marshall agrees. "Everybody was trying to book her when she went to La Reine, back in the day."

"Ain't she down at Spelman?" Walt asks as we get into the long line at Roxy's.

"Yeah, he needs to hide that girl somewhere, 'cause I know brothers is going crazy over her," Marshall comments.

Derrick sighs. "Okay, let's stop ridin' his girl and see which one of us can holler at the most honeys in here," he says, cooling off the heated girls/guys and complexion discussion.

We all get searched down for weapons, pay our way, get our hands stamped, and head up the stairs to the dance floor. I don't know why I keep wasting my money for these parties. All I do is go in and admire the best-looking women and the guys they're attracted to. Walt usually dances the most because he's always been the most sociable. Marshall usually finds someone in the crowd that he knows and starts to hang with them instead of with us—as if he's met up with a long-lost friend. And Derrick and I usually scan the crowds and chill.

"Ay, Wes, look at that girl right there," Derrick says, nudging me.

I look toward a girl my complexion in the middle of the dance floor. She's wearing all blue and looking sensational. But she's dancing with some thick, dark brown, hip guy who can dance his ass off.

I nod my head and smile. "Yeah, she's nice."

"Excuse me," another sister says, squeezing by me at the dance floor's outer edge. I almost get a hard-on from her just touching me. Damn, she looks good! But like that Positive K song, "I Got a Man" is what she'd probably say to me if I wanted to talk to her.

Derrick nudges me again. "Yo, ask her to dance, right there beside you."

I look to my left. A tan-skinned girl wearing all black is bobbing around to D.C.'s "Go-Go Rump Shaker" by Proper Utensils, as if we're not already tired of the original song by Wreckx-N-Effect and Teddy Riley.

I almost get ready to ask her to dance, but I procrastinate. As soon as I do, some other guy does and they're out on the dance floor.

Damn! I feel like The Pharcyde: *She keeps on paaassin' me-e-e byyye.* But it's no one's fault but my own. I wish women could know how hard it is to put your ego on the line every time you ask for a dance. I guess the "dogs" have the best principle: *If the first girl ain't wit' it, then fuck it, move along to the next trick.* Then again, that's not for me. I have too much respect for the black woman. But hell, that doesn't mean much if I'm afraid to even approach them.

I remember how I met Sybil up at UDC my sophomore year. We were both waiting on the L2 bus on Connecticut Avenue in front of the school.

"Is the bus supposed to be coming any time soon?" she asked me.

"Yeah, it should be," I said back.

It was during the spring semester. She had braided

hair, and she was wearing a pair of long, pink shorts and a white T-shirt with red roses designed on it.

"That's a romantic-looking shirt," I commented.

"Oh, this?" she asked, pointing to it with a grin. "Thank you," she said. In fact, she had so much positive energy that I was impelled to continue.

"Where did you get it from?"

"Virginia Beach."

"Do you have family in Virginia?"

"Yeah, how you know?" Her brown face glowed with friendliness.

"Well, I figure that most black people have family in Virginia or North Carolina."

She smiled. "Yeah, that's where a lot of the first slave ships ported."

I was surprised at *that* response. "So you're not shy about slavery?" Most American blacks seem to be, especially those who would like to move on and forget the past.

"No, I want to finish up at UDC and then get a masters at Temple University in African-American studies," she told me.

I was surprised again. "Oh, so you're going all out."

She laughed. "Yeah, I am."

We dated for three months before we started going together. But now that I think back to it, it was easy. I mean, it wasn't as if I had to "book her" or anything; she was just there for me to talk to. And I've had girlfriends before her, but they were always girls who went to school with me, like when I went to Banneker Senior High School.

Unfortunately, when I get out of UDC in May, if I don't go back to school for a masters or a PhD, I don't know if I'll have the balls to meet a woman at a club or something. I may have to go back to the old methods of family associates and asking my mom to fix me up with one of her girlfriend's daughters.

"Yo, man, stop daydreaming and ask that girl to dance," Derrick tells me.

I look a few feet in front of me to a light-skinned girl in loose-fitting blue jeans, a green blouse and a matching headband.

"N-o-o-o, she probably dances too 'phat' for me," I joke.

"Well, I'on know about you, but I'm tired of just standing here," Derrick says. He walks out and asks her to dance. She obliges.

Damn! This is going to be a long night. I turn around energized and ask a short, dark sister if *she* wants to dance.

She smiles and says, "No, that's all right. I just got here."

So what? I'm thinking. But instead of saying something harsh and selfish, I say, "Okay, I'll wait until you're ready."

She grins at me as if it was cute. And I think it was. But I doubt if she'll really dance with me; she's already looking through the crowds curiously. She's probably looking for the guys with the game and the money.

Aw, to hell with it! Maybe I need to hook up with Butterman after all.

CHAPTER 4

Butterman

My four-man crew finally hustled up ten grand. Me and Bink going up to New York tonight to make that buy on a quarter-kilo. I'm taking eight grand with me.

I roll my 3000 through Southeast at about eight-thirty, looking for Bink. He said he'd be out here on Martin Luther King Avenue, but this a long-ass street! It's kind of rugged-looking with a million old storefronts and some new ones. It looks like they're rebuilding a bunch of shit over here.

Oh shit, there go Bink right there! He's standing outside of a black Toyota 4Runner jeep across the street to my left, up near Portland Street's corner in front of a liquor store. It looks like he's out here talking that cool shit of his to these winos. A bunch of young'uns are watching him in amazement, like he's a ghetto don.

I blow my horn and holler out of my window at him:

"Yo, Bink!" I make a U-turn and whip up next to the curb.

"Yo, ain't that nigga name Butterman?" I hear somebody ask.

"Yeah," Bink answers. He hops in on my passenger side. "Right on time, man, jus' like my women." We giggle like shit. "Yeah, we gon' follow them niggas up," he says. "I already let my boys up New York know, so you in. You ain't have ta go up there though, B. I could'a got the package for you."

I wanna make my own connections up there, nigga! Fuck that middle-man shit, I'm thinking. "Tell you da truth, I just wanna go up to New York. I never been up that joint before," I lie to him.

"Oh yeah? Well, shit, New York is just like Southeast: twenty-four-seven live."

We roll out behind the black 4Runner, heading for I-95 North.

I ask Bink, "Yeah, why you stay in this shit down here when you paid like you is?"

Bink looks at me confused. He's wearing a blue velvet Kangol and a black leather jacket. He's looking as sharp as a pimp, as usual.

"I jus' tol' you, man; it's live as hell in Southeast. This where all the *real* niggas be at."

Yeah, you got that shit right, I'm thinking. I laugh. "You know, I was watchin' some talk show—I forget which one it was—and they was talkin' 'bout drug dealers an' shit, right. And this ol' lady stood up and said, 'The thing I jus' can't understand about these dealers is why they wanna stay in the ghetto even after they done got all that money.'

"Yeah, Joe, that shit tripped me out. 'Cause I ain't even gon' lie; I live in Silver Spring, Maryland, like a muthafucka. You ain't gettin' me to live around these damn fools out here, you'n."

Bink sits quiet. And yo, this shit is strange as ever for him. Bink is always saying some cool shit about something.

He nods his head in deep thought. "Look, man, on'na down low, it's like takin' a lion out of his jungle. You know what I'm sayin'? Niggas gotta have their jungles, 'cause the white man got his. I mean, like, that integration-type shit ain't for er'rybody, man, and them niggas that did that shit knew it.

"Martin Luther King wasn't no poor man; his family had money from jump. And how it all went down is like this: Them integratin' ma-fuckas wanted to have er'rything white people had, but they also wanted to separate themselves from the poor niggas. So when King started talkin' 'bout a poor people's march on Washington instead of another rich-nigga march, ma-fuckas stopped supportin' 'em. So, like, I stay in Southeast because that's where the people I love is at."

Bink nods to himself like he's satisfied with the shit he just ran down to me. I just drive and keep listening.

Bink says, "No matter how much cash you get, you gotta fit in wit' da people or you end up isolated. Like Michael Jackson."

I start to laugh while Bink continues:

"Yeah, man, 'nat ma-fucka got all'at money an' livin' like a freak: runnin' round wearin' disguises an' shit."

I'm laughing my ass off! We just now getting on I-95 North, behind the 4Runner.

Bink is still going at it: "I mean, it's just like Mayor Marion Barry—or *former* Mayor Barry. That nigga felt his best around real niggas. So when he got out of jail for that shit they set him up for, where did he set up at? Southeast."

Yeah, it was amazing that Marion Barry was able to win a City Council seat for Southeast's Ward 8 after he got caught sniffing blow in that hotel with that trick three years ago. He probably could have run for mayor again and won. For real!

It fucks me up how much street niggas like Bink know. But when I think about it, Bink been in the game for years and ain't did no time—me either—so you figure he has to be smart enough to understand the life to the extent of not getting caught. You have to always understand the position you're in as it relates to the world. That's why I'm all fucked up in the head now; I don't know where the hell I belong. But I guess I'm in this game more so for the power than anything else. I love the power to make things happen. I'm actually in charge and controlling shit.

My father been working for the federal government now for about twenty years, and with all the promotions and money and shit that he gets, that nigga still has to ask his authorities if he can make certain decisions. Even President Clinton has to answer to higher powers. I read about that white nigga being one of those Rhodes Scholars. My father used to talk about that shit all the time when I was in school. All them Rhodes Scholars kiss ass to older ranks just like any other nerdy fraternity. That Rhodes Scholar shit seems like *lifelong* ass-kissing. That's why I know that if Bill Clinton was a Rhodes Scholar, then he was kissing somebody's ass. And it don't stop just because he's the President.

We take it easy, cruising on I-95 North until we get up near Philly. Then these niggas in the 4Runner start ballin', doing over a hundred.

"Get them niggas, B! How much this ride do?" Bink shouts at me.

"One-forty."

"Well, push this muthafucka, man! *'Come on, Speed, we have to win the race!'* " he says fast and animated like they do on the cartoon.

We laugh like shit while I push the accelerator to a hundred. But that damn 4Runner is holding right next to us.

Bink rolls down his window. "We'll see y'all niggas in Brooklyn!" Then he looks back to me. "Now gas dis muthafucka, B!"

I push my 3000 to 120. We jet out ahead of the jeep, flying past the few cars that are still out. Them niggas in the 4Runner are holding tough on my ass.

Bink is enjoying the hell out of himself. "Man, I ain't had no fun like this since the last time I went to King's Dominion!"

We get up to Brooklyn, New York, by two o'clock in the morning. But don't ask me what part because I couldn't tell you. All I know is that young'uns are still outside; little niggas! Then again, it *is* Saturday. But still, young'uns at *two o'clock* in the morning?

We ride up to this brownstone apartment building that has like twelve soldiers surrounding it. Bink gestures for me to follow him up the steps to where these niggas are.

"Binnnnk! What up, hopps? What a nigga know?"

Bink slaps hands and gives one of those arm-to-chest hugs with this chestnut-colored New Yorker wearing fly-ass Karl Kani gear and tan Timberland boots. Bink's crew and dude's crew all greet each other and give each other pounds. I stand cool and wait for my introduction.

Bink says, "I'm holdin' down'na fort and hosin' down the women, general."

New York dude laughs like hell and turns to a few of

his boys, pointing at Bink. "This my ma-fuckin' nigga, G! Shit, how long we been knowin' each other, Bink?"

"Ah, ever since ya sister wanted me to be her boyfriend."

New Yorker giggles. "This ma-fucka be trippin', yo." Then he looks to a darker-complexioned dude wearing some off-white-colored gear and Timberlands. "Yo," he says back to Bink, "this my man Ted; him and my sister gettin' married next month. They had a little girl two months ago."

Oh shit! I'm thinking. *We fucked up now!* This nigga Ted don't look like he think it's funny.

Bink says, "Aw, man, 'nat shit is cool. I mean, I'm not gon' cry or nothin' like that. But she said we was gon' get married though, man. I mean, she promised me, Mark."

Bink drops his head like he's really hurt by it.

These niggas start cracking up out here. I didn't know Bink could act! This nigga be lunchin'. Even this dude Ted is laughing.

Bink shakes dude's hand. "Naw, for real though, congratulations, man," he tells him.

His boy Mark looks to me. "So this ya boy that wants the quarter? Butterman, right?" he asks me.

"Yeah, this my main man in D.C., Mark. Me an' him be havin' girl competitions," Bink answers before I can.

Mark reaches out to shake my hand. Then he pulls me into one of those arm-to-chest hugs. "If you in wit' my boy Bink, then you in wit' me, G."

"Aw'ight, I'm hip," I tell him.

He looks me over and then back to his sister's fiancé. "Yo, Ted, Butterman looks like Puerto Rican Mike. Don't he?"

"Word! He damn sure do. You got any 'Rican blood in you, G?" Ted asks me.

I shake my head and smile. "Naw, man, I'm pure nigga."

Mark looks to Bink and smiles, then he looks back to me. "Yeah, well, if ya ass get caught up in Spanish Harlem, them ma-fuckas damn sure gon' start speakin' Spanish to you, G. And yo, dey got some *mad*-fly bitches up that ma-fucka, hopps. On'na real!"

"Yeah, 'member that time we had that Puerto Rican in Manhattan, Mark?" Bink asks.

"Yeah, and she sucked *both* our dicks."

Bink grins like a kid. "Man, it was a good thing I went first, 'cause you messed around and pissed the bitch off." Bink turns to me. "Yeah, B, this nigga was grabbin'na whore by da head, talkin' 'bout some ol', 'Deep throat! Deep throat!"

Mark laughs. "Yeah, G, I was havin' Vanessa Del Rio flashbacks."

By now I'm thinking, *All this shit is real cool, but I'm ready to get what I came for and get da hell out'a here.* I'm tired as hell, and I have to drive all the way back to D.C.

We finally go inside the guarded brownstone and make the transaction. Then we end up hanging out in Brooklyn until daybreak.

I drive back home with my 3000 cruising on sixty. Bink falls to sleep. I'm probably gonna have to sleep for two days to get my head back in order.

I drop Bink off when we get to Silver Spring and let his boys drive him back to Southeast in their 4Runner. I walk into the crib, crash onto my bed and check my answering machine.

"J, this is Mom. I thank you for participating in your cousin's wedding last month, but you really have to come out to more family functions because a lot of people are asking about you. Now, I don't know what it is about your father and you, but you two really need to

stop acting like children and love each other like you
know you both do. Now, we have a family get-together
next month in Florida, so I'll call you back on it. Okay?
And Jeffrey, we love you, but you have to love us back.
Love is not a one-way street."

BEEP!

Yeah, fuck that shit! They all living in a fantasy world.
That light-skinned family garbage don't change nothing.
I went to my cousin's wedding because I didn't want to
break my promise to him. We used to be tight when we
were young. But now . . . fuck him! He got into that light-
skinned shit too. He was always asking me, "Why do
you associate with them?" talking about Red and my
boys whenever he came up to visit from South Carolina.
Man, fuck him! And that girl he married looks white to
me.

"Hey, baby, this is me. I see you're not in again, and I
didn't leave a message the first two times I called because they were just to say hello. But now I'm starting to
worry what girl's house you're over. I mean, I know we
love each other and all, but I wish you wasn't out runnin'
in the damn streets like you do. Young black men are
dying, you know.

"Anyway, call me when you get my message, okay?
Bye-bye, baby."

BEEP!

I'm smiling like a damn kid. That's my girl! I love that
damn girl!

Fuck it, I'm thinking about going back down to Atlanta.
I haven't rolled around on her smooth-ass dark skin in
weeks. And we squashed that weak shit I was talking
that other night. I mean, I was trippin' off of that weed,
that's all that was.

I'm probably gonna sleep all day today. Then I have to

get with that boy Shank and set everything in motion. And the last thing I have to do is get with Wes.

Man, that nigga Wes a hard nut to crack. I have to find out what he's searching for. I mean, I should just get him some pussy. I need to hook him up with a pretty-ass girl to keep him preoccupied. Then I can get him on my squad.

Wait a minute! Damn, that sounds like a good-ass plan! All niggas love some pretty-ass pussy. And Wes *does* stare at them. I amaze myself sometimes. Now all I have to do is catch you'n at a party.

Shank

I had to rob this junkie today for some spending money. I wasn't thinking about the motherfucker, but this nigga kept bragging to his homey on the bus about how he was going to spend some two-hundred-dollar unemployment check on some smack, some brew and some bitches. Fuck that shit! He was asking to get robbed. You know what I'm saying? So I simply got off the bus with his ass and stuck my gun to his face and pistol whipped him.

It's getting to be that time of the month again to pay the rent. And that motherfucking Butterman keeps giving me the run-around about hooking up for this put-down on the enforcement tip. I'm gonna be like Frank Nitti: executing all punks and suckers! Matter fact, let me beep this nigga right now.

I run outside and up to Rhode Island Avenue to use a pay phone. Some dude is on it already. I look down the street and start to walk to the next one. Two high-school-looking girls walk out in front of me with a little tan-skinned boy. He's wearing a down coat and some boots.

Young'un looks cool as hell, a young hustler about

five. All of a sudden, one of these bitches trips him on purpose.

"Yo, what da fuck you do that for?" I ask the bitch. That shit wasn't right!

She turns and looks up at me with this goofy-ass grin. I guess she's surprised that I said something to her about it.

Little shorty gets up and only whines a little as he brushes the cement pebbles off his hands.

" 'Cause he bad," the girl tells me, still grinning like a sneaky bitch.

"Oh, so I guess trippin' his li'l ass is gon' make him good then, hunh?"

The other girl faces me too now. I don't think she knows what happened. "What'chu do?" she asks her friend the bitch.

"Oh, I jus' tripped him 'cause a how bad he be ackin', shaw'."

"Why you do dat, girl? He ain't do nothin' t' you."

"I mean, he aw'ight; he ain't even hurt. Look at him. He took it like a man."

I walk by to use the telephone while these young-ass girls continue to argue about the shit. Now see, when that little motherfucker grows up mean as hell from people fucking with him, everybody gon' wonder why, just like when my mom used to talk that dumb shit to me.

I remember when we went downtown when I first moved here. It was a parade or something going on at The Mall.

My mom was dragging me by my arm. "Come on, got'dammit! Walk ya li'l ass up!"

I didn't even wanna go to that shit. I had some new army men toys and I wanted to stay home and play with them. I mean, you know how it is when you a kid and you get some new toys. You don't care about shit else but playing with them motherfuckers. But here my damn mom was, dragging me around the street, fucking my clothes all up while all these people looked on and shook their heads.

She looked down at me and pointed with her free hand. "You see dat white man ova dere on'nat horse?"

I looked to see one of those horse-patrol cops wearing a helmet, a black leather jacket, and shiny badges.

"Yeah," I said.

"Well, if you keep actin' up, I'm gon' get him to lock you up and take you away, you hear me? Now, do you wanna be locked up in a damn cage, boy?"

I shook my head. "No."

"Well, you betta walk ya ass up den."

I hated her fucking ass! But at the same time, she bought me stuff, fed me and was always in my face, so I just got used to her. I ain't never cry because crying was punk shit, you know? But I mean, that evil shit has an effect on you; that's why I don't let nobody fuck with me now. Matter fact, she the *only* one that can do that shit and get away with it. I guess it's because she's my mom. I was about to kick her ass though that time when I had to beat the hell out of Julius. But I ain't got time to be thinking about that. I have to beep this motherfucking Butterman.

I beep him on the pay phone and wait. It's a good thing some of these phones still got the numbers on them. I remember the city had a policy where they were trying to ban the shit, and a lot of the phones didn't have numbers to call back.

This short, older guy with a trimmed beard walks up to use it.

"Yo, Joe, I'm waiting for a call," I tell him.

"I'm not gon' be but a minute."

"I ain't got no minute, man. Seriously. It's another phone down the street."

"Now, why should I have to walk—"

I reach inside my jacket where my gun is. Joe shuts the hell up and walks. Then he turns back to say something:

"What's wrong with you young brothers today, man?"

He must be asking one of those rhetorical questions because he turns back around and keeps walking up the street. And fuck him! Ain't shit wrong with me besides my rent.

The phone finally rings after waiting for like five minutes. I counted to ten three times already, and if it's not this motherfucker calling me back, I'm gon' rob *his* ass when I catch him.

"Yo, it's B."

"Yeah, this is Shank."

"Where you at?"

"Rhode Island Avenue Northeast."

"What hundred?"

"What, you comin'na pick me up?"

"Yeah."

"Aw'ight, meet me out in front of Super Trak."

"Yeah, I know where that's at."

"How many minutes?"

"Gi'me fifteen t' twenty. I'll be drivin' a 3000."

"I gi' you thirty, jus' make sure I'm not waitin' for nothin'."

"Naw, you not gon' be waitin' for nothin', Joe. I got a job for you."

"Aw'ight den. Bring the noise."

"I'm out."

We hang up. I look east down Rhode Island Avenue to see if one of those 80 buses is coming. Yeah, here comes an 82.

I jump on the bus and pay my dollar. I didn't wanna

tell this motherfucker where I was; that shit would be too close to home. I mean, he wouldn't know it anyway, but you can never be too careful. I don't know Joe like that.

I get down to Super Trak and wait for a white Mitsubishi 3000 GT. That smooth ride comes rolling around on my left from the west side of Rhode Island. Out jumps some tall, light-skinned dude with a curly-headed temple-tape and a thin-ass mustache. He's wearing one of those cowboy-looking coats with the leather strings and shit hanging down. He ain't *that* tall, but he's tall enough. I'd steal his pretty ass with a left-hand body blow, an overhand right and a left uppercut. I'd stretch his ass out like I'm Terry Norris. But fuck that, you'n's about to put me down with some ends!

He stretches out his light-ass hand. "What's up?"

"Biz'ness. And that's a nice-ass ride."

He looks back at it and smiles. "Yeah, I had t' fuck 'er a few times before she hopped on my dick, you'n. But she aw'ight now."

I smile. *So this ma-fucka's a comedian*, I'm thinking. "Yeah, well, we ain't gon' talk here, right?" I ask him, cutting through the bullshit.

"Naw, let's roll out."

He opens the passenger door. I slide on in.

"Who you think gon' win the Super Bowl this week?" he asks me as we pull off.

"Dallas."

"You don't think the Bills can pull this one out?"

"Hell no! Once a choke, twice a choke, three times a fuckin' choke."

Now I got Joe laughing. That's good. It's always good to make niggas laugh; it makes motherfuckers feel comfortable.

He pops in that new Dr. Dre tape: *The Chronic*. "You hip to this shit, man?"

"Yeah, I got it."

"Yeah, this shit is slammin'," he says, bobbing his head like a bamma.

We ride east up Rhode Island Avenue toward my crib. *I wonder where da hell he goin'*, I'm thinking. "What'chu got a run t' make?" I ask him.

He looks at me with light brown eyes. "Naw. You got anything else you gotta do t'day?"

"Nothin' but signin'nis ma-fuckin' contract I'm thinkin' you gon' gi'me."

He smiles. "Aw'ight, what we gon' do is ride up to Baltimore and back while I break everything down to you. You cool with that?"

I nod to him. "Yeah." But I'm glad I got my .38 on me with an extra clip in case Joe tries some stupid shit on me. I'm not trusting him too well. I might have to kill his ass.

He nods back to me. "Aw'ight, for starters, I'm gon' give you a gran', and then five hundred dollars a week with bonuses when you have to beat down a nigga."

"That sounds good." *Damn good!* I'm thinking. But he's still talking:

"See, it's just like with a nation. You know what I'm sayin'? You always gotta have a military."

I nod my head, paying more attention to this Dr. Dre bass than this bullshit this motherfucker talking:

"But I'm mainly gon' have you travelin' wit' me and things to make sells. 'Cause see, we gon' be comin' in contact wit' a lot of hard niggas lookin' to rob somebody. You know what I'm sayin'? 'Cause we jive-like sellin' ounces now."

I start paying more attention when I hear him say "ounces." This nigga selling weight. I might have to ask for a raise. But I don't wanna get greedy until I see how much he's pulling in.

I nod my head and smile. "Ounces, hunh?"

"Yeah." He looks over at me with those light brown eyes and grins. I'm thinking, *This ma-fucka prob'bly got a million bitches.* He says, "I heard you got a rep for killin' niggas."

"Who tol' you dat?"

"I jus' heard the shit on the street."

"Oh yeah?" *I ain't kilt no muthafucka yet, but I ain't tryin'na tell him that,* I'm thinking. It sounds like people are out here lying on my gun. Ain't that a bitch!

"I heard that people are scared'a you," he says, still grinning at me.

Yeah, dat's why I ain't have t' kill none of 'em yet, I'm thinking. But I just nod my head and put my black shades on.

He says, "What do you think about when you kill somebody?"

What da fuck is wrong wit' dude? He keeps stressin' this bullshit! "What do you think about when you sellin' niggas drugs?" I ask him. He's getting on my damn nerves!

He sits quiet and smiles at me like a bitch. He says, "Oh, I see your point: all the shit is biz'ness, hunh?"

I don't respond to the shit. I look out the window at a state trooper giving some unlucky motherfucker a speeding ticket on this Baltimore-Washington Parkway we're cruising on.

"You don't talk much, hunh?" this pretty nigga asks me.

Yo, I'm gettin' tired of this bitch-ass nigga already. I'm gon' have ta pull his skirt up like Onyx.

I frown at him. "You s'posed t' be givin' me da rundown, right?"

"Yeah, you right. But I guess it ain't much left I can tell you."

Tell me how much money we gon' be makin', ma-fucka. "How many ounces you got?" I ask him.

"Oh, we got a few. A li'l somethin'-somethin', you know?"

Okay. Now the ma-fucka wants to get secretive. "How many people gon' be runnin' wit' us?"

"We got four, not including us."

"Hard niggas?"

"Two of 'em is, but the other two are sociable. You know, you always gotta have a mix of different-type niggas on your squad, jus' like a basketball team."

I nod, but I don't agree with that dumb shit. Fuck that bamma-ass soft nigga shit!

He says, "Yeah, so you get a little bit of diversity goin' on, you know?"

"If you say so. But soft pussies always get you taken under," I tell him.

"That ain't always the case, you'n. Sometimes hard niggas can ruin your shit. And they always gettin' locked da hell up, you know?"

Yeah, like ya man Red in jail now, ma-fucka. That's why you out here gamin' me, I'm thinking. But fuck it, I need the money.

Butterman gives me a grand and tells me I got my first day off "to think things over." Do you believe this motherfucker? He act like he some kind of corporate executive or something. But it's cool. I'm gonna go and chill over Carlette's crib up at the Howard Towers Plaza

I'm gon' get a phone put in my crib. I can buy me some Karl Kani gear and other hip shit that comes out. And I'm gonna buy a big-ass grub! YEAH, I'M IN!

I call up Carlette as soon as Butterman drops me off back in the District at Popeye's on Florida and Georgia.

"Hello," she answers.

"Where you been at?"

"Where *you* been?"

"Aw, girl, I was callin' you."

"Did you leave any messages, Darnell?"

I can tell she's smiling by the sound of her sweet-ass voice. "Fuck no. I'm tired of leavin' messages."

"See, then it's not my fault. Plus I went home for the Christmas vacation. Remember I told you about that?"

"Yeah, I forgot about the shit. But yo, I'm right next to Popeye's. You want some chicken?"

"No, I had some chicken last night."

"Oh yeah? Well, what'chu want then? I'm buying."

"Oh, you are?"

I suck my teeth and smile. "I jus' said that shit, didn't I?"

She laughs. "Okay, well, I want some Chinese food then."

"Oh, so you gon' eat da Chinese food, but you don't want no nigga food, hunh?"

"No, Darnell, I just told you I had chicken last night."

I can imagine her dimpled-ass smile through the phone. And I'm gonna spend the night and *tear that ass up!*

"Yo, is it that time of the month?" I ask her, just to make sure.

She laughs. "Unt-unh, it's over. Why?"

I can tell she's smiling again. She probably has pink cheeks from all that laughing.

" 'Cause we haven't been t'gether for a while. And what was all that damn laughin' for?"

" 'Cause you funny."

" 'Cause I'm funny? What do you mean by dat?" I talk like an Italian: "Am I amusing to you? What am I, a fucking joke to you? What am I, a clown? Is that what you mean by 'funny'?"

She's laughing her ass off at my *Goodfellas* impersonation. My dick is hard as hell just thinking about her.

"Oh, cut it out and come on," she says to me.

I grin. "You smilin', ain't'chu?"

"You know I am."

"Why?"

She giggles. Then she sighs. "That quarter didn't run out yet?"

"It was twenty cent, and naw. What? You don't wanna talk to me?"

"No, I don't."

"What?"

She's laughing some more. I'm out here lunchin' up like shit.

"I wanna see you," she says.

"Naw, fuck dat! I'm gon' make you wait like you made me wait."

"Why?"

" 'Cause you should'na went home."

"But my parents would've killed me if I didn't."

That recorded message comes on telling me to put more money in.

"Ah, ha, it's time to hang up."

I smile. "Aw'ight, girl, here comes the Night Stalker."

She smiling again with her pretty-ass dimples. I mean, I just know this girl like that. You know what I'm saying? You always know your main bitch.

"Okay. Bye," she tells me.

I hang up and straighten out my shit in my pants.

I'm about to say, "Fuck da food" and just head on over there.

I get to the Howard Towers Plaza-East with the bags of Chinese food and look inside to see if my man is at the front desk. Yeah, he is. This motherfucker lets me in without all that identification shit these Howard students go through.

Fuck that shit! I don't even have a driver's license yet!

I walk in after a student and look you'n in his eyes. He drops his head and goes back to reading some textbook he's reading.

I remember when I first caught his punk-ass slipping. It was right across from the McDonald's parking lot. I caught up to his ass when I had my .25 and told him if he ever talked shit to me again I was gonna kill him. I told him that snitching on me would only get him killed when I see him again.

Man, this motherfucker ain't said *nothing* about me coming up here yet after that. But the first time, I had to sneak up to Carlette's room because of him. Joe was steady talking that identification shit.

I get up to her room on the ninth floor and see some studious-looking guy talking to her out in the hallway. She smiles at me as I walk toward them. Nerd dude shuts the fuck up.

"Well, I'll see you in class tomorrow," he says to her.

Yeah, jus' get da fuck out'a here, punk.

I smile.

"Hi," Carlette says to me, grinning.

"Don't 'Hi' me. Take dese damn bags."

"Oh." She takes the bags and bumps her ass into me. She's wearing a black skirt and a white blouse with black panty-hose.

Shit! I love taking off panty-hoses and skirts for some ass. You know what I'm saying? That shit seems sexier than just pulling off jeans.

Her colorful, decorated room smells good and flowery, like it always does. I walk right in and take off my hat, jacket and black Timberlands to stretch out across her bed.

She walks into the room with shrimp fried rice on a plate and a big, green plastic cup filled with Hawaiian Punch. She always buys that shit.

She puts it on the floor and smiles at me. "Those are new socks?" she asks, talking about my feet.

"Why?"

"Because they look so white."

I grin at her. "Why da hell you worried about my socks? I mean, you know I like to stay clean. It's a habit."

She shakes her head, smiling. "Yeah, you prob'bly buy new socks every other week."

"So what? And why you put my food on'na floor?"

" 'Cause I keep tellin' you I don't like crumbs and food and stuff on my bed."

"Well, ain't we neat."

"That's right."

I smile and climb off the bed and hit the floor. Carlette brings in her plate and cup.

"How come you didn't ask me if I wanted some of that egg-foo-yung shit?"

She laughs and chokes on her food. "See what you made me do?"

"Naw, you da one laughin'. I ain't do nothin'."

"You made me laugh." She leans down beside me with her plate. I lean over and nibble on her ear. She pulls away.

I look at her surprised-like. "What's up wit' dat?"

"I don't want no shrimp fried rice in my ear."

I grin at her. "You silly."

"No, I'm not. You are."

"Fuck is this, Pee Wee Herman an' shit?"

She fucks around and chokes on her food again. "Would you shut up so I can eat."

"Yeah, but don't get too full, 'cause I don't want you throwin' up an' shit on me."

She looks at me strangely. "Why would I throw up?"

I smile and nod back to her bed. She twists her lips and says nothing.

"What, 'chu ain't got nothin' t' say?"

"About what?"

"You know what I'm talkin' 'bout . . . Fuckin'."

She sighs and stops eating. "Must you keep calling it that?"

"Aw'ight, aw'ight, makin' love."

"Well, it ain't that either."

"What is it then?"

She smiles. "Having sex."

I giggle like a clown. "Havin' sex, hunh?"

"Mmm-hmm," she mumbles through a mouthful of food.

"You know what?" I ask her.

"What?"

"Why we sittin' here starin' at a blank tube? Turn'na fuckin' TV on."

She smiles and gets up to turn it on. "Oh, that's right, today is Thursday. Damn! We missed *Martin!*"

I'm curious. "Would you *make love* to Martin Lawrence?" I ask her.

She frowns at me. "No. Why would you ask me that?"

'Cause I'm fuckin' curious! I'm thinking. "I'on know," I tell her.

"I don't even know him. And how you know I don't make love to you?"

"Because you said that we be havin' sex."

"That's because I don't know if I could tell you the truth."

"What truth?"

She smiles and looks away. "That I really do like you."

I try to keep my cool now. This the stage where girls start to play you. That nice shit starts to sound good to you and you lose track of your game. "Yeah, okay," I tell her, like I don't give a fuck.

We sit quiet on the floor and watch TV until twelve o'-clock.

"I'on think I can make it home," I tell her. I'm teasing to see what she says. I *know* I'm spending the night already. I don't go for that girls kicking you out of their crib shit.

She says, "You can stay over. I don't have classes until one o'clock tomorrow."

"How many days is your schedule like that?"

"Just on Fridays."

"Oh."

I take off my black Champion sweatshirt and climb into her bed.

She watches me and grins. "Aren't you gonna take more than that off to sleep?"

I grin back at her. "Naw, I'm gon' take it *all* off to 'have sex.'"

She laughs and turns off her lamp. Through the silence in the dark room I can hear her stripping off her clothes.

I start to unbuckle my belt for some all-night drama. And like Eddie Murphy said in *Raw*, "My dick don't get much harder than this."

Wes

"Ray, you haven't been showing the same sales capabilities you usually have. Is everything all right?"

I pack up my things to head home after another Friday night of throwing robotic sales pitches over the phone from my downtown telemarketing job. My brown-haired white manager—who isn't much older than I am and considerably younger than a lot of the other employees—is now asking me why I haven't been performing like usual.

Typical. Whenever you're held accountable for producing quality work, people tend to believe that you're incapable of faltering on occasion like the rest of humanity.

"Yeah, I've had a lot on my mind lately," I tell him.

Jon Fletcher pats me on my back as if I'm one of his "dudes." "Well, maybe you need to chill a bit with all that overtime, pal."

Now he's trying to flatter me with a little "blackness" in his word choice. "I've already thought about that with school back underway and all," I tell him.

"Oh yeah? Where do you go?" he asks with genuine interest.

"UDC."

He looks confused. "UDC?"

I look at him questioningly. "You're not from this area, are you?"

"No way, man. I'm from upstate New York."

"Rochester"

Jon's face lights up. "Yeah, how'd you know?"

"I guessed." *And I wonder if he would have been so surprised had I been white*, I'm thinking. It seems that even though a lot of American Blacks are educated in the 1990s, many Whites still feel that we don't know anything outside of the ghetto. And at the same time, white Americans are seldom criticized for knowing almost *nothing* about Blacks.

Now I'm curious. "Have you ever heard of Howard University?" I ask him.

He grimaces, probably straining to pull some knowledge of black culture from his Eurocentric mind. "Yeah, isn't that that black school?"

"Do you know where it is?" I challenge.

"It's down here somewhere, isn't it?"

"Yeah, in Northwest, off of Georgia Avenue. And by

the way, UDC is the University of the District of Columbia. It's located up on Connecticut."

"Oh yeah, I heard'a that. I just haven't heard it called UDC. So it didn't strike me right away. Anyway, guy," he says, slapping me on my back again. "I have t' get out'a here and go party."

"In Georgetown?"

His face lights up again. "Yeah, why, you hang out in G-Town, do ya?"

I head to the door that leads into to the hallway as I respond, "No, I just figured you did." *Because you're a white boy in "Chocolate City," Washington, D.C.*

It never fails to amaze me how little white people know about us and how little they think we know about them. Actually, many blacks in America know much more about white Americans than they know about themselves—myself included. It wasn't until getting involved with the African cultural lectures held by UDC's Pan Afrikan Student Alliance and the further agitation by "The Spear"—Jesse Mc Dade—and his WPFW radio show that I began to blossom in African awareness.

I head down the escalator at Metro Center to ride the Red Line train to Fort Totten and I'm stopped by a panhandler who steps out in front of me.

"You got any change on you, brother?"

I dig into my pocket and pull out fifty-six cents and toss it in his change-jingling cup.

He smiles with a hair-covered brown face. "Thanks, brotherman. You have a good day, now."

"You hear about those three white men that set that black man on fire down in Florida?" one middle-aged sister asks another as we wait for the train.

"Yeah, girl! And two white men raped a black woman in Maryland. And you know how much time they gettin'?"

"No. How much?"

"Eighteen months! You believe that? Eighteen months!"

"Unh-hunh, now that's a damn shame, 'cause you and I both know that if it had been two black men rapin' a white girl, they would have gotten twenty years to life! You hear me?"

"Ain't it the truth! Don't make no damn sense the way they do us."

The train arrives. I jump on it and take a seat next to an older black man. I pull out my *Urban Profile* magazine and start to read.

"Who you got this Sunday?" the older brother sitting next to me asks. He smiles through a thick mustache.

"Excuse me?"

"The Super Bowl: Who you thinks gonna pull it out?"

"Oh, I mean, I don't care."

He nods. "Unh-hunh, you ain't inta sports much, hunh?"

"Not particularly, no."

We sit quietly as the train pulls into the Rhode Island station where we both watch a curvaceous chocolate-brown sister boarding our car. She takes a seat across from us.

The older brother whispers to me, "A beauty, ain't she?"

I agree. "Definitely."

He laughs with deep rumbling spurts. "You got a girl-friend?" he asks quietly.

Now I'm starting to wonder if he's just friendly, nosy or doesn't have anything better to do.

"No, we broke off before Christmas," I tell him painfully.

"Well, shit, that's the best time to break up wit' 'em. 'Cause I tell ya, young brother, some of these women will rob you blind."

I get off at my stop and catch the bus to my six-story apartment building to find Marshall, Walt and Derrick all dressed and waiting for me at the entrance.

"Come on, slow-poke, it's already ten after ten and we wanna get there early," Walt says, peering down at me from his six-foot-five frame.

"The Mirage is not gon' up and fly away if we get there at eleven-thirty," I respond. "Besides, the crowds don't really come until twelve."

"Yeah, but we don't know how long it's gon' take for you to get dressed. You know you act like a girl sometimes when it comes to gettin' ready."

We take the stairs to the fourth floor. I open my door and let them all inside my apartment.

"Well, tonight I have all my clothes ready. And I bought some Karl Kani jeans, too."

"What? Some Karl Kanis? Yo, Wes tryin'na get fly on us!" Marshall screams.

"Yeah, that nigga ti'ed of dressin' like a bamma," Walt says.

I look to Derrick, who's usually quiet, to say something in my defense. And he does:

"I mean, why can't he go out and buy some Karl Kani? It's nothing wrong with that. I mean, at least Karl Kani is a brother."

"Yeah, but this is coming from the same guy that says we spend too much on clothes," Marshall retorts. "So unless he got some Karl Kanis on a twenty-five-percent-off sale—and I doubt if he did—he's contradicting himself."

"So what? He has a right to do that. Everybody contradicts themselves if they live long enough."

"Yeah, Joe, 'cause I den done many things I said I wasn't gon' do no more," Walt says.

I pull on my loose-fitting, forty-dollar, navy blue jeans

and a navy blue cotton vest over my off-white knit shirt and striped blue tie. I brush my freshly cut hair, put in my contact lenses and spray on the finishing touch of some Drakkar cologne.

"Yo, you'n, Wes got some Drakkar!" Marshall shouts, nosing in on me inside the bathroom. "Now tell me he ain't gettin' fly on us now."

"You got some Drakkar, for real?" Derrick asks me as I walk out into my small living-room area.

I smile embarrassingly. "Yeah, I went out and splurged a bit, so sue me."

"He might just book a girl t'night," Walt says, smiling and standing up from my tan, striped, second-hand couch to leave.

I grin as I walk to my closet. I know that I'll probably receive more of the same jiving when I pull out this new yellow down coat I bought.

"OH, SHIT! Wes lost it! We gotta get him checked out at the hospital!" Marshall shouts after eying my yellow Polo coat.

Derrick looks at it, smiles and says, "You know Ralph Lauren said he don't like Blacks wearing his clothes?"

"So? Fuck him!" Walt retorts from the front door. "That white nigga can't designate who his clothes are for."

At this point in my life I'm growing tired of feeling guilty for desiring a bit of the limelight, so I agree with Walt for a change:

"There are a lot of things that white people enjoy from us that weren't necessarily produced for them: jazz, hip-hop, blues, animation, slam dunks, and even their use of slang."

"I know. That's why them white politicians are talkin' that shit about rap music now, because it's starting to reach *their* kids," Marshall agrees.

We hop into Marshall's blue '87 Pontiac and head to Southeast to the Mirage nightclub.

"So this the weekend that you give me twenty dollars, Marshall," Derrick says.

Marshall smiles over the steering wheel. "No it ain't. Dallas ain't ready yet."

Walt yells, "You crazy, boy! You see how they handled San Fran? They gon' kill Buffalo."

Derrick laughs. "Marshall the only one that don't know," he says.

"Yeah, we'll see," Marshall responds to him.

"So, Wes, what made'ju decide to get buck wild and go out and buy some gear?" Walt asks me. He's looking back from the front seat. Derrick is in the back with me.

"Well, I just wanted to experiment and see if women really do respond to a dress code."

Marshall shakes his head and frowns. "What are you, retarded? Of course they do. Especially in D.C."

"Damn straight," Walt agrees.

Derrick smiles at me from my right. "I guess you gonna find out tonight," he says.

We get to the Mirage nightclub and wait inside of a nice-sized line.

Walt says, "I tol' you it was gon' be packed early, nigga," while slapping me on my back.

He leans over to a curvy, brown-skinned sister standing with her friends in front of us. "This my boy, Wes, from UDC," he says to her.

She smiles confusingly and turns to look me over.

"Hi," I respond, slightly embarrassed that Walt put me on the spot.

"Hi you doin'?" she says.

Walt smiles and backs away, giving me room to talk to

her privately. Derrick and Marshall stand behind me, awaiting my response.

"I'm aw'ight. How 'bout you?" I say. *I have to sound cool. I have to sound cool. I have to sound cool,* I'm telling myself.

"I'm okay," she says.

We both stand quiet until Walt instigates. "So he wants to know if you gon' dance with him when we get in."

She smiles at me with sparkling eyes. "I didn't hear him say that," she says to Walt while facing me. "But my boyfriend's gon' be here later on anyway, sweetheart. Nice meeting you," she tells me. She and her girlfriends walk inside ahead of us.

I grin at my letdown because it was fun while it lasted.

"You should'a said, *'What'cha man gotta do wit' me?'* " Marshall chants, quoting Positive K's popular rap song.

"I know, man, girls always talkin'nat boyfriend shit," Walt adds.

"But she acted like she was on him," Derrick says.

We all show IDs, pay our five dollars, get our hands stamped and pay a dollar to have our coats checked.

"Yes, yes, the pretty ones are in *here,*" Walt says, rubbing his hands together. "Ay, Marshall, you got that pen on you, right?"

"Yeah."

"Well, give it here, Joe, 'cause you ain't gon' use it."

"Aw, man, you crazy!"

We all laugh and weave through the crowd. I'm noticing already that I'm getting more looks than I usually receive. I'm thinking about letting my hair grow more on top to get a temple-tape. But I'm still undecided.

Marshall says, "Ay, Wes, that girl checkin' you hard, man."

I look around cautiously. "Who?"

He laughs deceivingly. "I'm just jokin', man."

Walt chuckles with him. "Yeah, his new gear den went to his head."

I smile as we roam over to the bar. Walt orders a Long Island Iced Tea.

"Walt, please don't get drunk and start cutting up on us," Derrick says jokingly.

Walt looks at me and winks his right eye. "This what you need to book bad girls, Wes," he says, holding up his drink. "Wearin' nice clothes is only *half* the battle."

"Don't listen to him, Wes. That nigga'll have you becomin' an alcoholic," Marshall says.

Derrick nudges me to the left. "She checkin' you out, Wes."

I turn to see a pimple-faced, tanned-skinned girl eying me. "No, she's okay, but . . ."

"You hear this nigga?" Walt interjects. "Now he gon' get picky on us like he got exquisite taste."

The guys laugh.

I smile at them. "What, I can't choose the girl I want to be with?"

"No, nigga, you get wit' any girl that wants you," Walt responds, taking another sip of his drink.

I laugh myself this time. I think this Iced Tea is doing a quick job on Walt. And tonight I seem to be the focus of attention with the guys. I must say, it feels good!

After a while they stop catering to me and move out and ask girls to dance. I feel a little more confident tonight, but it seems as if the prettier girls are all taken. There are a few girls left I could probably ask for a dance, but I'd rather search the party and see who else I can see.

I look onto the Mirage's raised dance stage at a girl my complexion wearing a cream-colored outfit that nearly matches my shirt. She's looking over the rail on to the lower dance floor with her face leaning into her hands as if she's bored. And from here she looks good, but kind of young.

A sister standing in front of me suddenly shakes her girlfriend to attention. "Ay, girl, there goes Butterman! He like dat, shaw'. *He is* like dat!"

I look to my right. A familiar light-skinned face smiles openly as J struts through the crowds. The hustler called Butterman makes his way through the Mirage audience as if he's a D.C. star! I hate this, but I'm still intrigued like everyone else.

He's wearing a rust-colored outfit with a huge gold cross hanging down from his neck, attached to a thick link chain. A crew of shorter guys seem to follow and surround him as he shakes hands and greets people. And still, he's smiling confidently in my direction.

I whip my head back to where the pretty girl once stood on the raised dance floor to find that she has left. I look through the crowds.

I turn to my right again to witness the hustler called Butterman now heading my way. *Shit!*

"Ay, what's up, cousin? You jus' the man I expected t' see."

I wonder what he's up to, calling me cousin, I'm thinking.

He grabs onto me and leads me through the crowd as if we're the best of friends. I mean, sure, I know J, but I don't think I want to be involved in his "biz'ness." And I don't call him Butterman either.

"Hey, J, where are you taking me?" I ask him while he pulls me along with his arm wrapped around my shoulder.

"Aw, man, stop girlin'. I want'chu t' meet somebody, Joe. And make sure you let me do all the talkin'. Aw'ight?"

As if I have a choice with the way you're pulling me, I'm thinking. But as I begin to look forward to our destination, my heart starts to pound when I see the pretty girl I had been watching earlier. She looks openly toward us from the left side of the crowded bar area.

"Hey, girl, this is my cousin, Wes," J says to her.

"Hi," she responds.

She looks outstanding close-up. She has short-cut hair with attractive curls and a perfectly smooth complexion that matches my own. She smiles at me through shocking, dark, almond-shaped eyes. I feel like I'm about to faint.

Keep your cool! Keep your cool! Keep your cool! I yell at myself.

J says, "Yeah, my cousin 'bout ta graduate from UDC this semester, you know? And like, him and his girl just broke up recently. So I figured you two could talk, since you single now, NeNe."

She smiles at J while I keep my mouth shut, wondering, *How did he know that I broke off with my girlfriend?*

"How you jus' gon' hook me up wit' somebody like that?" she asks him.

" 'Cause I know you like nice guys, and my cousin Wes is the nicest guy I know."

"How you know I want a boyfriend?"

Boyfriend?! I'm thinking in a sudden panic. *Wow, she's getting serious fast!*

"Look, Wes'll treat'chu much better than all these bammas try'na holler at'chu."

"But I don't want nobody right now," she says through a lighthearted smile. "I need a restin' period from guys."

"Aw, girl, stop that shit. If you really needed a restin' period you wouldn't be in here lookin' all lonely. Now you gon' talk to my cousin, and when he get his Red Acura out da shop, y'all gon' do all the things that you used to talk to me about doin'."

Red Acura? Since when did I have a red Acura?

"So, Wes, this is Raidawn, but we call her NeNe. And NeNe, this is my cousin Wes."

J pushes us together as if we're two toddlers and gives me a don't-fuck-it-up look. "Aw'ight, well, let me let y'all get to know each other," he says, fading back into the crowd to join his crew.

I look at NeNe, intimidated. J walks right back in between us, flashing money in his hands. "Here. And don't be all conservative with her, either," he tells me, handing me the green bills. I open them up, revealing two twenties and a ten.

"You not really his cousin, are you?" NeNe asks me once he leaves.

"Ahh—"

"Don't lie, 'cause I know you not. So don't even try it."

I smile admittedly. "Okay, I'm not."

Already I feel that I'm out of my league. She's as forceful as Candice at school. And she's even prettier.

"So, you really go to UDC?" she asks me, sticking by my side.

"Yeah, I really do."

She grins. "Are you sure?"

I grin back at her nervously. "Yeah."

"And what's your girlfriend's name?" she says slyly.

I smile timidly at her. "Like J said, I broke up with her."

"You call him J instead of Butterman, hunh?"

"Yeah," I respond, wondering if it makes a difference to her.

"So you must be like an old friend; or do you know him from school?"

"No, I met him at Georgia Avenue Day, two years ago, when I was vending with my mother."

"And he tol' you his name was J?"

"Yeah. Why? Does it make a difference?" I finally ask her.

"Yeah, 'cause er'rybody dat sells drugs and stuff with him call him Butterman or B or Butter. Only people who he don't mess with like dat call him by his real name."

"Oh yeah? Well, how come you know this?"

"Because he goes with my cousin," she answers simply. "He used to talk to my sister back in'na day."

I chuckle. "So he goes with your cousin and he used to talk to your sister?" I ask, just to make sure I heard her facts right.

She smiles, and it warms my heart like a Boy Scout camp fire. "Yup, and my cousin and my sister used to fight over him. But er'rything cool now, 'cause my sister fell in love wit' somebody else and got married. Yup, I got a nephew and er'rything. Ain't that deep?"

I nod my head and smile in agreement with her. I'm feeling more comfortable now. I'm enjoying her company.

"So what's your cousin's name; the one that J goes with?" I ask her.

"Oh, LaToya. Why; you seen him wit' 'er before?"

I shake my head and grin. "No, I just heard that she was really pretty."

NeNe beams at me. "Yeah, she is. But that runs in my family," she says, laughing good-naturedly.

"Hey NeNe? What's hap'nin, girl?" a heavy-set brown sister asks from our left.

"Ain't nothin', jus' coolin'."

The full-bodied sister looks at me and grins. "So who's your friend?"

"Oh, this is Wes, and Wes, this is Kailah," NeNe says absentmindedly. It seems as if she doesn't want to be bothered.

"What's up?" I respond to her friend. I lean up against the bar to maintain my cool pose.

"So is he ya new man?" Kailah asks NeNe, grinning.

Oh God, this is it! She's putting us on the spot! I'm thinking. I see why NeNe didn't want to be bothered with her; she's one of those nosy, instigating sisters.

"Mind your biz, girl. Mind ya biz," NeNe responds civilly.

"Well, I mean, you need to get a new man and stop sweating Damon all like that, shaw'," Kailah says with an attitude.

NeNe sighs angrily. "Could'ju leave us alone, please. Damn!"

Kailah frowns at her. "Whatever," she says, walking off.

NeNe stands quietly. She stares out into the crowd with a blank expression. Then she speaks without facing me. "He was my old boyfriend." I nod sympathetically, just listening to her. "He in jail now for drug possession, attempted murder and a whole bunch of other shit. That's why I ain't really been messin' wit' nobody."

Derrick quickly approaches us from our right and breaks the harmony that NeNe and I are slowly building.

"You still haven't danced yet, hunh?" he asks me. I don't think he knows that she's with me by his tone.

"No, I've been standing here talking to my friend," I tell him.

NeNe smiles at him and introduces herself. Derrick then sneaks behind me and jars me softly in my ribs. I guess he likes her as much as I do.

Silk's slow song, "Freak Me," comes on. That's the group that Keith Sweat produced. To my surprise, NeNe pulls me onto the dance floor. As we embrace and slow drag, I face Derrick. He gives me all kinds of male-talk hand signals referring to NeNe. I try my hardest not to laugh.

"You seem like a real nice person," she says, cuddling closer to me. I'm wondering if she can feel my raging erection through my jeans.

"I am, but a lot of women don't appreciate 'real nice' persons."

I hope I'm not sounding preachy. God knows I don't want to bore her off.

"Well, I think it's about time we start," she says, again surprising me. I can feel her smiling against my shoulder.

"So what are you trying to say?" I find the courage to ask.

"I'm sayin' that I might jus' talk to you, that is, if you're really nice to me."

I want to scream, "I'll be nice! I'll be nice! I'll be nice!" But instead, I remain quiet and let her do the talking.

"I mean, sometimes you can jus' tell when a person is about somethin'. And I had a lot of guys that wanted to talk to me when I went with Damon, but I was always too loyal and hard-headed when people told me how bad he was."

"And now?" I ask her inquisitively.

She draws her head away from my shoulder and smiles at me. "Well, if you can help me, maybe I can change."

I feel dizzy, like I'm about to fall back into the crowd. I feel sexy, like I want to kiss her. And I feel included, as if I'm really a part of something special in this world.

"Yeah, I hope I can," I tell her.

She drops her head back against my shoulder while the second slow song comes on: "Weak," by SWV.

"You're wearing Drakkar, aren't'chu?" NeNe asks.

"Yeah, you can tell?"

"Mmm-hmm. I love how Drakkar smells."

That's good. I love that she loves it! I'm thinking.

As soon as we finish dancing and head back to the bar area, J snatches me by my shoulder again and leads me into the men's bathroom. Using my peripheral vision I can see the utter confusion in Marshall's, Walt's and Derrick's eyes.

"So you like her, Wes?" J asks me inside of the bathroom.

"Like her? Man, I love her! She's beautiful, sweet and everything. I mean, what's *not* to love about her!"

J smiles. "You wanna take her home t'night?"

"Say what?" *I don't think I heard him right.*

J laughs. "You heard me, nigga. Stop actin' like a bamma."

"She's just gonna go home with somebody she just met?"

"Look, let me hook it up. Aw'ight?"

I have to know this, I'm thinking. "She's not a whore or anything, is she?" I ask, holding my breath. "Because she told me that she was loyal to her last boyfriend."

J frowns at me as if he's dissapointed with my thoughts. He shakes his head violently. "Naw, Joe, you ain't gon' bang 'er t'night, but she'll stay with you."

"How do you know?"

"Look, man, 'nat girl can hang late, but she's not a whore and she *is* real loyal. I mean, 'nat last nigga she went with for three years and nobody could touch her. She tol' you da truth about that shit, you'n! Now let me do the talkin', aw'ight?"

We walk back out to where my friends and NeNe's friends are all in proximity in front of the crowded bar.

"Hey, Butterman," one of NeNe's girlfriends says.

J looks over her well-curved frame, packed inside of a tight-fitting one-piece body dress. "Hey, nasty," he responds to her.

She frowns. "What I tell you 'bout callin' me dat shit, man?"

J laughs it off and hugs her. "Come on, girl, you know I'm jus' bull-shittin'."

"Yeah, aw'ight. Whatever."

"Anyway, NeNe wanted to check out my new car, so I'm gon' take her home t'night after I drop Wes off," J announces.

Smooth plan, I'm thinking. But will it work?

"Oh yeah, that's right," NeNe responds excitedly. "I forgot about'cha car. And it's about time you gi'me a ride," she says, bumping J like a little sister would. I'm wondering again how old she is.

"Yo, Wes, we'll jus' get wit' you tomorrow then, boy," Marshall says up-tempo. I can tell that he's happy for me.

"Yeah, nigga, we'll get back," Walt adds.

I look to Derrick. He nods at me happily.

"Well, let's get da hell out'a here den," J says. He bends over and hugs NeNe toward the coat room while signaling to his boys that we are leaving.

We get our coats and I notice a sharp-eyed, crow-looking brother dressed in all black. He leads our small caravan of five guys and one girl out of the door.

"Yo, watch where da fuck you goin', Joe," he says to a seemingly drunken brother who crosses our path.

"Oh, my fault, man."

"Yeah, jus' don't let that shit happen again."

"Yo, don't kill 'em, Shank. Be cool, man," J says to him.

Shank: what a perfect name for him.

We all step outside. J stops and talks to his other two boys. "Yo, Steve and Rudy, here's twenty dollars. Y'all go 'head and take a cab home. Cool?" he asks them.

"Yeah, as long as you payin', it's cool wit' me. Shit," says the one named Steve.

I look toward Shank, who walks in front of us with a quick, arm-swinging gangster stroll. He surveys the corner as we walk up behind him.

NeNe whispers, "Who's dat?"

"That's my new bodyguard," J says, smiling.

We approach his white Mitsubishi 3000 GT. Shank

waits outside the door. He's chilling with black shades on and a low-cut temple-tape.

"Hey, man, you look like a black Ninja," I comment humorously.

J laughs as Shank responds through a tight smile, "Yeah, well, get in'na fuckin' car before I chop ya neck off."

We all chuckle except for Shank. J opens the doors. NeNe and I climb in the back and Shank rides up front.

"Yeah, we got a lot of runs t' make t'mar, man. So like, we prob'bly gon' get out early around ten. Aw'ight?" J says to Shank.

"You da man," Shank tells him while he stares out of his window. I watch him as he pulls out a tape from his black leather jacket and jams it inside J's cassette player, stopping the car radio without even asking. "Yo, dis Diamond D from Diggin' In The Crates' crew," he says.

"Aw'ight," J responds to him.

I ask, "Hey, is this the same group that does that song: 'Sally Got A One Track Mind'?"

"Yeah," J answers.

I smile. "I like that song." I was really asking Shank, but he doesn't seem to talk much.

"So where you move to now, Wes?" J asks me.

Damn, he's smooth! I'm thinking. NeNe isn't even paying attention. She's bobbing her head to some rather different-sounding beats with an added percussion influence. I guess Diamond D really did "dig in the crates."

"In the Fort Totten area," I tell J, directing the way to my block.

When we park out in front of my apartment building, J says, "Ay, NeNe, let Wes call you a cab from his crib. I jus' remembered I gotta make a run out t' Rockville."

"Rockville? At one o'clock in'na morning?" she asks, shocked to attention.

"Look, girl, do I look like I'm in high school? Now come on, I'm runnin' late as it is."

NeNe sucks her teeth as Shank jumps out and stands in front of the car and looks up at my building.

"He's quiet, hunh?" I ask J while I climb out behind NeNe.

J smiles. "Yeah, dat's my killa. He's s'posed t' be quiet. Boy like Terminator X; he only speaks with his hands."

NeNe slams J's door after I make it out. "You got dis shit, J! You think you so-o-o slick!"

J winks at me through his windshield.

Shank walks backward and opens the door to get in. "Yo, you bes' handle that li'l temper she got on 'er," he tells me.

I grin at him as NeNe waits for me on the sidewalk. "Be cool, Ninja."

He shakes his head and smiles before getting inside the car. NeNe doesn't respond as J speeds up the street with Shank.

"I hope you got a neat apartment, 'cause I can't stand mess," she says to me. She smiles as we go inside and climb the stairs.

"Yeah, my room, I mean apartment, is real neat."

NeNe chuckles at my Freudian slip and says, "It better be."

We get inside and she just adores it.

"Oh, this is nice!"

"It's small, but it's my home for a while," I say, happy that she actually likes it.

"Yeah, but it's clean and jazzy lookin'. I like these black art prints you have on your walls, too," she tells me, searching over everything in sight.

"Yeah, I bought some of them up at P.G. Plaza and some from African vendors during the Black Family Reunion Day celebration."

"Oh, Wes, this place is so nice," she reiterates, now walking into my fresh-scented bathroom.

I stand inside my small kitchen pouring apple juice, amazed at how quickly things have turned around for me inside just one evening.

NeNe tries on my Polo coat and hangs it back in the closet. "Wes, do you have any incense?" she asks me, kicking off her shoes.

Hell, I guess she's not taking a taxi home, I'm thinking as I watch her. "Yeah, I have some," I respond, going immediately to my bedroom dresser to get it.

I bring it back to the living room where NeNe sits on my second-hand couch, watching a late night horror movie on TV.

"Sit right here," she says with her beautiful smile, patting the space beside her.

Oh my God! I simply cannot believe that this is happening!

I sit down beside her. She immediately leans her head against my shoulder. "I'm not a slut or anything, okay, so I jus' want you to know that up front, 'cause I don't usually do things like this. But I feel good with you and I like you, okay, but jus' don't try t' hurt me or nothin' like that 'cause I jus' came out of a tough relationship and I don't wanna go through that again."

"Okay," I tell her, still not believing my ears. Where has all this kind of story-book drama been in my life? How come I've never felt this excited before, this full-filled, this comfortable? Damn it, I'm simply in heaven!

"Wes, can you answer a question for me?" NeNe suddenly asks. She leans up and looks me straight in my contact-lens-covered eyes.

"Yeah. Sure."

"Umm, if I, umm, spend the night, are you gon' try anything wit' me?"

"No, of course not. I just met you and I respect you. A lot," I respond hurriedly.

GOD! It feels like my heart is burning a hole through my chest. This just can't be real!

She looks happily at me as if I've correctly answered a million-dollar question. "Okay, well, do you have anything that I can sleep in? And I need to make a phone call."

"Yeah, you can sleep in my bathrobe. I have a winter one and a lighter one for the summer. And yeah, you can use my phone."

I set my living room phone down beside her and she kisses my cheek. "You so sweet. But I jus' asked you that because I'm not fast or nothin', I jus' wanted to stay with you tonight. I mean, if that's okay with you."

"Yeah, it's okay with me. Definitely."

NeNe makes her phone call: "Hey, it's me. I'm at my girlfriend Brenda's house. I'll be home in the morning." She hangs up and smiles at me. "I live with my aunt; she's cool."

NeNe leans back into me as we continue to watch this late night horror movie: *The Evil Dead.* I have nothing to say about her lying to her aunt. Girls will be girls. And by now my erection has settled down. I'm feeling more relaxed now than I think I've ever felt in my life. And out of all the things that I've acheived thus far in life, I truly believe that nothing on God's green earth is as gratifying as the connection between a man and a woman. This is exactly what the doctor ordered to fulfill my growing sense of emptiness: L-O-V-E.

CHAPTER 5

Wes

You only live once, so I've now decided to live it up while I'm in the hot seat.

I bought some more "hip gear": Tommy Hilfiger shirts, Girbaud jeans, Calvin Kleins, a Karl Kani vest, Nike Airs and Cross Colours apparel. I also bought an African American College Alliance sweatshirt. It's always good to support the brothers too, while I'm out here spending money. But it hasn't been all of my money. J has been giving me a lot of "gifts," as he calls them.

I'm waiting for J now in front of UDC on Connecticut Avenue.

"Hey, Wes, so when you gon' take me out?" Candice asks me, startling me from behind.

I turn around and face her. "Oh, well, I didn't know that you had broken up with Antwan."

Candice looks as good as she usually does, but she kids a lot, so I'm not actually taking her proposal for a date seriously. I'm more or less stalling.

She leans into me, smiling with a flushed red face. The whipping February cold seems to have done her in. "I'm jus' playin' wit'chu, Wes. You get so serious all the time," she says, fighting to keep her scarf from blowing around in the wind.

See what I mean about the kidding? And I guess she can read the panic all over my face, especially since I have a new girlfriend and all.

J pulls up to the curb at the corner in his 3000 GT. Perfect timing to save my neck! He blows the horn and opens the passenger door.

Candice looks at me bewildered. "You be hangin' wit' him now?"

"No, not really," I tell her, walking toward the car.

"So you really are gettin' buck-wild, hunh, Wes?" she asks as I hop in.

I hold the door open. "Who told you that?" I ask her. It was probably Walt, because Derrick and Marshall don't know Candice as well as Walt does.

She smiles and backs away toward the Van Ness Metro station. "I'll talk to you about it tomorrow."

I shut the door and turn to find J grinning at me.

"She on you, man. You should holler at 'er and get that seven."

"No, it's nothing like that. She just likes to play around a lot."

J looks out into the traffic as we head down Connecticut toward center city.

"If you say so, you'n. But I know girls."

I smile agreeably. "Yeah, I bet you do."

"Oh, you *know* I do. But what's been goin' on wit' you and NeNe?"

"We're getting along just fine."

J smiles, and now I'm wondering what he's thinking. He says, "I heard she been spendin' the night a lot."

"So, who's been dispersing our business?" I ask him.

"Man, I know the girl been hangin' out late, and she ain't been at the parties, so she has to be with you."

"That doesn't mean she's automatically with—"

"DAMN!" J slams his car horn, cutting me off. "You see that shit, man? I hate non-drivin' ma-fuckas, Joe! You'n didn't even look where he was goin'."

I chuckle, after watching a green Toyota slash out in front of us without any warning.

J shakes his head in disgust. "Anyway . . . did'ju bang her yet?"

"That's none of your business," I snap. But truthfully, I didn't. Not yet. But we did get close once.

J laughs as we get closer to my downtown telemarketing job. He double parks outside in front of the towering building where I work on the eighth floor.

"So when you gon' come in and be my banker?" he asks me.

"I told you what to do already," I respond defensively.

J nods. "Aw'ight, so I call the Maryland Business Bureau and secure a company name for twelve dollars, then I take the forms to a bank and open up an account under an assumed business with all my named positions: president, vice president and the board members an' shit."

"That's all you have to do. But if you have a problem with naming positions, you can file for a sole-proprietorship."

"Yeah, I know."

"So what's the problem? You have everything under control. I mean, you seem to understand everything."

He grins at me again as we both watch a well-built sister enter my work building.

"She phat t' death. Ain't she, you'n?"

I smile out of the window at her. "I guess so."

"Well, anyway, as soon as I get the time to do all that, I'm gon' hook it up. And I'm gon' put'chu down as one of the board members," J says,

I jerk around and face him heatedly. "WHAT?"

J smiles. "Aw, nigga, stop girlin', man."

"No, don't do that, J. Seriously."

"Why not; it's gon' be legal, right?"

"Yeah, but your money's not, and I'm not trying to get mixed up into that!" I shake my head, feeling crossed. "See, I knew I shouldn't have taken any money from you. Now you gonna sit here and try to force me into this drug business after I've already told you that I don't want any part of it."

J looks solemnly out of his front window. I'll repay him his money if that's what he's thinking. "Look, man, I'm 'bout t' build up enough money so we can go into a legit business," he says instead. "Now, since I've known you, you been vendoring, organizing and conserving ya ends. You know? Plus, I can trust you, and it ain't that many niggas out here that you can trust wit'cha money."

He pauses and starts up again. "Anyway, workin' for this white man an' bustin' ya ass for little more than minimum wage ain't gon' get it. Now what I'm sayin' is that you have a chance to get hooked up with something that's gon' pay off. I trust you, man. That's why I'm sweatin' you like you a fat-ass girl. But yo, I want'chu t' think over shit, 'cause I ain't askin' for you to do *nothin'* but plan out ways to multiply da money."

He peers into my eyes through my new thin-rimmed school-boy glasses, and grips my arm. "You hear me, man? It's strictly biz'ness."

"Yeah, whatever," I say as I hop out of the car and head toward my work building. I just don't understand why J's sweating me. There are a lot of guys hungry for an opportunity to become *filthy* rich. But I'd rather re-

main clean. And that means no more taking money from
J. It was stupid of me in the first place! Of course he'd
want something in return: my soul.

I take the elevator, walk into the offices and head toward the lounge area. It's not quite three-thirty yet, so
the morning shift is still busy calling away. My shift
starts at four.

"You hear about them young'uns gettin' shot up over
in Southeast?" Eugene asks me, glancing through the
Washington Post in his hands. He dips his gray-haired
head in and out of the paper as he leans back into one of
the lounge chairs.

"No I haven't. But how many of them was it?" I ask,
wondering what the death toll is in D.C. by now.

"Four got shot and two of 'em died," Eugene answers.
He shakes his head. "What's wrong wit' dese young'uns
out here, Ray? I mean, I jus' can't un'nerstan' 'em."

I take a seat as I answer: "They're unfulfilled, and they
feel like they don't have a place in this society. So what's
happening is that they're creating their own culture
based on anger and destroying the enemy."

"Enemy? What enemy they got at sixteen and fifteen
years old?"

"Other sixteen- and fifteen-year-olds."

"But why?"

"Because they don't want anybody to dis or carry
them."

Eugene shakes his head again and grimaces. "You
know, I done sent three young'uns of my own off to do
something with their lives and now I got gran'chil'ren
wearin' pants hangin' all down off their behinds, using
filthy language and then gettin' mad at *me* when I call
'em on it. Now, I raised *my* three right, but something
went wrong when'*ney* had chil'ren for 'em to turn out

like dey is. One of my gran'sons is in jail now for tryin' ta shoot somebody."

He throws up his hands in disgust with the newspaper now on his lap. "I tell ya, Ray, I jus' can't un'nerstan' 'em."

I nod, thinking more so about Eugene still working at sixty years old than about the young'uns killing each other. I wonder how many of them even think about reaching sixty and having grandchildren. And Eugene may not have the best English grammar in the world, but he's one of our top sellers because he uses his friendly humor and wisdom to charm customers rather than sell them. That's one of the main problems in America today: everybody wants fast sales—even me.

Four o'clock ticks around and we all head to our stations, wipe the phones off with alcohol pads, and gather our pitch scripts. This week we're selling memberships and asking for contributions for the Clean Water Association, an environmental group.

After I get turned down by seven prospects, the young, white manager, Jon Fletcher, calls me into his office. While I head to the small room I notice that this fly brown-skinned girl named Sherry is watching me. She's been eying me for the past couple of weeks, probably after noticing my wardrobe improvement. She's never paid any attention to me before.

"You have a phone call. She says it's an emergency," Jon says with a smirk, as if he believes it's a lie.

"Hello," I answer.

NeNe's voice rushes across the line. "What time you get off?"

"Nine-thirty."

"Can I meet you there?"

"Yeah."

"Okay, I'll see you later then."

"Fine," I tell her, dazed at her forwardness.

I hang up and catch Jon staring at me.

"Was that your sister or something?" he asks.

"No," I respond flatly. I don't feel too talkative today. I head back to my station.

Jon rushes to his feet from behind his desk. "Hey, Wes, pal, I wanted to talk to you about something else, too."

I stop at the door. "Oh yeah, and what's that?"

"Well, you know, you've been doin' a lot of overtime lately—well, since you been here actually—and the company is now deciding that we won't need as many extra hours as before. So starting next week we'll have to cut back on your overtime."

Now I stare at him. "How long have you known this?"

Jon starts to turn red. Black Americans are not supposed to ask questions; we're supposed to bow down and take anything white America dishes out to us.

"Well, the management has talked about it. But you know, we just lollygagged a lot and never really brought it up when we were supposed to because we still had a considerable-sized budget."

"But now you don't?"

"Well, it's like, we do, but we want to make sure that we're able to *keep* a budget. You know what I mean? So we're gonna have to cut hours a bit, especially from our overtime workers."

"Whatever," I respond to him, walking out. *I bet his hours won't be cut,* I'm thinking.

Sherry's peeking at me again as I round the corner to my aisle. I feel like asking her what she's looking at. But right now wouldn't be the right time; I'm too pissed off.

I pass Corey Blair, another Georgetown-looking white boy with blond hair, who's been doing as much overtime as I have.

"Hey, Corey, are they cutting back your overtime hours?" I ask him after waiting for him to hang up on an unsuccessful sale.

Corey shakes his head confusingly. "Hell no, man! I need this money to pay my car insurance. No way are they cutting my OT." He smiles humorously. "Why? Are they cutting your overtime?"

"Yeah," I answer solemnly.

Corey turns a bit red too now. I guess he's feeling guilty. "Well, I mean, you've been here longer than I have so it's probably a thing where, you know, they're trying to equal out time. I mean, who knows? Maybe they haven't called me yet . . . But damn. That would be really fucked up if they were cutting hours. You know?"

I walk off rudely to get away from his rambling. I return to my station to finish up my five-hour Wednesday shift.

At nine-thirty-five I get off of the elevator at the bottom-floor level and find NeNe waiting inside the building for me. She's wearing a short, chestnut-colored fur coat and matching leather gloves. And boy does this make me feel good after just being cut out of a sum of one hundred and twenty-eight dollars per paycheck.

"Hi," she says, beaming. "Do I get a hug?"

"Of course you do." I hug her and step back. "This coat must've cost a pretty penny."

"Naw, my sister got it for me."

"That doesn't mean it's not expensive."

"Yeah, I guess you're right. But Wes, let's go to Friday's restaurant on Pennsylvania Avenue before we go home, okay?" She slips her left arm underneath my right arm and leads me out of the building.

"Well, I'm a little low on funds right now. I mean, I wasn't expecting to go to dinner or anything tonight," I tell her apologetically.

"I'll pay for it. But don't let this happen again," she responds playfully. "My mother taught me to always have a li'l bit on me to splurge, because you never know what might cross ya path when you're walking around broke."

"What if you don't have any money to carry?"

She smiles, sly and sexy. "Oh, well, I wouldn't know anything about that."

We walk down to Pennsylvania Avenue and jump on a 34 bus. We arrive at Friday's. It's very comfortable inside with a dimness that has a hint of romance. I must say, NeNe has made a good choice.

"Have you ever eaten here before?" I ask her as I look over the menu.

"No, but I've always wanted to."

She's wearing a yellow outfit which highlights the yellow stripes in my multi-colored Cross Colours shirt. She has a freshly-cut bob hairstyle that shines with professional care: the old En Vogue look.

"What about you?" she asks me in return.

"Nope, I haven't. But I do like this place."

She smiles while observing the pleasant surroundings. "I know; it *is* nice."

We both order Italian pasta meals with chicken, accompanied by salad and water. NeNe orders a medium-sized Sprite and I order a Coke.

"So how was ya day?" she asks me, sipping her Sprite through a straw.

"Terrible. I just had more than a hundred dollars taken from my paychecks."

She puts her drink down, eager to speak on it. "Don't even worry about it. As long as you in wit' Butterman, you don't have t' worry about money."

"Hmm. Why are you so sure about that?"

" 'Cause he likes you, a lot."

"How you know?"

"Because he would've never introduced you to me if he thought you wasn't right."

I'm starting to wonder if she'd say anything about me selling drugs.

"How would you feel if I started working with J?" I ask her curiously.

"What? You think I would tell you not to?"

"What would you tell me?"

"First of all, you're not the drug-selling type, so he wouldn't even have you doin'nat."

"So, what would he have me doing?"

"Well, when his friend Tub was still livin', Tub would break down all the money and make sure they kept things organized. 'Cause you know, a lot of times when guys hustle all they end up doin' is spen'in'-up the money."

I shake my head.

"What?" she quizzes me.

"I mean, you talk about the drug trade as if it's a regular thing."

She frowns at me. "Hmm, Joe, it is. It's so many drug dealers in D.C. that it seems like a normal career occupation."

"And that doesn't bother you?"

"Why, because some people are strung out on drugs? That's America's problem, not my problem."

"But what if someone close to you was strung out on drugs?"

"There is—my uncle. And he used to bother my mother for money until my father almost shot and killed 'im. Now my uncle is in Alexandria, Virginia, some-damn-where."

"And you're telling me that that didn't bother you?"

She plays with the food on her fork. "Of course it did. But it ain't nothin' I can do about my uncle. He gotta get his own life together."

Neither of us are hungry enough to finish our food. We order doggie bags and run to catch a 32 bus. We head for Seventh Street at Judiciary Square so we can catch the Red Line Metro to Fort Totten.

NeNe has spent the night with me five times already. She doesn't lie to her aunt about being at one of her girl-friend's houses anymore. That was just that first night. Raidawn is nineteen years old, turning twenty in August; a "grown woman" she calls herself. I'll be turning twenty-two in July, so I guess we're a perfect couple age-wise.

NeNe hollers as soon as we enter my hole-in-the-wall but neat apartment, "We should go to the movies this Friday, Wes!"

"To see what?" I ask, hanging our coats inside the closet.

She turns on the TV and pounces on my living-room couch. "Umm, *Universal Soldier*. And *Unlawful Entry* is comin' out. Which one?"

"Okay. Either one is fine with me," I tell her.

I sit down beside her on the couch. She immediately runs her long painted nails through my thick and growing hair.

"I need a haircut, hunh?" I ask her, feeling a bit embar-rassed.

NeNe's fingers massage my nape, where my hair *used* to blend into a fade. "Yeah, you should get another tem-ple tape."

"High like J's, hunh?"

She smiles. "Yup."

Now I'm starting to wonder if they ever did anything. Or maybe it's just that platonic love thing going on.

"You seem to like J a lot," I comment.

She grimaces at me, reading my ill thoughts. "Yeah, but not like *that*, Wes. But I like that you're jealous about it."

My brow raises in shock. "You *like* that I'm jealous?"

"Yeah, it shows that you care."

"But we go with each other. Of course I care."

She grins at me. "But even still, Wes, when a guy shows that he's jealous, it's like *proof* that he likes you."

"Yeah, but—"

NeNe kisses me on my mouth with her moist lips. "Shut up. You argue too much," she tells me, still teasing my lips with her tongue. By now my tool is gearing up to attention. And NeNe puts her left hand right where it feels good.

I run my left hand softly across her breasts. NeNe stops me with her free right hand.

"Don't be bad," she whispers.

"Why not?" I whisper back.

She giggles. "Because I tol' you not to."

"Well, how long do I have to be good?"

She giggles again. "Until I *say* you can be bad."

"Well, say it then," I demand seductively.

All the while she continues to tease me with her tongue and tickle my neck with her left-handed fingers.

Before I know it, we're wrapped into each other like snakes.

"You don't have ta get me your robe t'night," she tells me dizzily. By now my glasses are off, but I can still clearly see how sexy and pretty she is, even with my far-sighted vision.

"So what are you planning to sleep in?" I ask her.

She huffs in my ear, "Nothin'."

"And you still expect me to be good?"

"If I tell you to."

"Well, are you gonna tell me to?"

She smiles. "I'm still thinkin' 'bout it."

We get up from the living-room couch, turn off the television and head into the bedroom, still tingling with sexual vibrations. NeNe pushes me softly across my bed and stretches out on top of me. We resume our kissing as she wiggles out of her clothing. I virtually rip mine off.

"Do you have any protection?" she asks me.

I scramble nakedly to my tall dresser drawer and pull out my lubricated Trojan-Enz. NeNe slips underneath my quilt blanket as I snuggle back into bed with her and rip the condom package open.

"Take your time, Wes. We got all night. I ain't goin' nowhere," she tells me through a barely visible smile in the darkness of my silent room. I think I heard that line before in a SWV song. Or maybe it was Mary J. Blige. But now is not the time for musical commentary.

"I know," is all that I can muster as NeNe ravishes me with her hands, lips, legs and toes.

We destroy my neatly made bed with our pushing and pulling and tossing and turning and loving each other.

I roll over in exhaustion once we're done. NeNe edges her head to my chest. Her left leg wraps across my body as I lay stretched out on my back.

"Was it good?" she asks me.

"Aw, man, was it!" I respond breathlessly.

She chuckles softly and squeezes my ribs. "It was for me, too."

I smile and stare at the ceiling as I run my hands through what's left of her once neatly bobbed hair, which is now wet from our heated passion. I feel ticklish inside as if a swarm of butterflies were racing back and forth from my toes to the top of my head. And I want to shout to her, "Yes! This is life! I love you!" But I don't, because I don't think it would be too cool. So instead, I squeeze her back as hard as she squeezes me. And I let our satisfied silence shout it for me.

Butterman

"Yo, nigga, I got what'cha need!" I yell from my 3000 to my boy Drake from the old school. We go wa-a-a-y back.

Drake walks over, smiling and still looking like an oversized, light brown teddy bear. He's wearing a gray ski hat pulled down over his ears and a matching gray down coat.

"Yo, Joe, where you been at?" he asks me, extending his hand through my open window for a pound.

I smile. "To the moon and back, you'n."

He grins with kiddie-looking dimples. "Did'ju sell any drugs to Martians while you was flyin' around in'nis space mobile, shawdy?"

I laugh. "Yeah, dey some cool ma-fuckas, shaw'."

Drake looks over to Shank, who's sitting in my passenger seat.

"Oh, this my boy Shank," I tell him.

"What's up?" Drake says.

Shank nods his head in silence. He's listening to Kool G Rap & Polo on my system.

"Nigga don't talk much, hunh?" Drake says, smiling.

Shank looks over to him with penetrating eyes, like he got X-ray vision.

I chuckle to lighten things up. "Be cool, Shank. Don't kill 'im. He was just jokin'."

Shank shakes his head and looks out the window to his right.

"What's up wit'cha boy, man? I mean, I'm just tryin'na

be cool wit' you'n, Joe. See, that's what's wrong wit' niggas now: always thinkin' somebody tryin'na carry 'em."

Shank turns and looks at me. "Yo, dis ya boy? You
about ta lose that nigga, Joe. You betta tell 'im t' shut da
fuck up."

"Yo, I got ounces, man, so beep me when you ready," I
tell Drake as I pull off.

He nods, still thinking about responding to Shank;
that's why I'm jetting out, because I don't want these two
niggas getting into nothing. Drake was never one to back
down. He even gave Red a run for his money.

Me and Shank coast up Eighteenth Street in Adams
Morgan before either one of us says anything.

I say, "Yo, Shank, chill out a bit, man. Drake is cool. He
jus' got a big mouth sometimes."

"Niggas wit' big mowfs find big holes in'ney chests."

I chuckle. You'n a straight-up killer. "Yeah, but he
aw'ight," I tell him.

"Yo, we should get some grub while we up here,"
Shank says, checking out the flashing neon lights from
the restaurant signs.

"Yeah, but first I gotta check my boy Ahmad."

Shank looks over at me. "He a Ethiopian?"

"Yeah, how you know?"

"Shit, da ma-fucka name Ahmad and we in Adams
Morgan. Nigga gotta be an Ethiopian."

I chuckle again as we pull up into a parking spot.
"Damn, this must be my lucky night! I can't never get a
parking spot when I got a girl wit' me."

Shank smiles with a tight face, as if he's straining to let
it show. "Yeah, well, it's good t' make bitches walk."

I laugh like shit as I hop out. Shank gets out after me
and leans with his back against the door.

I run into this dark Ethiopian restaurant. Ahmad is
cleaning tables.

"Yo!" I yell to him and walk back out. He knows what I want.

Ahmad strolls outside wearing a rayon shirt, open at the chest. He's wearing purple slacks and black snake-skin shoes. He has a high-rounded Philly cut with thick black hair, looking like he's some kind of ethnic pimp.

"Yo, so you got some new weed for me?" I ask him.

Ahmad walks over to my car, ignoring my question. "This a nice baby."

"Yeah, she aw'ight. She got some good pussy though. I be fuckin' 'er all'la time."

We start laughing, standing out here in the cold and watching our breaths turn into the cold wind.

"Ain't'chu freezin', man? This ain't summertime, Joe," I ask him.

Ahmad shakes his body against the wind. "Nope, I can take it. Ethiopians are warriors."

He and Shank make eye contact. "What's up?" Ahmad says.

Shank nods his head, again in silence.

"I'll have it for you later on t'night," Ahmad says, turning back to me. "Come back around twelve."

I joke with him. "Aw'ight, I'm gon' buy a pound." Ahmad smiles. "Naw, I'm just jokin', man. Gi'me the usual."

He nods. Me and Shank hop back into the car, where the shit is still warm.

"God damn, man! February is colder than it was in December!"

"No bullshit!" Shank says.

We roll out and head up Sixteenth Street. This street is familiar territory for me. But my parents don't live up on The Gold Coast no more; they moved their integrating asses out to Fairfax County, Virginia, commuting on the Metro to get to work every day. Shit don't make no damn sense.

"I heard rich ma-fuckas live up here," Shank says, looking out the window at the four-, five- and six-bedroom houses with pretty lawns lined up on Sixteenth Street.

I make a right on Kennedy and head back toward Georgia Avenue. This is the same route I used to take when I rode my bike.

I say, "I used to live up here."

Shank smiles as if he already knew. "Yeah, you act like a rich nigga."

I grimace. "How?"

"Man, I can't explain'na shit. You just do."

"What makes me any different from other niggas sellin' drugs?"

"You act like you sellin' for a damn hobby. Other niggas be clockin' twenty-four–seven; you out here ridin' 'round in your car all day."

"Aw man, 'nat's 'cause I got runners workin' for me. I mean, when you start sellin' ounces, you ain't all out here on'na street corna wit' a couple bags hidin' in'na bushes and shit."

"Yeah, whatever you say."

We sit quiet as we roll around to where I told Steve, Rudy and Otis to meet us. I had to let Fred go. Joe was too lazy to work for me. And I'm pretty cool about shit, so I know he couldn't get put down with nobody else, except with some New Jack niggas who don't know nothing.

I'm still thinking about that shit that Shank said though.

"Ay, man, Bink rides around with his niggas all day, too. Is he actin' like a rich nigga?"

Shank looks at me. "How long you knew Bink?"

" 'Bout six years."

"Have you ever seen him look like he was poor?"

"Hell no! That nigga was always paid!"

Shank smiles. This nigga got me hooked on a string. I

ain't even gonna lie. I'm curious about what he's thinking.

"You ever heard about his pop?" he asks me.

"Naw, but Bink'll talk a little about 'im er'ry now and then."

"Yeah, well, his pop been in'na game for years. He from New York. And that ma-fucka Bink ain't never know what poverty was. The way I see it is like this: some ma-fuckas may live in a poor neighborhood, but that don't mean they poor."

"So how come dey livin'nere?"

"Because they used to da shit."

I frown at him. "No it ain't; it's because they don't know how ta move!"

"What if they ain't have no money for movin'?"

"Wait a minute. I thought you said that they wasn't poor."

"I'm talkin' about bein' poor in the mental state. It's kinda like *feelin'* poor."

Aw, man, this nigga is crazy! "I don't give a fuck if you don't *feel* poor! If you can't do the types of shit that middle-class and upper-class people do, then you ain't got no money."

"Whatever, man."

Shank looks out of the window while we wait inside the car for these niggas to show. And I still have some things to tell you'n:

"You know, it's a lot of people wit' no health care, no life insurance, no home insurance. No *shit!* Matter fact, a lot of these people don't even own their damn homes, livin' in fucked-up-ass apartment buildings from Section Eight."

Shank looks mad at me now. "Aw'ight den, you *a Richie-Rich*-type ma-fucka! How come you ain't somewhere in law school so you can get out and work for your father's company? And how come you ain't got no stocks and bonds, and other shit like that?"

I giggle like a silly-ass girl that's just been carried. "I got some stocks and bonds, nigga."

"Yeah, sure ya right."

Shank sits smiling as these three stooges come rolling around the corner with chips and sodas. I hop out of the car. "I hope that ain't my money y'all just spent!"

Steve says, "Naw, man, we got ends." It's good to see that he finally bought a new coat. People might start to think I got homeless people working for me.

They all pull out greenbacks and slip them into my hands.

"Yo, we got two more sales," Otis says with his fast-ass tongue. "You'n, we can sell a half-ounce to these niggas for six hundred or seven. These young'uns is New Jacks."

"Yeah, well, hold dat shit up until I count this money."

I walk to the car and jump in to count it up. Shank is still listening to Kool G Rap & Polo.

"Damn! Ain't'chu ti'ed a listenin' to that 'Ill Street Blues' shit yet? You try'na memorize it?"

Shank smiles. "Yeah, ma-fucka. Kool G Rap is da shit."

"He talk like he got a ball of *shit* in his mouth, ta me."

"He got a lisp," Shank says through a tight grin.

"Oh yeah? Well, how come only niggas in New York got that shit then?"

Shank shakes his head. "You lunchin', Joe."

I count the money up and the numbers is right on time. Steve then taps on my window.

"Yo, we got some new customers for later on."

"Yeah, well, fuck 'em 'til tomorrow, 'cause I got some other runs t' make."

"So what'chu want me ta say?"

"What da fuck? Tell them young'uns you got it hooked up f' t'mar."

"But they got money t'night, you'n. We might mess around and lose out on these niggas. I mean, if we sell 'em t'night, then we'll have 'em as constant customers."

"Look, I don't give a fuck! I'm not goin' back t' da crib t' get no more shit t'night. One damn day ain't gon' kill 'em, Joe. Damn!"

"Aw'ight, man. Now when'ney hook up wit' some other ma-fuckas to buy their package from, it was ya call."

I suck my teeth, roll up my window and drive off, heading back toward Adams Morgan. It's almost twelve o'clock now. I have to have me some of that weed Ahmad sells me. Tonight! I need it to calm my nerves.

"See dat? Now if you was poor you wouldn't let that sale go," Shank says. He puts his dark shades on.

"Yeah, well, fuck it, 'cause it's more ta life than jus' feedin' niggas' habits. Me and Bink got some ass lined up."

I'm smiling now as Shank sits silently. He's finally listening to the radio instead of that Cool G Rap tape. "Yo, you got any girls, you'n?" I ask him out of curiosity.

He smiles, slick-like. "Naw, rough niggas don't get no bitches."

"Aw, you crazy! My nigga Red had many girls pressed. But he messed around and got this girl Keisha pregnant, like a damn fool. And you'n, 'nat girl ain't got *no* damn sense!"

She is right about sayin' nigga all'la time though, I'm thinking. But fuck it! I can't help the shit.

Shank slips out another smile, which is rare for this nigga. He reminds me of Rakim. "Yo, you like Rakim?" I ask him while we inch down Eighteenth Street in Friday-night traffic.

"Oh, you ma-fuckin' right, Joe! Rakim is da Godfather!"

I laugh. "You really inta them rap songs, hunh?"

"A li'l bit."

"What about da go-go?"

He frowns. "Fuck dat go-go shit. I ain't never liked dat shit."

"What about Rare Essence: 'The Niggas That I Fuck Wit'?"

"Oh, that song is cool. I like the beat. But the rest of that shit? Man . . ." He shakes his head.

"What about Junkyard: 'Ruff It Off'?"

"I mean, 'nat song is cool, too. I just don't like *most* of that go-go shit. But if dey come *correct* wit' some bumpin'-ass beats like that ol' 'Sardines and Pork & Beans' song, then you gotta give it up to them niggas."

I jump out and buy two dime bags of killer from Ahmad. Then I make a phone call to these girls.

"Hello."

"Yeah, it's Butterman."

"Hey, sweetness, where you been at? I been waitin' for you for a hour."

"I'm in Adams Morgan. I'm 'bout to call up Bink now. Then we'a head ova ta ya crib by like one-thirty."

"Aw'ight, well, as long as y'all come, shaw', 'cause me and Kita horny like shit."

I hear Marquita laughing in the background. I can visualize that healthy-ass, light brown body of hers.

"Aw'ight, well, let me make this call."

I hang up, page Bink and put my code in. I'm late by now. But Tamisha got her own apartment. They gon' be there all night.

Bink calls me back after waiting out here in the cold. "Yo, nigga, you beeped me too late and now I got another date."

"What? You wanna be a rapper now?"

"Naw, but *you* always been one."

"How you figa?" *Bink mus' got me confused wit' somebody else*, I'm thinking.

" 'Member you used to wrap ya yellow-ass lips around my big, dark brown dick. I mean, don't tell me you forgot."

I laugh at that crazy shit. This nigga let me walk right into that one. "Aw'ight den, man. I got Shank wit' me, so I'll jus' take him."

"Yeah, well, I'll throw my balls in Marquita's mouth another day, 'cause I don't mind sharin'. Shank is my boy. He cool like dat."

My brows raise. "Yo, Kita suckin' balls?"

"Oh, I'on know. I was just bullshittin'."

"Oh, 'cause I thought ya old girl Shannon was da only one suckin' balls the way she did me last time."

"Aw, go 'head, nigga. Shannon only like men wit' big balls. And ya light-bright, li'l-dick ass don't qualify."

"Shit, I'm Big Daddy Long Stroke."

"Fuck out'a here. You a Little Daddy Half Dick."

I laugh like shit before I hang up and walk back to my 3000. Shank hops out and makes a three-minute call and hops back in.

"Yo, wanna go to these girls' crib wit' me?" I ask him.

"I thought you and Bink was goin'."

"Yeah, we was, but that nigga Bink is sellin' me out."

Shank thinks for a minute with his hand to his chin. "Fuck it! Aw'ight, I'm down."

"What, you had somewhere else ta go?"

"Yeah, but I've been spendin' too much time wit' dis one bitch anyway."

I smile at him. "Oh, so you *do* have a girl?"

"She ain't my girl, she jus' knows how ta treat me."

I rev up my smooth engine and roll out toward Fourteenth Street. Tamisha lives in Takoma Park, Maryland, so I use New Hampshire Avenue.

I don't know how this girl talked me into seeing her again. Maybe it's because them walls of hers are so damn good.

"So what this girl look like?" I ask Shank.

"Sade."

"For real?"

"Yup. She got a shiny forehead and er'rything."

I laugh. "So what do you mean when you say she treats you right?"

"She don't bother me, she feeds me, lets me spend the night, and she gives me the pussy whenever I want it."

I nod with a broad-ass grin. "Yeah, you'n, I see what'chu mean. That's my kind of girl too. But my girl is in Atlanta. She goes to Spelman down'nere."

"Yeah?"

"Yup. That's my baby, you'n. I *love* that girl."

Shank smiles at me. "So why you fuckin' wit' dese other hoes?"

I smile back. "Why you comin' wit' me instead of goin' t' see ya girl?"

" 'Cause, like Denzel Washington said in *Mo' Better Blues,* 'It's a dick thing.' "

I laugh like hell. "Yeah, well, it's a dick thing wit' me, too."

I park in the parking lot of Tamisha's building and roll up a couple of joints. "You want one, right?" I ask Shank.

"Ma-fuckin' right."

We lean the bucket seats back and get fucked up before going in to get some ass.

"So do you think you could ever be faithful to a girl?" I ask him.

Shank takes a hit and holds it. Then he blows it out. "For what?"

"You know, t' be a good man, an' shit like that."

"A good man? Fuck that shit, Joe! A good man is any nigga that lays his pipe right."

I geek off of the shit. "Yeah, you got that shit right. Once you make a girl scream and dig her nails in ya back, she ain't goin' nowhere. But I ain't never been'na one t' say I'on need a girl or call them bitches and hoes, 'cause I got too much respect for my mom and my sisters. So you know, I'll listen to that Dr. Dre and Snoop Doggy Dogg rap, talkin' 'bout *bitches ain't shit but hoes and tricks*, but I don't really feel that way.

"I mean, yeah, I love black pussy as much as the next nigga, but I don't feel like that makes me evil or nothing. 'Cause pussy is good for ya health, you'n. For real!"

We're laughing *hard* now. This weed got me talking out of my ass.

"But you know what I'm sayin' though, Shank?"

Shank takes another hit. "Naw, 'cause my mom been a *bitch* all my ma-fuckin' life."

I'm laughing so hard that my stomach is hurting! "Yo, why you say that, man?" I ask him, wiping tears from out of my eyes, still giggling.

"She is, man. Sometimes I felt like she jus' wanted t' fuck wit' me, jus' 'cause I was there and she ain't have nobody else t' fuck wit'. So whenever I see these evil-ass black women draggin'ney sons around, talkin'nat trash, I jus' be feelin' like fuckin' 'em up, Joe. I mean, I ain't wanna live in no fuckin' Washington. My mom fucked around and lied to me while I slept in'na back of her car. You believe that shit, you'n? The *bitch* lied to me!"

Damn! I'm still laughing and all, but I got this nigga talking a little bit, don't I? I guess I hit a nerve or something. Or maybe it's just the weed.

Shank stares out of the window as if he's in a daze, thinking to himself. His shiny black skin shimmers from a street light slashing inside the car. He's starting to look like them hard-ass African warriors that I used to see in library books.

"Yo, you ever heard of Shaka Zulu?" I ask him.

Shank's eyes pierce into a slit as he takes another hit. "Yeah, I saw that nigga on TV. My cousin taped da shit."

"What'chu think about 'im?"

"He was da man."

"And you ever heard of Nat Turner?"

He blows out more weed, feeling that herb like I'm feeling it. "Yeah, I heard a him; that ma-fucka from Haiti, Toussaint Ouverture, or something like that. Then you got Hannibal and Ghengis Khan and a whole lot of other tough ma-fuckas."

I frown. "Ghengis Khan? He wasn't black."

Shank grimaces. "Who gives a fuck? He wasn't white."

I laugh, overdoing it because of this killer we're smoking. "How you know about these people?" I ask him.

"What? I mean, how da hell you know?"

"From readin' and jus' hearin' about da shit. I mean, this *is* Black History Month."

Shank smiles. "Black History Month. What kind of shit is that? These white people got history all year long, and we got a fuckin' Black History *Month*. And yo, the shit is on the shortest month of the year at that."

"Yo, I didn't know niggas like you paid attention t' stuff like that."

Shank looks at me through sharp, dark eyes. "Niggas like me? See, I tol'ju you act like one of those rich niggas. You think ma-fuckas is stupid. Fuck it though, as long as you keep my pockets fat; I'on really care. And if you ever try any crooked-type shit on me, you'n, I'm gon' lynch'cha ass, jus' like all the rest of us get it."

"Yo, man, cool out an' shit, Joe. I ain't mean it like that. That's da weed talkin'."

He says, "Yeah, like they say, when you fucked up you do stuff that you usually suppress. But you be *thinkin'* 'bout da shit though."

"So you think that I think about black people like that?"

"Fuck what'chu think! I ain't hurt by it. Many ma-fuckas treat'chu like you don't know nothin'. But all you have to do is ask a ma-fucka."

"A lot of times you ask somebody somethin' and he don't know," I tell him, trying to compensate.

"So, that ain't no reason to assume that ma-fuckas is stupid. That's jus' how white people treat'chu an' shit. That's why I hate being aroun'nem ma-fuckas."

"Me too, man. I'm in the same boat," I explain, pressed like a girl trying to make up with her man for some more dick.

Shank smiles as he hops out of the car. "Yeah, sure ya right. Now let's go in here and get some ass, 'cause my dick is hard as Chinese arithmetic."

I laugh at that Eddie Murphy-type shit and get out with him, still trying to explain myself. But Shank's not listening.

It's Saturday morning. My head is still ringing from that nigga Shank. He really fucked me up last night with the things he said. Maybe I'm still more like my pop than I think I am. And that's fucked up!

I call up my girl and she answers on the first ring.

"Hey, baby, it's me," I tell her.

"Where were you at last night?"

"Outside."

"Doin' what?"

I frown. It's too damn early for this shit. "I mean, did'ju wake up on the wrong side of the bed or something?"

"No, Jeffrey, and I know you was out there playing that Butterman shit, acting a damn fool. I swear to God, sometimes I hate the hell out of you! All I ask is for you to call me every other day, at least, and you can't even do that. I mean, not even to call and leave a message on my machine, saying that you been thinkin' 'bout me or nothin'."

She sounds fed up. I shake my head. "Damn! Well, what can I say?"

"I'on know, but I'm up working on this paper that I started on last night while I was waiting up for you to call me. And I bet'cha ass ain't even check ya messages. Did you?"

"Naw."

"I know you didn't. So what you need to do, J, is check your machine to hear what I had to say to you, and then you call me back later on. Okay, 'cause I'm busy right now."

I say, "Cool," and hang up. I'm too damned tired to argue.

Shit! If people only knew how much dumb stuff I go through. I'm flipping damn near twenty thousand dollars a week now and still got problems. Life is a pinball game for your ass. And I still have to set up that bank account like Wes was telling me.

I need that nigga Wes! I'm getting all kinds of money now. I don't want to waste it. Yeah, I know exactly what I'm gon' do for Wes' ass. Hooking him up with NeNe wasn't enough.

I push my answering machine button and let it play:

"Yo, B, this Bink, nigga. What's up? I mean, is you tryin'na get some ass or what? Call me up, man, and let me know what time it is."

BEEP!

"Hey, Junior, this is big sis, Joyce. Look, me and Chester are going down to Florida for a little winter get-away this weekend. And I know you were talking to Mom about needing to just get away from it all. So call me back. We're leaving in the morning at seven."

Seven? God damn, it's ten o'clock already! They been gone.

BEEP!

"You know, Jeffrey, I'm real tired of this. I mean, maybe you trying to play me out like a ho now. But then you wanna call up out of the blue and start talking that stuff about how you love me and how you need me. I mean, it's confusing me, baby.

"What do you want with your life, J? You can't just do one thing one day and some totally different shit the next. You just end up running in circles.

"Now look, I love you like I'm crazy, and I gots to be crazy wit' all these fine-ass Morehouse guys runnin' around down here while you up there throwing your hot dick around. And I know you are. Just don't get me no diseases.

"I'm out. But just remember that you were never there for me when I mess around and turn into a lesbian or something. I love you too much to mess wit' another guy, but I still have emotions of my own to be fulfilled.

"Anyway, call me when you've finished fucking some-body else. I'm just sitting in here in my bed, teasing my-self. Well, . . . bye, J."

BEEP!

Shank

I ain't seen my mom since I left Southeast in October. Talking with Butterman last night got me thinking about her.

Yeah. It was messed up the way me and Moms broke off. I was in my room listening to Ice Cube's new album, *Predator.*

"How da hell you gon' tell me what I'm not doin' t' get a damn job?!"

"Well, how come I can get *two* jobs then, Julius?"

" 'Cause you a bitch! The white man likes hirin' bitches for work!"

"Look here, don't call me no bitch, motherfucka!"

Man, fuck them. They were always arguing about some shit. I just turned my box up louder and ignored it.

Bloom! *Da fuck is goin' on?* I was thinking after hearing a crash against my wall.

I leaped the hell up and ran into my mom's room. Julius had her dumb ass pinned up against the wall. He was trying to get a good punch at her.

I hit that motherfucker with a left jab, an overhand right, and a right hook to the body. That motherfucker curled up on the floor like a snail. Then I kicked him in his ribs and punched him in his fucking mouth and started trying to pin his ass to the floor so I could unleash on him.

Next thing I know, my mom's dumb ass is punching me in the back of my head.

I looked at her like she was crazy. "What's wrong wit'chu?"

"You leave him the hell alone!"

"He was jus' 'bout t' beat'cha ass!" I shouted in shock. She was really fucking crazy!

"I can handle my got'damn self, boy!"

"Aw'ight, fuck you den!" I said, stomping out of their room.

Then she rushed me in my back! "You don't disrespect me like that! I'm your got'damn mother!"

I said, "You gon' be a got'damn zombie if you don't get da hell away from me!"

I saw my little light-skinned sister in the hallway with tears in her eyes.

"You betta not lay a hand on me!" my mom was still screaming.

I wanted to say, "Oh, but *he* can beat'cha ass though, right?" But looking at my sister stopped me. So I jetted to my room and slammed my fucking door.

And here my mom come banging on the shit. "You a evil person, Darnell! You need to realize when people need help. And you don't try to hurt a person who needs help."

She was talking about Julius and his damn habit again, and I was tired of that shit.

I said, "Yo, fuck him and fuck you! He's *ya* husband! He ain't gettin' no ass from me! And if I help 'im, I'm gon' help his ass to a graveyard!"

She said, "Well, maybe you need t' get the hell out of this house then!"

"Fuck dis slum-ass house! I'll get da hell out right now! I ain't gotta take dis shit!"

Three days later, this man down the street from us had a daughter moving out of her apartment in Northeast, off of Nineteenth Street and Rhode Island Avenue. I packed up my clothes, took the four hundred dollars that my mom gave me, and got the fuck up out of there for my *own* spot. And I bet she think I'm homeless now. But I got news for her ass. I got furniture, a big screen TV, a VCR, a telephone line, and food in this motherfucker! Yeah, *this* nigga living *right!*

I get up and walk to my small-ass kitchen to cook some eggs. I'm thinking about Carlette now. That's fucked up, because I just got some ass last night from that girl Marquita. And yet I'm still thinking about Carlette's ass.

This girl got me sweating her like a bamma!

My telephone rings. I hope it ain't Butterman. I'm trying to chill today; fuck you'n.

"Hello."

"H-i-i-i, Shannnk. It's Kita. I just wanted t' say good mornin' an' t' tell you that I had a good time last night."

"You had a good time last night?" *Hell is she talkin' 'bout?* I'm thinking.

"Yeah, you know. Don't tell me you forgot."

"Naw, but I'm cookin' right now. Call me back in a few."

"You cook?" she asks me like she's shocked.

"Yeah, what da fuck? A nigga gotta eat, right?" *Bitch!*

She laughs and shit. "I'm sorry. I didn't mean to offend you."

I'm sorry too; I'm sorry I gave you my damn number!

"Yeah, well, just call me back later on."

"Okay, but umm, where you live at, 'cause Tamisha was gon' drop me off to come see you."

"Hunh?" *Is this girl crazy? I'm not tellin' her where I live.*

"I wanna come see you," she says.

"Aw'ight, well, look, call me back and we'll talk about it."

I hang up on her before she can say any more dumb shit. The nerve of that bitch: calling me up and asking me where I live, talking about she wants to come see me just because she gave me some free pussy last night! Bitches are out of their fucking minds!

I sit on my living room couch and eat a scrambled egg and toast sandwich, watching *X-Men*. Wolverine is like dat! I bought a couple of his comics.

After the show goes off, I run down to the lobby and check my mail from yesterday. Shit, my cousin sent me a letter!

I dash back upstairs and read it while sipping on some orange juice.

Yo, this is Cal.

I know who da hell it is, nigga! Ain't no other motherfuckas writin' letters an' shit. I shake my head and smile. Then I drink some orange juice and start to read it.

Yo, cuz, those new comics from Milestone Inc. I was telling you about just came out. I got all of them. They got one called *Blood Syndicate*, then *Icon* and *Hardware*. And yo, them shits sold out in the first week. I can't wait to graduate now. I'm going straight up to New York. Greenwich Village is where all the artists hang out. I'm telling you, Nell, I'm gonna have my name on something next year, whether it be comic books, paintings or poetry.

Oh yeah, man, Oz is bugging out. I had to beat his ass last night cause he came in the house trippin'. He was pressuring Moms to give him some money for that drug shit. It's fucked up, man. I was reading this article before that said that people often take their anger out on their loved ones because they know they can still be forgiven. Because, you know, if they hurt somebody that don't love them, then they might end up dead.

You got that shit right, you'n, 'cause I don't give a fuck about Julius!

Yo, ock, you been to the movies lately? Smile. I know you have, Nell, so don't even front on me. Yo, did you see *Hoffa?*

Yeah, that movie was aw'ight. But I wouldn't see it twice.

Under Siege?

Yeah, that flick was cool. It had a lot of action in it.

Aliens-3?

The second one was da shit. But this joint spent too much time with them dumb-ass prisoners. That movie was gettin' borin', Joe. Dey ain't even have no fuckin' weapons!

Sniper?

Oh yeah! Sniper was like dat! That muthafucka was one of those psychological movies. It was slow in'na beginnin' though.

Teenage Mutant Ninja Turtles-3?

Aw, man, hell no! I ain't go see that trash. But I checked out Batman Returns. *And yo, that joint was a little raw for a superhero movie. I guess I'm too used to watchin' that soft, Superman-type shit.*

Yeah, I'm just joking about the Ninja Turtles. But that movie *Sniper* reminded me of you. You see all the trauma they was going through in that movie, man? You don't wanna go through that shit, Nell. I'm telling you man, you better do like Ice Cube says and "Check yo'self before you wreck yo'-self." Anyway, I ain't trying to preach to you, but that cold killer life is crazy, Nell. Or should I call you Shank now? Ha ha ha. Remember that time we was about to fight because I refused to call you that dumb shit years ago? Yo, you was bugging, man. But anyway, I know you ain't into writing letters or nothing so I'll just keep you up to date on shit.

Love, peace 'n hair grease—that's that Big Daddy Kane shit. He got a new album coming out soon.

Audi 5000—Boyeeee

This motherfucker lunchin'! He crazy as hell if he thinks I'm gonna give up all this money to try that poorman's art shit. I'm making five hundred dollars a week, just to drive around in a 3000 GT and beat down a few niggas every now and then. And fuck it, if I have to kill somebody . . . I got to do what I got to do. It ain't no thing but a chicken wing, you know what I'm saying? But I mean, I do think about rappin' every once and a while.

I'm bored like shit, sitting here watching cartoons. I feel like calling Carlette up but I don't want to sweat her. As soon as you start really liking a girl, that's when the bitch starts playing you. All these rappers ain't talking that shit for nothing. Bitches are slimy! But fuck it, I still feel like calling her up though. I mean, this girl just lets me chill, and she don't bother me. Like this girl Kita is getting on my nerves already. I can tell she gon' be a pest. But Carlette is just what a nigga needs to have some peace of mind, you know? Everybody needs peace of mind. That's why niggas mess around and marry white bitches; they're tired of arguing and shit with these black women. Marrying white bitches ain't for me though. I wouldn't even know what the hell to say to a white girl. But I see how them other niggas feel.

I call up Carlette any-fucking-way.

"Hey, girl, what's up? What'chu doin'?"

"Trigonometry."

"Triga-what?" She laughs. "Naw, I'm jus' jokin'; that's that geometry-type shit wit' formulas and all. You could draw angles and shit wit' rulers. I used t' like that class in high school."

"Yeah, well, I don't. And trig is more formulas than geom," she says tiredly. She don't sound too talkative today. Or maybe she upset about me not coming over last night.

"Yo, I ended up havin' to do some other shit last night. Aw'ight?"

Aw, man, look at me soundin' like a bamma! Damn, I can't even take it back now. See what bitches do to you?

"Oh, I wasn't worried about that."

"So what'chu do last night den?"

"Nothing."

"Nothin'?"

"Nope."

"Well, I'm gon' make it up to you t'day."

"Oh yeah? What time you coming over then?"

"Like in an hour. So be downstairs for me. Aw'ight?"

"All right."

"Okay, let me get ready."

"Aw'ight, bye."

See that shit? That's my kind of girl.

I get down to the Howard Towers Plaza-East and meet Carlette in the lobby. She's reading this big, black book.

She lets me in. The girl at the front desk doesn't say nothing about no I.D., so we walk right to the elevators.

"Are you goin' somewhere?" I ask her. Carlette's wearing a bright green skirt with white stockings and a T-shirt, as if she's getting ready to go out.

"I was."

"So what—I'm stoppin' you now?"

"No."

"So how come you not goin' no more?"

She smiles. "Because I have company."

"You have company? Who?"

"You, Darnell."

I smile back at her, trying to stay cool. I feel like a damn kid with a new set of army men. This girl is good for a nigga's ego.

I walk into her room and perform my regular routine:

I take off my jacket, hat and Timberlands and stretch out across her neat bed.

She kicks off her shoes, props up her two pillows and lays beside me. She's still reading her book with her knees up and her back against her pillows. And she smells good as hell, like she always does.

"What's dat'chu readin'?" I ask her.

"Elaine Brown and the Black Panther Party."

"Oh yeah?" I lean across her body and pick up the book's cover jacket from off the floor. "*A Taste Of Power,* hunh? Damn, she looks kinda good!"

"Why, because she's light-skinned?" Carlette is smiling at me now, like she got me on a tough question or something.

"Naw, because she has smooth skin, some pretty-ass eyes and she looks clean and healthy. Now! You thought you had me stumblin', hunh?"

She smirks like she's been carried. I toss the cover back to the floor.

"I thought you said you was doin' trigonometry?" I ask her, teasing.

"I was, but I'm finished."

"No you ain't. Now, get back and do that damn homework, girl."

I give her a soft push, and she giggles.

"You sound like my father."

"How?"

"Because he's always asking me about my homework."

"Yeah, but is he cool though?"

"Yeah."

"Would he like a nigga like me?"

"I don't know."

"Aw, don't lie. Ya pop would prob'bly have a heart attack." I mock how her father would probably be: "'Carlette, out of all the young, potential men at Howard University, you get yourself involved with a street person'."

She laughs like shit. I must have hit her pop right on the nose. But it's cool. I know I can't keep no educated bitch like her. I'm just in it while it lasts. And she probably is too.

"You always make me laugh," she says, blushing.

"I'on know why."

She sucks her teeth and smiles. "You know why."

"No I don't." I get up off the bed and walk over to her stereo system where she keeps all of her cassettes and CD's. "Oh, you got Digable Planets' album, hunh?"

"Mmm-hmm," she mumbles with her face still inside that Elaine Brown book.

I pick up the CD and read the title. *"Reachin' (a new refutation of time and space).* Oh shit, you got my nigga 2Pac's album, too!" I pick up 2Pac's cassette tape.

"Yeah, I like him," she says, all excited. She lifts her head out of the book for *him.* "That's why I got his cassette, so I can listen to it in my car."

I grin at her. "So would you make love t' 2Pac?"

She sucks her teeth and smiles again. "No, Darnell. I don't know him."

"Yeah, aw'ight. I bet if that ma-fucka had a concert at da Cap' Center, you'd be up in his hotel line."

"No I wouldn't! But he is supposed to be up here next week though."

"Oh yeah? Where at?"

"At the Howard University Hip Hop Conference."

"So you goin'?"

"Oh, I'on know. I heard it costs like seventy-five dollars for the weekend."

I frown at her. "Seventy-five dollars? Them ma-fuckas is crazy. It must be for rich Howard students only."

She shakes her head, grinning. "You know, I don't

know why everybody thinks Howard students are so rich. I mean, it's a few like that, yeah, but most Howard students are getting financial aid and student loans like at any other school."

"So how come they talk so much shit about Howard den?"

"Because it has an old reputation."

"Yeah, I guess so, hunh?"

I hop back on her bed and wrap my legs around hers. I tug on her hips with my hands while she's still trying to read.

"Ain't it a little too early for this?" she asks me, grinning.

"No, not if my shit gets hard."

She smiles, but she doesn't laugh. "Do you like that song by Dr. Dre and them? 'Bitches Ain't Shit but Hoes and Tricks'?"

Damn, she try'na pull a Joker's Wild on me! "Naw, I'on listen to it much. Why?"

She's still smiling, as if she thinks I'm lying. But I *don't* listen to it that much.

"Do you call girls bitches and hoes?"

Oh my God! Is she fuckin' me up or what? "Yo, why you askin' me somethin' like that?"

"Because I know you do. You probably can't even help it because you've been doing it for so long."

"So that shit wouldn't bother you?"

"No, as long as I wasn't called no bitch to my face, what can I do about it? But I read before that black men degrade their women because they're afraid of them."

I frown at her. "*Afraid of 'em?* Afraid of what?"

She grins, like she knows some shit that I don't know. "Of gettin' their feelings hurt in a relationship."

"So what that got to do wit' callin' a girl a bitch?"

"It's like, if you call a girl a bitch and you say that you

don't care about her, then you'll be more prepared, emo-
tionally, to walk away from her if she gets close to hurting you."

Damn! That makes good-ass sense. She might be right.
"Where you read this at?" I ask her.

"I don't really remember where I read it, but that's just
how I think about it. And you know, sometimes you read
things and forget the source and you kind of add it to
your own thoughts."

"Yeah, I know what you mean. I do the same kinda thing
wit' my lyrics, mixin' and minglin' different styles."

"You can rap?" She looks all surprised.

"Yeah, a li'l bit," I tell her, being modest. I think I'm a
bad motherfucker!

"Can you write poetry too?"

"I'on know. I never tried. But my cousin can write
poetry."

"Is he a writer?"

"Oh, Cal is all kinds of shit. That's my nigga! I just got
a letter from him t'day."

Carlette finally closes her book and leans closer, up
against me. She runs her fingers over my chest, making
my shit hard. And I guess we're about to get into something.

"Darnell?" she asks me, looking all sexy.

"What?"

"Do you call me a bitch when you talk about me?"

*SHIT! Yo, she messin' wit' me good! You see how bit—, I
mean girls, get?*

I'm smiling because this shit is crazy. "Yo, why you
keep stressin'nat shit?"

"I'm just asking. I mean, I'm not gonna be hurt by it."

"Yeah right. Why you askin' then?"

"I don't know. I just keep thinking about how girls
don't really ask their boyfriends stuff like that."

Boyfriend? Aw, she really try'na pull a Joker's Wild on me now. I say, "Oh yeah?"

"Yeah. So I figure if we really ask guys about it, but not in like an angry way, I think guys would really think about it more before they did it."

She got that shit right. 'Cause she done messed my head all up!

I chill with Carlette all fucking day and end up falling asleep listening to that Digable Planets, poetry-type shit.

I sit up and listen to Carlette talking to somebody out in the hallway. Then she shuts the door and comes back into the room to watch TV with the lights off.

"Yo, who was that?"

"My friend from class."

"Do you ever go out wit' 'im?"

"No."

It's funny, but in all of the five months that I've been fucking with her, we ain't never went no-damn-where. And she got a car!

"Yo, how come you never asked me ta take you out or nothing?"

She shrugs her shoulders. "Because you never said you wanted to. So I just thought that you were busy."

"Busy? Doin' what?"

"I'on know, whatever you do all day."

She sits on the floor and leans up against the bed. I lean up on my elbow and play with her long, brown hair.

"So do you go out with other ma-fuckas?"

"Not motherfuckers, but other guys, yeah."

I laugh. "Yeah? And do they come over here?"

"Sometimes."

Oh shit, it's happening! I'm getting jealous! I want to ask her if she ever "had sex" with them. But that question ain't gon' sound right.

"We don't do nothin' though. And I only let *one* other

guy spend the night, because he was from back home in Ohio, and he was down here for homecoming last year."

Good, she read my damn mind. "And he ain't even touch you?" I ask her, still digging like a cold miner.

"No! He's like my little brother! And he was down here trying to get with any girl he could."

"Yeah, so how come you don't fuck wit' nobody like that?" I ask. *Damn, what da hell is wrong wit' me? But I gots t' know. The shit is startin'na bother me.*

"Because I tell them that I'm already involved with someone. I'm not a loose girl, running around with a bunch of guys. But if a guy asks me to go to the movies or something, I'll go, as long as he knows that it doesn't mean anything more than that."

"And what about with me?"

I can tell she's grinning, even though she's not facing me. Her cheeks are rising. I can see them from the light shining off of the television. "What about you?" she asks me back.

I chuckle at the shit and fall back on the bed. Carlette gets up on the bed with me. I dip my head between her nice-sized titties. "What time is it?"

She leans over me to look at her clock. "Nine o'clock."

"So we can still catch a movie, hunh?"

She kisses me. "Mmm-hmm."

I kiss her back. "Fuck it. Let's go then."

I wake up Sunday morning, still over Carlette's crib. I look over at the clock. The shit says 8:32.

"Carlette?"

"Hunh?"

"I'm 'bout t' roll."

I get up and start putting my clothes back on.

Carlette stretches. She turns over on her back to face me. "Hold up."

"Naw, you don't have t' walk me out or kiss me or nothin'."

She stretches some more, under the sheets with no clothes on. "I had fun last night," she says, smiling.

"Yeah, me too. That *Universal Soldier* shit wasn't half bad. And oh, the sex was jus' what a nigga need after a date."

She smiles at me. "Chauvinist."

"Naw, that's for old white men an' shit."

She laughs. "Boy, get out of here."

I grab her 2Pac tape off of her stereo cabinet. "Yo, let me check this out."

She waves for me to take it. "Go 'head."

I walk to the door, putting my black hat back on and slipping the tape into my pocket. "Yo, I'll holler at'chu when I get in."

CHAPTER 6

Shank

*D*addy's home.
*So? You say that like that means something to me.
You been gone a mighty long motherfuckin' time for you
ta be comin' home talkin'nat 'Daddy's home' shit.*

Damn, this nigga 2Pac is getting personal as hell with
"Papa'z Song." I been listening to his tape all this week:
Strictly 4 My Niggaz. I mean, I know how he feels though;
I ain't never known my pop either. All I know is that he
was in Vietnam, in the war. And he hated white people.
But fuck him! I'm here now. I don't need that mother-
fucker—unless he got some money.

I went and bought this Maya Angelou book, too: *I
Know Why The Caged Bird Sings.* That's a long-ass title,
but I bought it because it was the only book I ever saw on
my mother's shelf. Plus, the whole country been talking
about some poem Maya Angelou recited for that presi-
dential function. It seems like every time I turn the TV on
they're still talking about it. And that shit was last

month! I mean, that poem must have been powerful, like a sawed-off shotgun, hunh? Or a MAC-10?

I ain't tell Carlette I bought it though; she'd probably get all excited and shit because she's been talking that Black Man education shit to me lately. I think that Black Panther book been going to her head. I mean, every nigga knows we need to kill these white motherfuckers . . . But I don't see niggas doing it.

Anyway, this book was the only one that my mother had. But I never saw her reading the shit. It just sat on her shelf right next to her Bible, haunting me, because I always wondered why she had it. I mean, if she had a bunch of other books, then it wouldn't have had the same effect. And as far as the Bible? Man, every nigga, I think, got a fucking Bible. We the most religious people on this earth.

Like when I was riding home from Carlette's crib Sunday morning, a bunch of church women got on the bus. I was sitting up in front because I was too tired to walk to the back. Then one of them well-dressed-ass church women sat beside me.

"Young man, do you know Jesus?"

I mean, she was sweet and all that, but I just got up and moved to the back. That shit is just like them religious people who pass out that *Watchtower* paper with white people all over it.

Your God can't look like your enemy! I don't know who said that shit, but Professor Griff had it on his second album.

Showbiz & A.G. fuck with that political stuff too: "Runaway Slave":

And you surely don't catch hell 'cause you an American, 'cause if you was an American you wouldn't catch no hell. You catch hell 'cause you a black man!

Yeah, that's from Showbiz & A.G., sampling Malcolm X. They slow the shit down, but you can still tell it's Malcolm. Nobody talks like Malcolm. But he dead now, and Farrakhan ain't been saying much lately.

It's almost twelve o'clock noon on Thursday. I'm supposed to meet Butterman at Super Trak by one.

Money been rolling in like a motherfucker! I'm about to ask this nigga for a raise. I want a G a week.

I hop off the bus and cross the street to find this motherfucker Butterman already here at Super Trak, sitting inside his GT.

"Yo, man, why don't I jus' pick you up from ya spot instead a meetin' down here all da time," he says as I hop in.

"For what? You wanna gi'me some ass?"

He grins. "Naw, Joe, I'm jus' sayin' that it would be more convenient."

I ain't saying shit to that. Maybe he'll stop sweating me.

"And I hope you ain't got that damn 2Pac tape t'day. I'm ti'ed of hearin' that crazy shit he be talkin' 'bout."

"Why is it crazy?"

"Look, that ma-fucka sound mad at the world, Joe."

"And you ain't?"

"How? I mean, we got shit goin' on, you'n. We paid da hell up! And it ain't like that nigga 2Pac ain't got no money. That nigga 'bout t' be in his second movie when that *Poetic Justice* movie comes out. And he got two tapes out already. So why is he still talkin' shit?"

" 'Cause shit is still messed up for niggas." *You rich-ass ma-fucka! Hell you know about problems an' shit!* I'm thinking.

"Yeah, whatever, man. That nigga crazy t' me."

We ride up Georgia Avenue to go meet these silly-ass niggas he got working for him.

Yo, I swear to God, if I wasn't working for this nigga

myself, I'd rob his ass blind. You'n is a *punk!* That's why he got me working for him in the first place.

"Yo, yo, Shank! See you'n right there?"

He points to this tall, stringy-looking nigga to my right, walking up Georgia.

"Yeah."

The stringy nigga turns right, walking down a side street.

"That's Bean, the nigga dat tol' me t' watch my back."

I hop out of the car in traffic. "Shut da fuck up!" I holler at the cars blowing their horns at me. Punks!

I jog down the street and catch up to you'n. He turns down an alleyway like a stupid-ass victim. "Yo, you got da time on you?" I ask him. I say the shit like I just happen to be heading in the same direction.

He stops and looks down at this gold-plated watch. I steal his ass with a right hook to the jaw. God damn, he hit the ground already! I hate that shit! I ain't had a good fist fight in years.

Butterman rolls the GT inside the alleyway with us. We're around the trash Dumpsters in back of these Georgia Avenue stores. "Yo, wake that nigga up, Shank!"

I search him down first and pull out a compact .45 semi-automatic. Damn! I've seen one of these in a handgun book; it has one of those wooden-ass handles, looking pretty as hell. I toss the .45 inside the car with Butterman. I start to smack this motherfucker until he comes back to the world.

The nigga looks up at me in a daze. "Yo, you'n, what's all'lat shit for?"

"It's for talkin'nat trash, nigga!" Butterman shouts from the car.

Joe named Bean turns toward him.

I take out my .38 and slam the butt into his face with my safety clip on.

"SHIT, MAN!" the nigga hollers like a bitch.

I slam him with my gun again and he starts to struggle. I kick him in his head with my Timberlands boots. "PUSSY!" I stomp him, kick him, pistol whip him.

"God damn, Shank! That's enough, man! Fuck that nigga, Joe!"

I take my gun off safety and aim it at his head.

"Yo, man, be cool, Shank!" Butterman is yelling.

My heart is roaring like thunder. I feel my hand on the trigger. Blood is rushing through my arms. I feel hate. And I feel like killing this nigga.

Butterman is whispering now. "Be cool, Shank." It must be some witnesses in the area.

The string bean nigga looks up at me in defeat. He doesn't even beg for his life. Fuck him! He's a pussy anyway!

I click my gun back on safety. I walk to the GT and hop inside in silence. Butterman jets down the alley and turns left, away from Georgia Avenue.

I settle down, picking up the .45 from the floor. I hold it in my hands. It's heavy, hard and powerful. Niggas will hear me with this. Niggas will fear me and respect my ass when I have to use it.

"Got' damn, man! Was you gon' shoot you'n?"

The car has stopped in a driveway. We must be at least twenty blocks away from the scene. This neighborhood looks like Maryland; it has a bunch of open space with grass and trees.

I yell, "Fuck dude, man! You'n gave up. He was ready t' die. He didn't even fight back."

"*Fight back?* You was beatin' his ass, Joe! How da fuck was he gon' fight back?"

Butterman is sweating and looking nervous. Pretty motherfucker's a *bitch*. I knew he was.

I look him in his face. "Yo, man, what'chu hire me for?"

"Yeah, but damn! I mean, he had already gotten'na point."

I frown at him, pissed the hell off. "Look here, ma-fucka: Joe lucky he still breathin'. I put my life on'na line er'ry time I smash a ma-fucka, man. Now he'll think twice before he thinks about gettin' revenge. That's how you gotta do a punk. That's why niggas is scared'a the white man. But if I ever go up against 'im . . . I'm gon' kill his ass."

Butterman sits with nothing to say. I guess he's trying to get his heart out of his throat. Poor, punk-ass nigga. He probably wants to go back to his mommy now. So fuck it! Let me get my raise.

"Yo, I need a G a week, you'n. And I know you got the money, so don't run no game about da ends not meetin' on me."

He nods his head, slow-like. "Aw'ight. That's cool."

Aw, you punk muthafucka! I know it's cool! I'm thinking.

He says, "Aw'ight. If that's the way it has t' be done, I got another stop fa us t' make."

We ride down North Capitol Street and make a left to get to Florida Avenue. We pull up in Northeast, around H Street. This the other side of Northeast from where I live on Rhode Island. New York Avenue kind of sepa-rates the north and south sides of Northeast. And this south side is jive-like rougher than my side. But I grew up in Southeast anyway. So fuck these punk niggas over here!

A bunch of motherfuckers sit strategically on steps and corners. And yo, this shit don't look like the place to try no hero stunts. So if this nigga Butterman is thinking about Clint Eastwood movies, he got the wrong damn scene. But we'll see what happens. Fuck these niggas!

We hop out and walk toward another alleyway behind the H Street stores this time. I got my .38 inside my belt and my .45 inside my leather jacket. When we get around back, some chubby brown dude with a goatee walks out toward us, smiling like he's invincible.

"Hey, Butter-bitch. I ain't think you was gon' bring ya ass around here no more. I heard ya bamma ass got shit rollin'."

I recognize one of his boys.

He speaks to me, all like he on my dick. "Yo, Shank. What's up?"

I nod to him, but he walks over to shake my hand. "Yo, we cool and all, but I ain't out here for shakin' hands." I look to Butterman. "Yo, go ahead and take care of what'chu got t' do."

Dude with the goatee looks toward me. "What? Y'all got'chall own shit, right? We ain't got no biz'ness here. I heard y'all niggas got a New York connection."

I look to Butterman. "Yo, what'chu got t' talk to dis nigga about?"

Shit gets tense. The nigga that knows me turns away. I guess he realizes that I'll kill his punk ass.

Chubby Goatee says, "I'm sayin', me an' B ain't got no biz'ness."

He's bitching now. I guess he's realizing that I'll kill his ass too. Punks! And they got at least ten motherfuckers around the corner.

Butterman smiles. "Yo, you'n, er'rything cool. I just wanted to know if you wanted to buy some weight from me."

Goatee hunches his shoulders and raises his eyebrows. "Ah, well, we'll see, man. I mean, I got my connections already."

I turn around and catch another motherfucker eyeing me, as if he's sizing me up. "What, I got a fat ass or somethin', you'n? Fuck is you starin' at?"

"Ay, man, stop that Rambo-type shit, shaw'. We ain't

got no beef wit'chall. It's enough money for er'rybody in'nis shit," he says.

I start to walk back toward the car.

Butterman says, "Yeah, so Max, beep me if you wanna buy some weight. Aw'ight?"

"Yeah, I got'chu."

Butterman follows me out of the alleyway and back to the street. We hop in the GT and make a right turn onto H Street. We're heading back toward North Capitol now.

Butterman smiles. "Yeah, Joe, you'n tried to carry me before. Punk-ass nigga."

That's dumb shit, I'm thinking. "Yo, you'n, you should'na done'nat dumb shit, Joe. And if you would'a tol' me what we was about t' do, I woulda said 'Naw'. Now, the only reason them niggas didn't shoot us is because dey was caught off guard. And I knew one of their trigga-men; he went to Anacostia wit' me an' Bink. But now, them niggas is embarrassed. So you done made us some unnecessary enemies."

"Yeah, but Max and his boys ain't really got no back. That's why they stay over here in Northeast. I can roll wherever I want, 'cause I'm cool wit' er'rybody."

"Not if them motherfuckas pass da word that you try'na be a big boy. Then we gon' have er'ry crew in D.C. ready to fuck us up for steppin' out like dat."

"How? I mean, that shit is jus' between us and them."

"Yeah, and we got about six ma-fuckas, and two of 'em is pussies." *Not including ya punk ass*, I'm thinking. Damn this nigga stupid!

"Steve'll be down."

"I ain't talkin' 'bout Steve. I'm talkin' 'bout Otis and that new ma-fucka Pervis you got workin' for us."

"Pervis is gettin' us sales in Maryland. And like I told'ju before, you'n, biz'ness ain't always about havin' a bunch of roughnecks on ya squad."

"Yeah, well, I hope you know what da hell you doin', 'cause you just made situations more heated, man. I'm tellin' you now."

"We aw'ight, man. Fuck Max."

We get back to Steve, Rudy, Otis and Pervis. Pervis rides a green 300 ZX Turbo with gold-chrome, five-star hammer rims. Smooth-looking car. But he still a *bitch.*

"Yo, we got like *five* sales set up f' t'night," he says. Motherfucker's rocking to some go-go music, blasting from his car. He's wearing some blue suede shoes and slacks, with a long black leather coat. Nigga look like he's trying to be a black gigolo.

Butterman says, "Yeah, well, first things first. I wanna count at least *five* Gs, right now."

They all pull out knots. Butterman goes through his regular routine of counting the money inside of his car.

He hops back out and walks over to us. "So we got how many sales?" he asks Steve.

"We got three right now, but we got prospects for two more."

Butterman looks at me, then Pervis. "Ay, Pervis, I thought you said we had five."

Joe giggles like he's high. And I don't trust his wanna-be-hip ass already. I'll fuck him up! All Butterman has to do is give the word. But I feel like busting Pervis up anyway. And then I'll take his car . . . Punk!

"Aw, man, them niggas is sold, Joe," he says, facing Steve.

"Dey ain't have no money, man," Steve answers. "They could'a been'na po-leese or anything, you'n."

Pervis frowns and looks nervous. "Aw, man, you actin' paranoid."

I look at Butterman to give me the okay to bust Pervis up. But he doesn't.

He heads back to his car. "Yo, wait here wit' dese nig-gas while I go get da shit, Shank."

I nod and take a seat on the steps of the house we're in front of. An old, ragged man walks up to us, fiending.

"Yo, man, go see dem Jamaicans. We ain't got no small-time shit ova hea no more," Rudy tells him.

"Hunh?"

"I said, we ain't got shit for you, man!"

"Oh." The old man turns and heads off, wearing some dingy-ass jeans and a dirty old wool coat.

"Yo, you betta watch how you talk about them Jamaicans, Joe," Pervis tells Rudy. "Them niggas'll fuck ya ass up. Them Jamaicans don't be bull-shittin', you'n! I 'member I was in New York one time, in Queens, and these ma-fuckas rolled around the corna in jeeps, like twenty deep, and started sprayin' niggas."

"So how come you still livin'?" Steve asks him.

"Oh, 'cause I was watchin' from this window an' shit. I was ova dis girl crib, gettin' me some pussy."

Steve smiles at Otis and Rudy. "Yo, this nigga be lyin' more than me, you'n. He a lyin' ma-fucka, Joe. Nigga prob'bly never been to New York."

"Aw, man, you crazy! How you gon' tell me? I got cousins all over New York."

Rudy looks at *me* and smiles. "Yeah, da nigga got lies all over his mowf, too. You know, Shank?"

I nod to him. And Rudy's the roughest motherfucker out here, besides me. "Yeah, I know," I tell him. "And sometimes niggas get fucked up for lyin'. Ain't that right, Steve?"

Steve looks at me and then to Pervis. "Sometimes it bees like dat."

I look to Otis. "What'chu think, O?"

"Man, I'on know."

"Why, 'cause you ain't never busted nobody up?"

"I mean, I had a few—"

"No da fuck you didn't!" I shout at him.

Fuck this! I get up so I can explain a few things to these punks. "Aw'ight niggas, here's the scenario: two ma-fuckas hop out of a car on five of us. We all packin', but we don't really know what these niggas is gon' do. So what do we do?"

"We ask them what's up," Steve says.

"Then what?"

"If they wanna buy a package, we do biz'ness. If not, then they can get da fuck out'a here," Rudy adds.

"But what if these ma-fuckas pull out guns and start demandin' shit, like in a stick-up?"

Rudy spits to the curb. "Fuck it! We cap them niggas, Joe!"

"And what da fuck would *you* do if somebody did *this?*" I pull out my compact .45 semi-auto and stick it behind Pervis' coat, where it can't be seen by onlookers.

"Man, stop trippin'," he says, bitching.

"*Trippin'?* Nigga, I don't like you!" I shout at him. "You da one trippin'. I've hated punk muthafuckas like you all my life. 'Cause you know whadda happen if somebody really pulled out on us? Ya punk ass would run, Joe! Like a bitch!"

These niggas all quiet the hell up. And I still got the .45. It's underneath Pervis' arm while I stand in back of him.

"Man, this shit ain't even called for, you'n," he says to me, looking all helpless. But ain't nobody gon' help him; they know what time it is.

I shove my gun into his ribs. "Yes da fuck it is! 'Cause it's punk-ass, entertainin' niggas like you that always get people taken under. I hate muthafuckas like you wit' a passion! You know why?" He doesn't open his mouth to say shit. "Speak up, ma-fucka! Assert'chaself!"

He sighs like a fucking girl. "Why, man?"

I holler into his face, " 'Cause you a spineless pussy! And if we ever have a shoot-out, I'm gon' shoot'cha ass *first!*" I search him for a gun and shove his ass toward his car. "Now get da hell out'a here before I kill you."

He stumbles toward his 300 ZX.

I walk to his driver seat and point my gun at his window as soon he gets in. "Roll dis shit down." He does the shit. "You got a piece in'nere?"

"Naw, man. I ain't packin'."

These other niggas are just standing around, watching, like they ain't got nothing else to do.

"Yo, Steve?"

"What's up?"

"Search his car for a piece," I tell him.

Steve opens the passenger door and gets in.

"What I do to you, man?" Pervis asks me. His eyes are begging for mercy. And I can see his chest rise and fall with his heartbeats.

I stick my gun to his cheek. "Yo, you find a piece in there, Steve?"

"Naw, he ain't got nothin' but a bunch of rubbers and some weed."

"Take that shit and make him buy some more. And I would take ya coat, but I ain't got no place t' carry it."

"I'll take that shit," Rudy says, stepping up to the car.

"Naw, fuck this nigga," I tell him. I don't want to prolong the issue. I want this spineless motherfucker out of my face before I end up shooting him.

I slip my .45 back inside my jacket. I look at Pervis with steady eyes. "Yo, look here, Joe." He turns to face me with his chest still heaving and tears rising in his punk-ass eyes. He probably pissed on himself.

"Don't'chu ever get in a game that you afraid of, nigga. If you can't stand the heat, den get da hell out.

And another thing. If you got some tough-ass cousins in New York, then tell them ma-fuckas to come down here and meet me. Maybe we can drink a few beers and laugh about'cha punk ass. 'Cause you know what, Joe? I don't give a fuck if niggas is from New York, Jamaica, Compton or the Fifth Ward, Texas; a nigga wit' heart is a nigga wit' heart. And Shank don't back down t' no-fuckin'-body."

I let the motherfucker drive off. This cold-ass February weather whips past me and shakes my stance. But I feel unmoved. And you know what? A nigga ain't got nothing when he's castrated. "That's why the white man always goes for a nigga's balls, just like a bitch" my uncle in Jersey used to tell me. He in jail now, but he stood up for his. You know what I'm saying? We got to get our shit straight. We got to go out like warriors. Or die like bitches. And I ain't no *bitch*. So fuck all the punk shit! I'm a cold-ass warrior!

Wes

"I'on know why Riddick Bowe talkin'nat shit, you'n; he ain't fightin' nobody. Anybody can knock some old-ass Michael Dokes out," Walt says.

"Yeah, but nobody thought Bowe had a chance to win a title after the Olympics. Him and Rock Newman came a long way, Joe," Marshall rebuts.

"Yeah, he talkin'nat trash; 'I beat the man that beat the man that beat the man' after he beat Holyfield," Walt retorts.

Derrick smiles from the couch; he's sitting next to me as usual. We're all inside Marshall's basement apartment on Thirteenth Street Northwest, off of Euclid. "You can't beat 'em, Walt."

"Shit, you crazy! I'd knock that fat nigga out."

We all chuckle.

"So what'chu gon' do for a job now, Wes?" Walt asks me. "You gon' go work for Giant's again?"

"Nope. I think I wanna take a resting period."

Marshall frowns from the floor. He's in his usual spot in front of his TV. "So how you gon' pay rent?"

"I'll find a way."

Walt grins. "That nigga 'bout to hook up wit' Butterman and start hustlin', that's how."

"Hell, why not?" I say just for the hell of it.

Marshall shakes his head while cleaning his thin-rimmed glasses against his shirt. "Man, you should'na fucked up that telemarketing job."

"What was he supposed to do, jus' let them jerk 'im around?" Derrick says to my defense.

"He ain't have t' call 'em racists white assholes, though," Marshall retorts.

Walt laughs. "He should'a called 'em some cocksuckin' sons of bitches. That's how dey talk."

We all howl with laughter.

"That's just how poor, white trash talk," Derrick says. Then he looks to me. "You did what you had to do, man. White people always be lyin' and hooking each other up at our expense."

"Yeah, but you gotta keep your job no matter what white people try da do," Marshall responds.

Walt frowns, stretching out his legs from the smaller couch. "Man, fuck that! He did the right thing. Nigga jus' ain't got no job now."

We all laugh again. I figure it's no sense in me being upset about it. I have to keep moving on.

"Yeah, you missed Khallid Muhammad up at Howard University, man," Marshall says, facing me with his gold glasses back on.

"He been hangin' out wit' dat girl twenty-four–seven. She prob'bly got 'im pussy-whipped," Walt says for more laughter.

I smile. "So what was Khallid Muhammad talking about?" I ask Marshall, ignoring Walt.

"Man, he came right out and said, 'If The Nation of Islam killed Malcolm X, we wouldn't lie to *you*, we'd tell you we killed him. Then we'd ask, 'What do you wanna do about it?' But we didn't kill Malcolm X'."

"Everybody should know by now that it was a set-up," Derrick adds.

"Spike Lee said they did it," Marshall says.

"Spike Lee don't know what da fuck he talkin' 'bout!" Walt yells. "That nigga need to stick to his movies. But he was right when he said that the white man created AIDS." Walt gets hyper. "Oh, I believe that shit, you'n! They been sayin' that shit for *years!*"

"What else did he say?" I ask Marshall.

"Oh, man, a bunch of stuff. You know them Nation of Islam speeches be three hours long. But he was lunchin', Joe. He came out here talkin' 'bout 'This ain't the zoom, zoom, zoom in'na boom, boom. This the real deal t'night. There ain't gon' be no zoom, zoom, zoom t'night'."

We all howl with more laughter.

"I'm tired of that damn song anyway," Walt says.

Derrick nods. "They played it too much."

"So what'chu think about the civil rights movement now, after Thurgood Marshall died, Wes?" Marshall asks me out of the blue.

I respond, "What civil rights? We need our own work places now. That civil rights garbage didn't work. White people still racist. And Clarence Thomas? Give me a break."

Derrick laughs. "Yeah, he fucked around and said

okay to the Ku Klux Klan's right to burn a cross on your lawn."

Walt grimaces. "Yo, if any white ma-fucka burn a damn cross on *my* lawn, I'ma fuck 'em up. That shit is fightin' words for a nigga, Joe. For real!"

"No bullshit," Marshall agrees.

"Arthur Ashe died too," Derrick comments.

"Aw, man, fuck him," Walt says, frowning. "He was one of them ass-kissin' niggas."

"But at least he married a black woman," Marshall says.

"But he had AIDS," Walt retorts.

"Yeah, but he wasn't a faggot. He got AIDS through a blood transfusion."

"Whatever, man. The ma-fucka died of AIDS, and that's fucked up. Period!"

"No, what was really fucked up was how they exposed it in the media," Derrick says.

"Oh yeah, you know they'a do that t' one of us in a minute," Marshall agrees.

We sit quiet for a while, watching cable television before I head up another discussion:

"So Black History Month is almost over."

Walt laughs as if I've just made the funniest joke in the world. "This nigga trippin'. *Black History Month.* And niggas be proud of that shit, too."

"Why not be proud?" Derrick asks. "I mean, we even got every state honoring Martin Luther King now."

Marshall nods. "Yeah, that's right, 'cause Arizona finally gave in."

Walt shakes his head. "Y'all niggas is crazy. I mean, I just can't understand that dumb shit. Here we are in a country that kicks our ass every day and yet we gon' be proud of some Black History Month."

"Naw, *you're* the one that's crazy," Derrick retorts. "We can't let white people or anybody else take our achievements from us."

"I know. We did a lot of shit in this country," Marshall adds.

Walt grins. "Yeah, and most niggas is still poor and stupid."

Now I come in on it: "If we make Black History Month an everyday celebration, then we can close the gap between the conscious and the unconscious. But the major deterrent is that the public school system, which is controlled by the greater white supremacist institution in America, won't allow it. I mean, we've had African-centered scholars researching our history for years, but the only way to reach our youth with it is to have our own schools."

"Here this nigga go wit' that lecturing shit," Walt says, cutting me off before I can continue.

Derrick smiles. "See that, Walt? That's why people are poor and stupid, because they don't want to listen. We might be sitting next to the next James Baldwin here."

"No, I'm not James Baldwin," I retort. I don't have anything personal against him, but I'm a new black man from the hip-hop generation with a different philosophy from Baldwin's integrationist approach.

Marshall smiles. "Wasn't James Baldwin a faggot?"

Walt roars with deep down laughter.

"That's beside the point," Derrick responds. "It's what he was fighting for that was important."

"Okay, and what was the faggot fighting for?" Walt asks, still giggling to himself.

Derrick shakes his head. "You pitiful sometimes, Walt. Sometimes I ask myself why I even hang with you."

"I ask that shit to myself about hangin' wit'chall niggas er'ryday. I mean, I really sit down and go, 'Damn!

Now these boys don't get no pussy; they can't run no ball, and they sit around talkin' about politics and gossip like a bunch of fuckin' girls.'"

Walt breaks out and laughs again at his ruminations as Derrick continues to shake his head.

Marshall says, "'Cause we cool. And you know that we goin' somewhere in life. So you know what'chu doin'; you try'na stay on a winning team. 'Cause when push comes to shove, you know that them other niggas you be fuckin' wit' ain't gon' be about shit."

Marshall shuts Walt up. And I must say, I don't think I could have said it any better myself. Walt is actually having a moral fight to be down with us instead of his wanna-be roughnecks, because he knows that ultimately, we'll be the real survivors. Or will we?

I'm forgetting that I just lost my job for standing up for my black manhood at work. So what will the future hold? Will I learn to accept racism, fight it, or simply run away from it?

After a while I call my answering machine and get a message to call NeNe. But I don't want to. I know they're going to tease me about being "pussy-whipped" again. Especially Walt. But I believe he's jealous. I think he'd *love* to be whipped by a pretty girl like NeNe.

"So when you takin' that test for graduate school?" Marshall asks me, breaking our silence.

"Oh, the GRE exam? It's one coming up in April."

"So you really thinking about going on to graduate school?" Derricks asks.

Walt chuckles. "He might as well be a teacha. Nigga always lecturin'."

I smile. "Yeah, I'm just wondering how many people I can really reach."

"Hey, man, every soul counts," Derrick tells me.

"Yeah, but you better get a PhD if you wanna make

some real money, you'n," Marshall comments. " 'Cause that other small-time teaching ain't worth it."

"I know, Joe. Them teachas be gettin' jerked," Walt says.

I try to sneak on the phone and call NeNe while everyone is still conversing.

"Who you callin'?" Marshall asks me, smiling. I think I've just been busted.

"You know who he's callin'," Walt says. "He callin' his girl up."

"So what?" I shout, no longer caring if they know.

Derrick chuckles. "They jus' jealous that *they* ain't in love."

"*In love?* That nigga only been with her for like a month. How he gon' be in love?" Walt asks as if he's shocked Derrick even used the word.

"Love works in mysterious ways," I tell Walt with a smile, as NeNe answers the phone.

"Yeah, that's ya dick talkin' to you, nigga. You ain't in no damn love. How he gon' be in love? That nigga don't know nothin' about love. Hell he talkin' 'bout?"

Marshall laughs. "Would'ju shut'cha jealous ass up so he can talk to his girl."

"I'm gon' be in ya area in a half an hour, 'cause my girlfriend givin' me a ride," NeNe says over the phone.

"Okay, I'll be home by then."

"Oh my God! You hear this nigga? Now I know he pussy whipped," Walt interrupts, minding my business.

I put my hand over the receiver while I chuckle.

"So you got er'rything?" NeNe asks me.

"Yeah, I got everything."

"Okay, I'm leavin' now."

"All right, I'll see you." I hang up and motion to Marshall. "You giving me a ride, right?"

"Yeah."

Marshall jumps up and grabs our coats from the closet.

"So what'chall gon' do?" Derrick asks me.

"Oh, we're supposed to have a candlelight dinner tonight, over spaghetti."

Walt frowns. "This nigga even cookin' for her."

"Yup," I admit as Marshall and I step out toward the door.

"So how does she treat you?" Marshall asks me once we settle into his car. We ride down Columbia Road toward Michigan Avenue.

"She treats me *real* well."

Marshall grins. "So did y'all do shit yet?"

I smile. "Why is that so important to guys?"

"Aw, man, come on. Women talk about it too. You read Terry McMillan's books. You should now that by now."

"Yeah, well, I'm not one to kiss and tell."

"You told me when you slept with Sybil."

I smile embarrassingly. "Well, I shouldn't have done that."

"Aw, man, you gon' front on me now?"

I smile at him innocently, but with no response. We turn left on Twelfth and Michigan Northeast, heading to my apartment building. NeNe and her girlfriend are waiting inside a black Honda Civic when we arrive.

"Damn, they beat us here!" Marshall says in shock. NeNe's girlfriend must live closer to my house than what she thought.

We all hop out and go through the introductions before NeNe and I head up to my apartment. Marshall and NeNe's girlfriend drive off in their cars.

"I see you have a new hairstyle," I tell my sweetheart. "It's pretty, too."

She pats her hair delicately and smiles. "Thank you." She smiles as I hang up our coats. "So, have you missed me?" she asks.

"Yeah, I missed you all yesterday."

She giggles, looking gorgeous in a casual black and purple outfit with matching purple earrings.

I joke with her. "So, I see that Prince must have gotten to you today, hunh?"

"Funny," she says, opening the refrigerator. She pulls out the Ragu spaghetti sauce and the ground turkey. She doesn't eat beef. And I respect that a lot. But I still eat it. It'll take years for it to kill you. Or at least that's what I believe. A vivacious attitude is the key to longevity in life. Health can be overrated if your spirits are still low.

We get everything ready and set our plates in front of us. A yellow candle glows in the middle of my small kitchen table. I can't even fit the table in my micro kitchen, so I have it off to the left of the living room.

"So what's new?" NeNe asks, gazing at me as we start to eat.

I swallow down my first bite. "Well, for starters, I quit my job tonight."

Her eyes pop open in surprise. "Why?"

"Because I caught these two young white males talking about how they were gonna spend their weekend in Florida while they sabotage my damn overtime hours."

She smiles. "That's the first time I heard you cuss. You must've been pissed off, hunh?"

"Well, 'damn' isn't that bad of a curse word. But yeah, I *am* pissed. And the thing that's so frustrating about it is that it's hard to *prove* when they're screwing you. They always try to call you incompetent."

She giggles. "I know, that's how it be."

"Oh yeah? So where have you worked before where it's happened to you?"

"I used t' work in'nis restaurant in Maryland. And they always gave this white girl the best hours. I mean, they had me working on Friday and Saturday nights.

And those nights are good for tips, but I wanted to go out my damn self on the weekends. I'd rather work during the weekdays and on weekend mornings."

"But the white girl had those hours?"

"Yup. And I hated that bitch! Fat-ass thing. She had the nerve t' have a black boyfriend, too. But he was a bamma; he wasn't nobody."

Every time she uses that word "bamma" I start to feel guilty. It's only been since she's known me that I've been dressing "hip." Last year she would have called me a bamma too.

"So what'chu gon' do about a job now?" she asks me, staring at me with her sparkling, almond-shaped eyes. God, she's gorgeous!

"Well, I still have money in the bank. And if push comes to shove, I always have my mother."

"What, t' move back in wit'er?!" she responds radically.

"No, to borrow some money until I can get back on my feet."

"Oh, I thought you was gon' give up this apartment."

Okay, is it me or the apartment she's after? I'm thinking. Hmm, maybe Walt is right: we have only known each other for a month.

We sit silently and munch as I contemplate how rash she responded to me losing my job, and the possibility of losing my apartment. I can feel pressure in our relationship for the first time since our first night together. I didn't know if she liked me or not then. But then again, I'm always slightly nervous around NeNe. She adds the sexual excitement that Sybil lacked, but she also adds a rush of insecurity. I really don't know how long I can expect to be with her with no rep and no money.

"Who's that?" she asks me, responding to a car horn.

"Some neighbors are probably going out or something." I look at my watch and it says eleven-thirty. It's Thursday night.

"No, it sounds like somebody's calling you."

"Oh yeah?" I get up and walk to the window. "Guess who?" I ask her.

"Who?"

"It's your big brother, Butterman"

"Stop playin'!" She leaps from her seat and dashes to the window with me. "Oh shit, is that ya car?" She dashes to the front door. "Come on," she tells me, running down the exit stairs.

I walk out behind her. J approaches me, smiling. Then he hands me the keys to a red Acura Integra sitting out in front of us.

"Er'rything cool wit' it, man." Then he whispers away from NeNe, "But you gots to get new registration and all."

NeNe opens the passenger door and hops right in. "Shawdy, dis car is like dat!" She looks to me. "Come on, Wes, let's drive it."

I look to J solemnly as NeNe closes the door and waits for us excitedly.

I shake my head. "Why you do this to me, J?"

J starts toward the driver side, grinning. "Man, stop girlin' and come on."

He hops in the back as I follow him in. I gear up on the steering wheel and check out the dashboard: hi-tech, cruise control, automatic, tape cassette, air conditioner and pure comfort. I can't lie, I feel like I've just won the lottery!

Key to ignition. Smooth kitten purr. And we're off!

"We can go everywhere now, Wes! We can go to Virginia Beach when it gets warm. We can go to my cousin's house in Pittsburgh, 'cause I been dyin' to ride on a river-boat out there. Oh God, Wes! We can do er'rything."

NeNe turns on the radio. That stupid "Dazzey Dukes" song is on. But I'm too dazzled to complain. I drive down South Dakota Avenue, loving it.

"Yo, turn around and take me back to Georgia Ave, up near Ibex. I got my car parked up there," J hollers from the back seat.

I make a quick U-turn and head up South Dakota Avenue to Riggs Road. I stay on Riggs and cross North Capitol Street toward Georgia Avenue.

We stop on a street alongside the Ibex nightclub. I let J out.

"Yo, Wes, let me talk to you for a minute," he says.

I leave the key in the ignition while NeNe bobs her head to the radio. I follow J toward the Ibex club at the corner.

Girls are staring as if we're *both* celebrities. I know Butterman is a wanted item, but I'm just a UDC student with a pretty girlfriend. But now I have the keys to an Acura!

"Look, man, don't even sweat da car, 'cause that shit is jus' because I love you. I mean, I ain't never bought nobody a car, not even my girl. But that's 'cause I want'chu to be down wit' me, Joe. Now, look, you ain't gotta sell nothin', jus' keep accounts on what we spend. And you can type the shit if you want. I'll keep the joints at my crib if you scared to have 'em in yours.

"The bottom line is this: I don't know of that many niggas like you that I can trust wit' money. And as far as the drug biz'ness? . . . Look, you a upstandin' young man, right? I mean, wouldn't you rather have the money so you can start a biz'ness of your own? That's what them white niggas do. Man, all them ma-fuckas got financiers. But we don't. So I'm jus' tryin' to set things up so we can roll like that and eventually pump the money into a legal business.

"I mean, I'm not like these other niggas sellin' drugs, man. I got real plans for this money, Joe. For real! So what's up, man?" J presses me.

He extends his hand and looks at me as if he'll break down if I don't say yes. But *all* I have to do is book-keep. That's how many unethical Jews have made a killing. But I don't want to be like them. Nevertheless, I need the money. And who else is giving me this kind of an offer? WHO ELSE?

I extend my hand and take the handshake. "Yeah, man, I'm in."

J smiles like a wide-eyed toddler. "Yo, you made the right decision, you'n. It ain't no sense in you sweatin' for them white niggas. You gon' get *paid* now, man! Watch! You made the right move."

Butterman

"Yo, B, what's up, man? Is we gon' take dat ride or what?" Bink asks me from behind.

"Yeah, hold up. Let me finish talkin' to my boy."

I turn back to Wes, who's wearing a rayon shirt and some blue slacks. He's finally pimping some slammin'–ass clothes. "Well, I'll talk to you tomorrow, man. Go 'head and get back to y'all dinner."

Wes looks at me confused. "How you know we were having dinner?"

Oh shit, I'm fuckin' up! I smile and laugh it off. " 'Cause y'all look hungry, nigga. Now go 'head an' check out dat ride, Joe."

Wes shakes his head and walks back up the street to-ward the Acura. She sweet as hell, too. For real! I wouldn't mind keeping that Integra for myself if he ain't want it. Fuck it, you know? Butterman could've been switching

up cars! Then these niggas would really be on my dick.
I'm already like dat. Now I'm about to get buck-wild!

I turn and face my main man. "So what's up, Bink?
Let's take dat ride, nigga."

I stroll over toward my car. Bink follows me with a
cool-ass grin.

He says, "Fuck you all excited about? What'chu jus'
got some pussy?"

I laugh as I open the car doors. "Yeah, man, somethin'
like dat."

"Well, gi'me dis bitch number den. 'Cause she mus'
got some good ass; she got'chu actin' like it's your first
shot."

I laugh, making a right turn and then a left. We jet
down Thirteenth Street, heading to Hains Point.

"So Marc, up in New York, been tellin' me dat you flip-
pin' like a ki' a week now?" Bink says as we roll.

"Yeah, somethin' like dat. But I thought *you* was flip-
pin' more than'nat."

Bink nods. "Yeah, but I ain't the one t' sell 'n tell. You
know."

I smile. "Man, I ain't thinkin' 'bout competin' wit'chu."

"That ain't da point. What I'm sayin' is that you always keep ya name down low; that's how you make ya
shit last. Niggas start gettin' flashy, and then stupid shit
start hap'nin'."

I nod. Bink got a point. Maybe I should stop thinking
about this high-profile shit.

"You heard about Smiley gettin' busted last week,
right?" Bink asks me.

"Naw, da po-man got 'im?"

"Yeah, Joe. I'm surprised you ain't heard about dat shit."

I shake my head. "Naw."

"You hear about that shoot-out, back at The Met?"

"Yeah, two ma-fuckas died, three injured."

꜋

Bink nods. "Mmm-hmm. On the quiet side, B, that was Smiley's crew that did it. They got a contract out on'nat boah name Cuppy."

"Cuppy? Yeah, I know you'n. He used to be back Southwest when me and Red and them used t' swing back dat way."

"Yeah, well, how 'bout dis: ma-fuckas heard that he was gon' drop a dime in court on Smiley. And the prosecutors use dat bullshit where you snitch on a nigga and get a lesser sentence, or you get that mandatory ten years for drug traffickin'."

"Man, 'nat's fucked up! I always thought that mandatory sentencin' was crazy. I mean, a nigga can get less years for killin' somebody."

Bink says, "Yup, this white man know what da hell he doin'; he'a let us kill each other, but he don't want us t' get wit' no money.

"Ain't that a bitch? So now it's more niggas stayin' in jail for drugs than any other crime."

I park down at Hains Point while Bink rolls a couple Js to smoke.

"Yo, yo, it's da po-man," I whisper to him.

Bink holds the weed under the seat. A white-and-blue District of Columbia cruiser drives by with two black cops.

Bink giggles. *"Crooked awww-ficer, crooked awww-ficer. Why you wanna put me in'na cawww-fin, sir?"*

We laugh like shit as Bink hands me one of the joints.

"Yeah, you'n, da Getto Boys is my niggas. Dey be kickin' facts for ya ass," he says.

I nod. "Yeah, ya boy Shank be listenin' t' all dat rap shit."

"Oh, Cool-ass Nell can flow. Boy been flowin' rhymes since high school."

"You older than him, right?" I ask Bink.

"Yeah, I'm a year behind you. 'Cause you turn twenty-four next month, right?"

"Yeah, how you know dat?"

Bink looks at me as if I've just said something stupid. "'Member you had that big-ass party two years ago?"

"Oh, oh, oh—my fault. Yeah, dat party was da bomb."

Bink nods with a cool-ass smile. "You damn right it was. That's where I met this girl Angela."

"Oh yeah? I know her."

"Did'ju bang 'er?" Bink asks me, grinning.

I shake my head. "Naw, man, she said I had too many girls. Plus my girl knows her."

Bink laughs for no damn reason. "I know you didn't wax'er, nigga. I jus' wanted t' see if you was gon' sit here and lie t' me. 'Cause my long, brown dick was the first to *work da walls, work da walls. Come on!*"

Bink laughs. He's trippin' off of that Rare Essence song. "Yeah, yeah, nigga. And she was grippin' me like I was killin'nat ass."

I smile. "You still wit'er?"

He shakes his head. "Naw, she went away t' college and got wit' one of them ma-fuckas. But she calls me whenever she comes back home though."

I'm curious now. "Yo, you think you can compete with them college niggas for a girl?"

Bink frowns at me. "Nigga, is you crazy? I be schoolin'nem college ma-fuckas. I done banged so many girls from Howard, UDC, American and George Washington, that it don't make no sense. I even had this one girl from Georgetown. Now tell me I ain't da man!"

I laugh. "Yeah, 'cause some girls act like dey don't fuck wit' street niggas."

Bink smiles. "Believe that shit if you want. Matter fact, Nell fuckin' a girl from Howard now. We met her when we was up at Kilimanjaro's in October. Me and Nell was on, right. And he jus' walks up t' dis bad-ass light-skinned babe and says, 'Yo, I wanna call you when I leave here. So what's up wit' dat?' And man, this bitch got all excited, talkin' 'bout some: 'Oh, well, I don't know, 'cause I'm just out here to have a good time.' And Nell said, 'Well, you gon' have a good time wit' me, too.' And yo, do you know this bad bitch giggled and ended up writin' down her number! That shit tripped me da hell out!"

I laugh, then get serious. I'm feeling the weed now and grooving.

I say, "Yeah, why dat boah Nell; that's his real name, right?"

Bink nods "Yeah" while I continue.

"Why you'n so crazy, man? He be talkin' 'bout killin' ma-fuckas constantly. We don't need all dat drama."

Bink takes another hit, slanting his eyes. He holds it in and blows it out. "Hey, man, some niggas got that rough-ass edge t' life. I can't call it. I mean, some ma-fuckas rub Nell the wrong way, some niggas don't. But don't tell 'im I told you his name though, 'cause I'on want that crazy nigga after me."

We laugh like shit, higher than two motherfuckers. But Bink is still talking.

"Naw, really though! That boy Shank is cool, it's jus' that street life that got 'im livin' harder than ten other hard niggas."

I nod. "Yeah, it's messed up how some niggas is mad at the world like that."

Bink sits quietly, like he's in deep thought. "Yo, all of us have that shit a li'l bit. Some ma-fuckas jus' got more discipline than others."

I smile, thinking about asking him something else. "Yo, I heard your pop had shit goin' on for years."

Bink looks at me confusingly. "You ain't know?"

I shake my head. "Naw."

"Yeah, man, nigga like me ain't never been poor. And see, ma-fuckas expect you t' be poor because you live in a black neighborhood now, like I was tellin' you before. But things don't have t' be that way. And this drug game is open 'cause the white man is allowin' it to be open."

I nod. "I *been* sayin'nat; that's jus' how ruthless he is."

Bink says, "Yeah, now how 'bout dis, right: if all these jobs is s'posed to be evaporatin' in America, then how come these big-ass companies still advertising all this bullshit to us? Them ma-fuckas know we gon' get money from somewhere. I mean, 'cause if you think about, niggas ain't *got* no money—so they say—but yet we buyin' more shit than any other race livin'."

"Yeah, you got that shit right."

Bink nods, still running his mouth. "Now, I'ma tell you somethin' else, right: 'member when'nare was a shortage of weed in the late eighties and early nineties?"

I smile. "Yeah, I remember that. It was hard as hell t' get some weed."

"Well, yo, the white man was trying t' get niggas hooked on blow. Now he got 'em, and he fuckin' many households up. And after all the hustlers go t' jail, it's gon' be younger and younger niggas sellin' drugs."

I tell him, "Yeah, and I read somewhere that all these new prisons gon' have all kinds of cheap-ass nigga labor."

Bink nods, smiling at me. "Exactly. That's why I keep my shit down low. They try'na put us back in slavery. Sister Souljah know what she talkin' 'bout! And that's why I buy from different sources, so that they can't track me. So my boys in New York is cool and all, man, but don't let'cha connections get limited, 'cause that's when brothers go under."

I nod. "Yeah, I hear you. That shit makes sense."

Bink grins at me like a kid. "Yo, you keep gettin' lessons from me like dis and I'ma have t' start chargin' ya ass up."

I laugh. "You lunchin', man."

Bink shakes it off. "Naw, I ain't lunchin'. I'ma tell one more thing: weed is *in* now. Ma-fuckas wearin' blunt shirts, hats, drawers, all kinds of shit. And I'm about to start sellin' pounds of that shit. I'll fuck around and start growin' weed in my backyard. For real!"

I start laughing, but Bink looks serious as shit.

"I ain't jokin'. I mean, you gots t' stay hip to the signs of the times, and weed is da shit now."

I'm still giggling as I try to respond. "Yeah, well, maybe I need to invest in some."

Bink nods, smiling. "You motherfuckin' right."

It's Thursday, March 4, 1993, a week from my twenty-fourth birthday. Today I'm going to visit my boy Red at Lorton after getting this fresh haircut up on Georgia Ave.

Georgie's telling another one of those funny-ass, old-timer jokes: "So da young man went inside the store and told the lady, 'Ma'am, I done forgot what my Ma tol' me t' buy from this here sto', but since you look about her age, I figa I could ask you what a woman would want if she sent me with two dollars.' And the older woman looked down at the young man and said, 'Well, wit' two dollars, I'd send my boy t' da store t' by me some new stockings.' So he comes marchin' back in'na house and says, 'Ma, I gotcha ya stockings!' And his big-ol' mother comes wobbling out from the kitchen and shakes her head. She looks down at him and says, 'Boy, I done tol'ja a million times dat'cha daddy's gone and I surely ain't plannin' on goin' out here and gettin' pregnant by none of dese sorry-ol' niggas. Now go on back t' da sto' and buy me some fatback, hog maws, blackeye peas and cornbread like I told'ja.'

"So the young man starts walking back to the store. But then he stops and runs back to his house and says, 'Ma, I got an idea!' His mother comes back out from the kitchen and says, 'Junior, what'chu got t' tale me, boy?' And Junior says, 'Well, I was jus' thinkin' 'bout how you can get me a new Pa by wearing these stockings t' church this Sunday. 'Cause I heard Reverend Smith tell Deacon Jackson one day.' And his mother said, 'And what did Reverend Smith say t' Deacon Jackson, boy?' And Junior said, 'Well, Ma, I heard him say, Jackson, I can't help it! Lawd strike me down, 'cause I Jus' loves me a fat-assed woman!"

We laughing like shit. Them old-timer jokes are something else! I'm gon' learn how to tell them dumb jokes myself. I'm gon' practice that shit.

"Yo, where you be gettin' all these jokes from, Georgie?" I ask him.

"From plain, long livin', boy. But see, you young'uns ain't gon' be able to tell no *good* jokes because you don't listen enough, and you got short attention spans. See, so t' get *these* jokes, you have t' know how the story all comes together. But naw, you young'uns all want it fast nowadays. You all like that Eddie Murphy stuff. But see, Richard Pryor had them long, story jokes. And before him you had Redd Foxx. But you young'uns wouldn't know nothin' about him; Redd Foxx had grown-up jokes."

"I heard Redd Foxx before."

Georgie frowns at me. "Now, boy, go on and get'cha hair cut, 'cause I'm ti'ed of you bullshittin' me. You ain't never heard no Redd Foxx stand-up. Hell, you still watchin' *Sanford & Son* reruns."

Niggas start laughing again while my barber finishes

up my cut. But I'm gonna learn how to tell them damn jokes. Fuck what Georgie's talking about.

I head over to Keisha's crib. She opens her door, looking all sad and shit.

"What's wrong wit'chu?" I ask her.

"J, you might as well go on somewhere else, you'n."

"Why? What'chu talkin' 'bout?"

"I called up dere t' Lorton t'day. And dey said dat Mitchell was on lock-down for assaulting a guard. Aw, man, I feel so depressed I jus' don't know what t' do. Dey prob'bly beat 'im down bad, shaw'. I hate not bein' able t' do nothin' about dis shit, man, I swear."

She starts sobbing and shit with tears running down her face, looking pitiful. Damn! I hate this sad-type shit.

"How long they say he's on lock-down for?"

"Aw, you'n, I'on know," she whines, crying some more. "I'on feel dat good about dis shit at all. Dey try'na kill 'im, J. Dey try'na kill 'im. 'Cause you know how he is, you'n."

Aw, fuck! She gettin' worse, cryin' all ova da place now.

I sit down on the couch with her and pull her head to my chest. She sniffs against my leather coat. "It ain't nothin' we can do, man. It ain't even shit we can do!"

Damn! Now she making me feel sad and helpless. And Little Red already crying.

"Yo, well, look, let's ride up t' Baltimore Harbor and get some seafood or something, 'cause you gon' need t' get out da house," I tell her.

"I'on wanna go nowhere, Joe. I'on wanna go nowhere."

Man, this scene is pitiful, I'm thinking. I get up and get her and Little Red's coats from the closet. "Come on now, Keisha. Let's go."

She shakes her head like she's half crazy. "Naw, man. I ain't goin' nowhere."

I stand her up and try to put her coat on. She falls back

on the living-room couch. Then her Mom comes downstairs. She's as big as Keisha is, but a lighter shade of
brown.

"Now, Keisha, go 'head, now! I ain't try'na have you
mopin' 'round in here all day, girl. Go 'head and go
somewhere, 'cause you got yaself in'nis damn mess."

Keisha stands up sniffing, and puts her coat on. "Come
on, boy," she says, extending her hand to Little Red.

We walk out and get inside my 3000. Nobody really
says shit for the whole thirty-five minute ride to Baltimore. Keisha doesn't say anything to me until we have
the seafood out in front of us: stuffed shrimp, crab, lobster, flounder; every fucking thing. I ordered the works,
you know, because I got it like that.

Keisha looks into my eyes with a shrimp in her hand,
still looking pitiful. "I jus' wish dat'chall could do somethin' right wit'chall lives instead'a all dis crooked shit,
man."

*Aw, here we go. As soon as things get a little rough, this the
first thing people start sayin'*, I'm thinking. I'm not giving
up my pull. Fuck that! I worked too hard for mine! Tell
this bamma-ass shit to the next nigga.

I look away from her, frowning, but Keisha still talking
crazy.

"You listenin' t' me, Joe? Y'all don't have t' live like
dis, man. Y'all don't." She drops her shrimp back on her
plate. Now she looks like she's about to start crying and
shit again. "Why ain't it no other way t' make money like
dat, man? Hunh?"

She's gettin'na hell on my nerves, but I'm try'na stay cool!
"Come on now, Red gon' be aw'ight," I tell her, helping
Little Red break off a piece of the lobster.

Keisha shakes her head at me. "No, I'm talkin' 'bout
you now. I mean, Tub is dead, John-John takin' drugs,

DeShawn jus' disappeared; now what'chu gon' do, *Jeffrey Kirkland?*"

"I'm gon' keep gettin' fuckin' paid; that's what *I'm* gon' do!" I yell across the table at her. I look around us to make sure that I didn't draw too much attention. Damn! I hate to get loud with her like this, but she's fucking with me!

She grits her teeth, balls her fists and glares at me. "I hope t' God dat dey put'cha pretty ass in jail so dey can fuck you!" she yells back.

She jumps up from the table and grabs Little Red's hand and their coats. I shake my head and ignore all these bamma-ass niggas and white people staring at our booth. I pull out three twenties and a ten and leave it on the table. I follow Keisha and Little Red as they rush out. We get back in the car and ride home the same way we came: neither one of us are saying anything.

I drop Keisha and Little Red off. Keisha slams my damn door. I shake my head again. Fuck her! I never really liked her heavy ass anyway. That's Red's girl.

I ride back to my Silver Spring apartment building and park in the parking lot. I walk up to the door and dig into my pocket to pull out my lobby key. Some white man comes out before I put my key in the door, so I try to walk in behind him.

The middle-aged white man grabs the door. "Excuse me, do you live here?"

I yank the door open and show him my key. "Yeah, I live here, muthafucka! Now get da fuck off the door!"

He looks at me as if I'm crazy and heads on his way. Shit! I'm already pissed the hell off, and this damn white man gon' ask me if I live here! I guess he thinks this apartment building is too plush for a young nigga to live in. And that's exactly my damn point. I mean, why should I kiss some white motherfucker's ass all my life? Fuck that shit! Is that what niggas live for?

Well, not this nigga. I got my own fucking game. I got my own power. I make my own decisions. And I'm not going out like my father. I don't care how much money he makes; my father's a pussy, like all the rest of these niggas that live like him. The white man won't never let them in. It's just like this white bastard trying to keep me out of my own damn building. For real!

We gots to run our own shit! OUR OWN FUCKING GAME!

CHAPTER 7

Butterman

I did everything Wes told me to do to get a company name from the Maryland State Small Business Bureau. Now I'm all dressed: suit, tie and shoes, to game this bank teller up and open an account.

I got like, sixty thousand dollars in cash at the crib after buying that Acura, so Wes told me I'll have to put my money in the bank, little by little. They have this government policy where they have to report cash in excess of ten thousand dollars. It might take me two months to get all my shit in the bank, but I figure it's better than laundering money through some bamma-ass store like a lot of these other niggas are doing.

I park my car downtown and put four quarters in the parking meter. These damn parking ticketers are crazy! Fuck if they think they're giving me a ticket!

I straighten out my blue tie and walk into the bank with five thousand dollars in cash and all my papers of corporation, including two newspaper clippings. I had to state that my company is open for business in two publications.

It's three women opening the accounts: one black, one Asian and one white. I guess they're an equal opportunity employer, hunh?

I walk over to the white woman because she's the only one who's free. Plus, I kind of think it's better to bullshit these white people. I still know how to talk to these bamma-ass niggas.

"Hi, can I help you?" she asks. She's wearing a gray women's business suit, you know, with a matching skirt instead of pants.

I give her a "good nigger" smile. "Sure, I would like to open up an account for my P.R. agency." I sit down in the seat in front of her desk.

"Okay, that would be a checking account."

"Ah, both, please, checking and savings."

She smiles. "All right. Do you have your articles of corporation?"

I hand her all my shit and she hands me some papers to fill out. I fill the form out and give it back to her.

"Okay, for a company account you have to maintain at least two thousand dollars within the account at all times or suffer a ten dollar penalty per month. Now for the savings, the minimum balance for an account will be two hundred dollars."

I smile at her and show her all my teeth. "Okay, I have four thousand dollars for the checking and one thousand for my savings."

I give her the money and she counts the shit two and three times. God damn! These banks don't bullshit about that money.

She stands up and hands me a receipt. "Well, thank you very much, Mr. Kirkland. You should be receiving your account book and company checks in the mail in a week or so."

I stand up and shake the white woman's hand. She's smiling with pink-ass cheeks, looking all bammafied, just like in one of those commercial advertisements and shit!

"Thank you," I tell her.

She smiles again as I turn around and walk out.

Yeah, my shit is rolling in! I'm gonna make it legal! I'm the fucking man! I'm like dat! I'm *cysed!*

Tomorrow is my birthday: Saturday, March 13. I call up Wes to take him down South Carolina with me so he can see this light-skinned, bullshit family of mine up close. I mean, besides my old boys: Red, Tub, John-John and DeShawn, Wes is the only new nigga I can fuck with like that. I don't want them other young'uns to know what kind of fucked-up-ass family I come from. Plus, Wes is the only one that could fit in with my family anyway. Shit, they'll probably like his upstanding, studious ass. For real!

Me and Wes ride in his Acura down I-95 South.

"So everything at the bank went well?" he asks me.

It feels good not to be in the driver's seat for a change. I got this bucket seat leaned back and I'm cruising, enjoying the sights. The weather's getting warmer now.

"Yeah, man, that shit was easier than I thought it would be. *Much* easier."

Wes smiles. "I told you. I mean, I don't see why more Blacks don't know how easy it is to open up a business account. It's really nothing to it. You just send in your company name, take out a few newspaper articles, and then open up the account for business."

"Yeah, but I'm worried about how quickly I can get the rest of my fuckin' money in'nere," I tell him.

"Well, one way in which you can speed up the pace is by giving cash to people who have their own small businesses. They deposit the money into their accounts and then you get them to write checks back to your company."

"Yeah, that shit'll work!" I smile. "See, man, I needed you on my squad earlier. I could've had a million dollars by now if I wasn't wastin' money. That's what happens when you really don't know what to do with it."

"Yeah, well, I've been putting most of the money you give me in the bank now myself. But you know, it's something else how I just seem to buy larger things with more money. Like two days ago I bought a high-tech CD player that costs nearly four hundred dollars."

I laugh. "That's what money is for. You supposed to treat'chaself."

"But what I'm saying is that I used to frown on spending that kind of money on things you can do without. Now, since I have the money, I went right out and turned into a hypocrite."

Wes smiles and shakes his head. I look over to my right at an unlucky driver pulled over by a state trooper.

"Yo, you'n, you give somebody enough money, and any nigga'll turn into a hypocrite. That shit is the American way."

We laugh like hell, and Wes pops in Arrested Development's tape.

"Hey J, what do you think about female rappers like Boss?" he asks me.

"Oh, shaw', dey slammin'! They like dat!"

Wes grins. "So you agree with how they figure to equate bitchdom with niggerdom?"

I chuckle. "You makin' up words, nigga?"

He smiles. "You know what I mean."

I nod, more seriously. "Naw, I don't agree wit' dat shit.

I want my women soft and pleasing. But I want them to stand up for themselves when they have to. I mean, that's how *my* girl is."

"Yeah, I heard a lot about her."

"NeNe told'ju?"

"Yup. And I like how you two set me up for this."

We both smile. "I mean, I had t' get you in somehow," I tell him.

"NeNe and I haven't been getting along as well since then."

I nod to him. "She told me."

We sit quiet for a while, listening to "Mr. Wendal."

"Who do you have for the NCAA March Madness?" Wes asks me.

"Oh, I got Duke. Them boys is still like dat. People be try'na sleep on 'em."

Wes smiles at me. "I heard you went to Duke for a year and dropped out."

I nod with a grin. "NeNe got a big fuckin' mouth."

"Who you telling? She tells you everything about *me*."

We share another laugh.

"So where's this guy *Shank* been hiding out?" Wes asks me.

"Man, I got him runnin' with the workers now, 'cause he be actin' crazy. I think that nigga watched that movie *Juice* too many times."

Wes chuckles. "So he's pretty hard, hunh?"

"Yeah, Joe! That nigga's crazy! He one of them 2Pac-actin' niggas. *'Strictly for my, strictly for my, strictly for my niggaz.'* That ma-fucka out his mind!"

Wes smiles. "You ever heard that song 'Trapped'?"

"Yeah, but I ain't really listen to it all that much."

"Well, you need to. That song's a political, hip-hop classic in my book. 'Trapped' sums up everything. I feel trapped every day. America *is* a trap for us young black men."

I ain't responding to that. I don't want him going on one of his political tangents.

"Yo, them girls from Jade look good as shit, you'n. What'chu think?" I ask him. I'm trying to change the subject away from that political stuff he's talking.

Wes says, "I think they're selling sex. Just like Public Enemy said years ago: *'You singers are spineless, as you sing your senseless songs to the mindless. Your general subject, love, is minimal; it's sex for a profit.'* "

Aw, this muthafucka lunchin'. For real! "Yo, man, this ain't the sixties. Niggas into makin' money now." I laugh the shit off, but Wes is still serious.

"That's what bothers me about our generation. But hell, we have to eat to live. So like I said, they have us trapped."

We don't say much to each other until we pull up into the parking lot of my aunt's crib in South Carolina.

"So, this is where you're from?" Wes asks me as we hop out.

"Naw, we originally from *North* Carolina, but then er'rybody broke out."

We head up the painted wooden steps to my aunt's front door.

"Here he is! My birthday nephew has come back home to us!" Aunt May hollers through her elegantly-decorated house. She grabs my cheeks between her hands and kisses me. "Boy, look at these little bones on you. You been eating right?"

I smile. "Yeah, I been eatin' right."

She frowns at me, then laughs. "So who's your friend?"

I turn to Wes. "Oh, this my business partner, Wes."

Wes extends his hand. "Pleased to meet you."

"Unh-hunh. So what kind of business you two doin'?

'Cause you know it broke your mother's heart when you stopped going to Duke to hang out with them hoodlum friends of yours."

See dat shit? I can tell I'm not stayin' long, I'm thinking. My aunt is starting that guilt-trip shit on me already. "We got a P.R. firm to promote and manage go-go bands," I tell her.

She frowns at me. "Go-go bands? Boy, you still into that ol' pot-and-pan music? That ain't no real music. And then you have them little girls dancing to that stuff as if they some kind of prostitutes. Oh yeah, I've seen that stuff."

I shake my head and smile at her. I mean, it's typical for adults to reject the culture of the youth. But I ain't saying nothing because I don't feel like arguing.

My aunt leads us into the basement. "Well, go on down there and meet everybody who hasn't seen you in a while. I gotta finish cooking this food. And your mother and sisters should be here in an hour or so. They called not long after you did."

Wes chuckles as we head down the basement stairs. "You see how this shit is, man?" I whisper to him. "It's gon' get worse. Watch."

"Hey, Junior! You just in time to join our argument! Now we down here discussing that Alex Haley TV series about us mixed bloods," Uncle Jim says. He's gained a lot of weight but he ain't fat yet. He's lost some of his straight hair, but his green eyes are still sparkling. And everybody in this damn house could use a suntan, except for Wes.

I smile embarrassingly. These high-yellow niggas down here debating light-skinned shit already.

"Now, we ain't all light colored 'cause of no damn rapings. I know my wife was one of the finest women in

North Carolina A&T. I had to date her for a year before she started liking me."

"What about you, Junior? You got any young woman for us to meet yet?" Aunt June asks me. She's my father's sister, looking a bit like *my* sister Joyce. She's sitting on the couch with my younger cousins. They're all watching some movie on the big-screen TV.

"Naw, not yet," I lie to her. I'd never bring Toya up against this *bullshit!* I love her too much for that. Our relationship is just between us anyway.

Wes walks over and starts introducing himself and chatting to my relatives. Everybody is sitting around making a lot of noise.

"And you see that woman Eddie Murphy married? Oh, she's tall and beautiful! He really lucked up to be able to marry her," someone says.

I look to Wes to find him shaking his head at me with a smile.

"Well, what do you all think about this Miss USA from Detroit?" someone asks. By now I have my eyes glued to the TV. These niggas never fail to amaze me with this damn gossiping. And it just seems to increase whenever we all come together like this.

"I don't know, but I *do* know all this jungle rap music is prostituting the minds of our young folks in America. Especially these young black children," Uncle Jim says after watching a McDonald's commercial. "Now, Jeffrey, please don't tell me you listen to that kind of music, boy." He's not really asking me. He makes statements as questions sometimes, especially when he's really expressing his mind. I guess the shit is a habit.

I slip my face in between my hands. Wes continues to converse with these lost niggas. I mean, I ain't saying that I'm all revolutionary or nothing like that, but these niggas are pitiful; that's why I don't like being around my family.

"You have to understand that hip-hop culture is coming from a group within America who have never had a voice before. It's a culture that has to release itself no matter how violent or sexist some of it sounds," I hear Wes saying.

"If these youth really want to express themselves, then what they need to do is get more education and show this white man that they are clean, educated and worthy of just treatment," my uncle argues.

Wes shakes his head with a patient grin. "We've been trying that approach for years, and nothing has really—"

"Well, I don't see what's gonna come from these young men cursing and yelling and raising all kinds of hell," my Uncle Jim says, cutting Wes off.

"It's only through *that* process of raising hell that America seems to listen to black folks," Wes responds.

My uncle faces him, shaking with anger. "Young man, you are not old enough nor wise enough to sit here and tell me what I know. I am fifty-two years old, and I've gotten everything through hard work and respect . . ."

Wes done got his ass in hot water now. You can't argue wit' dese ma-fuckas. It ain't like they really want to listen to you. You gots t' say, "Fuck 'em," like I do.

"Are you a college graduate, young man?" my uncle asks Wes.

"Not yet."

"Well, when you get a degree, and then a masters, then you can tell me what you *think* I know . . ."

I look to Wes to get him out of the shit, but this boy is still sitting here trying to debate with my uncle. Wes is *not* gonna win! He must think he's Moses!

"Are you gonna cut the cake?" my little cousin asks

me with a big, happy-faced smile. Kids always like that cake-cutting shit.

"Yeah, just as soon as they're ready for me," I tell her.

"Okay," she says, running back up the steps.

"Jeffrey?" my mother yells down at me. "Can I speak to you for a minute?" She's standing at the top of the basement. I walk on up to see what she wants, hearing Wes still debating his political heart out.

My mom grabs my hand and leads me through a packed room of relatives, all needing damn suntans.

"Hey, J, my girlfriend's sister still wants to meet you," my sister Jo (Josephina) says. She's the younger one; twenty-seven. Joyce is thirty.

I shake my head, telling her that I still don't want to meet this girl as my mom guides me outside and onto the painted wooden patio.

"J, what's this bullshit you're up here telling people about some damn P.R. firm? What is wrong with you?"

I give her an honest kid look. "Look, Mom, I just set the company up yesterday. I've decided to straighten up and fly right." I'm hoping she eats this shit up.

She looks at me sternly with hazel eyes and sharp features. "Do I look like one of these young fools in love to you? You can't lie to me, J. You never could. Now, I wanna know what you're doing with yourself."

"Look, Mom, y'all wanted me t' come me down here for this big party shit—"

"*Shit?* Jeffrey, don't you *dare* talk to me like—"

"Well, how I'm s'posed to talk to you when you trippin' on me like you is?" I yell at her, cutting her off.

She gives a strong sigh and looks away. Then she looks back to me. "I wish your father didn't have to make his trip to Chicago, 'cause then we could all—"

"We could all do what?"

"—talk about whatever happened between you two, Jeffrey!"

We stare at each other speechlessly. I figure I can't win an argument with these people, so why even try?

"Can we join this party, Mom, 'cause I have nothing else t' say."

She walks back inside without saying anything. I walk in behind her and cut the cake while they all sing that "Happy Birthday" song to me. I bullshit with my cousins and introduce them to Wes. Then I tell them I want to show Wes around the neighborhood.

"Yo, man, head for 95 North," I tell Wes once we start driving.

He looks at me confused. "You're not going back?"

"Fuck no, you'n! Let's get da hell out'a here."

Wes shakes his head. "This is cowardice."

"I don't care, man! Let's roll!"

We ride quietly for the first thirty minutes. We listen to Wes' Heavy D & The Boyz cassette, *Blue Funk*.

"Fuck them!" I finally let out.

"Yeah, I see what you mean," Wes says, keeping his eyes glued to the road. "But we still shouldn't have left this way."

I shake my head, still disgusted. I look at Wes behind the wheel. "Look, you'n, they already call me the monster of the family. So fuck 'em! I mean, that shit was s'posed to be *my* party. But them niggas in'nere whisperin' an' shit about rumors they heard about me instead of talkin' t' me. And my bamma-ass cousins be actin' like girls, man. I'on really mess wit' dem like that no more. All'lem mafuckas is pussy whipped."

Wes smiles. "What about you?"

I smile back. "Shit, I ain't whipped, nigga. I got *her* whipped."

Wes giggles. "Sure you do."

We ride on and I start to feel lonely again. Usually I talk to my girl or smoke some weed when I get like this. But this is Wes. I can trust *this* nigga with my feelings.

"You know I went to Georgetown Day School and Georgetown Prep when I was little," I tell him.

Wes looks surprised. "For real?" he asks, facing me.

"Yup. I had to beg my parents to let me transfer t' Wilson after the ninth grade."

Wes chuckles. "You were in the big league?"

I shake my head. "Man, fuck that bamma-ass shit, you'n. You don't get no respect from being wit' 'dem mixed-up people. I mean, they some fake-ass people. That's why I hate them white-acting niggas. Red and Tub and them was the first real friends that I had. I didn't have to create no facade for *them*. I could find myself and be myself. That's why I love being wit' down-ass niggas, man. I mean, they got that . . . that . . . I don't know, jus' that cool feelin' of togetherness. You know what I'm sayin'?"

Wes nods. "But it's not just 'down-ass niggas' that have that togetherness. A lot of people have that same love for blackness. My friends have that love for me. And none of them are 'down-ass niggas,' but they'll do anything for me. *Anything.*"

I nod back to him and take a deep breath. "We got a million different crews, man, and ain't nobody listenin' to the other sides."

"You got that right," Wes says, nodding.

"I figa if these rich niggas was all that, they could start to run their own shit instead of kissin' white peoples' ass all'la damn time. You know what I'm sayin', Joe?"

"Yeah, now you're talking."

I look over to Wes and smirk. "Fuck you think I'm preachin'?"

Wes laughs. "No, but I just want you to know that I agree with you."

"Hmm, well, anyway . . . all I got is my girl, man. I got my girl and my boys."

"Well, what am I?" Wes asks me.

I smile at him. "You my nigga."

I start to laugh, but Wes sits quietly.

"I'm not your nigga, J. I'm your friend. We can start with that."

I'm thinking, *Yeah, fuck what he talkin' 'bout. Friends come and go in the wind, but ya niggas is really in it with you, you know? Ya niggas is down for shit. Ya niggas feel how you feel and believe in you. A lot of these so-called friends is some fake-ass ma-fuckas.*

"Are you into Digable Planets?" Wes asks me, breaking me away from my thoughts.

"Yeah, they aw'ight. Most of the time I don't know what the hell they're talkin' about though."

Wes smiles. "On this one cut called 'La Femme Fetal,' the brother Butterfly says, 'Isn't it my job to lay it on the masses, and get them off their asses, to fight against these fascists.' And that shit is deep. But first we have to fight against ourselves. We have to stop using this 'nigga' reference. Then we have to listen to those who have the knowledge."

"You mean niggas like you," I say with a smile, cutting him off.

"*Brothers* like me," he responds demandingly.

We sit quiet again as we reach North Carolina. It's starting to get dark.

"You never seen a picture of my girl, have you?" I ask Wes.

He smiles. "No."

I dig in my wallet and pull out one of my many photos of my dark and beautiful girl. Wes takes it and glances at it, trying to keep his eyes on the road.

"She's *very* pretty," he says.

I smile. "I know. It was a bunch of nigga—" I stop and grin at him. "I mean, ma-fuckas after her."

Wes shakes his head and smiles back at me. "Mother-fuckers isn't a better word than nigga. They both come from the same self-degrading mentality."

Yo, I'm getting pissed the fuck off now! "Aw'ight, man, look, that's enough of this dumb shit!" I snatch my girl's picture back. "Now, if you think you gon' get people to stop sayin' 'niggas' or 'muthafuckas,' then you crazy out'cha mind! That's like sayin' we can stop the world from turnin'."

"One day the world *will* stop turning."

"And that's when we'll stop sayin' the shit!"

Wes looks at me with pity in his eyes. "Look how confused you are. On one hand you criticize your family for being colorstruck, but then on the other hand you do the same degrading things to black people that your family does to you."

I grin in agreement. "But the difference is that I'm down with niggas."

"Are you? Or are you just down for yourself?"

"Whatever, man."

We finally pull up to Wes' crib, out in front of my 3000. We hop out and stretch our legs. Wes looks over and shakes his head at me.

"What?" I ask him. I'm tired of him talking that brother-man shit.

He sighs. "Here I am, helping you to calculate and hide your drug money, while I drive around in a drug-bought car, but yet I'm trying to preach to you about what black people need to do to correct themselves." He shakes his head, looking all guilty and sorrowful.

I walk over to him. I smile and put my arm around his shoulder. "You know what, man? As long as this white man controls da money, it ain't no nigga livin' that can say everything he's doin' is all right. 'Cause if anything, we need to be fuckin' his country up and tryin' to break away from it. But we don't, right? Naw. Fuck no! 'Cause we love this damn country, Joe!

"Now what me and you need to do is smoke this weed I got in my car and dream about gettin' some pussy. 'Cause that's all a nigga got left in this country, you'n, dreams and pussy."

Wes laughs. "Well, I don't take drugs."

I frown at him. "Weed ain't no drug. Weed is a spiritual herb."

Wes smiles. "You know, I've always wondered how it feels though."

"Oh yeah." I walk over to my car and pull out a dime bag and some Top paper from under my seat. I throw my arm back around Wes and we head to his building's entrance. "Now you can't front on the herb. Even the Digable Planets is down wit' dis. And all them militant niggas from the sixties smoked weed, too. I read up on'nat shit."

We walk up the steps. Wes says, "I'm not experimenting for that reason. I have my own plans in mind."

"Whatever, man. As long as we get on together, I'on care what'chu thinkin'. But I love you though, Joe. For real!"

Wes stops and looks at me. "You don't know what love is. You haven't had enough pain yet."

I laugh and wait at his door. "Hell you think this is, *The Five Heartbeats?* Nigga, please! Now, come on and open this door so I can call my girl up."

"Long distance?"

"Yeah, it's long distance, nigga! And don't worry about it. I'll fuck around and pay ya whole phone bill. Now come on and open'nis shit up."

Wes

"I need you t' ride me to my cousin's house," NeNe says.

"But I'm not going that way."

"So?"

"So why should I drive all the way over to your house in Northeast to take you way over to your cousin's house in Southwest, when all *you* have to do is jump on the Metro like you used to?"

" 'Cause you got a car, and your girlfriend shouldn't have t' ride no damn Metro!"

"I don't see why not, because I'm getting tired of being your chauffeur."

"Wes, you know what? If it wasn't for me, you wouldn't even have that car."

"Thanks for reminding me."

"Oh my God, Joe! Why you carryin' me like dis?"

"I don't know what that word means."

She sucks her teeth. "Oh, don't act smart."

"Well, look, I'm about to take a nap. Is there anything else you have to say to me?"

BLANG! She hangs up violently in my ear. I don't care. I am sick of her! She's driving me crazy! Sometimes I find myself wishing I had Sybil back. I have all the free time in the world for Sybil now. I don't have any job, and I have access to hoards of money. But this also makes me bored because I often find myself with little to do all day.

I lay out on my couch and click the television on with my remote control. It's amazing: all these cable channels and nothing worth watching! We need some drama-based black shows on TV instead of all these silly sit-coms. *Roc* is about the only black show worth watching. *Martin?* He's okay, sometimes, because he deals with some worthwhile issues every now and then. But I can't believe NBC just dropped *A Different World;* it was fast becoming one of the best shows we had. All they had to do was get rid of Dwayne and Whitley and let the new-comers shine. Then again, Dwayne and Whitley were the stars of the show.

I still haven't warmed up to *The Fresh Prince of Bel Air.* I think the uppityness in that show displays all that's wrong with the wealthy blacks in this Westernized world now.

Look at me! I'm actually sitting here worrying about TV shows. Man, I have to get out and do something. But I don't even know what. I feel weird being around Marshall, Derrick and Walt now. I mean, it's hard as ever to explain to them how I've gotten myself involved with Butter-man. Not to mention trying to explain an Acura Integra to my mother. I've even been smoking marijuana. And it's not because of any peer pressure or anything. I actu-ally wanted to experience the real deal of weed and cut through all the hype I hear from others. I want to experi-ence what goes on in the mind of a brother who just doesn't "give a fuck."

I jump up and grab my keys and tan Nautica jacket. The weather is getting warmer now with April nearing. I ride up South Dakota Avenue and make a left on Riggs Road, heading for Georgia Avenue. Maybe I'll bump into Shank and the rest of Butterman's workers.

I ride around corner after corner until I finally spot them, all out conversing in front of a housing tenement's steps.

I park the car as near as I can get to them and hop out. "Hey, remember me?" I walk up to the one named Steve.

He smiles, flashing yellowish teeth in need of some se-rious Topal toothpaste. He could use a better diet as well. "Yeah, I remember you. You still wit' NeNe?"

"Yeah, but she's driving me crazy," I tell him.

"Shit, a girl like that can drive me crazy all she want,"

the one named Rudy says, looking healthier and taller than Steve.

We all laugh, except for Shank, who sits solemnly on the top step. He's wearing all blue today instead of black. He even has on a pair of blue Nike Airs.

"Hi you doin', Ninja?" I say, to try and liven him up.

He shakes his head and smiles. "Am I wearin' all black t'day, ma-fucka?"

"No."

"So how da hell you figure I look like a Ninja?"

I chuckle carefully. I don't want to piss him off. He already looks as if he's bored and dying for some action. "I was just joking, man," I say to him.

"Well, you betta find somebody else to joke wit' before I cut'cha tongue da fuck out'cha mouth."

The rest of them start to giggle, but I read through the tough talk to see if he can back it.

"So you have a knife?"

"Yeah, ma-fucka."

"Let me see it then."

Shank smiles and looks toward Rudy. "Yo, man, you betta take this nigga somewhere before I kill 'im."

Rudy laughs. "Yo, he aw'ight. Shawdy jus' fuckin' wit'chu."

I sit on the steps below Shank and listen to their discussion.

Steve takes the spotlight. "Yeah, like I was sayin', you'n, I could be a comedian. I'm funny as shit. I'd do a skit called *How Come?* And I'd be like, How come niggas wit' the least amount of money talk the most shit? You ever notice that? That's why bums don't ever stop runnin'ney damn mowf."

We all start laughing. Even Shank sneaks in a chuckle as Steve continues:

"And how come bitches always look better when'ney

wit' da next ma-fucka? You ever notice that? Man, one time I took this girl from this nigga. And you know what? She stopped lookin' good to me. Maybe it's me. I mus' turn out the ugliness in a girl."

We all laugh some more. Steve *is* a comedian. But he can do without the hard language.

"Yeah, and how come these radical niggas ain't never got no money? You ever notice that shit? They be talkin' all'lat revolutionary shit and sellin' bean pies and Kente hats. And them ma-fuckas expect you t' be down wit' dat dumb shit, too, you'n. Them niggas are crazy."

I'm laughing, but it's actually true in many cases. Preaching revolution is not a skill that can be marketed within a European-dominated society. Even many white radicals are poor, except for the ones who go through a reactionary parental breakage. That's when kids go against their parents' wishes, like with J and his "Butterman" image. All *he* has to do is straighten up and do what his parents want. J doesn't have to worry about being poor. But I couldn't even go to Howard University like I wanted to because tuition cost too much and my mother didn't have the money. So I ended up working, moving out for space and going to UDC.

"Yeah, man. And how come girls always be sayin' somethin' stink, but yet they can't smell when'ney shit is stinkin'. You ever notice that shit? Bitches be talkin' 'bout some, 'damn, somethin' stink in here!' And I'm like, 'It's you, *bitch;* you ain't wash ya shit out this mornin'!"

He's getting nasty and hilarious now. It's not right, but I can't help but laugh at it.

"Yeah, Joe, we gotta get'cha ass a contract, 'cause you be lunchin' like hell," Rudy says, wiping out his eyes with the back of his hands.

I look over to a brown-skinned, baby-faced guy, whom I haven't seen with J before.

I extend my hand to him. "What's your name, man? I'm Wes."

"Otis," he says, accepting my shake.

Shank frowns. "His name should be Othelia."

Rudy and Steve start laughing. Otis looks as if he wants to say something but he doesn't. I guess he's scared of Shank. But I'm not. Shank hasn't shown me anything to be afraid of yet. All I see him doing is looking tough, talking tough and being very anti-social.

I instigate things. "Don't let him talk to you like that, O."

Steve and Rudy look to Shank as if they expect him to do something.

"That nigga know what time it is," Shank says.

I look to Otis. He drops his head in defeat and kicks a soda around in front of him. So that's how it works. Once you intimidate someone you can make them accept anything that you care to dish out.

I sit silently and observe the block. Things seem so peaceful on this nice, sixty-degree day.

Up coasts a royal-blue 300 ZX with those flashy rims. "Yo, Steve, what's up, man?" the dark-skinned driver hollers past his passenger.

Steve walks over to the passenger side.

"If they got money, we deal," Rudy says.

"Aw'ight, hit us back in like an hour," Steve says as they drive off.

"What that nigga talkin' 'bout, Joe?" Rudy asks Steve.

"Oh, they ready to get a package."

"Do they want a half-ounce? 'Cause I hope you let 'em know that we ain't sellin' no fuckin' quarters t'day. Fuck that shit! Either they got money for a half-ounce, or it ain't no sense in talkin'.'"

We sit quietly for a while until a rusty tan Pontiac drives up.

"Yo, Steve!" the brown-skinned guy in the passenger

side yells. He's wearing one of those black bandannas wrapped around his forehead. His bushy hair sticks out on top.

Steve leans up from off of a nearby fence and walks to the car. "Damn, as soon as B gets here, we gon' have like five customers."

"Po-man!" Shank calls out.

I look down the street to my left. I don't know whether to run or stay calm as the white-and-blue cruiser eases up the street. No one else seems to worry, so I remain calm like everyone else.

Shank eyes the black officer sitting in the passenger side, eye-for-eye as they pass.

"Punk-ass ma-fucka," he says once it's over.

"You don't like cops, hunh?" I ask him.

He faces me with a smirk. *"Do you* like them ma-fuckas, man?"

"Well, what about when they're out protecting somebody?"

"Protecting somebody?" Rudy intervenes. "When you ever see a cop protect somebody?"

I think about it. "Damn, I guess you're right."

"They don't protect nobody but the President and rich white people," Shank adds.

"How 'bout dat shit, Joe? 'Cause 'member that L.A. riot last year? They said that the cops all went to protect the white neighborhoods in Beverly Hills and Bel Air. That's why nobody was there when'nem people was burnin' stuff up and robbin' stores in South Central," Steve says.

I nod my head in agreement. I'm actually amazed that they're even giving opinions on such things. I guess the media's perception of young black men being brainless and apolitical has rubbed off on me as well.

"So what do you think about the new police brutality trials in L.A. that they're getting ready for?" I ask Steve.

"Ain't nothin' gon' change. I mean, even if them white cops is found guilty, what'chu think they gon' do; suspend them ma-fuckas without pay? That's dumb shit, you'n! They ain't goin' ta jail."

"No bullshit," Rudy says, agreeing. "Now let three *black* cops whup some *white* ma-fucka's ass. Them niggas would get lynched, you'n. For real!"

I look to Otis, who's just been giggling on and off and not saying anything since Shank challenged him.

"And what do you think, Otis?"

"Man, I think—"

"Shut da fuck up! And fuck what'chu think!" Shank snaps.

"Ay, Shank, man, why you keep fuckin' wit' me, you'n?"

Shank jumps up and punches Otis in his mouth. "Come on and fight back, nigga."

Otis throws a lazy right hand. Shank slips outside of it and lands with a punishing overhand right. Otis loses his footing and ends up on his back before Rudy grabs Shank off of him.

"Yo, Rudy, let 'im fight for himself," Steve says.

Shank grins as if he's loving it. "Yeah, let da ma-fucka get it on wit' me."

Rudy lets him go as Otis climbs back to his feet and puts his hands up. He dances around as if he has a ring on the sidewalk.

Shank stalks him, flat-footed. "Stop jumpin' around, ma-fucka. This shit ain't no Kriss Kross."

We start laughing as Shank catches Otis with a quick left jab. He blocks Otis' left and doubles up with a right/ left to the body. Then Otis finally nips Shank with a desperate right jab.

"Yeah, good one, ma-fucka! Come on!" Shank taunts.

Shank scores another overhand right to Otis' face. Shank hits him with a left. Otis throws his head down and rushes in. Shank grabs his head as they tumble to the ground. They tussle for a few seconds before Shank ends up on top with a gun to Otis' chest.

"Fuck you gon' wrestle me for, punk? I should shoot'cha ass."

Shank gets up using Otis' chest for leverage. He brushes himself off and walks back over to take his seat at the top of the tenement's front steps.

"Shit, you couldn't get but one punch in, Otis?" Rudy says, laughing.

"What'chu tryin'na say, Rudy?" Shank asks.

"Man, I ain't sayin' shit, you'n," Rudy responds, still giggling. "I'm just noticin' that Otis got stole."

We all giggle while Otis gathers himself together.

"That's aw'ight," he finally says, spitting blood into the street from his stance at the curb.

"If you thinkin' 'bout gettin' revenge, shoot me in my chest like a man. Don't shoot me in my back; that's punk shit," Shank tells him.

Otis doesn't respond. We go back to watching cars ride by.

"That's your Acura down there, Joe?" Steve asks me.

"Yeah, you see me ride up in it?"

"Yeah, but like, I wasn't really thinkin' 'bout it."

Shank looks up at me as I stretch out my legs. "How long you had it?"

"Like, two weeks."

"Oh, so that ride is brand, spankin' new, hunh?" Rudy says.

"I guess you can call it that."

Steve asks, "Yeah, well, what time is it, Rudy?"

Rudy twists his left arm and looks down at his watch. "It's two-thirty."

"Two-thirty? Shit! Butterman ain't gon' be here for another hour then. You know how that ma-fucka always be comin' late."

"Yeah, he says it's his good luck charm to keep the po-man off guard," Otis says for a change.

"Yeah, he act like we givin' the cops our meeting times or somethin'," Rudy responds.

Steve laughs. "Butterman know what he doin'." Then he looks to me. "Yo, you'n, ride me down to my crib for a minute. I live down near Howard University, off of Fourth Street. We can roll right down Fifth Street and get there in like, ten minutes," Steve tells me all in a hurry.

I start walking toward the car. "All right, come on."

Rudy shakes his head. "Don't trust that nigga, Joe."

"Aw, man, shut up. Dis Butterman's boy!" Steve yells back.

I make a U-turn and cross Georgia Avenue toward Fifth Street. I then make a right and ride Fifth Street straight down and into Fourth Street, right past Howard University's dorms and library.

"See that shit right there," Steve says, pointing to my left.

I look over to a construction sight of a new dorm. "Yeah."

"They built that shit fast, you'n. For real! It was like a whole different sight this time last year."

I nod my head as Steve tells me to make a left. We then coast into a block of three-story housing tenements.

"Park right here," he tells me in the middle of the block.

He hops out and runs inside one of the buildings. As soon as I get out to wait, three young boys walk up to me immediately.

"'Das ya car?" the first light-skinned boy asks me.

"Yeah. You like it?"

He nods his head as a darker boy walks up to touch the door. "Can you take me for a ride?" he asks me with an innocent smile.

"I don't think your mother would like that. She might think you got yourself kidnapped."

"Unt-unh," he says, shaking his head. "No she won't."

"*I* can go for a ride," says the third one. He and the second one look similar.

"Are you two brothers?" I ask, pointing them out.

"Unh-hunh. He older than me," the second says of his brother, who announced that *he* could ride.

"Well, how old are you?" I ask the the older brother.

"Five."

"Five? And you're not in preschool or anything yet?"

"I was, but den my mom took me out."

"Why?"

" 'Cause he was too young," his younger brother says.

"Nont-unh, he was bad in school," their light-skinned friend interjects.

"No I wasn't!" the five-year-old retorts loudly.

They start scrambling for my attention. Each one is pulling on my arm for me to listen to his particular story of why the five-year-old is no longer in school. I laugh, trying to give each of them my attention as they hustle for position and eye contact.

"Byron! You and Tommy get'chall asses back in front of this house!" a voice yells from a third-story window. I look up to see a mean-looking black woman, my complexion, wearing a scarf over what appears to be curlers.

The boys run back behind the fence that's in front of their complex.

"Come over here, man" the first light-skinned one says. The two brothers look on to see if I'll actually come.

And what the hell! I smile and start to walk over, climbing over the small fence.

The five-year-old runs and jumps on me.

"Would you leave that man alone," the voice inside the third-story window yells out again.

Now I feel leery, knowing that she's watching me. I look up to her and smile while her two sons continue to tug and pull at my arms and clothes, along with the other little guy, all jockeying for my interest in them.

"Get off of him, would'ju!" the mother persists while being ignored by the boys. She then shakes her head at me. "You'll have to excuse my children. They must think you're their father or somethin'," she tells me.

Steve finally comes dashing out of the next building. "Come on," he says.

I start to walk away. The three boys freeze as if they've just been paralyzed. I turn back while walking slowly. "See you," I tell them with a smile. I guess they see it as another father figure leaving them.

"When you comin' back?" the five-year-old asks.

Damn! What am I supposed to say to that? "Ahhh, I don't know," I respond hesitantly.

"He ain't comin' back here!" their mother shouts out of the window again. She smiles at me as I look up at her once more. "You don't have to lie to my children. They get enough of that from their father."

I then look back to the three boys, who eagerly await my response. "I'll be back tomorrow," I tell them. Then I go to join Steve.

Steve shakes his head with a smile. "You ain't never been in no 'hood like this, hunh?"

"Why you ask me that?" I ask as I unlock the car doors.

"I can tell. I mean, you lookin' all confused and shit. Them niggas can live without'chu. Hell, dey gon' be aw'ight. You act like them li'l ma-fuckas gon' die if you leave 'em."

I smile as we head back up Fourth Street. But I'm in deep thought. Steve is right; I've never been around *real* poverty. I always talk about it and the masses, but I've never really been a part of the chaos. I always knew that I had a future. I always knew that I would make it. But now as I look at the lives of just those three boys and a mother, I realize that *they* all are looking for some kind of savior, someone to pull them out of hell. And even if I were to try, how much pushing and pulling would it take for them to trust in their own ability to succeed when no help is available? That is the true essence of survival.

Shank

I only read a couple of chapters of Maya Angelou's book so far, and I can't see what the hell my mom has it for. I mean, Maya Angelou grew up in the South. My mom lived in Jersey all her damn life! The only comparison I can make is that they're both black women. But that ain't nothing! It's a lot of books by black women.

Anyway, I've been hanging out with these silly niggas that Butterman got working for him. I guess he scared of having me with him now after I beat down that boy Bean. Fuck it though! As long as I'm still getting my grand every Monday, I don't give a fuck!

I'm trying to get Otis ready though, just in case we have to take care of some motherfuckers. But he's all right. I'm just trying to make sure he don't punk out on us. And that boy Wes? I don't know about you'n. I mean, he just been hanging around us instigating shit and asking questions like he gon' write a story or something. He'd probably call the shit *Niggas In The Eastcoast 'Hood*.

I know Butterman bought Wes that Acura, too. I ain't

fucking stupid! I mean, how this nigga just gon' pop up out the blue and roll around us in a brand-new Integra. Something ain't right about that shit. If he wasn't hanging around us I wouldn't be thinking about it. But since he is, there has to be some connection between him and Butterman. But I know that motherfucker Wes ain't selling no drugs. He don't seem like the type.

I get dressed in some springtime clothes because it's almost April now. It's getting warmer outside.

I throw on my blue Calvins, a white Polo shirt and my green jacket. It ain't wintertime no more, so I ain't trying to wear all black; that shit is hot as a motherfucker when it gets warm. But yo, you still got these bamma-ass young'uns out here wearing that all-black gear.

I jump on an 82 bus and ride down Rhode Island. I get off and walk my regular way under the Metro bridge, past McDonald's and past the bank to catch a G bus at the corner of Fourth and Rhode Island Northeast.

"Hey, main man, I got some cologne," this tall, skinny nigga asks me. He pulls out several small bottles from his tan jacket.

"Naw, I'on wear dat shit."

He smiles at me, wearing some dingy-ass clothes. "You need to, main man, 'cause the women out here love good-smellin' mens, especially when it gets warm."

How da hell you know what women like, you homeless-lookin' muthafucka?

I stand at the bus stop and lean up against the glass walls that surround the bus stop's bench. It ain't that many people out here riding the buses yet. I guess it is kind of early for niggas on a Saturday. It's only like eleven o'clock. But we got customers coming down from Maryland and Virginia to make buys now. So we have to do business early sometimes to avoid all these nosy motherfuckers. And if I ain't up there, these silly-ass niggas might fuck around and get robbed. That's why I got my compact .45 with me every damn day.

The bus finally pulls up. I get on and ride it to Georgia Avenue.

"Transfer, brother?" another dingy nigga asks me when I hop off.

"Naw, man, I'm usin' mine."

"Oh, okay den, young brother."

I cross the street and wait for the 70 bus. When the shit comes, this old-ass man is talking crazy on the bus.

"What'chu fightin' for? Some turf? Niggas ain't even got no damn turf, but they fightin' for turf," he says. He's moving around in his seat like he has a live stage audience watching. "These young'uns always out here talkin'nat shit. Well, fuck you! Fuck you, nigga! You ain't got *nothin'!* What'chu got? That's why the white man got'cha ass in jail now, nigga! FUCK YOU! You ain't *got* no damn turf!"

I'm shaking my head and smiling with the rest of the passengers on the bus. This motherfucker's crazy!

"What, 'chu gon' shoot me, nigga? Why, 'cause I'm in ya damn turf? Well, FUCK YA GOT'DAMN TURF!"

He gets up and sits back down. "Fuck it. FUCK IT! That's why the white man got all you niggas now. Even in Africa niggas was fightin' ova some GOT'DAMN TURF! That's why the white man got'cha. Fuck ya got'-damn turf!"

He gets up and gets off at New Hampshire Avenue.

This black woman with a Jheri-curl giggles from my left. "It's some crazy people out here."

I smile. But that motherfucker was talking some real-ass facts! He was right! We are fighting over turf; that and respect. But all humans fight over turf and respect. That shit ain't nothing new. Bamma-ass nigga. Fuck him! He just mad because he don't have nothing to fight over.

I get off the bus further up Georgia Avenue and walk around to where these niggas are.

"Yo, Shank, we got a sale already," Otis says. He's been on my dils-nick lately. I guess he's trying to stay cool with me. But you can't really trust a nigga too much after you beat his ass.

"Yeah, so how many ounces did Butterman leave y'all?" I ask him.

"We got seven," Rudy answers.

I take my regular seat up on the top step. This middle-aged woman comes out from the apartments behind me. I move to let her by. But she stops out in front of me.

"Is there any reason why you all have to stand in front of my home with this shit every day?"

"I'm waiting for a ride to come pick me up," Steve tells her.

I nod for Otis and Rudy to follow me around back. Steve handles most of the deals anyway.

"She ain't say nothin' to us any other time we was out here," Otis says, once we get around in the driveway.

I look up to her back window and see the shades move. I shake my head. "I can see this bitch is 'bout ta 'cause us problems." *Damn, I shouldn't call her a bitch. I mean, she got a right to tell us to move away from her property. But this shit is public property anyway. The city or some white ma-fucka prob'bly own this whole block.*

Damn! That crazy-ass man on the bus was right. We don't even have no turf, for real.

"We need ta get a new spot anyway," Rudy says.

"Where at, 'cause most of the area is used up already. We got niggas on like, e'ry hot-ass block around here," Otis says.

Rudy looks to me. "Fuck it then, we'll jus' kill a few ma-fuckas and take their shit over."

Otis giggles. "You betta stop watchin' that *New Jack City* shit, you'n. This ain't no movie."

"Naw, but for real. We supplyin' most of this area anyway. So we jus' tell niggas they buy from us or else."

Hmm. Sounds like Rudy gettin' a bit too ambitious. I might have ta watch his ass.

Steve comes jogging around back. A gray 280 ZX follows him. I choke up on my wooden-handled .45. Rudy pulls out the ounce. Steve and Otis watch both corners.

"Aw'ight, but we might be movin' soon, so keep that beeper number," Rudy says. He pockets the money. The gray 280 ZX backs up and pulls off.

Steve nods his head. "Yeah, I can tell we gon' make a killin' t'day. It's warm out, you'n. Bitches is startin' t' come out . . ."

"No bullshit," Otis says. "I met this fourteen-year-old yesterday, you'n, phat t' death."

Rudy frowns. *"Fourteen?* Muthafucka, my sister's fourteen! I'll kick ya fuckin' ass if I catch you messin' wit' some young'uns like that, Joe! And ya ass is like, twenty-two."

Twenty-two? Got'damn! I ain't know I was younger than all these ma-fuckas like that, I'm thinking. Fast-living niggas usually look old. But Otis got one of those little baby faces with no hair. And Rudy don't look that old either. But Steve look raggedy as shit, with fucked-up-ass teeth.

"How old is you, Rudy?" I ask.

"Oh, I'm turnin' twenty-three next month."

"I ain't know you was that old," I tell him.

Steve smiles with them fucked-up teeth of his. "Yeah, you'n, you the youngest out here."

"Unh-hunh," Rudy says, nodding. "And you notice how the younger a ma-fucka is, the rougher these niggas is gettin'."

I smile. "So what'chu try'na say, Rudy?"

"I'm sayin' that these young'uns is crazy as hell, an' gettin' crazier. I ain't stutter." He smiles back.

Steve says, "Yeah, I wonder if their mothers is feedin'nem the wrong kind of food, you'n. These young'uns is out dey minds."

I smile. My mother did feed me some fucked-up food. I'm not talking about the kind you eat; I'm talking about the mental food she fed me. I mean, she was always fucking with me! And I can't understand why, and shit. That's why I'm reading this Maya Angelou book to try and figure my mom out. And fuck it, I'm gon' call my mom a *bitch* until I see a reason to call her something else. She ain't really did nothing to make me feel like a son. I mean, it takes more than just feeding and clothing a motherfucker to be a mother, you know.

"Yo, Steve, here comes another one!" Rudy yells.

I snap to attention and I go for my gun inside my jacket.

Rudy laughs. "Got'damn, Shank. You got da jitters dis mornin', you'n?"

Otis cracks a smile and turns away when I eye him.

"Naw," I say to Rudy.

I walk to the curb and watch the streets. Steve makes another sale. And this shit is getting boring. I'd rather be at a movie somewhere. Or better yet, over Carlette's crib, butt-naked, watching her TV and having breakfast in bed. I mean, since I got money now, I'm really getting kind of tired of this hustling shit, standing around waiting for niggas.

"Yo, you goin' t' see *Who's The Man?* Shank?" Steve asks me.

This boy must be readin' my mind. "Yeah. That movie *Posse* is comin' out, too."

"Ay yo, here comes that nigga Wes," Rudy says with a smile.

Wes pulls up in his red Integra and rolls down his window. "Where's a safe parking space around here?"

Steve giggles. "Hell we look like, a hotel? Ride ya ass around the block and find one."

"All right. I'll be back."

"Yeah, well, don't bring no guns like no *Terminator*, 'cause Shank is a muthafuckin' sharp shooter," Rudy says, bullshitting.

Wes looks at me and smiles before he drives off.

"Yo, you know you'n been comin' around my way to play wit' dese bad-ass kids," Steve tells us. "Yo, dat mafucka a saint. I mean, I ain't never met no nigga like that."

Wes comes walking around the corner wearing a tough-ass Tommy Hilfiger shirt. "So Shank is a sharpshooter, hunh?" he says to no one in particular.

I take out my gun and aim it at his heart. But you know, my safety clip is on.

"Yo, yo, yo, man, he cool!" Steve shouts like a bitch.

I chuckle and put my gun away. "Shut da fuck up, man. I'm jus' jokin' wit' 'im."

Rudy shakes his head. "Please don't joke wit' me like that, you'n, 'cause we a fuck around and have to kill each other out here."

"Oh yeah? So you wanna draw wit' me, Rudy?" I ask him, facing off.

Rudy turns his back to me and shakes his head again. Punk-ass nigga.

"Yo, Steve!" Otis yells.

A maroon Sidekick jeep pulls up. "Yo, you got that?" this boy yells out to Steve.

Steve looks back to me. I move into position with my hand on my .45, inside my jacket. Rudy moves to my right. And Otis positions his ass too.

"Yo, Wes, get ready to duck if you have to," Rudy says on the down low.

Wes glances toward the Sidekick and backs up.

"Y'all got da money?" Steve asks them.

"Look, man, fuck that! Is we gon' do business or what?"

This edgy-looking tan-skinned dude inside the jeep is stalling. He got two boys with him. But we got these niggas surrounded if they try anything.

He looks around at us. "Yo, what's up wit' all dis?" he asks, referring to our strategic positions. "What, 'chu don't trust us?"

"I'm sayin', man, this the third time you came around here wit' no money. I mean, we thinkin' you try'na set us up by now. We don't know you like dat."

"What, nigga? I'd shoot'cha ass right here if it was all like dat!"

That's my cue! I run up on the driver side. Before I can quite reach it, one of you'n's boys yells, "YO, YO, TAKE OFF!"

I bust three shots and fuck up their windows. Rudy busts two shots and hits the body. These niggas fly up the street and make a left turn.

"Shit! Where you park at, Wes?" Steve yells.

Wes starts to run around the corner. "Around this way!" he yells from in front of us.

We all run behind Wes and squeeze into his Integra.

"Yo, ride us around Emery Park so we can beep Butterman," Steve says, sitting up front with Wes.

I wanna tell Wes to chase them niggas, but they probably too far ahead by now and Wes would probably bitch anyway. Or maybe he wouldn't? I don't really know.

He whips the car to Georgia Avenue, across from Emery Park. We all hop out. Steve beeps Butterman on a pay phone.

We sit and wait for the call. I expect Wes to leave, but he doesn't.

"Yo, Butterman gotta buy us a damn car, you'n," Rudy says.

"So what happens now? Does this mean war?" Wes asks all of a sudden.

"You muthafuckin' right!" Rudy yells at him.

"Yeah, I knew them niggas was crooked," Steve says from the phone.

A woman comes out of a nearby store and heads toward the phone. "We about to use this phone," Rudy tells her. She looks at all five of us and decides not to argue.

Butterman calls back.

"Yo, these boys jus' tried ta get us," Steve says. Then he listens. "Naw, dey ain't get none of the shit." He listens again. "Yeah, they pulled off right when Shank started bussin' . . . Aw, man, we had all kinds of sales hooked up for t'day . . . Maryland? But what do we get out'a dat? . . . Oh, for real? Well, cool den . . . Aw'ight den, I got'chu." Steve hangs up and smiles at us.

"Yo, B said t' chill for da rest of the day. We gon' regroup t'mar, to go get them niggas."

"So what about all this money we was gon' make t'day?" Otis asks.

"He got some sales out in Maryland, so he said for us to hold the shit that we got and don't worry about it."

"Aw, you'n, that's dumb shit! We s'posed t' hit them niggas back as fast as we can. Now them ma-fuckas might come back wit' two and three carloads," Rudy says.

That's the same thing I been thinking. But I'm just chilling, leaned up against Wes' car. We don't even know where to find these niggas.

"That's right," Wes says.

What? This ma-fucka down? I look at him and hide my smile.

"What, 'chu down t' ride around and find them, Wes?" Rudy asks him.

"Do you already know where they're from?" Wes says.

Rudy looks to Steve. "They from back Northeast, right?"

"Yeah, back Max and them way," Steve tells him.

Oh shit! Now it's on! Max and them is gon' try ta get cysed *if they ain't still scared. It's been like a month since me and Butterman carried 'em,* I'm thinking.

"Max and them way? Got'damn, Joe! Them niggas be like thirty thick back there," Rudy says with big eyes. I guess he's not down no more.

"Man, 'ney ain't got that many, but they got enough," I tell him.

"But they ain't wit' Max and them, and if they team up on us, it might mess around and *be* thirty," Steve says.

"So? This ain't no L.A. It ain't like all them ma-fuckas is gon' come around here shootin' shit up. A lot of them boys ain't got no heart," I argue.

Rudy nods. "Yeah, you right. But yo, we gotta get some more niggas. So let's jus' chill da rest of the day and think shit over like Butterman said."

Everybody nods and agrees. Wes ends up taking everybody home around Northwest. But I live in Northeast, so he has to drop me off last.

I tell him to drop me off at Super Trak up on Rhode Island Avenue. Before he parks and lets me out, he throws in some jazz-type music with Guru rappin' on it. So I chill for a few.

"Fuck is this?" I ask him.

"Oh, you haven't heard it yet? It's *Jazzmatazz* by Guru from Gang Starr, and a bunch of jazz artists."

"Naw, I ain't heard it."

I listen and lay back into the cushioned seat.

"Look, ah, Shank, if it's cool with you, we can hang out. I mean, if you're not doing anything."

I smile. *You'n sounds like a bitch. I mean, a girl and shit.*

"Yeah, it's cool wit' me. I ain't got nothin' t' do."

"Okay, well, let's chill at my house for a while. My nerves are shot to hell."

I grin. "What, 'chu was scared?"

He exhales like he's been holding his breath all this time. "To tell you the truth, I was petrified."

I start laughing. We pull off and make a left down Twelfth Street, leading toward Michigan Avenue. I say, "It sounded like you was ready to go get them niggas to me, you'n."

"Yeah, I was. But that's just because we were in the thick of it and my father always told me never to run out on your friends."

Friends? He calls them niggas friends! And he don't really know me, either.

Steve was right; this motherfucker is a saint!

"So you would fight, hunh?" I ask him, just for the fuck of it.

"Well, don't get me wrong; it's not like I'm into gang-banging or anything like that, but I'd never run if it was time to do battle. And a lot of my friends think that that's weird because I'm so studious and all. But I figure once you make a man run when he's supposed to stand and fight, he's no longer a man.

"Even so, fighting inside of a drug battle is stupid. We would have been riding around, chasing after those guys, and if we would've gotten pulled over by a cop, we would've been arrested for drug possession, possession of illegal handguns and anything else they could pin on us."

Yeah, he's right. That shit would've been stupid. But I was in the thick of it too. You start makin' all kinds of mistakes when you stop thinkin'.

"So what kind of battle would you fight in?" I ask him.

"Huh, are you kidding me? I go to battle every day against every image of *shit* that that white man projects at *me* about *you*. I mean, I'm not gon' lie, Shank; since the first time I was around you I wanted to sit down and talk. But sometimes it seems impossible. Because it's like, why in hell would he want to listen to me?"

"What'chu got t' say to me?"

He smiles as we pull up to his apartment complex off of South Dakota Avenue. "Well, we can smoke some marijuana and talk about in my apartment."

Smoke some marijuana? Joe don't look like the smokin' type either.

We walk inside his apartment on the fourth floor. His crib is the same size as my mine! He has black artwork on his walls. I got movie posters and rap artists and shit on mine. My favorite ones are Big Daddy Kane and Eric B. & Rakim , from back in the day. And this *Deep Cover* poster from last year.

I sit down on this tan couch and check out Wes' RCA VCR. He has a RCA television too. I guess he's into that buy-American shit.

"So," he starts. The motherfucker went and put some glasses on. "We can chill and talk about shit now."

I smile. Wes don't even sound right cursing. I guess he's doing the shit to appeal to me. But I don't care if he cusses or not. I mean, just because I curse don't mean other people have to sit around me and do the shit. Be your motherfucking self!

Wes hands me a rolled J and sits down beside me. He sets another J on the table in front of us.

"You know, I always wondered what I would say if I had the chance to talk to a real-ass nigga, as some of us like to call guys like you," he says to me. He lights the J as he talks.

I offer him the first toke, just to see if he'll really smoke. And yo, the motherfucker hits it. Hard!

"Yeah, this marijuana is what they call a hallucinogen; and, it's similar to a barbiturate. It's like a natural type of sedative that calms the nerves. At the same time, it gives you a heightened feeling of connectedness to everything around you. I didn't realize that until I actually tried some."

He passes it to me. I take a toke, and this smart nigga keeps on talking.

"The African medicine men, the Native American Shamans and the high priests of the Orient all inhaled some type of barbiturate to bring forth that calm that the body's natural alertness fights against. "You see, the body is a war zone in itself. A battle is being waged as we speak, inside our bodies, to keep us healthy. So the entire essence of having health, Shank, is war, the body's constant fight against disease."

"Yeah, dat shit sounds about right," I say. "'Cause that AIDS shit is supposed to mess up your immune system so that ya body can't fight no more."

"There it is. And then a common cold can kill you."

Joe got some straight-up killa! I'm startin' t' feel this weed already.

"And guess what, Shank?"

"What?"

"The white man is *your* disease, *my* disease and everybody else's disease."

I nod as I take another hit. "I know."

"No, you don't know. You know why I say that?"

"Why, ma-fucka?"

"Because *America* is your hallucinogen *and* your barbiturate; the American streets . . . I mean, this system has young black men running around in circles, killing each other up while *he* makes all the real money. And oh sure, he'll allow Butterman to get 'paid,' but it's no sweat off of his back. Butterman's making pennies."

I smile at his ass. "Well, dem ma-fuckin' pennies is doin' me *right*. And I know Butterman bought'chu dat car, since we gettin' all friendly an' shit."

The motherfucker smiles. But I ain't mad or nothing; I'm just letting him know that I ain't stupid.

"You see that, Shank? Now black people call that being street-smart, you know, the fact that you can know things about the games being played in the street. But they don't expect you to be worldly nor organized. That's where *I* come in. And the game in America is to keep *me* too afraid to talk to *you*. But the advantage that I have is that I wasn't reared in America."

I look at him and pass the J. "Where'd'ju grow up at?"

"All over the world, Mexico, Germany, wherever my father had to go on base."

"He was in the Army?"

He shakes his head, slow-like. "The Air Force."

I nod. "Yeah, I heard the Air Force has the smarter guys."

"Yeah, them and the Navy."

"Oh yeah? Did you ever see that movie *Under Siege?*" I ask him.

We finish the first J and Wes lights up the second one. If he can take it, I can take it. I can't let no little school-boy out-smoke me!

He takes a hit. "No. But what did you like about it?"

"How you know I liked it?"

"Why did you bring it up?"

This nigga playin' mind games now. "Anyway, man, they had that shit about Navy SEALS in it. Is they supposed to be like Green Berets or something?" I ask him. I take the J from him.

"Yeah . . . and in simple words, they're all assassins, just like you, Shank. And you know what America does to its assassins?" I open my mouth to speak, but he doesn't wait for my answer. "They send them on *Rambo* missions where you're not supposed to come back. Or they lock you up after you do some ridiculous crime. And even if they let you live, you live in fear, having nightmares and wondering who the hell is after you or who you'll have to kill next. Yeah, Shank, I know all about it. My father told me."

I take another hit and start coughing. "So what happened to 'im?" I ask Wes with watery eyes.

"Germany. They killed him. My mother won't even talk about it."

I look in his face for a minute. "That's fucked up." And he got me thinking about my own father now. But fuck it. Ain't no sense in talking about that Vietnam shit. I mean, talking about it ain't gon' change nothing, is it?

"No, you know what's really fucked up, Shank?" Wes asks me. "You. I mean, once your war in the streets is over, what are you gonna do? Where are you going? Who will you be? *That's* fucked up."

I shake my head and smile. "Yo, man, you always talk like this?"

He takes another hit. "How do you mean?"

"I'on know, man." I hunch my shoulders. "Fuck it."

Wes grins. "Well, actually, I don't. Usually I sound more preachy. Now I'm just making plain sense. And I hate to admit it. But it's the weed that makes it all fall into place. The weed makes it simpler, until I've mastered the method."

The method? I'm thinking. "What fuckin' method?" I ask him.

"The method of connection. It's a spiritual high that all of us have inside, but we have learn how to reach it. The

Nation of Islam is able to do that with many of our men, especially 'real-ass niggas' like yourself."

I laugh. "Yo, man, I'm human like you. Why you keep talkin'nis 'real-ass nigga' shit?"

"But isn't that what you project? Isn't that what you want to be? I mean, I saw how you punked out Otis that day. Why? Because he wasn't real enough for you. You feel safer when everybody around you is *down*, down to kill a nigga."

Yo, dis weed is makin' Joe sound like he a medicine man or somethin', a Voodoo doctor, puttin' a spell on me.

I laugh. "Yo, man, you lunchin' like shit."

He nods with a smile. "I heard that you're into rap music."

"Yeah." *Butterman prob'bly told him that. I wonder what else they talked about.*

"Can you write rhymes?"

"Why?"

"I'm just asking, you know, because it's amazing that some people can memorize entire rap songs, but nevertheless, they can't make up their own."

"Hmm, I got *my* own." *I got skills like shit!*

"So have you ever thought about getting put on someone's label?"

"Man, it's a million ma-fuckas try'na get on labels! What da fuck makes you think I can jus' get put on?"

"What, are you scared?"

"*Scared?* What I got to be scared about?"

"You know, that you might not succeed at getting your record out."

Damn, he got me! Am I scared of goin' for mine? "Naw, man, I wouldn't say I'm scared. It's more like . . . why should I go through all that dumb shit t' get put on when I know I got skills?"

"So why go through all that 'dumb shit' in the street when you know you're tough already? I mean, you looked liked Pernell "Sweet Pea" Whitaker when you kicked Otis' ass."

I shake my head. "Yeah, but I'on know if he can get wit' dat Mexican muthafucka, Julio Chavez. That muthafucka be destroyin' niggas."

"But the point is that Whitaker believes he's gonna win, right?"

"Shit, everybody dat steps in'na ring is thinkin'ney gon' win."

"So how come you don't think so?"

"What, wit' rap music?"

"Yeah, with rap music."

I hunch my shoulders. "Man, I'on know."

"See that? You're punking out. It's the same principle, Shank. I just fail to believe that someone could only desire to be a gangster. There has to be something else that you're interested in. So if you had the money, would you have the heart to go after what you really want?"

I ain't got nothin' t' say t' that, 'cause I'on really know.

"It's the same principle, Shank. Young fathers punk out when their girlfriends, or flings, say that they're pregnant. It's the same principle. Many unemployed people punk out when it's time to go in and fill out an application for a job. It's the same principle. Black employees punk out when they know, in many cases, that their white bosses are discriminating against them for pay raises and promotions. It's the same principle, Shank! You hear what I'm telling you?

"These same blacks that have all kinds of money punk out when someone with the economic know-how asks them to invest in a worthwhile project instead of sitting on dollars and wasting it. All these damn athletes and singers and entertainers that we have, but yet we still produce nothing because we don't put our money into production. We put our damn money into consumption! And that goes for all of us! You hear me, Shank?"

We meet eye to eye. This motherfucker is dead serious!

"Yeah, man, I hear you."

We both lay back on the couch. And after smoking two joints, I'm hungry as shit.

"Yo, man, let's get some food."

Wes smiles. I know he's hungry. He gots to be! "Okay," he says.

Now instead of just grabbing some Chinese or Mc Donald's-type shit, this guy drives way back over to Northwest to order soul food from the Florida Avenue Grill to support black business. This motherfucker is lunchin'! But yo, this soul food grub is slammin'!

"So, what do we do now?" Wes asks me. We're sitting at the intersection of Florida and Georgia Avenues, heading east. We're waiting for the light to turn green. I look at Wes' car clock and the shit says ten-thirty.

"Yo, let's go to the East Side," I tell him.

"The East Side? Man, I always wanted to go there."

"Yeah?"

"Yeah, but my friends didn't want to go, except for Walt. But Walt always goes with his cousins, you know, because they're 'real-ass niggas' like you."

I smile and shake my head. He's still talking that "real-ass nigga" shit.

We get up to the East Side and cruise in line. Cars are lined up pumping go-go music that I'm not really into. Maybe it's because I'm originally from Jersey. Anyway, they gonna have more of this go-go shit inside. But I ain't been to the East Side in a while, so fuck it!

We ride around and park. We walk toward the door with all these prostitute-looking D.C. girls. I mean, I ain't never been in a city where women dress as nasty as these bitches. They wear cut-up jeans, shit hanging off their backs and shoulders, and flowery body suits; just plain nasty shit. I think the only place that can compete with D.C. whores in nastiness is Florida, you know, with that Two Live Crew shit.

"Wow, I see why my friends never wanted to come here. These are some rough-looking people, wearing a whole bunch of color. You ever notice that? How come black people love to wear so much color?" Wes asks, laughing. He's doing that Steve *How Come?* shit.

We walk through the crowds, downstairs in the hip-hop section. I watch both of our backs. I can tell Wes ain't never been in tough territory before. He don't even realize that people are watching him. But I got his back! So any nigga acting stupid is gonna get hurt. I'm gon' make it back to his car to get my gun before they do. Matter fact, I should get the keys, just in case.

"Shannnnk! What's up, boy? Where you been at, man? I heard you moved to Northeast somewhere," this cool-cap-wearing, toothpick-chewing nigga says to me. He all on my dils-nick, and I don't even remember his damn name. I just remember he used to hang back my way near K Street in Southeast.

"Yeah, I moved," I tell him. I ain't really trying to have no conversation.

"So what'chu been up to?" He reaches out his hand for a shake. I look over his shoulder to watch after Wes. This motherfucker's wandering around like he's dying to be sized up in here.

I shake dude's hand and move by him. "I'm makin' money, you'n, that's all."

Wes is talking to some fly brown-skinned girl who's wearing gold shoes and a gold belt. Her hair is dyed gold too. I guess the bitch, I mean, girl, is trying to coordinate. *You know, you gots ta co-or-dinate.* I smile. I ain't gon' call this girl a bitch if she knows Wes. She might be cool. Makes me feel like seeing my girl tonight.

"Hey, Sherry, this is my boy, Shank," Wes says, introducing her to me.

Sherry looks at me and then back at Wes, as if I'm working for him. I can tell she's thinking that, because her eyes are getting all big, like she has new respect for Wes. It's a trip how girls fall for that *Bodyguard*-type shit. They think anybody is important if he got a tough-ass friend with him.

Wes dances with her. But I can see his eyes following all these other scandalously-dressed girls. I can't blame him though. These go-go bitches dress freaky and dance even worse. Makes a nigga want to pull the rest of their clothes off and fuck them.

I look around and spot a bunch of guys looking in Wes' direction. They're all looking jealous, like they wanna start some drama with him. But I can't have that shit! Wes is cool with me. He don't even have to pay me to watch his back in here.

I walk over to him, hard and slow, as if I'm ready to kill somebody. I get his attention and whisper to him, "Yo, you should try t' take this girl t' ya crib."

Wes smiles and nods his head. I turn around and make sure I look in every direction at these punk motherfuckers who are staring at him. And guess what? Now these niggas are turning away. I guess they see that I got my boy's back.

I go back to where I can watch some more freak-dancing bitches on stage. Fuck that, they are *bitches!* That's why these guys are always in here cheering these nasty-dancing freaks on. I'll fuck my little sister up if I *ever* catch her doing this freak-dancing shit in a club. That shit ain't right! I mean, how can a girl expect for you to treat her right after you see niggas freaking her and telling her to get nasty and take her clothes off in a party?

"Yo, Shank! What's up, man?"

It's three more young'uns from my old neighborhood.

"Yo, you hear what happened to Wiley, man?" one says, looking sad.

"Naw, what?"

"He got shot by a sixteen-year-old."

"He died?"

"Yeah, young'un shot 'im in'na head, three times."

DAMN! That's fucked up! But I can't do nothin' about it. The nigga's dead now. Fuck it. And I remember I used to hate that muthafucka, until we got to be cool that summer.

"When'nis happen?" I ask.

"Man, like three weeks ago, right around the corner where we used to hang out. 'Cause you know, Wiley been hustlin' around the projects for years. But now some new niggas is try'na house shit."

"Some new niggas? Who?"

"People was sayin' it was BJ and them. But I heard that niggas from New York is backin' 'em up. An'ney paid young'un'na take Wiley out."

I nod. "Niggas from New York, hunh?"

"Yeah, man, you know how that drug shit is. Niggas'll go anywhere t' get paid. 'Cause I got cousins from up here housin' shit down in Virginia now. Then you got brothers from Philly, New Jersey and New York down in Norfolk." He shakes his head. "Man, you'n, that's jus' how it is."

I nod, and we do some more small talk before you'n joins his boys. I catch motherfuckers peeking at me and turning away. I guess they're trying to find out who the hell I am. It's funny how it's always some new niggas trying to step up in the ranks. But if they fuck with me . . . they getting *capped!*

"So I'll drive you home in the morning," Wes says to this girl Sherry.

Damn, he must have taken me seriously! She down with him, too! I mean, I said that shit to him just to let them people know that I was with him.

Everybody crowds outside after the party. Me, Wes and Sherry head back to Wes' car. I'm still watching for niggas. So the first thing I do is grab my gun from under the front seat and slip it inside my jacket. Sherry sees me, but she doesn't say nothing. I guess she know what time it is.

We ride back to Rhode Island Avenue, Northeast. I get Wes to drop me off at the 7-Eleven around the corner from my building. I ask him to hop out with me as I squeeze out the back on Sherry's side.

"Yo, man, this shit is between me and you. So don't tell no ma-fuckas you dropped me off up here," I tell him seriously.

He looks me in my eyes like *real* men do. "Don't even worry about it. You have my word. And I understand exactly where you're coming from."

I nod. Then I smile, thinking about this girl Sherry that he has in the car. "So you gon' get busy, hunh, shawdy?"

Wes smiles. "You know what? This girl didn't even notice me before I starting wearing hip gear. She used to work with me at this telemarketing company for like, seven months." He shakes his head. "It's amazing how people change when you get some money."

I smile at him. *I guess she is a bitch,* I'm thinking. "Aw'ight den, man."

I walk off. Wes backs up and heads up Rhode Island toward South Dakota. I walk into my crib, kick off my Nike Airs and scramble to my bed. I fall out, tired as shit. I'm not even trying to take my clothes off.

* * *

The telephone rings loud as hell Sunday morning. I answer it after it rings five motherfucking times. "Hello."

"Yo, it's Butterman. We gotta get together about gettin' them niggas that tried t' take y'all yesterday."

"Aw'ight, man, but let me get da hell up first," I tell him.

"I got somethin' else t' tell you too, you'n."

"What?" I'm hoping that this shit ain't long so I can go the fuck back to sleep.

" 'Member dat boy Bean dat'chu busted up?"

"Yeah, what about him?"

"Yo, that ma-fucka shot somebody last night up on Fourteenth Street Northwest. He shot you'n seven times."

"So?"

This motherfucker laughs. "I just thought I'd tell you that shit, you know, 'cause you wanted to kill 'im. But they got his ass in D.C. Jail now. He goin' up, man."

I sigh heavily. "Is that it?"

"Yeah, jus' beep me when you get up."

"Aw'ight," I grumble.

I hang up and stretch out on my bed. That nigga Bean had heart enough to shoot somebody seven-ass times. So? Fuck him! I beat you'n's ass so bad that he would run from my damn shadow. But just in case . . . maybe I shouldn't let the next motherfucker live. You know what I'm saying? My life might depend on killing a nigga so they can't get me back.

Chapter 8

Wes

"I don't think that D.C being a state is gon' change anything. I mean, it ain't like we gon' have more jobs just because we a state," Candice says, dressed in a silk turquoise outfit while I'm sitting here in class, staring at her.

Professor Cobbs's brown face looks pained. "So you mean to tell me, Miss Moreland, that you don't think the District of Columbia could create more jobs if we had control over our own tax dollars?"

Candice frowns. "How? I mean, jobs come from skills and stuff. More government money would just go to these greedy officials.

"Like Sharon Pratt Kelly. I heard that she got a penthouse built off of D.C. tax dollars."

My small class of senior political science majors laughs. I chuckle myself, but it's true. Mayor Sharon Pratt Kelly did have a luxury penthouse apartment remodeled with the use of D.C. tax dollars.

"That's why it's important that we hold our public officials accountable," Professor Cobbs argues. He straightens out his gold-and-blue striped tie. His camel-colored sports jacket swings loosely as he paces the front of the class, wearing casual blue jeans with a white shirt and brown dockside shoes.

"All we seem to do is talk about our officials. And I mean, you guys are political science majors, *Candice*, so you should know better."

Candice sucks her teeth and smiles. "Whatever; 'cause even if we write letters and stuff, all they gon' do is ignore us."

Professor Cobbs shakes his head as the class period ends. "Candice, why did you major in political science?" he asks, as everyone gathers their things to leave. A few of us lag behind to hear her response.

Candice smiles. "Oh, I'm try'na go to law school. I just took political science 'cause it ain't that hard or nothin'."

Someone behind me laughs and says, "Yo, Joe, you should'na said that."

Professor Cobbs nods and responds to Candice with a smirk, "Oh really?"

"Man, I ain't even gon' lie about it."

He shakes his head as Candice walks off. Then he looks to me. "Hey, Ray, how come you've been so quiet these last few weeks? I could usually count on you to help me out in here."

"Yeah, well, I've just been thinking a lot about going to grad school and all," I lie to him. Actually I've been more caught up in life *outside* of class.

Professor Cobbs gets excited by my response. "Oh yeah? That would be a great move, Ray, and I could write you a recommendation. You have good grades, so grad school shouldn't be a big problem for you. You've been one of the most enthusiastic students I've had in years."

I feel sick to my stomach as I beef up my lie. "Yeah, well, you know, I just think it's kind of grim that there's not that many black male teachers in this country and all. Especially with the great need of positive role models that we have."

"Aw, man, don't I know it," he says with his face lit up in understanding. He's making me feel even worse. But I *could* still go to grad school though. It's not as if I've totally ruled it out.

"Do you know Mark Thompson?" he asks me.

"Heard of him, seen him, been around him, but no, I don't really know him."

Professor Cobbs chuckles. "Well, I'll give you his number; he's a good guy to know." He takes out one of his business cards and writes on the back. "Now, you call him up and tell him that I referred you," he says, grinning.

I take the card. "Okay, will do."

I head out into the hallway, make a right and walk down the exit steps.

Candice is reading the *Afro-American* newspaper right in front of the first floor escalators that lead down to Connecticut Avenue. "Hey, Wes?" she calls to me glowingly.

I smile as she snuggles up close to me. She's tempting me with her warm body and her sweet-smelling perfume. And I know she wants something.

"Yes, Candice? What can I do for you?"

She smirks and bumps me with her hips as I feel my pants tighten.

"I need a favor from you," she says softly.

"Homework?"

"No."

"A ride home?"

"Almost, but not quite. I need you ta ride me up to my old job so I can get my last paycheck."

"Where is it?"

"Bethesda."

"How far in Bethesda?"

"Right around the corner from the Metro station, off of Wisconsin Avenue."

"So how come you can't take the Metro then?"

She sucks her teeth and squeezes my left arm. "Come on, Wes. Please."

I smile. "Okay. I don't have anything else to do."

We ride the escalators down to Connecticut Avenue. I walk over to buy some corn chips from the Ethiopian woman stationed inside at a food cart.

Candice chuckles. "Er'rybody be eatin'nem corn chips."

"So?" I respond playfully.

"Don't get smart," she snaps.

"Hey, Wes! What's goin' on, man?" I turn around to find J extending a right hand to me. He's wearing a bright red Polo jacket and tan jeans. I shake his hand and notice the ostentatious gold nugget bracelet immediately.

"When did you buy this?" I ask him.

"Aw, Joe, it's jus' a li'l somethin', man. Stop sweatin' it." He faces Candice and makes her blush. "Hey, sexy."

"Hi."

He looks her over, grinning. "So you sweet on my boy Wes?" he asks her.

Now *I* feel like blushing. *Damn, this is embarrassing!* I'm thinking.

Candice smiles. "I'on know."

"You don't know?" J looks to me. "Hey, man, you betta ask her." Then he laughs and gets serious. "But for real though, man, I gotta talk to you."

He pulls me over to the side. "I heard you been hangin' out wit' my niggas again."

"Yeah, a little bit," I tell him.

J shakes his head, seemingly in disgust. "Fuck is

wrong wit'chu, man?" he whispers. "I mean, I didn't hire you to hang out wit' dem niggas, Joe. I hire you ta be yourself and take care of the damn money. Now, if they would'a got you locked da hell up wit' 'em, then what? Ya ass would'a been lookin' stupid."

He shakes his head again as he looks around at the sunny, April weather sights—mostly at how the UDC women are dressed. And I guess he's pretty much right; I was taking a needless risk by hanging out with his "runners." But I still learned a lot.

"Look, man, I got a dumb-man's joke for you, you'n," he says lightheartedly.

"A dumb-man's joke?" I smile and shake my head. "I don't mean to be rude, but I have somewhere to go."

J looks toward Candice, who is still standing to the left of us, waiting patiently.

"Aw, man, she ain't goin' nowhere. That girl look like she in love."

"She's hardly in love," I tell him through my grin.

"Yeah, 'cause ya game is weak. Anyway." He gets serious again. "Yo, here it go—right: A poor, homeless black man was offered ten million dollars by a rich, white millionaire—"

I cut him off. "If he's a millionaire, I would think that he was rich."

J quickly frowns. "Listen, man! Damn!"

I listen impatiently.

"So the rich, white man says, 'Would you take my ten million dollars as a token of my innermost compassion for your terrible situation?'—right. And the poor, homeless black man says, 'No, suh.' 'Well, would you take my red Jaguar valued at sixty thousand dollars?' 'Nope.' 'How about a thirty-thousand-dollar entry level position at my company?' 'Unt-unh.'

"So then the rich white man laughs and says, 'What

about my wife? She has fifty-eight years on her, and she's no longer the good-looking dame that she used to be.'

"The poor nigga shakes his head. 'Oh no, suh. I'd neva take a man's woman. That'a come back t' haunt ya.'

"So the white man says, 'Jesus Christ, man! Here I am, a good Samaritan, feeling guilty for you helpless Negro people, and you won't even allow me to help you. Now, look, man, is there anything else that I can get you? *Anything?*'

"Then the poor black man smiles with one front tooth and says, 'Gi'me three dollas f' some wine."

J laughs and shakes his head as I start to chuckle. "Dumb muthafucka! Now that's the type'a niggas you was hangin' out wit', man. Stay ya ass away from them. Them niggas don't know their face from their ass."

He shakes my hand again as he heads off to his car.

I'm still smiling as I walk back to Candice.

"What was all that about?" she asks me.

"Nothing. He was just telling me a joke."

Candice and I are heading up Connecticut Avenue toward Bethesda, Maryland, as she fiddles with my car radio.

"Oh shit, it's Tupac!" she yells. His new single, "I Get Around," pumps through my four car speakers.

I grin at her while she turns it up and rocks rhythmically in the passenger seat. "How come so many girls like him?" I ask her—not because I don't like him, but because I'm curious.

" 'Cause, Joe, he rough like that, man," she answers, still rocking. "And he's sexy."

"What about my friend, J?"

She pauses to think. "Oh, I'on know about him. I mean, he act like he stuck on himself."

I smile as we make a left turn and head toward Wisconsin.

Candice points to the building. I let her out at the curb. "I'll be right back out," she tells me, leaving her pocketbook inside the car. I guess she trusts me more than NeNe does. NeNe always takes her pocketbook with her—even to the bathroom. Or maybe it's not really trust, but something else her mother told her never to do; leave her pocketbook unattended.

Candice jumps back in after a seven-minute wait with my blinkers on.

She shouts, "Damn! I hate that shit, man!"

"What are you talking about?"

"Naw, Joe, they always be takin' money out ya check."

"Well, do you know what it's for?"

"Yeah, man, but still."

I smile and shake my head.

Candice turns down the radio and gives me her undivided attention. "So, Wes, who you messin' wit' like dat?"

Uh oh, I'm thinking. *Here comes the big question.*

"I have—" I think better of telling her the truth and lie "—like, a few associates, but no steady girl or anything."

Man! This lying is really becoming a habit.

"Well, how come, like, you never asked me out?"

I feel like my heart just increased its temperature by thirty degrees. My chest burns with anxiety. "Because I know that you still go with Antwan," I lie once more. Truthfully, I'm afraid that I may not be able to handle Candice.

"Me an' him don't really talk like dat no more."

I sit quietly with no response.

"So what's up, man? Is we gon' go to the movies this weekend or what?"

Maybe it's my new high temple-tape haircut. Or

maybe it's my new gear. Or maybe it's the car and a new surge of coolness. But this all feels *GREAT!*

"Friday, Saturday or Sunday?" I ask her.

"Oh, it don't matter t' me. Shit, we can go all three days." She laughs as we cruise down Fourteenth Street Northwest.

I let Candice out at the corner of Fourteenth and Harvard Streets, right out in front of her apartment building.

"Oh, I'm moving out to Silver Springs next month, 'cause this neighborhood is crazy. I'm tired of all these damn bums, beggin' an' shit. You know?"

She smiles at me and dips her head back inside the car window. "You wanna kiss?"

I smile, trying my hardest to say anything. But nothing comes out of my mouth but air.

"Psych. I'm just playin' wit'chu, you'n. Chill out an' shit, man. Damn!"

She winks at me as I watch her awesome body strut off toward her building. And I guess I don't even have to say it; I have another hard-on.

I use my old key and walk into my mother's house on Bunker Hill Road Northeast. I've parked my car around the corner. I still don't have the heart—or the stupidity—to tell her about it.

"Raymond, is that you?" she hollers from the kitchen, hearing the door close.

"Yeah, it's me, Mom!"

"What took you so long?" she asks me, still from the kitchen. My mother never stops what she's doing, so she ends up talking at you and around you most of the time.

I walk into the kitchen and watch my mother's slightly rounded form working hard at fixing appetizers for a small get-together she's having tonight.

"Everybody's going to be so proud of you next month when you graduate, boy. I am just so pleased with you."

My mother turns around and faces me momentarily. Her red hair and freckles don't exactly complement the green suit and yellow blouse she's wearing. But you never tell your mother anything like that, or it's off with your head.

"Get on up out of that chair and give your mother a hug, boy!" she says to me.

I do as she says, embarrassed. I mean, why must she continue to hug me so much? I'm about to graduate from college, and I'm turning twenty-two years old this year for God's sake!

"This a nice jean shirt you have on," she says, looking me over. "How much it cost you?"

"It ah, was forty dollars, but I got it on sale for twenty-two."

"From where?"

"Marshall's, up at City Place Mall."

"Unh-hunh. This is a colorful tie you have on, too. I see a lot of young guys wearing the jean shirts with colorful ties now." She laughs. "I guess everybody wants the Boyz II Men look."

"Yeah, I guess so."

"So are you gonna participate in the rally for statehood this year?" she asks me, finally letting me go. "You know Jesse Jackson will be there, probably to soak up all the press." She smiles and gets back to work.

"Hey, Mom, do I have to stay here long?" I ask her. All she wants to do is show me off to her friends while pinching my cheeks and whatnot.

She faces me again. "Well, Raymond, honey, a lot of my friends haven't laid eyes on you in years. Especially since you just *had* to move away from me and all."

I'm not even trying to go there, I'm thinking. We've had that discussion a million times before. And I still feel the same—a man has to move out and move on. But you know, I still love my mother. It's not as if I'm neglecting her or anything.

When her friends finally get here I go through the regular routine: answering everyone's questions as I sit innocently as a white dove, dying to be excused.

By nine o'clock I'm finally allowed to go. I run around the corner through the April rain like a kid on a sunny Saturday morning and hop into my car. I'm heading straight for Marshall's house. I know all the guys are there; I called them earlier to make sure.

"Well, look what the rain blew in," Walt announces when he opens the door for me. He's dressed in a blue and white Adidas warm-up suit. As I run in out of the rain with no damn umbrella, Marshall and Derrick are playing John Madden's football game by Nintendo.

Marshall looks up at me while I stand dripping on his door mat. He smiles at me. "Yo, man, don't sit down until you finish dryin' up."

Walt laughs, but Derrick remains concentrated.

I look onto the television screen. "Who's Dallas?" I ask.

"Derrick," Walt answers.

The Philadelphia team has Dallas 34-10.

"No wonder Derrick looks so serious," I comment.

Now Marshall laughs. "Yeah, man, this nigga must've thought it was a flashback of the Super Bowl, but I ain't havin' it."

"If it was the Super Bowl, you'd have Buffalo," Derrick says.

"Yeah, whatever, man."

"Anyway, like I was sayin', Chris Webber still gon' be number-one draft choice. I mean, that time-out shit was the coach's fault," Walt interjects from his usual stretched-out spot on Marshall's smaller couch. He's referring to Michigan's loss to North Carolina for the NCAA Basketball Championship.

"We'll see," Derrick says.

Marshall shouts, "YES!" as he runs his quarterback into the end-zone for another score. "You can't stop Cunningham, boy!"

Derrick looks increasingly frustrated.

"Ay, yo, you hear about Randall Cunningham's wedding to some tall, light-skinned girl? You'n, 'nat nigga spent like eight hundred thousand dollars," Walt informs us.

"Yeah, that don't even make no sense," Marshall responds.

Derrick is still speechless.

"I mean, wit' all the homeless people all around the world, and he gon' spend a million dollars for a damn wedding day!" Marshall adds distastefully.

"Look, fuck that! If you got the money, you can do what'chu you wanna do. Fuck them homeless people! They can't play ball!"

Still looking on from the doorway, I shake my head and smile at Walt's frankness.

"That's typical of Walt to say," Derrick finally says.

"Aw, man, you just mad 'cause you gettin'nat ass whipped."

We all giggle except for Derrick. "Aw'ight, man, shit! You won," he says, tossing the controller to the floor.

"Yo, man, what'chu try'na break my shit?" Marshall responds angrily.

Walt cracks up. "That nigga a sore loser."

"Whatever," Derrick says. He stretches out on the longer couch, where we usually sit.

Walt peers at me. "Ay, man, sit ya ass down, you'n. Don't let that nigga have you standin' around like a bamma. Fuck Marshall!"

I smile and take a seat next to Derrick.

"So where you been at, Wes?" Derrick asks me.

"Yeah, I heard you got a slammin'-ass Acura Integra now. What's up wit' dat, Wes? You holdin' out on ya boys or what?" Walt says.

Everybody quiets down and stares at me, waiting for my response.

I let out a weak sigh. "It's a long story."

"We ain't goin' nowhere. We got all damn night," Walt says with a smile. He stretches his legs further out from the couch and clutches his big hands behind his head.

"I'm a bookkeeper," I admit. But nobody says anything, so I continue, "Butterman wants me to make entries on all the money coming in and going out. Plus I helped him set up a bank account under a fictitious company name."

I sit uneasily as the room turns into a morgue.

Walt clears his throat. "So I guess you gettin' paid now, hunh?"

"I mean, it wasn't like I really planned it."

"Hey, fuck it, Joe. Money is money."

Walt seems to be the only one speaking to me now.

Derrick stares. "Is this what you wanna do with your life, man?"

Walt sucks his teeth. "Aw, Derrick, man, he gettin' it on, Joe, gettin' paid. What da hell is you talkin' about?"

"Well, let him answer the question himself then," Derrick says.

"Look, it's just a meantime thing. I mean, it's not permanent or nothing. I mean, a lot of big business people started off illegal and then went straight," I respond. "It's not that big a deal, to me. Well, at first it was, but not any-more."

"When you get shot-up in the crossfire, then it's gon' be a big deal," Marshall says from his usual spot on his blue floor rug. I feel like going back home now. I knew that this would happen. But I couldn't expect to dodge them forever.

"Aw, y'all sound like a bunch'a girls. Wes ain't out there sellin' drugs; he's just a bookkeeper, like he said," Walt defends. And I *know* I'm wrong if *Walt* is defending me.

"Yeah, but this is Mr. Conscientious Scholar *here*. He ain't supposed to be participatin' in drug sales in *no* ca-pacity. I mean, this is Mr. Hard-work Stay-honest *here*," Marshall responds, mocking me.

Derricks chuckles. "Whatever, man. Do what you wanna do then, but just be warned that the shit ain't safe, at all. And I think I'd rather ride in Marshall's car. I mean, it's a lemon, but at least it's not hot."

Walt shakes his head and frowns. "Y'all some cheesy-ass niggas, man. I mean, y'all gon' sit here and talk that shit t' Wes when we all been cool too long for that dumb stuff, Joe. For real!"

He stands up and looks over at me. "Well, yo, man, it's gettin' late. I'm about t' head t' da crib. So take me da fuck home, Wes, 'cause I ain't afraid t' ride in'nat car."

Derrick and Marshall share a silent glare. I get up and head out the door behind Walt. Then Walt steps back in for a moment as I run through the rain to open the car doors.

"What did you say?" I ask him. We ride east on Florida Avenue.

"Oh, I jus' tol'lem niggas that they petty, man."

I shake my head solemnly. "No, they're right. I have a whole lot of thinking to do."

"Yeah, well, I wish that ma-fucka Butterman asked me

t' be his bookkeeper, 'cause I wouldn't give a fuck. And you probably can't even go t' jail for nothing like that."

"Yes, you can. And the feds like to use small, innocent guys like me to rat out on the bigger boys."

Walt laughs. "Yeah, you right about that shit. So ya ass betta not get caught."

I ask him curiously, "Do you think I would tell if I did, like if I got grabbed by the DEA somehow?"

Walt grits his teeth for a moment. "I'on know, man. Like, I know you wouldn't tell if it was any of us. But how close are you with this Butterman nigga?"

I nod. "That's a good question, a damn good question."

I arrive back home by twelve o'clock and check my C&P phone mail service.

"I guess you busy again, hunh? See, man, guys ain't shit. And I thought that you was different."

That's it? Hell, I guess NeNe's really pissed off at me.

I listen halfheartedly to my other messages from UDC classmates. They're all talking about getting together for study sessions for the upcoming finals. I guess everyone wants to use me. They've all been using my brains throughout my years at school—at Banneker High and at UDC—while I wallow in despair and loneliness as an unknown hero. I mean, who really gives a damn about what I want and what I feel? Who really cares about me fulfilling my own personal goals? Everyone seems to have all these expectations of me, but I can't have any say-so in what the hell I want to do, as if I'm some damn intelligent puppet!

I call NeNe back. She sounds irritated when she answers: "Yeah, who dis?"

"It's Wes."

"Oh, hi," she says blandly.

We just sit on the phone with neither of us saying anything.

"Well, did'ju call me to breathe in my ear or what?" NeNe asks.

"No. I mean, *I'm* feeling bad, *you're* feeling bad, the world is starving, and there's a war in Somalia."

"Hmm. You lunchin', Joe."

She's smiling. And right now I feel like saying something crazy. What else are you supposed to do when you're feeling desperate? "You think you can spend the night tonight?" I ask her.

She pauses. "Why should I?"

Now I pause. "Because two humans bonding together in the middle of the night is the best cure in the world for unhappiness."

I can tell she's smiling again. And her slight giggle confirms it. "Yeah, and that's why so many young girls out here wit' babies now."

Damn! I wasn't expecting for her to say something like that, I'm thinking.

"So you gon' drive me ta work t'mar mornin'?" she asks to my surprise.

I perk up. "Of course I will."

Another short silence creeps over the phone. NeNe says, "You know, I shouldn't even do this with the way you been treatin' me lately."

I don't say anything. She's been driving me crazy lately too, but she's still my girlfriend—even if I *have* slept with Sherry three times. And what about Candice? Will I be able to hold her off?

"Well, come and get me, boy," I hear NeNe telling me as I continue to muse.

"Okay. I'll be over in a half hour."

"Aw'ight now, don't keep me waiting."

I put on a dry sweatshirt and head out the door with my umbrella. It's still raining outside, but it's not as bad as it was earlier. And I don't feel as bad as I did earlier either. Maybe the key is to live life like a football game, always looking forward to the next play to score another touchdown. Only thing is, when time runs out on you, that's it. So hell, maybe it's best that I play this game of life to the fullest. I mean, bench-warmers don't get any respect anyway—right? Or am I just rationalizing bad decisions and my present situation?

Shank

The Mad Man

It's time to get out
when a criminal mind can't sleep at night
daytime comes and I still can't think right.
These violent thoughts keep exploding like dynamite
now I'm asking myself, "Yo, maybe I ain't wrapped tight?"
'Cause only a Mad Man runs from flashing lights.
They tying me down like I'm wild from a full moon
then locking me up with no bail.
I'm in hell
and can't tell
as I yell
if it's night or it's day from the darkness of my prison cell.
I need to be free, like a whale
so I rebel
'cause I'm a Mad Man.

Then I'd sample Da Lench Mob's "Guerillas In Tha Mist":

That's how it's done. So ya betta run yo'—run yo'—run yo' ass out da jungle.

Then Onyx's "Bitch Ass Niggas":
Bitch ass niggas I'ma have ta pull ya skirt up.
Then Gang Starr's *The Illest Brother:*
You got to be the illest brother just ta claim respect.

I'm walking down the street, my head's up high, my .45 is
packed,
waiting for some suckers to attack,
and then BAP, BAP, BAP
they get capped
'cause I'm strapped, black.
They must've thought that I would duck 'em,
but now I bucked 'em.
I hope their mothers love 'em
'cause the way I'm thinking is, Fuck 'em!
They shouldn't have tried to rob a Mad Man with a weak
plan,
now them suckers are chilling six feet under brown land
and their mother's dropping tears in the sand
'cause I'm a Mad Man.

   That's how it's done. So ya betta run yo'—run yo'—
run yo' ass out da jungle.
   Bitch ass niggas I'ma have ta pull ya skirt up.
   You got to be the illest brother just ta claim respect.

Give me a tranquilizer. I'm too hyper. I need to be calmed
down,
my gun is pulled at every fucking sound now.
And on the 4th of July, I had to shoot up a whole town.
Them niggas wouldn't quit
with that firecracker shit
and they thought I was a joke
so every motherfucka got smoked.
Now they wanna make a movie off my ass in Hollywood

I signed on the dotted line, "You better make my shit good."
Then I shook hands and stepped
with a larger rep
and for niggas that slept
here comes The Mad Man.

That's how it's done. So ya betta run yo'—run yo'—
run yo' ass out da jungle.
Bitch ass niggas I'ma have ta pull ya skirt up.
You got to be the illest brother just ta claim respect.

I'm still on edge. I can't help it, I'm hyper,
thinking like a sniper.
If I was on G.I. Joe, I'd be a fucking viper
jumping out of airplanes with a Mac 10
BANG! BANG! BANG! Motherfuckas I'm out to win.
I'm giving all my enemies blood showers . . .
and killing so many suckers I can't even hear the fuckers
holler.
I'm collecting more blood than a blood packer
when I'm attacking ya,
and then I howl while I'm after ya,
even giggle while I'm hacking ya.
A silver bullet won't kill me, silly
and fuck the Holy Water,
I'll swallow the shit down and burp
right before I slaughter ya.
And now I got the whole world in my hands
'cause I'm a Mad Man.

That's how it's done. So ya betta run yo'—run yo'—
run yo' ass out da jungle.
Bitch ass niggas I'ma have ta pull ya skirt up.
You got to be the illest brother just ta claim respect.

They're dropping bombs on me.
I guess they're thinking they can kill me like Godzilla
but I'm still a killa
and getting illa
and fuck Michael Jackson and his band,
I'm the real Thrilla.
Punk motherfuckas can't play my rhyme on prime time
'cause a nigga like me is too hard and too legit.
Candyman and Dr. Giggles, the type of niggas I'm running
wit'.
We gave MC Hammer a visit, that's why the nigga quit.
And if you battle me
you'll get your fucking tongue ripped.
So see me at your door with my red eyes
my knife and some blood flies, nigga
don't act surprised.
You gots to figure a lot of suckers died
from my ruthless-ass hands
'cause I'm a Mad Man.

That's how it's done. So ya betta run yo'—run yo'—
run yo' ass out da jungle.
Bitch ass niggas I'ma have ta pull ya skirt up.
You got to be the illest brother just ta claim respect.

Hold it right there, motherfuckas!
I ain't done yet, sucker.
Matter fact, I'm just starting to sweat, yo
so give me some more bass drum . . .
yum, yum, here I come,
and cutting off heads is fun
like chewing bubble gum.
Give me some wild-ass cherry
or better yet, some strawberry funk

and if I'm dead drunk
you best believe I had a Bloody Mary.
When my movie comes,
yo, Joe, I'll have a lot of fans.
Niggas'll leave aisles at the show with bloody hands,
make a hundred mil' in demand.
'Cause I'm the motherfucking Mad Man.

That's how it's done. So ya betta run yo'—run yo'—
run yo' ass out da jungle.
Bitch ass niggas I'ma have ta pull ya skirt up.
You got to be the illest brother just ta claim respect.

Yo, this rhyme is hype as shit! That motherfucker Wes got me *cysed!* And I mean, Butterman all laying low and all, so I ain't been out in the street that much for like, two weeks. That's still punk shit to me. I'd kill them niggas as soon as they step. But fuck it, I'm still getting paid. You know what I'm saying? I can't complain.

I saw that movie *Who's The Man?* That flick was cool. It had a bunch of rappers in it, but they all did good. Especially Salt, from Salt N Pepa. Yo, you wouldn't even think she was a rapper she did so good.

Now I'm waiting for *Posse* to come out in a couple of weeks. That joint gon' have my man Big Daddy Kane in it. Black cowboys! Ain't that some shit? But it was probably black cowboys out in the West, you know? I mean, us niggas did every fucking thing else. Why we couldn't have been cowboys too?

I finished reading that Maya Angelou book, *I Know Why The Caged Bird Sings.* And man, she been through a whole *bunch* of shit! Like, her mother's boyfriend molested her in St. Louis when she was like six or seven or eight. Her father's girlfriend stabbed her when she was a teenager and shit. Then, she fucked around and lived inside of cars with a bunch of other homeless kids out in California some-damn-where. That's all some crazy shit! You know what I'm saying? But she loved the hell out of her brother Bailey though. I guess the only person I've ever been that close to in my life is my cousin Cal. I mean . . . yo, like . . . I love that nigga. And I ain't no damn bitch for saying that either! That's my fucking cousin!

Damn! I ain't got a *thing* to do today. I'm sitting here in my living room watching videos, bored like shit. They showing this cheesy-ass PM Dawn video on BET. I mean, this video is some stupid, punk-sounding song. How this nigga get a record deal? That's that new Big Daddy Kane single. But it's true though. It's a lot of no-skills-having motherfuckers with record deals.

Fuck it! It ain't no sense in me sitting around doing nothing. I might as well head over to my girl's crib, up at Howard. I mean, she still ain't *really* my girl, but I call her my girl anyway, you know? We been together for six damn months now.

I throw my blue Polo jacket on and head out the door. That H-Town video, "Knockin' Da Boots," is coming on. But I don't feel like watching that shit. They play it too much already. Even on The Box they order that video all day long.

I turn off my TV, lock my door and head for Rhode Island Avenue to catch one of these slow-ass 80 buses. Ain't nothing coming yet, so I run across the street to 7-Eleven and buy a Pepsi. I check out the magazines before I get in line. Halle Berry married David Justice from the Atlanta Braves. They on the front cover of this month's *Ebony*.

Now I'm checking out these rap-type magazines. Most of this shit is a bunch of photos. I mean, fuck them pull-out pictures! If I buy a magazine, I want some real-ass interviews on the rap artists, not their pictures. I got Big Daddy Kane and Rakim and them on my wall, but I'm not trying to throw no Jodeci or Boyz II Men shit up. Especially not all of these other New Jack niggas. These magazines must be for bitches. And they don't have *THE SOURCE* up in this joint. I guess they must have sold out of them. They don't have that *RapPages* joint that Wes had over his crib in here either.

Damn, I need something else to read while Butterman finishes bitching from these punk-ass Northeast niggas. Or wherever the hell they from.

I run back across the street and jump on an 82 bus that's just arriving. Now it looks like two more busses are right behind us. Ain't that some shit? That always happens!

I get over to the Howard Towers Plaza-East and look to see if my punk-ass boy is at the sign-in tables. YES! That motherfucker is here. I walk past and look at him. He nods his head to me. I nod back and head for the elevators. I ride up to the ninth floor and walk to Carlette's room. I stop at the door before I knock. Somebody the hell in here giggling and shit!

Yo, I swear to God; if this bitch got some other nigga up in this joint . . . I knock on the door like I'm the police.

"Who is it?"

Oh, damn, it's her fucking roommate. "Is Carlette here?" I ask her.

She opens the door. She's dressed in some baggy-ass, faded blue jeans and an oversized white T-shirt. This tall-ass dude she got with her is wearing the same-type shit.

"Do you have to knock so hard?" she asks me.

"Yeah," I tell her, walking past to Carlette's room. I know they gonna stand out here and talk trash about me, but fuck them. And I'd rough that punk motherfucker off.

I shut Carlette's door. "What are you doing here?"

Carlette asks me from her bed. She's stretched out across the shit, face down and looking inside some book. She's wearing a black skirt with black stockings and a green silk blouse. Man, I *love* how she dresses! My shit is getting hard already.

I take my jacket off and jump on top of her. "I was feeling horny."

She smirks, playing-like. "Oh, that's all you want me for?"

"Naw, I took you out t' da movies a couple times, didn't I?"

She smiles. "Yeah, you did, but that don't mean nothin'."

I reach up for the top of her stockings and start to pull them down.

"Umm, excuse me. But what are you doing?" She's grinning at me and shit, like I'm joking with her.

"I'm takin' ya clothes off. It ain't that time of the month yet."

She laughs. "Yeah, but I'm studying for a test." But she's still not trying to stop me.

I pull her clothes to her ankles and take off her black patent-leather shoes.

She says, "I don't believe you."

"Why not?"

"Because we just did it last night."

"So?"

"Didn't you get enough?"

I pull up her skirt. "Naw. Are you sore?"

"No."

"Well, be quiet then."

I spread her legs and climb on top of her with my pants down and hit it from the back. She intertwines her fingers with mine and moves with me.

Oh God, she got some good pussy! Damn, damn, DAMN!

I get up off of her and look for a towel to wipe myself off with.

"It's in my bottom drawer," she tells me, rolling over on her bed. "Now see, you done got me all messy."

I smile. "So? Get up and wash yaself off."

She duck-walks to the dresser and pulls out another towel. Then she walks to the door to see if her roommate is still out in the kitchen area. "You lucky they left," she tells me.

"Why?"

" 'Cause I'd make you lick it off of me."

I look at her come-dripped legs and cringe. "Yeah, you nasty as hell, girl."

"*Nasty?* How? You the one who wanted to do it to me in the middle of the day."

I shake my head and smile. Carlette heads to the bathroom.

"Are you coming back here later on?" she asks me after washing herself off.

"Why?"

She sighs. "What, I can't ask you a question?"

I grin at her while she changes her top bed sheet. "What if I do?"

"Then I wanna talk to you about something."

Oh shit! I'm thinking. *I don't like how that sounds.*

"What, are you pregnant?"

"No, Darnell. I am not pregnant, okay?" She shakes her head, grinning at me. "I told you I was on the pill."

"Yeah, so, what do you wanna talk t' me about?"

"You'll see when you come back."

"Yeah, aw'ight." *Sounds like she's gon' try another Joker's Wild on me. But she do got me curious.*

I walk back out into the blue-carpeted hallway and catch the elevator so she can get back to studying for her test. I don't really have nothing else to do while Carlette is studying, so I'm heading down to Georgetown on the 34 bus. I hope I don't get stopped by no cops down here. I don't leave the house without one of my guns on me. I'm packing my .25, and this Polo jacket is lightweight. I didn't want to carry my .38 or my .45 because I'd have to hide it inside of my pants. It's easier to hide the .25 with this springtime gear. I ain't planning on ever carrying that bullshit-ass .22. I'd pull that shit out and somebody might laugh at me. Matter fact, I'm thinking about giving it to Carlette, since she so much into that Black Panther shit.

I walk up and down Wisconsin Avenue doing that window-shopping-type shit. They got all these dress clothing stores with suits, ties and shoes inside the showcases. Then you got antique stores, a few book stores and all these expensive-ass white restaurants.

All these wealthy-ass, affluent white people are walking past me. Most of these motherfuckers are Georgetown students. And the rest are just rich preppies. This probably the only part of D.C. they know. Except for when they go to RFK Stadium in Northeast to see the Redskins play. I mean, this old-fashioned-looking Georgetown area might as well be another damn city. You know what I'm saying? These white people don't really live in D.C.

"Transfer, main man?" this bummy brown nigga asks this college student on M Street. He shakes his head and walks on.

The bummy dude looks to me now with droopy dog-eyes, looking all pitiful. "You'on got no transfer, do you, brotherman?"

I shake my head. "Naw."

"You got any change?"

Fuck it. I reach into my pocket and give Joe two dollars. He looks at the bills and back to me. But he still don't look too happy. That makes me feel like taking my ducats back. You know?

"You'on have to do this, man. I just needed fifty cents to ride the bus back to Southeast."

I frown at him. "What, 'chu wanna give it back t' me?"

This motherfucker smiles. "I'm just sayin' that it was nice'a you to do dat for a brother, you know? I mean, I ain't gotta tell you how hard it is for a nigga out here." He shakes his head. "I mean, you know how shit is for us."

"Yeah, I know."

I walk down M Street seeing more homeless-looking niggas begging for spare change. This shit don't make no sense when you figure that a lot of these white people up here are rich. Then these motherfuckers wonder why we out robbing people. We should be robbing *their* asses, for real! You know what I'm saying?

I jump on a 32 bus and head back downtown. It's always white people on these 30 buses until you get to the southeast side of D.C. Then you see nothing but niggas on the bus. But every now and then you'll see like a "poor white trash" person or a white businessman that looks like his car broke down. It's a lot of white people in Capitol Hill on the southeast side though; and then in them big-ass houses back Pennsylvania Avenue. White people always have the best shit. That's fucked up!

Anyway, I hop off the 32 bus at Fifteenth and F Streets Northwest. I walk across the street from the Treasury Department building.

"Look, Mom, there it is!" a little white boy shouts to his mother. He's pointing his finger upward-like.

I turn around to see what he's looking at. And damn, I should have guessed it; he's all excited about the Washington Monument.

I stand here and stare at the shit myself. That statue looks like a long-ass white dick. Seriously though! I mean, what is the significance of a damn statue that goes straight up in the air? You know what I'm saying? That ain't no amazing shit to me. Anybody can build *that*.

But you know what? I heard people say that that shit does represent a white dick. No joke. And I heard that no building in Washington is allowed to be taller than the monument.

Ain't that a bitch! So like, the white man is saying that he wants the biggest dick in the city. Then motherfuckers go right down there and take pictures of his dick, send postcards of his dick, sell posters of his dick.

Wait a minute. I don't believe this shit! I'm out here lunchin'. But it sounds true. I mean, white men are always talking about how big the black man's dick is. So this motherfucker went right ahead and built his own big white dick for everybody to see. And even niggas come down here, year after year, and pay tribute to the white man's big dick.

I start laughing at my thoughts. This white family turns around and glances at me with pink, fake-ass smiles on their faces. I guess they're thinking I'm just another crazy, jet-black nigga. But fuck them white people! I know what the hell I'm laughing at!

I head to Fourteenth and F and catch a 52 bus going up Fourteenth Street. A bunch of Hispanics is getting on this bus. And when you get all the way up Fourteenth Street, these Hispanics are every-fucking-where. They even got their own damn stores in Adams Morgan. Two years ago them Hispanic motherfuckers had a riot. They were saying some of the same things that niggas cry about, you know—about America's racism and the lack of jobs and discrimination and all that-type shit. But all the niggas that I know just went up there to snatch some free-ass gear.

I jump off the 52 bus at Fourteenth and U. They got a whole bunch of new stores up here after rebuilding. I remember when this shit looked like that movie *Escape From New York* for like five years. I mean, U Street was *all* fucked up! And it took the city long as hell to build the Yellow and Green Line Metro stations. Shop-keepers were complaining because it messed up a lot of their businesses. I can't blame them motherfuckers. They wouldn't do that in no white neighborhood! But fuck it, Ben's Chili Bowl is still here.

I get on a 96 bus. I ride it back to Georgia Avenue, heading to Carlette's crib. When I get off, this Hispanic dude damn near hits my ass while I'm crossing the street. Motherfucker better watch where he's going. They should ban them piece-of-shit, put-together-ass foreign cars them Hispanics drive anyway. Them niggas act like they can't buy no new ones. All their cars be out of them car lots. I ain't lying! And then they put them horns and shit in them and give them all these crazy-looking paint jobs.

I get back to the Howard Towers Plaza-East and walk in behind some students. My boy ain't at the desk now, but I made it in without him anyway. Carlette should be finished by now. It's almost seven o'clock.

I get off on her floor, turn the corner and spot that same nerd who was talking to her out here a few months ago when I came over.

"All right," she tells him as I walk up.

Nerd dude waves and walks down the carpeted hallway toward the elevators.

I point to his back. "What's up wit'chu and dude?"

Carlette pulls me into her kitchen by my arm. "Come on, he's just my friend."

I smile at her. "So you in here cookin' for me, hunh?"

She stirs a big pot of pasta boiling in hot water. "I'm cooking for *both* of us."

I look inside the pot. This shit looks like some big-ass pieces of pasta paper. "What da hell is that?"

She laughs. "It's lasagna. I have to lay it on top of the cheese and the tomato sauce."

"Oh."

I head to her bedroom and take off my Nike Airs and my jacket. I get ready to stretch out across her bed, but she got a newspaper and books spread all over it. I pick up the newspaper and read the large print headline: VIO-LENCE INITIATIVE: THE GOVERNMENT'S PLAN TO SEDATE BLACK YOUTH

Carlette comes in while I'm reading this article in *News Dimensions* newspaper. Some crazy-ass white man is saying that inner-city niggas are like wild African monkeys and that they need to be calmed down with medicine when they're young. And yo, this white man talking about giving them psychiatric medicines at five years old and shit!

This doc is crazy! Them motherfuckers are just kids!

"I'm doing a report on that," Carlette tells me.

"Oh yeah?" I'm still reading it.

I throw it back on her bed when I'm finished and shake my head. "Damn! Yo, they can do that?" I ask her.

She nods. "If black people don't complain. They're already using Ritalin and talking about using this drug called Prozac. But that's what I wanted to talk to you about."

I sit down on the edge of her bed and pull her toward me. "What?"

She pulls away and smiles. "No, I'm serious. I want you to help me with my homework."

I frown at her. "Help you wit'cha homework?" *What da fuck is she talkin' 'bout?*

She grins like a fucking she-devil. "I need you to answer some questions for me."

"Like what?"

"I want you to remember when you were young."

"Yeah, what about it?" I ask her suspiciously.

"Were you angry?"

She sits on the floor in front of me with a notebook and a pen in her hand.

I look down at her like she's crazy. "Wait a minute. What da hell is dis?"

She sighs and looks up at me all innocent-like. I know she gon' try to sweet-talk me now. Watch.

"Did I ever ask you for much?"

See what da fuck I mean?

"Aw'ight, aw'ight, I'll answer your damn questions. But first, what is it for?"

"I'm doing my final research paper on 'The Angry Black Man'. That's my title."

"For what?"

"I just told you, it's for my final."

"In what class?"

"Sociology."

"Sociology?"

"Yeah."

I grimace. "Oh, so you try'na use me as a guinea pig."

She smiles. "No, I'm not. I just need a tough guy like you to answer some personal questions."

"Are you gon' use my name?"

She looks at me as if I'm stupid. And I guess I am from the way she's looking at me.

"Of course not, Darnell."

I'm thinking about it. A few questions shouldn't be

that bad, but I'm still feeling funny. I mean, first that college boy Wes gives me a damn lecture, and now this Howard bit—, I mean, my girl wants to quiz me for some research paper.

"Come on wit' it then," I tell her.

She leans up and kisses me. "Thanks."

I smile and shake my head. She got me feeling like a silly-ass bamma. But fuck it!

She leans up on the floor with her back to the wall. She says, "Okay. Would you call yourself angry when you were little?"

"Yeah."

"Why were you angry?"

"My mom did it."

She stops and looks at me. "Your mom did it?"

"Yeah, that's what I said."

"How?"

"I'on know. Like, she was always fuckin' wit' me. And I remember this one damn time she burned me with a cigarette an' shit."

"Why?"

"Because I was hard-headed."

Carlette sits quiet. She acts like I just fucked up her whole interview. She's sitting there looking all sad.

She finally shakes her head. "Man, that's messed up." She says it with a cracked voice, almost like she wants to cry.

I suck my teeth. "Man, fuck that. I mean, I was aw'ight."

"But still, burning your kid with a cigarette? See, that's why people are talking about having licenses to bear kids now."

She's getting all dramatic about the shit. I mean, it was only a little burn. I didn't even cry.

She sighs again and starts over. "Okay. Did you know your father?"

"Naw."

"Did your mother talk about him?"

"Not as much as my gran'mom did before she died."

Carlette looks confused. "Why did your grandmother talk about him?"

" 'Cause I guess he got on her damn nerves. I'on know."

"Well, what kind of things did she say about him?"

"She called him a devilish man."

"A devilish man?"

"Yeah, my gran'mom called er'rybody that shit—my uncles, my cousins, me."

Carlette shakes her head like she can't believe it. "Okay, okay. Did you ever have any events where your family had a good time?"

I smile. "Yeah. Me and my cousins used ta throw rocks at cars an' shit. Then we used to chase stray cats and dogs with sling shots. Get in fights with other niggas. Aw, man, girl, we had a bunch of fun."

She bursts out laughing. "No, Darnell. I'm talking about, like, family reunions and stuff."

"Oh yeah." I think back to the time. "We ain't really get along though. Like, my gran'mother had the Bruce family up in New York, but she ain't really like dem mafuckas. And the Halls? We only had small shit, and we'd always get into family fights and whatnot."

Carlette shakes her head again. "This is so depressing. I mean, sure, every family has fights and stuff, but what good things do you remember?"

"Umm, me and my cousin Cal used to draw comic-book shit, and go to the movies a lot, make Kung Fu weapons. Run ball with my uncle and his friends. A whole bunch of shit."

Now she smiles. "You used to read comic books?"

"Still do."

"What kinds?"

"Any kind. But da shit is Wolverine, from the *X-Men*. He like dat!"

She nods. "Yeah, I've seen him on TV. But he's ruthless though."

"Yeah, that's why he da shit."

"So, you like being ruthless?" She's starting to take notes again.

"Sometimes you gotta be."

"Why?"

"Ta let ma-fuckas know you ain't bull-shittin'."

"Why is that so important to young black men?"

I smile. "Why is it so important for girls to get their hair done?"

She smiles back. "Is it that simple?"

"Damn straight! Would you go with that nerd dude you had up here?"

She grins. "He's not a nerd."

"Answer the question."

She looks away. "No. Okay?"

I laugh. "Yeah, I know you wouldn't."

"Anyway." She looks back down at her notes. "Okay, here's the big question. Do you feel that white society has contributed to your being angry?"

Now I look at her like *she's* stupid. "What da fuck you think?"

She smiles. "Okay then. Why?"

"Why what?"

"Why do you feel that white society has added to you being angry?"

I frown. " 'Cause dem ma-fuckas got all'la money."

"What about poor white people?"

"Fuck 'em. I hate 'em."

She cracks the hell up. "Okay, Mr. *Ice Cube*. This is not *Predator*, okay?"

"Yeah, whatever. Next question."

"Okay. Why is black-on-black crime more prevalent if white people are the real enemies?"

I rub my chin and look past her. "I'on know. Like, niggas be try'na carry you all da time."

"'Carry you?' That means like to diss you, right?"

"Yeah. Niggas be frontin' and showin' off and talkin' shit, and all that makes you wanna fuck 'em up."

"You never beat up a white boy?"

"Not me, 'cause dey never fucked wit' me. But I know niggas that used t' go down Georgetown jus' ta fuck up some white people."

"Why?"

"Because dey wanted to."

"But why?"

" 'Cause they don't fuckin' like white people!"

"But you don't like white people either, right?"

"Fuck no!"

"So how come you didn't go?"

Yo, I'm gettin' tired of this now. "I told'ju! White people ain't never fuck wit' me."

"So how come you hate them?"

She got me there. I sit here and blow out air. "Because it's their damn fault that we in this shit in the first place."

"So why not try to get out?"

"How?"

"I don't know. By gettin' an education and bettering yourself."

Okay, I knew dat shit was comin'. These Howard ma-fuckas always talkin'nat get-an-education shit. But I got somethin' for her ass.

"Yo—right. I know dis ma-fucka whose family is educated and got money. But he say that them ma-fuckas is puppets for the system. And he say that the only power niggas really have in this country is in'na streets. So he's out in the streets even though he don't need to be because he say he don't want to end up like his punk-ass father! Now, what'chu think about that? Your father's educated, right? What kind of power he got?"

"He gets to make his owns decisions and he's helping black people to get healthy! My father loves black people. But he says that people like this friend you're talking about have to learn to have faith in themselves and that nobody can give you power, you have to learn how to get it the legal way and go after it."

"Yeah, well, how much money does your father give back to poor niggas after he charges them the hell up, and what would he say about you fuckin' wit' me?"

"I don't know what he'd say about me talking to you, and I don't know how much money he gives to charity!"

"Fuck charity! I'm talkin' 'bout niggas, not da fuckin' American Way! That ain't nothin' but white people, t' me, that and that Red Cross-type shit."

"Well, you have to earn money. This country is not the Salvation Army. People know that. So we need to all grow up and realize that this is a capitalistic system."

I smile at her, still thinking about Butterman. "Well, this nigga say that's what he's doin', capitalizin', just like the white man capitalized on slavery in Africa, opium in China, Native American land over here, and drugs and alcohol now. So what about that, Miss Educated?"

Carlette looks at me with sharp-ass eyes, like how I look when I'm about to bust somebody up. "The difference is that we're doing it to our *own* people!" she yells up at me.

We both sit quiet for a while. I ain't mad or nothing. I mean, if I had money and the peace of mind to go to college, I would. But I don't.

"So you got any more questions for me?" I ask her.

She looks like she's pissed the hell off, but she looks

sad-like too. She says, "I just think people like you are being used. And I mean, I like you a lot, but it never seems like you wanna listen and do something positive with yourself."

I suck my teeth. "Stop fuckin' cryin'. You know damn well we ain't no match made in heaven."

She looks up at me with tears in her eyes. "Why not? Because you don't think that you could have me?"

Oh my God! I'm thinking. *Do you believe dis shit? I mean, as stuck up as most of these Howard girls is, she gon' sit in here and cry on me jus' 'cause I'm bein' truthful.*

I ain't saying nothing to that.

"Yo, what's up with the lasagna?" I ask her, just to get off of the subject.

She gets up without speaking to me and walks out into the kitchen. I guess she's trying to make me feel guilty. Fuck that shit though! I'm not sweating her over that *petty* shit. That's for punks.

I push all of her stuff off the bed and lay back and chill like I usually do. And if she got anything to say about it, then I'm leaving. I mean, fuck her! You know what I'm saying? Ain't no girl driving me crazy!

Carlette comes back in the room. I'm waiting for her to say some off-the-wall-type shit. Then I'm breaking out. Hell if she think she got me on a string. I ain't no damn yo-yo.

I get ready for her to say something about me pushing her books on the floor. But she lies down beside me and doesn't say Jack shit. She's staring up at the ceiling.

"What's wrong wit'chu?"

She still says nothing to me.

"Oh, you gon' ignore me now, hunh?"

She rolls over on me and hugs me, burying her face into my neck. "I'm not no bitch, and I still like you," she says.

I'm smiling like a motherfucker! And I feel like laughing, but I'm not. I mean, can you believe this? This girl must really like me! And this shit feels kind of good to me.

"Fuck it," I tell her. "You cool wit' me an' shit, too. Aw'ight?"

She mumbles, "Mmm-hmm."

I hug her back real hard. She must really like me. I still can't believe it.

Butterman

"Yo, you wanna race that shit up on V Street, you'n?"

I look to my left. This grinning, dark-skinned nigga is leaning over his passenger seat in a yellow RX-7. He got the '93 model. I guess he must think that car is pretty fast.

"Naw, man, I'on fuck around like that."

"Fifty dollars."

"Naw."

He shakes his head and smiles. The light turns green and you'n jets out like he's at the Indy 500.

"See ya!"

Yeah, fuck you. Dumb nigga must don't have shit else to do. But I do.

I get up Georgia Ave to pick up Steve for this late-night trip to New York. Steve's out here talking to some tall, skinny, brown-skinned girl on the sidewalk. I double park and blow my horn and wait for him. He runs over to the car and hops in smiling.

"Yo, you'n, I was jus' 'bout to get me some ass. But I'll jus' catch that ho later on."

I look him over. He's wearing a gold Champion hoodie and black jeans. And Joe needs a damn haircut.

"You can't get no better girls than her, man?" I ask him.

He looks at me confused. "Ay, look here, you'n, er'ry-body ain't the man like you. I thought you knew dat shit."

I don't respond to him. I'm too busy thinking about my money situation. I mean, the cake is rolling in, but these niggas in New York been having problems. The weather is getting hot, so young'uns are acting crazy *everywhere.*

"Why you all quiet t'day, B?"

I shake my head as we speed on I-95 North. "Shit is fuckin' up, man. These niggas down here got us makin' runs t' white boys out in Maryland, and my boys up in New York is havin' damn shoot-outs."

"I thought you said it was good biz'ness wit' dem white boys out in Maryland."

"Oh, it is. But sometimes it's hard to trust them white boys. You know, sometimes them white niggas get all fucked-up and do stupid stuff, like tellin' people who they dealin' wit'. That's why I told them my name is Butchy."

"Butchy?" Steve laughs and shakes his head. "Man, you'n, the way I figure, it's better to deal wit' dese white boys, 'cause at least they ain't out here try'na stick you up like niggas do."

I nod my head and push my 3000 to ninety.

Steve looks over to me. "Ay, man, is you try'na get a ticket or what?"

I look to my car clock. It reads 9:31. "Naw, man, I'm jus' try'na get up here and back as fast as possible."

"Yo, I heard you was up Deno's last week?" Steve asks me. We all the way in Baltimore already.

"Yeah, I was up in'nere."

"Was Northeast Groovers up in'nere?"

"Yeah."

He nods his head, smiling. " Dey like dat, ain't they, you'n?"

"Yeah, they aw'ight."

He takes a tape out of his hoodie pocket and puts it in my system.

"Yo, don't play that shit yet. I like this Super Cat song."

Steve smiles at me. And that ain't no pretty sight. For real!

"Yo, man, you needs ta stop smokin'," I tell him.

He leans over and looks at his teeth in my mirror. "Yeah, I know. But that nicotine is somethin' else, man. It's hard as hell t' stop smokin'. And I been doin'na shit since I was fourteen."

"Yeah, aw'ight, but shut up for a while. I can't hear myself think."

Steve looks at me like he's shocked. Then he bats his eyes at me like them cartoon women do. "Okay, Butter-man. Anything you say, baby."

I shake my head and smile. "You lunchin' like shit, man. Now shut da hell up and put that N.E.G. tape in."

"Yeah, you'n, 'cause dis shit is slammin'!"

We get up in Brooklyn and park the car in front of these brownstone apartment houses around the corner from my connection people.

"I thought you said them niggas is aroun'na corna," Steve says.

I never took him to New York with me before. He's as nervous as I was when Bink first brought me up here.

I grin at him as he feels for the .25 pistol I gave him last year. He has it stuffed under his hoodie and inside the front of his jeans.

"It's cool, man. These niggas know me," I tell him.

We hop out my 3000 surrounded by these Brooklyn, Brownsville boys flooding the steps and the corners.

That's how shit gets in the spring and summertime. *Everybody* comes out.

"Yo, what's up, G?"

I shake a hand and nod. "Yo, what's up, man?"

"Ain't nuttin'. Jus' maxin', you know."

Me and Steve walk by as more Brooklynites nod their heads to me. I don't know if a lot of these young'uns really like me, but as long as they don't try to carry me I ain't really worried about it.

We pull up to my connection spot. This light brown nigga steps up in military fashion. He's dressed in all brown and even wearing a Cleveland Browns football cap.

"What up?"

I don't notice him. I've never seen him before. And my heart is racing like shit. But I can't let this nigga know.

"Yo, man, is Ted an'nem here?" I ask him, keeping my cool stance.

Steve has his eyes glued to me to see how I'm responding.

You'n asks, "Who you?"

"Butterman."

He looks me over. "Wait out here."

"Aw'ight."

I expect for you'n to run inside the crib and get Ted or somebody I know. But he's just sitting here in front of us as if he forgot what the fuck I said.

"Umm, yo, G, is he here or what?" I ask him. I'm trying to sound like these New Yorkers to cool this nigga out.

He looks at me real fucking hard like Shank would. Then he pulls out a nickel-plated gun like he's Clint Eastwood. "I said wait da fuck right here, nigga!"

OH MY GOD! THIS SHIT MIGHT BE IT! I'm thinking.

Steve ain't budged to try and reach for his .25. And it's a good thing he's not, because this nigga could shoot both of us five times before Steve could get his gun out. Then again, he coulda shot this nigga through his hoodie. But I don't even know if Steve has his hands on his gun. All I'm seeing is his chest rising for oxygen.

"Yo, Pete, them niggas cool, G," somebody says. But I'm too stiff to try and see who it is.

Pete keeps his gun out and looks to Steve. "Lift that shit up." He's pointing his gun directly at Steve's stomach, where the .25 is.

OH MY GOD! OH MY GOD!

I'm taking a long-shot to save our lives. Maybe Joe is a bodyguard like Shank is to me. Maybe he won't shoot us. Maybe he just wants to see if Steve is packing a gun like Shank always does with niggas.

Steve blinks at me like he's about to faint.

"Yo, man, go 'head and show 'im your gun. I mean, it's cool like that. Ted knows me like that, you'n."

When I say "you'n," Pete looks at me strangely.

SHIT! I FUCKED UP! NOW THIS NIGGA KNOWS WE'RE NOT FROM AROUND HERE!

Steve lifts up his hoodie and shows dude the gun.

Pete steps in closer. "Get'cha fuckin' hands up!"

He takes the .25 out from inside Steve's pants.

God damn! I ain't been through no shit like this since that night I got robbed out in Southwest D.C., two years ago. That was right before me, Red, Tub and DeShawn went to war with these Southwest crew niggas. And Tub messed around and got shot and killed that night. Maybe now it's my turn.

"YO-O-O, it's cool, Pete!" I hear a familiar voice saying. This dude named Bones comes down from the crib and shakes my hand. He's a thick-built brown dude wearing all black Levi's denim and some brown shoes. He looks back to Pete, who still has Steve's gun in his hand. "Yo, gi'dat nigga gun back, man. He cool."

Pete gives the gun back hesitantly. "Yeah, a'ight, hopps. I'on know who da fuck these niggas is."

Bones nods to him. "I got it." He leads us inside. "Yo, shit is beefed up right now, G, 'cause these wild-ass kids rolled around here sprayin' shit up yesterday." He smiles to me. "You know how people act when it gets hot."

I smile back, feeling relieved. These New Yorkers call anybody a "kid" if they're not from their crew.

Ted walks out in blue jeans and a T-shirt looking dead serious. He shakes his head to me. "Yo, man, this the wrong-ass day t' come up dis ma-fucka, G. My man Mark got shot up yesterday, and we 'bout to go huntin' after these niggas like Schwarzenegger."

"Damn, so you ain't got no ki's for sell?"

"Hell, naw. Not right now. We try'na move our shit out before the police and the DEA start crackin' down on a nigga. They hit these kids from Fort Greene for like four ki's last week." He shakes his head. "Yo, I ain't gotta tell *you* shit, hopps; that's a hun'nit fuckin' Gs, *and* some! You know?"

I nod. "Yeah, niggas is actin' up in D.C., too."

Ted nods back. "Yup. It's that jealousy and greed, man. Word. I mean, it don't matter how cool you is in'nis ma-fuckin' biz'ness, G, niggas is always out t' take you under."

Steve nods *his* head. "That's just what I was tellin' B earlier."

Everybody looks at Steve as if he wasn't supposed to say nothing. And I think he gets the message: shut the fuck up while we're talking business.

"Anyway, man, when you think we be able t' get this shit back on?" I ask Ted.

He sighs and runs his hands through his New York-style Afro. "Man, I can't call it. The way things been goin', I might fuck around and be dead or in jail next time you come up here. You know what I'm sayin', G?" He laughs as if it's a joke. But I'm not laughing at that shit. That shit sounds *serious!*

He says, "Yo, hook back up wit' Bink. Bink got some connections down in Virginia now."

"Yeah, he tol' me."

"Oh, word?" Ted hunches his shoulders. "Well, that's all I can tell you right now, man."

He shakes my hand. And ain't no sense in me hanging around if these niggas are in war mode. I mean, you should see this damn crib! It's like eight dudes sitting around loading up guns and shit in the dining room and in the kitchen. Me, Ted and Steve are out here in the living room. And it looks like they moved most of the furniture out already.

I look in Ted's eyes. "Aw'ight then, man, I'll see you when I see you."

"A'ight den, G."

Me and Steve head back outside, past this nigga Pete and around the corner to the car. Steve hops in and sits quiet until we cross the Brooklyn Bridge into Manhattan.

"Yo, you'n?" He shakes his head. "I ain't never goin' back to that muthafucka, G. Fuck them New York niggas. Them niggas is crazy. Dude wit' da gun reminded me of Shank, Joe! So you can take Shank back up there. Fuck that! My New York trips is retired!"

"You crazy as hell, Joe!" I shout back at him. "I'm only usin' Shank for strickly killin' niggas. 'Cause if that would've been Shank up there wit' me ... man ... we prob'bly would've been dead. For real! 'Cause Shank prob'bly wouldn't have went for that give-up-ya-gun shit."

* * *

"So what'chu think you would'a did in'nat situation, Shank?"

It's two days later. Me and Shank are sitting inside my 3000 waiting for Bink out on Martin Luther King Avenue and Portland Street in Southeast D.C.

Shank laughs. "Yo, man, niggas can tell if you scared. Steve was prob'bly 'bout t' shit on himself. But it ain't nothin' you can do if a nigga got his gun out before you, but die. Especially if this guy was as serious as y'all say he was."

I nod my head. "Yeah, he was serious, aw'ight."

Bink heads back over to the car after talking to his crew.

"Yo, is that Mighty?" Shank asks him.

"Yeah."

Shank nods. "Yo, let me get out and fuck wit' dat nigga."

Him and Bink trade seats in the passenger side of my car.

"B, ride aroun'nis corna so I can see if this girl is out here," Bink says.

"Aw'ight, let me tell Shank." I holler over to Shank. He's out here slap-boxing with Bink's boy Mighty.

"Yo, Shank!" I wait for him to look over to me. "We be right back, man!"

"Aw'ight, nigga, I ain't'cha bitch! Do what you gotta do!"

I smile and get back in the car. "Yo, that boy Shank be lunchin', man. But I feel safe as hell wit' dat nigga. An'- nat boy still a teenager."

"Boy got heart," Bink says point-blank.

We ride back down MLK Ave and make a left into these light-brown-colored apartment buildings. Southeast has like, a million apartment buildings. So I guess Bink is right; this shit *is* like New York.

This young, tan-skinned girl runs over to the car after noticing Bink in his blue velvet hat and gold-framed, lensless glasses. He just wears them joints for sport.

"Is your sista in'na house?" he asks her.

"Yeah, she in'nere," the young girl tells him.

"Well, tell her Bink out here t' see her."

"So what's been up, man?" I ask him, watching the girl run to her building.

Bink looks me over. "You, shawdy. You da man. You been gettin' popular as shit the last couple of months. Niggas been talkin' 'bout you all the way out in Howard County."

I smile. "Stop playin', you'n."

"Psych, naw. But for real though, you gettin' too big too fast, man. And as friend to a friend, brother, once a nigga gets too big, it ain't nowhere he can go but back down. 'Cause you know why; this still the white man's land. Now go ask Rayful Edmonds."

"Damn, I ain't heard nobody mention his name in a while."

"Yeah, Rayful Edmonds was the man in D.C. And soon as that nigga went down and got locked up in like, eighty-nine, a million, zillion ma-fuckas wanted to take over. It ain't been no peace in D.C. since."

"Yeah, but my game ain't *nowhere* near his! *Nobody's* shit is!"

Bink smiles at me. "It's ninety-three, baby. It don't matter no more. If you doin' anything, people wanna know about it. And most of these young'uns act like they done lost their damn minds."

"So what'chu try'na tell me? You ain't gon' hook me up wit' dat Virginia deal?"

He smiles again, teasing me and shit. "Me and my boy Dave was back Georgetown wit' some weed last weekend—right? We had like three ounces. Sold it all to them white boys up there and came back with like, eight hundred dollars.

"Now, of course, wit' blow, you can flip more money faster. But right now, weed is the hip thing to do."

"So you tellin' me t' hook up with some weed?"

"Naw, I ain't tellin' you *shit*. I'm jus' suggestin'. 'Cause see, with all the crazy shit goin' on with the blow and all these young'uns runnin' 'round shootin' up each other, and then them damn jump-out boys arrestin' ma-fuckas; shit is a lot safer right now if you sell weed, you know?"

"Yeah, I hear you."

This older, tan-skinned girl comes out of the house wearing an all-orange body suit, big earrings, high curls and gold shoes.

"Damn, man! That girl looks like she can glow in'na dark."

Bink laughs. "She does."

"Hey, shaw', you still takin' me to the movies one of these days?" She's leaning into the open window on the passenger side. And I'm watching the nice-sized titties and the big ass on this girl. I guess now Bink gon' mess around and make me want some pussy tonight. Maybe I can give Latrell a call. She been calling me up complaining about me being too busy to fuck with her anymore.

"Ay? Ay? Ay, boy?"

"Who you talkin' to?" I respond. I was daydreaming about some ass out the opposite window while this girl was calling me, trying to get my attention.

"Ain't'cha name Butterman, shaw'?" She has gum in her mouth. She's chewing it like she really wants something else to munch on. And if Bink don't get this girl in check, she might end up being with me tonight.

"Yeah, that's what they call me."

She looks me over and smiles. "Well, damn, shawdy, you sure look as good as they say you do."

"You never saw me before?"

"Not up close."

"Hey, hey, hey? What da fuck is this? I didn't call you out here t' fuck wit' him," Bink says. But Bink so damn cool you can never really tell if he's serious or if he's joking.

Somebody calls her and she jerks her head back out of the passenger side window. "HUNH?" She looks back to Bink. "I be right back, aw'ight?" Then she looks to me. "And don't let your friend go nowhere." She winks her right eye at me before she runs off.

"Yo, is she down or what?" I ask Bink as soon as she leaves.

"Yeah, she'll let you fuck her."

I chuckle. "Damn. You make it sound like you'on give a fuck."

"Yeah, I mean, I had that ass already. She ain't my main girl, so I don't deal wit' her er'ryday. She's the type that *will* fuck another nigga. All my number-one girls just want *my* dick."

We smile at each other and laugh.

"Yeah, that's how it should be."

Bink nods. "Always."

Man, don't ask me exactly how this shit happened, but Shank is in the back seat and this girl dressed in the orange and gold named Eva is coming with me "Wherever you wanna take me."

"Super Trak, Shank?"

"Naw. Howard."

I smile. I guess now Shank wants some ass tonight too.

I drop him off at McDonald's on Georgia Ave. It's eleven-thirty-four, Thursday night.

"And Shank, remember I'm 'bout to get that beeper for you. Aw'ight?"

"Yeah." Shank walks off toward them Howard University apartments.

Eva says, "I 'member he use ta go t' Anacostia. People ain't fuck wit' him, shaw'."

I laugh. "He was a raw-ass nigga, hunh?"

"Umm, not really. It just seemed like you didn't mess with him."

"So where you wanna go?" I ask her. I don't know why though. I already know I want some ass from this girl. She's phat to death! For real!

"Let's go to De Unique's, out in Maryland. I heard Junk Yard *and* N.E. Groovers s'posed t' be out dat joint tonight, shaw'."

Yeah, I can see now. I don't know if this girl is lying or not, but she wants me to show her off. But I'm not trying to go out like that.

"Yo, let's not go to no club, 'cause I'm too tired for that shit."

She looks at me with big, playful brown eyes. "Well, what then?"

"Let's like, go to a hotel and chill. Go get some weed and somethin' t' drink and—"

"Unt-unh! I don't believe you think you jus' gon' turn me out like that, shaw'! I mean, I ain't no one-day, late-night ho! You musta bumped ya damn head somewhere!"

My pager goes off while she's running her mouth about not trying to give me no ass. This number called my pager like five damn times already. I don't know who it is, but anything is better than hearing this whore kicking this fake-ass game to me. I mean, I already know she's a whore. Why should she want me to treat her differently?

I pull my 3000 over and park, further up Georgia Ave. "Yo, I'm gon' call back this number. I'll be back."

Fuck that shit! Either this girl gon' gi'me some pussy, or I'm takin' her ass back home.

I jump on the pay phone and dial this number.

"Yo, it's B."

"MUTHAFUCKA, y'all killed my cousin, you'n! Ya ass is dead, nigga! Two t' ya fuckin' head!"

"Yo, stop playin, you'n. Who da fuck is this?"

"Ask ya boy Rudy! *All* y'all ma-fuckas is dead!"

Joe slams the phone on my ear. *Aw, shit! Are these niggas trippin' or what?*

I walk back to the car thinking about Rudy. I hope that nigga ain't did nothing stupid. Damn, I hope he ain't do no dumb shit!

"Yo, I got some runs t' make," I tell this girl Eva.

"Why, your girlfriend jus' paged'ju?"

I look at her sternly. "Yo, look, do you wanna get a taxi home, 'cause I ain't got time for this."

"WHAT? Oh you'n, you mus' really think you like dat or somethin'! Y'all light-skinned muthafuckas always be trippin' like dat, Joe! You gon' drive me the FUCK *back* home jus' like you picked me up!"

"BITCH! I'll throw you the FUCK *out* on the highway if you talkin'nat trash! Now shut da fuck up! Aw'ight?"

I can feel blood rushing to my face while I think about this nigga Rudy. I mess around and almost hit a car in front of me. But at least this damn girl shut her damn mouth! I guess she can see that I'm not in the mood to be played with right now.

A taxi lets two girls out back down around Howard. I swerve right in back of it.

Eva looks at me like I'm crazy. "What'chu doin'?"

I hop out with my keys. "Come on!"

"Come on, where?"

"Look, jus' get da hell out'a my car and get in'na taxi."

She gets in slowly. I give her twenty dollars.

"What I do t' you, shaw'? Why you treatin' me all like dis?"

She's trying to look all innocent now. And I guess I did go crazy. I mean, I even called her a bitch. But niggas are fucking with me right now. And I have to find this boy Rudy. TONIGHT!

"Look, umm, I jus' got a stressful phone call and my nerves are screwed up right now."

Her eyes get big with interest. "One of ya boys jus' got shot?"

"Look, I'll talk to you about it later. Aw'ight?"

"Aw'ight, man, but calm ya'self down, shaw'. Damn!"

I shut the taxi door. I still might be able to bang her. But not right now.

I run back to my car and head for Steve's crib around Fourth and W, in back of Howard.

I hop out and say "Hi" to a few of these young'uns, but I ain't in the mood for no small talk. Steve is standing over by this small gate in front of his three-story project crib. He's talking to another ragged-ass-looking girl. I'm glad I didn't have to grow up in this type of shit. I see why these niggas are hopeless.

"Yo, Steve, come here, man."

I can tell he's high. Boy got that dazed look in his eyes.

He says, "What'chu doin' back in my neck'a da woods, Joe? You ain't got no ho for the night? I'm tryin'na get mine now."

Kill that damn noise, nigga! "Yo, man, what's up wit' Rudy?"

"Hunh? Why you askin' me? I ain't Rudy's keepa."

"Ay, man, don't fuck wit' me, you'n. Has Rudy been talkin' crazy shit lately?"

"Like what?"

"Like about killin' niggas."

Steve shakes his head and leans to the side. He's wearing that yellow hoodie again with a blue Dodgers baseball cap. "Naw, man. Not that I know of. But I ain't seen that nigga since last week."

He leans some more, smiling like a drug fiend. "Yo, matter fact, the last time I seen'nem, ya college boy gave him a ride an' shit."

AW, NAW! I'm thinking. "You talkin' 'bout Wes? Wes gave him a ride home?"

"Naw, 'cause they was headin' back Northeast somewhere."

"Northeast? For what?"

"How da hell I know? I was doin' my *own* damn thing."

"Aw'ight. Fuck it!"

I run back to my car hearing that ragged-ass girl he's with talking about me: "What the hell is his problem?"

Fuck her! I don't have time for that shit. I'm gon' gather up all my information before I step to Rudy. I mean, some nigga gon' beep me up and tell me I'm about to take two to the head! Aw, fuck that shit! IT'S ON!

I beat on Wes' door. "Yo, Wes! Y-O-O-O!"

He opens the door squinting his eyes and wearing a paisley-colored bathrobe. I walk in and stand in front of him. Fuck sitting down! This shit is serious!

He turns a lamp light on. "This couldn't wait until the morning?"

I just stare at him. "Yo, man, what's up wit'chu and Rudy?"

"What do you mean?"

"I mean, I thought I tol' you t' stay away from them dumb-ass niggas, man."

"I haven't been around them."

"Oh, so you tellin' me dat Rudy wasn't ridin' in ya car last week, right?"

He looks at me like he's amazed that I know anything.

"No. I didn't say that."

"So what'chu sayin' t' me, Wes?"

NeNe walks out from his bedroom wearing a blue ter- rycloth bathrobe. I guess they were in here mashin' off.

She smiles at me. "I thought that was you." She walks over to hug me, but I hold her away at arms length.

"Yo, come on now. I ain't in the mood."

"What's wrong?"

"Nothin'. Me and Wes is talkin'."

I wait for NeNe to head back to the bedroom, but she just stands here in front of me like a zombie. I shake my head impatiently. "Ay, NeNe, can we get some privacy out here? Damn!"

She looks to Wes. He nods his head. Then she looks back to me.

"Aw'ight then."

I look back to Wes.

"So what's all this about?" he asks me.

"I'm askin'na fuckin' questions here, nigga! Now why was you drivin' Rudy back Northeast?"

"He asked me to drop him off at his cousin's house."

"Where at?"

"Edgewood Terrace Apartments. I was heading home anyway, and that's not that far from me. So I simply dropped him off and kept going."

"But how did'ju hook up wit'im in the first damn place?"

"I blew my horn at him on Fourteenth Street."

"Fuck was you doin' on Fourteenth Street?"

Wes goes silent. Then he says, "I was just up there coming from my friend's house."

I look back to the bedroom thinking about NeNe. This nigga Wes is out here banging other girls on her. He must think I'm stupid. But I ain't even gon' comment on that right now. I can use that shit against him later.

I frown at him. "I can't believe this shit, man!" *Damn, this nigga's hard-headed!* "I don't give a fuck if Rudy's cousin lived at the corner! I told'ju t' stay away from them niggas!"

"What the hell? They're human just like us! I can give him a ride!"

"Yeah, and you can end up dyin' that same day jus' for bein' seen wit'im."

Wes looks away from me and doesn't say anything. I guess he knows that I'm right. And I hate to come down on him like this. But I ain't done yet! I got more questions to ask.

"Yo, was Rudy talkin' 'bout killin' niggas t' you?"

"No."

"Did he talk about anything while y'all was ridin'?"

"Like what?"

"Don't bullshit me, man!"

"What? I mean, what's going on?"

"Look, man, did he talk t' you about some shit or what?"

Wes looks me in my eyes and takes a deep breath. "He was talking about money."

"Money? Like how?"

"You know, since you've been dealing in Maryland and all, he kind of felt that you were cutting him short."

I frown at him, wanting more information. Quick! "And?"

Wes looks at me confused. "What?"

I lose it! "What da fuck he say he was gon' do about it, man? Dis ain't no damn game!"

"Well, what happened?"

"Ain't shit happen, *yet!* Now what did he say?"

Wes looks away again.

This muthafucka's stallin'! I can't believe this nigga! I mean, I put him down wit' dis shit, not fuckin' Rudy! "Ay, man, if you don't tell me what da hell is goin' on, then I'm jus' gon' assume that you down wit' dis nigga, Joe. Now tell me what he said he was gon' do."

"Are you threatening me?" Wes looks me in my eyes.

I stare right back at him. "I might have t' kill you if it comes t' dat."

He doesn't budge. And I ain't planning on budging either.

Wes opens his mouth. "He said he was gon' start running with his cousins."

I nod my head, feeling more relaxed about the shit. Now I know what time it is. *Fuck Rudy!*

"Thank you, man. That's all I needed t' know."

I go straight to business over a pay phone. "Yo, Tee, you still got that guns-and-ammo stock?"

"Man, you know it. Guns is hotter than July right about now, Joe. But what's been up wit'chu, B?"

"You'n, I got problems. And I need some guns and ammo t' solve 'em."

Tee laughs. I ain't been out in Maryland with him in Oxon Hill for months. But now is the time. This nigga got all kinds of guns. And I'm about to ante up and hire some new recruits, some more killers like Shank.

"Niggas is actin' up back there, hunh?" Tee asks me.

"Yeah, man. But I'll call you up t' come out there tomorrow mornin'."

"Cool. What'chu need?"

"All semi-automatics. No Uzis or nothin', 'cause I don't want no bystanders shot up, you know?"

"Yeah, I hear you. I just got two nine-double-m Glocks last week. How 'bout them?"

"Yeah, that shit'll work. And you got any small, powerful shit that I can keep inside my belt?"

"Yup. A nickel-plated .32. But yo, when you come up here, man, I got all kinds of pieces. I'll let'chu check shit out tomorrow."

"Aw'ight, you'n. I'll hit'chu back t'mar."

I hang up the pay phone and walk back to my car out here on Riggs Road in Northeast.

A black Corvette with tinted windows rolls up past me before I can get inside my 3000. Damn, my heart-rate is increasing for anything now! And yo, this ain't no good feeling. So I figure it's better to get whoever these niggas are before they make a move on me. And Rudy? Man, fuck him. I don't know what he done got me into. Boy don't know his face from his ass.

I get back to my Silver Spring apartment and chill. I don't feel like listening to my messages and shit. I'll just call my girl tomorrow. She'll be coming home soon. School season is almost over for college. Maybe it's best to settle all this drama before she gets here. Matter fact, I know it's best.

I watch my ceiling fan twirl around and around and around from my bed. I'm remembering the good old days: girls, house parties, the go-gos, fist fights and more girls. We had shit going on! We had much back, and much fun. But niggas are crazier now. I'm gon' have to act crazier too, just to stay on top of things.

Damn, Red! Where you at, nigga? I know you in jail, but I need ya tough ass right about now.

Damn! I'm laying here lunchin'. I guess all I really got

right now is Shank and my money. But I know more nig-gas that will kill for some ducats. I'll get them to take care of business, then I'll just continue to lay low. I mean, fuck it, I got money in the bank anyway; damn near eighty thousand dollars. I got another forty thousand right here under my bed.

Yeah, getting with that boy Wes was genius shit. But he's starting to mess up. Maybe this game is more than he can take. That boy acting like he don't know how to control himself now. Nigga fucking around. He lying. He hanging out with stupid-ass runners. Damn . . . I feel like I did him wrong. But fuck it! He'll get it together. But he gonna have to learn to think a lot faster if he gon' run around out here in the streets. Because the street is a whole different classroom. For real!

CHAPTER 9

Shank

They keep showing this Waco, Texas, story again and again on the news today. Motherfucking FBI burned down their religious complex, with that crazy-ass David Koresh and all his followers still inside of it. White men are crazy! That's just like that Jim Jones shit years ago when he had all them holy niggas commit suicide. Then you got Charles Manson. And that crazy-ass white cannibal nigga Jeffrey Dahmer. I mean, I ain't never heard of no black people eating niggas. You know what I'm saying?

They caught this black dude wearing a baseball cap who's been riding around shooting people in Mt. Pleasant in D.C. That nigga's out of his mind! They've had his ass on that D.C. Crime Solver shit since March. Something wrong with you'n to just ride around and shoot people just for walking. I'd never do no dumb shit like that. I mean, for what?

Butterman went out and bought me a damn beeper with a six-number memory, the time and all this other stuff on it, special codes and call waiting. I don't really like the idea of him being able to track me down all day. I never was into these beepers. A nigga will see me when he sees me. I don't want motherfuckers paging me up all day. That shit would drive me crazy. But I gave my pager number to Carlette though. That's my baby! Every nigga needs a girl like her. She sweet as hell . . . Well, hell ain't really sweet, but you know what the hell I mean.

Anyway, I'm wearing all green today: green Calvin jeans, a green Champion hoodie and green Nike Airs. I like these light, track-type shoes—in case you have to jet out. Especially now, because the beef is on with these Northeast niggas. And dumb-ass Butterman went out and got two criminals. Both of these niggas are older than me. They both been in and out of jail.

These niggas are stupid if you ask me. They talk like it ain't shit to go to jail. Fuck that! I ain't looking forward to going to no Lorton. Then again, you never know.

It's after three o'clock, and all these young'uns are jumping on the E2 bus. I'm heading over to my boy Anton's house up Kennedy Street Northwest. You'n owe me two hundred dollars! And it ain't like I need the money—I got many ducats now—but I'm saying, this motherfucker asked to *borrow* it. And I think I want my shit back now.

"Aw, you'n, he ain't got da heart to shoot dat nigga. I'd bust dat ma-fucka if it was me, you'n," this young'un is saying. Motherfucker looks like a little brown half-pint nigga. Hell is he talking about? I mean, these little niggas love to come to the back of the bus and talk that shit.

"I know, Joe! That nigga be ackin' like he all like dat an' shit. That's why Tyrone was 'bout ta fuck you'n up last week," this bigger nigga says. He look like he don't even belong in no high school. He got a full-ass beard. Joe probably got left back three times.

"Tyrone can't fight, you'n! He a punk!" a girl says. And I bet *she* can't beat that nigga. She's talking shit. Matter fact, I think I'm gonna fuck with her. She a cute and tall, smooth-faced girl. She looks like my cousin Lisa in East Orange, New Jersey.

"Yo, can you beat you'n?" I ask her with a grin.

She looks at me like she's startled—like I just turned her light on in the dark or something. I mean, why all these young'uns act startled when somebody says something to them? I guess they must be used to being ignored and shit, you know? That's why them motherfuckers are always talking loud and saying nothing. I guess they just wanna be heard.

She smiles and looks away from me. "I'll beat his ass, Joe." She looks into her lap when she says it. You know how kids look when their parents ask them why they did some stupid shit? Yeah, well, she got that look. But her little high-school friends bust out laughing.

"Shit, Tyrone'a beat dat ass, girl. You can't beat you'n," the big dude says to her. He's laughing like hell.

"Yo, how old are you?" I ask him. I look him straight in his eyes. But he don't look straight in mine. He glances at me and looks back and forth to his hands, his lap and to his friends. Everybody's quiet now.

He says, "Eighteen."

These young'uns start lunchin' again, laughing like shit and jonin' on him.

"That nigga like twen'y, you'n, still in high school," the half-pint nigga says.

Big dude jokes back. "Shut da hell up, you'n! That's why my grades are betta den ya shit. Ya ass ain't gon' graduate."

"Who ain't gon' graduate, Joe? You crazy like shit, you'n. I'm passin' all my classes."

All these high-school young'uns are getting louder and louder, just like they used to do on the buses from Anacostia. But niggas ain't never say nothing to me. I don't feel like hearing all this shit on the bus today either. I mean, I'm an *elder* to these young motherfuckers now!

"Yo, y'all gon' have ta cut all this loud shit out. I know y'all ma-fuckas got manners. I'on feel like hearin' all this shit."

A couple of them snicker. But most of them shut the fuck up. You can almost hear a pin drop in here. I didn't know it would work *this* damn good!

My stop comes up and I get up to get off. These young'uns are talking again, but not half as loud as they were before. But this is when little motherfuckers start talking bolder.

I turn around and face these young niggas. "Yo, anybody wanna jone' on me when I get off can do that shit right now so I can shoot 'em." I smile when I say it. But these niggas get the point. I know they still gon' talk trash, but at least they'll wait a couple of stops before they do it now. That's just how it is. Niggas always gon' talk shit. Always did. Always will.

My boy Ant is chilling on the corner with these Kennedy Street niggas I know from Emery Park. I met most of these niggas while hanging out with Steve and Rudy. And fuck Otis and Pervis! I ain't never hang with them punks. Hanging with niggas like them will mess your rep up and have *bammas* thinking they can carry you.

"Y-o-o-o, Shank," Ant says with his right fist raised in the air.

I nod to him while I cross the street. He's wearing a blue Boss sweatshirt and black jeans with light brown

Timberland boots. It's getting a little hot for them damn boots. It's almost May. But you know how niggas love their Timberlands.

I walk up and shake a couple of hands in front of all these Asian-owned stores.

"Yo, I heard ya boy Butterman is on the list," this stocky nigga named Cap says to me. He's all smiling and shit, like it's a fucking joke. He's wearing that all-black gear with one of those nylon jackets that has the zipper on the left sleeve. Nigga needs to buy *the real*, some leather, like I got. But it's too damn hot out here for leather though.

"Am I on the list too?" I ask him.

He looks down and around and smiles. But he don't look straight at me. He's doing the same type shit that them little high-school niggas do.

"Man, ain't nobody try'na hit you. Niggas know what time it is wit' da Shank."

Yeah, get off my dick, nigga. I think this motherfucker knows something, too.

"So where you hear this shit from, Cap?"

He looks at me and smiles. "Hunh? Oh, I mean, I jus' heard, man."

He's doing that sucker shit now, trying to squirm his way out of answering my questions. Punk-ass nigga should have never opened his mouth. But that's what happens to sucker-type niggas when they talk that nonsense to the wrong motherfucker. And I'm the wrong motherfucker to talk shit to. Believe that!

"Heard it from where, man?" I slip my hands inside my hoodie pocket. My .38 is inside my belt. These niggas are getting nervous now. Even Ant.

"It's jus' been out in'na streets, you'n, that he got shit on with some Northeast niggas; that's all I'm sayin', man."

I back up against the wall so I can see all these niggas—and anybody else who might come up from the
back or from the sides. I slide my left foot up against the
wall and look to Ant. You'n ain't really saying too much.
I guess he ain't got my fucking money, hunh?

I ask him, "Yo, you got anything for me, Ant?"

He nods his head and reaches into his back pocket. "I
only got seventy-five t'day, but I'll have the rest by da
end of this week."

I take the bills and look back to Cap. But I'm still talking to Ant. "So what's been on the street about shit up
around here, Ant?"

Ant looks to Cap. He looks back to me and shakes his
head. "Ma-fuckas jus' sayin' that Butterman's time is
up."

I nod. "Oh yeah? Why it's like dat, Ant? Why my
nigga time up?" I don't really like Butterman all like that,
but I'm just trying to see what people are saying about
him.

Ant opens his palms toward me. "You got me, man.
Niggas is jus' jealous."

I look back to Cap. "Is that what'chu heard, Cap? Niggas are jus' jealous? Or did you hear some other shit?"

Cap looks to his boys. They're all surrounding me, but
I'll shoot all these motherfuckers right here. And you
know how it gets; nobody wants to be the first to die.

Cap says, "Man, you ackin' like we tryin' t' cut'chall
short, you'n. I ain't got nothin' against Butterman."

"Didn't you used t' sell up on Georgia Ave?"

"Yeah, but—"

I cut his ass off, like I'm a detective. "Didn't Rudy and
them take ya shit over?"

Cap looks to his tall boy wearing one of those lumber-
jack-looking shirts. Dude a tall, light-skinned nigga with
light brown hair. His hair is high like Butterman's, and

he got a temple-tape too. But he don't look shit like Butter-man. You'n got scratches all up and down his face like he got his ass kicked a lot.

He says, "Yo, it ain't even about that up here, man. We doin' our own thing around here."

One of their other boys makes a sale in the alleyway to a skinny brown woman about thirty-five. She's shaking like she's fiending.

I don't say nothing to tall dude. He's probably their main man. If I carry him, I'm probably gon' have to start shooting. But I still have to let him see where I'm coming from.

"Yeah, dat's cool. But what I'm sayin' is that it would look like punk shit if I jus' let ya man talk about my boy like it's nothin'. I mean, what would you say if a ma-fucka said *ya* boy was on a hit list?"

He nods his head. "Yeah, I know what'chu sayin', youn. I got'chu."

Now everything is settled. But I still got my hands in-side my hoodie pocket. I'm probably gon' have to hang around a little longer than I planned. You know, you gots to chill until everything is definitely cool and it ain't no misunderstandings.

"You got a cigarette, Ant?"

Ant pulls out a pack of Newports and gives me one. He lights it with a lighter from his back pocket. I don't even smoke cigarettes that much, but I figure this is the quickest way to cool everything out with these niggas.

"So what's been up with that li'l young'un wit' da fat ass you was talkin' to, shawdy?" I ask one of their young'uns. He's a cool-looking brown nigga with curly-ass hair. Bitches probably sweat him. He reminds me of Bink—my nigga.

He smiles. "Oh, I got that ass jus' last night, you'n. She fucked around and was a virgin like shit."

Ant says, "You bust 'er out, hunh young'un?"

"Fuckin' right."

"How old is she?" I ask him. I take my third drag and hold it.

"Fourteen."

God damn! My little sister's about to get up there in age, an' shit. Maybe I need to call her up and see how she's doin'. Young'uns might be tuggin' at her little panties already, little cool niggas like shorty. Then I'm gonna have ta pistol-whip a muthafucka.

"She was bleedin' an' er'rything, and shit, you'n." Shorty shakes his head. "Whew, she had me scared like shit."

We all start laughing.

Big, light-skinned dude says, "Yeah, that's what happens when you bus' out virgins, nigga. *You* musta been a virgin too, an' shit."

Shorty sucks his teeth. "Fuck out'a hea, you'n! Bitches know my name!"

A white 300 ZX pulls up with tinted windows and parks. Everybody's watching this Z for cover. And motherfucking Rudy jumps out.

"Ay, Shank, I been lookin' for you, man. Let's take a ride."

He don't say shit to nobody else. He's treating these niggas like they're nobodys.

"What's up, Rudy? When you get dis?" Ant says, walking over to hop on Rudy's dick.

Rudy frowns at him. "Come on, you'n, don't sweat it." He looks back to me. "Come on, Shank."

I pluck away the cigarette bud and hop in on the passenger side.

Rudy hops in and shuts his door like it's hard to close or something. This car looks good on the outside, but everything is worn out inside. But hell, I can't complain; Rudy just got me away from them niggas.

I lay my seat back and chill. Rudy drives down Kennedy and makes a right down Fifth Street.

"So what's up, Joe? Where we goin'?"

Rudy smiles at me and makes a left on New Hampshire Avenue. "We gon' park and talk out in Takoma Park for a few."

I nod. "Talk about what?" I heard he's going for self now. And Butterman think he shot some motherfuckers. But I don't know that until *he* tells me. I mean, you know how rumors and shit get around out in the street. That's why I'm always skeptical.

We get out on this quiet-ass road in Takoma, Maryland, and park. Rudy faces me looking all excited. He says, "I got my own connections, you'n. I'm runnin' wit' my peoples now."

I'm looking at him like, *So da fuck what, nigga? What da hell you want from me, a cigar?* "Yeah, and?"

"Look, I'ma tell you how the shit is, aw'ight? Dat mafucka Butterman think he's slick, you'n. He makin' his own fuckin' money out in Maryland off them white boys, an' we ain't gettin *shit!* I mean, that's jus' how these niggas get when you runnin' for 'em, you'n. Them ma-fuckas try t' keep you broke an' stupid. But I ain't takin' no shorts out hea, Joe. I'm goin' for *my* shit!"

"Now, yo, here's the plan—right." Rudy's grinning like a damn kid. I mean, you should see this nigga! He says, "Yo, I found out where Butterman lives. And what we can do is get him after he counts his money in his car. We run up on him, right, rob him, take his fuckin' keys, shoot dat ma-fucka in his head and let him stay in'na car. Then we go to his crib and take all'la money and go in wit' my cousins.

"We got, like, fifteen niggas deep wit' my cousins and them. And we'a fuck them niggas up from back Northeast. 'Cause like, Butterman a pussy, Joe! He ain't got no heart! And them ma-fuckas from Northeast know our faces."

This nigga's all out of breath now. All I want to know is if he really shot one.

"So you popped one?"

Rudy looks me eye to eye. "Yeah, you'n. I hit two of 'em, but I only kilt one."

"Where was y'all at?"

"They caught me back on Benning Road; that's where I bought this car from. And like, at first, I was gon' jus' run, but them niggas was still in'nat Sidekick. So I waited for them ma-fuckas t' try ta make their move. Then I ran up this alleyway and two of 'em tried to chase me." He stops and shakes his head with a smile. He acts like he's proud of himself.

"I waited for 'em to get close, you'n. Then I jumped out on 'em, like, 'Bang, bang, bang, muthafuckas!' " He shows me with his hand. And this is some deep shit! That's the same thing I wrote in my rhyme! I still ain't killed nobody yet, for real. I guess Rudy got one up on me now.

"I got dat first nigga in his chest. But dat second nigga tried to run back. I think I hit him in his leg. But after that, I hopped over like, three-ass fences and ran like shit until I got to the Metro."

"What'chu do wit' da gun?"

His eyebrows raise. "Man, I threw dat shit in'na sewer and kept goin'. Fuck a gun! I can get another gun wit' no problem. I got me a Glock right now." He reaches under his seat and pulls out this big, black 9 millimeter. "Yeah, boy, I'm goin' for mine. Fuck Butterman!"

I wanna ask this motherfucker how it felt when he killed somebody. I ain't feeling too good about hearing it, believe or not. I guess that preaching shit that Carlette been doing is rubbing the hell off on me.

"So what's up, man?" Rudy asks me. He puts his Glock back under his seat. "All you gotta do, you'n, is act like you still cool wit' him. And then we can set 'im up."

How I know you ain't gon' set me up, too, you crazy-ass muthafucka?

This shit is fucked up, man! This ain't no rap song either. This is real!

I nod my head as if I'm down with him. "But yo, what'chu gotta do though is stay away from Butterman and us for a while. He on alert right now 'cause them niggas beeped him and said they was gon' kill all of us. And even them young'uns up on Kennedy Street know.

"So what'chu do, right, is give me time enough t' figa shit out. Then, like, gi'me ya beeper number and I'll call you up on it. But we gotta wait until shit cools down, 'cause that plan ain't gon' work until Butterman think he's safe again."

Rudy smiles and nods back to me. I guess he's going for that game I just told him. I don't like Butterman all that much, but I'd rather roll with him until I can see exactly what I'm gon' do. It looks like I got myself right in the thick of this crew shit. This the same damn reason why I never hung out with niggas. I mean, I ain't really down to die or go to jail for nobody but my family in Jersey. But now it seems like I might have to kill or be killed.

Rudy reaches out to shake my hand. "Gangsta chronicles, you'n. That shit sounds *on*."

I'm fucked up now. I might as well do the shit I've been thinking about doing lately, before everything falls down on my head . . . I'm gon' rob me a fucking white man. Tonight! Just for the hell of it. You know, so I can say that I did the shit before I die.

I'm riding a 90 bus into Adams Morgan. A lot of white people live around here. It's easier to rob a white mother-fucker up here than it is in Georgetown. Once you're in Georgetown it's hard to get the hell out of there. Your ass would have to run like fifteen blocks before you could get out. But in Adams Morgan you can slip around and run through these Hispanic areas until you get back to Fourteenth Street. Once you get back to Fourteenth Street you can chill. Cops ain't gon' chase you as much around the black neighborhoods.

I get off the bus on Eighteenth Street and walk up and down these long-ass hills. I robbed niggas before, so it ain't no thing. I just have to check out my surroundings first.

I walk up a street that has less apartment buildings and more houses. I don't like them tall apartment build-ings; people can look out the windows and call the cops on you. They'll have your clothing description and everything. But I'm set to outsmart their asses. I got a yel-low Champion shirt under my dark green hoodie. I went home and threw my black Timberlands on and switched guns. So after these motherfuckers see the dark colors, I'm gon' change to light and throw this cheap-ass black baseball hat I got on in the trash somewhere.

A middle-aged white man wearing a red sweater is about to get in his car. It's a shiny black Jetta, looking brand-spanking-new.

I slip my dark shades on with my hood. I run up on him and hold my .45 to his head. You have to do it quick before they get a chance to act brave.

"Be cool and get'cha wallet out if you love ya kids."

He does the shit calmly. "I don't have much money."

I snatch his wallet out of his hands and find seventy dollars and all kinds of credit cards and shit. Fuck that!

I throw his wallet to the ground after taking the seventy fucking dollars. *This ain't shit!* I'm thinking.

"That's all I have," he tells me. I didn't even ask him. I guess he read my mad face.

I slug his pink ass with the butt of my gun, right to his jaw. *Please let me knock dis muthafucka out! 'Cause if I don't, I'm gon' end his life for seventy fuckin' dollars!*

The nigga falls and doesn't budge. WHEW! I'm out of here!

I do a cool-ass jog. I have to make myself look normal. But my heart is pumping like a motherfucker.

I throw my extra clothes and hat in a trash can up on Seventeenth Street.

Damn! Here comes a H2 bus on Mt. Pleasant. I jump on, pay my dollar and sit in the middle to look normal. I usually would sit in the back, but that's the first place a cop would go to find a nigga.

I ride the H2 to Georgia Avenue and get off. I run to catch a 70 bus and ride it down to Rhode Island. I jump off at Seventh Street and run across to catch a G bus. I'm hoping this shit hurries the fuck up! Motherfuckers ain't too cool with me around here. This where I robbed them New Jacks for seven hundred.

I jog down to Third and Rhode Island with my heart pumping fast before a G4 bus catches up to me. I ride it over to the Northeast side, get off and relax a bit.

Whew! Shit! Why da fuck am I so nervous about robbin' one white ma-fucka? Them white niggas rob us all the damn time, with rent and taxes and fucking hospital bills and services. But not for a cheap-ass seventy fucking dollars! This shit is stupid!

I get back to the crib after eleven. I turn my TV on and the damn news is on again. SHIT! They got a nigga's mug shot for robberies and rapes out in Howard County!

They say he was posing as a gas man. Howard County is the whitest place you can get! Joe in *big* trouble!

God damn! My heart is beating like I'm about to have a heart attack. This shit ain't even me. But wouldn't that be a bitch? I rob *one* white man for seventy fucking dollars and end up with the police after me!

I fall out across my couch and chill. White people don't even carry real-ass money on them. That motherfucker probably has his real-ass money in stocks and bonds and stuff like that. I heard Wes talk about Butterman putting his money in an account too. Ain't that some shit? I mean, it's cool with me, but that nigga Butterman is a trip. Maybe Rudy is right about him trying to cut us short. But I'm still getting my grand every Monday. I saved up five thousand dollars now. So what the fuck am I doing robbing a white man for seventy fucking ducats?

That's just how they get us niggas. We get like we backed up against a wall, then we break down and do stupid shit. I mean, Rudy got me in a bond now. I'm gon' either have to kill him and stay with Butterman or help kill Butterman and go up against this Northeast crew with Rudy and his cousins. Either way is no way out. Unless I get the fuck up out of here. But that's punk shit.

Damn! What da hell should I do?

I remember my cousin Cal telling me after we finished watching *Juice* at the movies in Trenton, two years ago: "You see that nigga, Bishop? That's how you get when you kill a man. It's no way back to fightin' wit'cha hands *or* your mind. You feel that rush like you can kill *anybody*, anybody that got beef."

Damn! What da hell should I do?

I call up Carlette on my new cordless phone. At least I can be with her one more night. I mean, it feels like I don't have that many left now. The walls are closing in on me.

"Hello," she answers.

"Yo, I'm glad you home."

"Why?"

" 'Cause, you get to see my house t'night."

She's smiling. I know her. Believe me. "Why now?" she asks me.

" 'Cause I don't feel like leavin' my crib."

She pauses. "I'm not even dressed."

"Get dressed and call me back."

She gets quiet. "Umm, maybe we should do this another night."

I don't really know what to say. "I need to be wit'chu t'night." *Damn! That shit sounded weak!* I'm thinking. But it's the only thing I can say besides threatening her with something stupid.

She sighs. "Okay. You live up on Rhode Island Avenue, right, on the Northeast side?"

"Yeah. It's a 7-Eleven right up around Nineteenth Street?"

She gets excited. "Yeah, I know where that's at!"

"How many minutes?"

"Prob'bly like thirty."

"Aw'ight. Hurry up then."

"Okay."

I press the OFF button and take a deep breath. If I didn't have her, I don't think I could sleep tonight.

I wait thirty minutes and walk around the corner to the 7-Eleven. Carlette's blue Toyota Tercel pulls up right as I cross the street. She opens the passenger door and I get in.

"Ride back down a half a block and make a right."

She does what I tell her and parks on my block.

"This looks real quiet," she says behind me, walking up the steps to my building.

"Yeah, it's jus' what a nigga need, some peace and quiet."

I open my door on the second floor and take my shirt off. Carlette walks in behind me and puts her black Coach pocketbook on my couch. She looks around my poster-decorated walls like it's some kind of museum. And yo, no lie, she's the first person to step foot in my crib or even know where it is, except for my family. So I guess she's really getting close to me now.

She's wearing this tan leather outfit and still looking around my living room. "This is all right!" she says while checking out my stereo system and speakers. It's placed inside of my entertainment shelf. It's all black and six feet tall with my television, stereo and a bunch of tapes and CDs on different shelves. I bet she's shocked to see a crib like this from a nigga like me. I even got some Persian-type rugs on my floors now.

I pull her close to me. "This leather smells good."

She smiles. Her hair is done up in one of those Shirley Temple do's with curls all over the top.

"Well, I got bad news," she tells me.

"What, you pregnant?"

She pulls away from me, shaking her head. "No, I am *not* pregnant! Why do you keep asking me that?"

'Cause I wish you were. Then I would know that I'd have somethin' left from me in this world when I die. But I don't have the heart to say no shit like that. Even though it's the truth.

"Well, what's wrong?" I ask her.

She walks toward my bathroom, alongside the kitchen. "It's that time of the month."

I smile. "That's cool. I ain't want no sex t'night anyway."

She starts running the sink water and peeps out the door, looking all cute and shit. "You lyin'."

"No, I ain't. I just wanted to be with you."

I walk past her and head to my bedroom. She comes in

behind me and checks out my new black dressers and my black satin-quilted bed; it's a full-size.

"God! I would have never known that you were so . . . so—"

"What, a nigga can't have a slammin'-ass apartment?" I'm smiling at her. And I'm glad this is how I'm ending this crazy-ass day.

Carlette walks back to the bathroom, closes the door and comes out wearing a blue satin teddy. She's carrying her leather outfit and her big, black Coach bag. She puts them on top of my smaller dresser in the left corner and jumps in my bed.

I lay back and let her rub on my chest. I look down at her light-ass hands, gliding across my black-ass chest. "Damn! Look how light you are," I tell her.

She giggles. "Look how *dark* you are."

I smile at her. "Our kids would prob'bly be tannish-brown or that red-brown, Indian-lookin' color."

She grins. "And would their father be able to be around them?"

I grimace. "What'chu mean by dat?"

"Would you raise them?"

"Damn right I would raise 'em!"

She chuckles and falls down against my chest. She damn near looks white on me! This shit is weird. I feel like I might get lynched for this.

"I love your skin," Carlette tells me. She's drawing circles on my stomach with her painted nails.

"Why?"

"Because it looks so deep. It shines without lotion or baby oil. And it's so smooth."

I laugh at the shit. Then she goes inside my drawers and makes my dick hard as she cradles it with her baby-soft hands.

I grab her hand out of my pants. "Yo, I thought you said it was that time of the month."

She smiles up in my face. "It is. But we can do it in the shower."

I frown at her and push her away, play-like. "You really is nasty."

She cracks the hell up. "Stop callin' me that before I start to believe it and not wanna make love to you anymore."

I lay silent. "Do you know what'chu jus' said?"

"What?"

"You said 'make love' to me."

She looks off of my chest and in the direction of my long dresser to my right. "I know."

"So you sayin' you love me? How you gon' love me an'nis the first time you even been t' my crib?"

She pauses like she has to think about it. I'm interested to hear her answer.

"I do love you. I love your honesty. I mean, even when you don't say nothin' you tell the truth."

"Hunh? What da hell dat mean?" I'm giving her a "dumb-nigger" look, but I know what she means. All real niggas tell the truth without speaking. It's the law of the strong. That's why you know which niggas are real and which niggas are fake-ass punks. But do you have to kill a man to be real?

Carlette's still drawing on my stomach. She says, "It's like, you're so serious—even when you say stuff that's funny—that no one could ever read you wrong. I mean, it's like, I know just what you're telling me. Like when you called me t'night, you needed me."

She squeezes me tightly. And I ain't got nothing to say. All I know is that she's right, and I'm glad she's here with me. Fuck being hard when you're really hurting inside. It may be punk shit to cuddle up with a girl like this to some niggas. But fuck them! *I* need this kind of attention! Maybe if my mother gave it to me I wouldn't be in this crazy shit in the first damn place.

I'm in some type of hospital. I have on light blue cotton pants and a matching short-sleeve shirt. I'm pushing some kind of cart in front of me. It looks like a food tray with wheels that they use in the hospitals. It's other people in the hallway with me, but it's not like anybody's paying me any kind of attention.

Now I'm sneaking inside of a fire escape. I open the bottom door to the outside. Sirens are going off with lights, trying to locate me. I run across some grass field and slip underneath a barbed-wire fence.

Shit! I cut my arm on the edge of the fence. They got dogs after me now. But it's like, I can hear the motherfuckers barking, but I don't see them.

I run across a highway and almost get my ass hit by an eighteen-wheeler truck. I walk inside some bar and it ain't nothing but white people in it. I look up at their television and the news is on.

OH SHIT! They got my mug shot! And they know my real name!

I run out the bar hearing police sirens, but I don't see no fucking cops. My heart is beating fast like shit, and I'm sweating now.

Somehow I'm back in Southeast on my mother's block on K Street. But nobody's out and it looks like a ghost town.

I beat on my mother's door. "MOM! Let me in! They after me!"

My mom opens the door looking all pissed off at me like she always looks. She got fucking rollers in her hair.

"Got'dammit! What'chu do now, boy?"

BOOM! BOOM! BOOM! BOOM! BOOM! BOOM!

"Open up, it's the police!"

"Oh shit, Mom! Hide me, Mom! Please! Don't let 'em get me!"

"Where, boy? I ain't got no place to hide you in'nis small-ass house."

I run to the back of the stairs and kick a hole in the wall. "Hide me in here and block off the hole with a dresser."

My mother starts to push me in the hole, but I can't fit.

BOOM! BOOM! BOOM! BOOM! BOOM! BOOM!

"We're breaking the door down, ma'am!"

My eyes are big as hell! My heart feels like it's about to jump out of my fucking chest!

"OH SHIT, MOM! HURRY DA FUCK UP!"

"WHO YOU CUSSIN' AT, BOY! I'M TRYIN', DAMMIT!"

"DARNELL! DARNELL!"

"HUNH? WHAT?"

Carlette is staring at me and shaking me around in the darkness of my room like she just saw a fucking ghost. "Are you okay?!"

"What'chu talkin' 'bout?" Damn! I know what she's talkin' about. I musta been lunchin' like shit in my sleep. And now she fucked around and caught me!

"You were shaking like you were having a seizure or something." She shakes her head, still looking shocked. "God, you scared the hell out of me."

I lean up and sink my face into my hands. I pull my knees up to my chest. *Damn! I'm fuckin' up in'na head*, I'm thinking.

Carlette hugs onto me. "Are you okay, Nell?"

I sigh. Ain't no use in acting like I'm hard now. She done messed around and caught me slipping. I guess too much has happened today for my mind to take it all.

"I'on know, girl," I tell her. "I jus' don't know."

I lay back on my bed. Carlette lays her head across my chest and starts stroking on my stomach again with her nails. All I'm thinking about is lyrics for some reason. I guess something's telling me that my rhymes are my salvation:

It was late one night. I was out, taking a walk, Joe.
A car pulled up behind me with no lights, cruising slow.
I looked to the driver, he said, "Yo, what's up, brother?"
So I thought it was cool and didn't think about ducking for
   cover.
All of a sudden I saw the 12-gauge shotgun.
And BOOM! I didn't even get a chance to run.
Then SMACK! My back hit the concrete.
Is this the end, Joe? Is my life complete?
God damn! I'm only dreaming, and my heart has a fast
   pace.
I'm having nightmares, like my man Scarface.

Wes

Professor Cobbs yanks me to attention before I can get out in Dennard Plaza to talk to the guys up at school. "So have you contacted Mark Thompson yet?" He's wearing his usual prep look with an attention-grabbing green-and-orange tie.

"Not yet, but I still have his number."

"Well, have you taken the GRE exam?"

"Yeah, and that little study guide you gave me came in handy."

He nods with a smile. "That's why I gave it to you."

I know I look anxious to catch up to my friends, but Professor Cobbs doesn't look like he's finished with me yet.

"So what do you have planned for this summer, Ray?"

he asks me with an intense look on his face. I can feel that he's going to proposition me with something.

"Work, work and more work." I'm hoping I can head him off with a busy-sounding schedule before he can zap me with some grand idea of his.

"I have this summer program—Y.B.M.C.—that I'm trying to find young, upcoming guys like yourself to take part in as counselors."

"Y.B.M.C.?"

"Young Black Men's Club."

I nod. "Oh, well—"

"And if you have any spare time, I'd love for you to participate." He shakes his head, seemingly as if he's in great pain. "We gotta do something out here to stop these young boys from killing each other."

I nod, feeling guilty as ever and halting my planned rejection. I believe I'm trapped in the thick of it now. The money and attention I've been getting lately is really hard to part with. But I've finally found the courage I need to call it quits.

"So you think you'll be interested in anything like that? We're located in Southeast."

"Southeast?"

Professor Cobbs smiles, knowingly. "If you wanna deal with this monster for real, you have to start with the most vicious head."

I smile back at him. "I guess so."

He grabs my shoulder the way older brothers do us younger brothers when they're really trying to communicate with us or convince us of doing something they deem important.

"So how 'bout it, Ray? You think you wanna help me out? You can tell a couple of friends, too, but only if they're serious. I don't want any half-steppers."

He's grinning at me while I think it over. He's still caressing my shoulder as his guarantee. I feel like he's more telling me than asking me.

"Yeah, I guess I'm in, but let me call you on it after I check my summer schedule and all."

He finally backs off of me with a smile. "Great! I knew I could count on you, Ray. We're not totally in the dark. We still have a *few* good soldiers."

He shakes my hand and heads for the down escalator to Connecticut Avenue. "Okay, Ray. I'll be talking to you."

I nod. "All right."

I head in the opposite direction toward U.D.C.'s Dennard Plaza area. As soon as I enter the yard I spot Candice talking to Marshall and Derrick on the benches to my right. Walt is to my left, talking to a brown-skinned sister in a big pair of blue jeans.

"Speak of the devil!" Marshall says to Derrick and Candice, who have their backs turned toward me.

"Hey, Wes," Candice says, facing me.

Derrick just smiles. We've made up—partly—after that rainy night when I first revealed my money sources and my car to the guys after hiding it for so long. I guess I took it harder than they meant it. They still see it as being hypocritical, even though they haven't disowned me yet. But I think I have some good news to tell them for later on.

"Yeah, it's me, the trouble-maker," I joke with a smile.

Marshall and I could pass for twins. We're both wearing our thin-rimmed school-boy glasses and colorful vests with our blue shirts, blue jeans and brown shoes. Derrick's wearing the Boyz II Men look: all denim gear with a colorful tie. And Candice shocks me with her black leather short-and-vest outfit over laced stockings, while Walt wears his typical jeans, tennis shoes, and a Polo sweatshirt.

Hell! When did I start paying so much attention to what everyone's wearing?

"So you ready ta drive me home?" Candice asks, grabbing my right arm. I guess she's showing off her affection for me in front of the guys.

I feel slightly nervous. I mean, we've slept together and all, but this is definitely going to add fire to the flame with the guys.

"Ahh, are we all hitting Marshall's house tonight?" I ask Derrick. I'm trying my best to make Candice look less obvious. Of course it's not working. The guys are eying her new affection for me like hungry vultures. And here comes Walt to throw the salt and pepper on me.

"I thought Wes wasn't ya type, Candice?" he says, smiling.

Candice laughs it off. "Uuuw, you'n, why you gon' say dat shit? You know me an' Wes always been cool like dat, Joe. Why you playin' me?"

She lets my arm go and throws love taps in Walt's direction to release some of her embarrassment.

Walt backs away from her. "Naw, naw, I ain't try'na hear that. Nigga get a car and some new gear and all of a sudden he's your type." He points at her to the other guys as he continues to back away, still grinning at her obvious embarrassment: "See how girls are t'day, you'n?"

She gives up trying to hit him and turns back to me. "Well, anyway, are you driving me home, Wes?"

I look to the guys as if they can help me out of this jam. They respond with blank stares.

Walt says, "Well, take her home, Wes. You da man now."

Candice sucks her teeth. "Nobody asked you nothin', *Walt!*"

Walt just smiles.

"Well, I'll see y'all later on. We're all going to Marshall's, right?" I ask them.

"We thinkin' 'bout goin' to the movies t'night, man," Marshall tells me quietly, as if it was some kind of secret.

"Okay, I'll go."

Derrick looks me in my eyes with no mercy. "You remember what I told you?"

He's referring to not wanting to ride in my drug-money car.

"Yeah. We can all ride with Marshall," I respond to him.

Walt frowns. "Man, look, fuck that dumb shit, you'n! I'm ridin' wit'chu, Wes. We'll jus' follow them niggas up there and listen t' ya bumpin'-ass system." He looks back to Derrick and Marshall. "Y'all some cheesy-ass niggas, man. I can't believe y'all."

Neither respond in front of Candice.

"Well, I'll see you later," I tell them.

Candice and I take the escalator down to Connecticut, cross the street, and walk around the corner to my car. A pink parking ticket is sitting inside of my window wipers.

Candice spots it and laughs. "See dat shit, Joe? That's that Sharon Pratt Kelly try'na increase her salary."

I just shake my head and take the ticket. "I bet the meter just ran the hell out, too."

Candice giggles. "They prob'bly waited for that shit, shawdy, 'cause them parkin' people get bonuses for writin' tickets."

"Yeah, I bet they do."

I drive Candice to Fourteenth and Harvard Streets North-

west, but she doesn't get out. She sits there in my passenger
seat as if I have something important to tell her.

I look into her seductive, light brown face. "Well?"

"Well, what?" she quizzes.

"You're home, right?"

"And?"

"Aren't you getting out to go in?"

She shakes her head defiantly. "Not until you tell me
where we are in this relationship."

*Oh my God! I knew this would happen. Now I'll have to tell
her the truth, just as I had to do with Sherry. But I should have
known that this would happen in the first place.*

"Well, like Walt said, I didn't know you liked me all
like that." I'm stalling to get her to loosen up her vice
grip on my neck. It actually feels like I'm having a hard
time breathing right now—even though my windows are
down and the weather is great.

Candice gives me a hurt and evil look. "Aw, don't even
play me like dat, man. You know what we did. I don't
just let anybody spend the night. And I even got up and
fixed you breakfast."

I sigh and look out my window away from her.

"So what's up, Wes? Are you gon' ask me to go with
you or not?"

"I have to think about it."

It honestly doesn't look like I can tell Candice that I
have a girlfriend the way I told Sherry. I can't lie to myself; I have more respect for Candice, I like her more, and
more importantly, I'm still kind of afraid of her social status and the whole glamorous way in which she carries
herself. She's liable to make me the talk of the school if I
diss *her.* Then she'd want to know who my girlfriend is
and the whole nine yards.

God, I've turned into such an idiot these last couple of

*months! I think it's best for me to get out of this thing. In fact,
I know it is.*

Candice looks confused. "You have to *think* about it?
Well, you should'a had all the time in the world to *think*
before you jumped into my damn bed!" She gets out and
slams the car door with her bags in hand. "Thanks for da
ride," she says slyly, with all of her sarcasm.

I take a deep breath and drive off. Candice would be a
great catch for a lot of guys. But I have better rapport
with NeNe. I mean, we've been together for only three
months, but NeNe doesn't give me half the jitters that
Candice gives me. I just feel like I'd have too much to
prove in order to keep Candice. And I'm really not up to
that kind of a challenge.

I pull over to my mother's on Bunker Hill Road and
park around the corner again. I use my key to enter and
walk straight into an unexpected trap.

"Hi, Wes."

I turn to my left to find Sybil resting against my
mother's black furniture in the living room. My heart
skips a beat before I can say anything. She still has her
hair braided, and she looks kind of good. Her brown face
has a glow of confidence. She's wearing a Kente-designed
blouse and a royal blue skirt. I guess things have been
going quite well for her.

I force myself to smile. "Well, what a surprise this is."

My mother walks in from the kitchen wearing all
green again—sweatpants and matching shirt—and
slings her left arm around my shoulder as we both face
Sybil. "Guess who I saw getting off the bus today, who I
talked into having dinner with us?"

I smile at her humor. But inside I'm hating this. I've
never told my mother about NeNe either. I've just been
living myself a double life, now, haven't I?

"How did you talk her into it?" I ask through the laughter my mother's remark has stirred between these two conscious black women. My mother has always adored Sybil.

"I begged her," my mother jokes before laughing again. "No, I just can't allow you two to break off right when you're both graduating in another week. It just doesn't seem fair."

Everything is stale for a second before my mother tries to add spice to the situation. "Well, come on over here and talk to Sybil while I finish cooking this vegetarian lasagna." She pulls me over to the couch, sits me next to Sybil, smiles at both of us and rushes back to the kitchen.

Sybil looks at me and sighs. "Well, how've you been?" I guess she wants to settle all this tension that we're both feeling as quickly as possible.

"Okay, I guess. And you?"

"I've been all right. You know, I'm still working at my job and all. They even offered me a full-time position during the summer."

I guess I've forgotten how much her employers like her. Sybil's already been helping out the black cause by filling a counselor role at a halfway house for troubled teenaged girls in Northeast.

"It looks like I'll be doing the same thing you're doing this summer with this group called Y.B.M.C," I tell her.

Her brow raises with interest. "Y.B.M.C.?"

I chuckle. "That's what I said. But no, it stands for Young Black Men's Club, and it's in Southeast."

She nods. "That's good. You know there's a cultural art and poetry club in Southeast, too, on Martin Luther King Avenue when you first cross the bridge."

"Oh yeah? What's the name of it?"

"Eight-Rock."

I nod. "Yeah, I've heard of that."

She says, "Yeah, well, I've been reading my poetry over there every now and then. You know the black arts movement is about to explode all over the place."

"Like the sixties, hunh?"

"Bigger than the sixties."

"You think so?"

"Yeah, because the time is so urgent that kids are gonna start living and dying with their art. I mean, it's the only way out for so many lost souls, Wes. It's like a bird's only feathers to fly. Art is that which does not cost money. And the artistic ones will learn to soar with their God-given talents because the white man can't take that away from them."

"Well, the white man seems to be putting a price tag on rap music and taking that away. And that's the most vital poetry that we have going right now."

"Only for the meantime, before this explosion of stage and written poetry starts to inspire the grassroots again."

I cut her off. "But the grassroots are still going to need some type of economic support. And see, back in the sixties you had organizations that gathered the money they needed to funnel into their different programs. But this generation seems to be broke."

Sybil frowns. "Yeah, we be broke, while our drug brothers be dopes, getting rich while they be selling coke, and our children be goin' up in smoke for the man, in this treacherous, treacherous red, black and blue land."

I smile. "That was good. I forgot how you can just make poetry up from anything."

Sybil looks away from me. "You forgot my phone number, too?"

Man! I can't get a break. "Where did that come from?" I ask her.

She sighs. "When I called you in *December*—" She looks at me pointedly when she says December. "—I was confused about how happy you were in the relationship. I wanted to give you time to rest and gather your thoughts because I understand that I was getting a bit serious. And—"

"But you said not to call you—"

"Until you thought things over," she says, finishing my sentence. She looks away again. "I guess you had a whole lot of thinking to do, hunh, Wes?"

She leaves me speechless except for an answered question here and an answered question there while we eat a "pre-graduation dinner" with my mother. My mother then drops Sybil off at the Brookland Metro station and drives me home. I'm feeling kind of silly about this, since I have a car now. But hell if I was going to tell her "Mom, I'll take the bus home" or something to get out of her driving me. She's always driven me home. Last time I ran out of the house before she could say anything about it. Plus, she still had company over, and I told her I was going to Marshall's house anyway.

"So, how did things go?" she asks me as we pull up in front of my building.

With my peripheral vision, I can see J sitting inside of his car to our left. There's no reason to get nervous or anything. My mother doesn't know he's here for me.

"Well, Mom, I mean, Sybil and I haven't been talking all that much lately, and—"

"Don't you both go to U.D.C. Don't you see her?"

"Not really. Most of her classes are at the other campus down near Howard now, on Eleventh Street."

My mother frowns. "And you mean to tell me that you two just—" she snaps her fingers "—broke up just like that?"

"Not really. It's a longer story. But I don't have time right now to tell it to you. I'm going out to the movies with Marshall and them tonight."

"Mmm-hmm. And does that boy Walt still hang out with you all?"

I smile. My mother always asks me about Walt. She always wonders how he ended up hanging with us instead of "out go-going some place" with his crazy self.

"Yeah, he still hangs with us, Mom," I tell her.

"Hmm. Is he gon' graduate next week?"

I smile again, knowing the type of response my mother's liable to give. "In December."

"Yeah, right."

I shake my head at her, still grinning. "Why are you so down on him, Mom? I mean, what happens to all this conscious spirit when it comes to guys like Walt? What, he doesn't have an opportunity like I do?"

My mother laughs it off. "Go on, boy. He's your friend. You know I love 'im. I jus' like talking about him a lot."

"Why? Why not talk about Marshall or Derrick? Why do people always talk about the wild seeds?"

"Because the Lord put the wild seeds on this earth to be talked about, that's why."

We smile at each other as I climb out of my mother's green Ford Pontiac.

"Hey, Mom?"

"Yeah."

"Is green your favorite color or something?"

"Who wants to know?"

We share another laugh as I shut her car door.

"You make sure you get back with that good girl, you hear me?" she yells through the open car window.

I smirk. "Yeah, I hear you."

As soon as she drives off, J hops out of his car and begins to walk in my direction with a big grin on his face. "Hey, man, what's up?"

I walk into my building expecting for him to follow me before I speak to him.

J follows me up the stairs with my visible anger and confusion. "You ain't mad at me for that dumb shit last week, is you?"

"No, I just didn't want my mother to see you talking to me in her rearview mirror as she drove off."

J smiles. Then he chuckles. "What she say about'cha car?"

"I didn't tell her."

"You didn't tell her?"

I open my door and let J in. I close it back before I look him eye to eye. "What did *your* mother say when you told her how much drug money you're making?"

J drops his head and looks away from me. Then he looks back up with a smile. "She said, 'Great! Keep it comin'!'"

I smile back at him. "Yeah, sure she did."

I get ready to head to my bedroom so that I can finally give J his record book back. But he grabs my arm.

"Yo, man, I ain't mean'nat shit I said to you last time in here, you'n. I was lunchin' a li'l bit, man. Niggas called me up talkin' 'bout some ol' 'Two t' ya head'-type shit."

"That's what Rudy was involved in?" I ask him.

"Oh, I'on really know. I was just askin'. But don't worry about that shit now. Er'rything is taken care of."

Sounds fishy to me. But I'm not going to even ask him about it. "Okay. I understand."

J extends his right hand. "Aw'ight. We cool den."

I shake on it. I walk into my bedroom and pull his ledgers from deep within my closet. When I walk back out into my living room, J has spread a considerable amount of green cash out across my couch.

"We gettin' busy like a muthafucka, man! This eighteen thousand dollars!" He looks up at me with the energy of a child.

"Yeah, well, not me. I'm calling it quits, J. I can't stand the heat. So here's your car keys."

I toss the ring of Acura Integra keys on top of his drug money.

J looks astonished. "I thought you said it was cool about that dumb shit, you'n. I mean, damn, Joe, I said I was trippin'."

He looks serious for a minute. Then he just busts out laughing. "Yo, you'n, you got me in here soundin' like a girl an' shit. Now stop lunchin' on me like that, Joe. Seriously."

I keep a straight face. "I am serious. I can't do it no more, man. It's as simple as that. And if you have to kill me . . . then do what you have to do."

I don't really mean this at all. I'm hoping J gets the point I'm trying to make and not have me killed for real. But I doubt if Shank would do it. We've gotten pretty familiar. I think he likes me.

J nods his head in slow, meaningful nods, as if he's actually thinking it over—having me killed. My heart is starting to race, but I have to do this. I just have to!

"Aw'ight, man, 'cause like, things 'bout t' get a li'l rough anyway." He picks up the car keys and throws them back to me. "You can keep the car, man. The shit is in your name now anyway. You even got tags for it now."

"Yeah, but I can't keep hiding it from my mother."

He chuckles. "Where is it at?"

I smile. "Around the corner from her house."

He laughs a good hard one.

"Yo, you somethin' else, man. But yo, I was jus' thinkin' 'bout'chu that night I left here. And man, you already put me down on how to get my money in'na bank. So we cool at that."

He looks into my eyes as he stands with his money

gathered back into his hands. He wears a Rolex watch on the left wrist and a gold nugget bracelet on the right. He reaches out to shake my hand. I reach out to receive it.

"My books, nigga," he says, slapping my hand away.

"Oh." I give the small, brown ledger book to him.

"Psych, man," he says, extending his right hand again. This time I'm hesitant.

"Come on, man. I'm on'na up-an'-up." We shake hands and smile at each other. "So what'chu gon' do about money?" J asks me.

"Get another job. Since I have a car now, maybe I can ride all the way out in Maryland or Virginia someplace and get something worth my while."

J pauses. "You know, it should be automatic for guys like you to get a job, man. I mean, good, clean niggas like you should keep a damn job, you'n. You should be da fuckin' manager! You know what I'm sayin'?"

"Yeah. Exactly."

He smiles and nods to me as he walks out. "Yo, you need me ta ride you back t' ya ride."

"Ahhh, no, I'll get it tomorrow morning when my mom goes off to work."

J frowns. "What about school?"

I grin at him. "School is over with."

"Aw'ight den, man. That means my girl'll be home soon." He closes the door on my smile.

Wow! That was tough! But it's over with and it was easier than I thought it would be.

I plan to sell the car and put the money in the bank along with the other four thousand dollars I've saved while keeping J's records. He's made over $200,000 since February. That's no joke! But a lot of it gets wasted on trivial stuff like girls, outlandish amounts of pocket cash, guns, gear and other expensive gadgets. Then again, what would a drug dealer be without those things? Then he's had to pay off all the runners and keep cash to make buys. Not to mention paying off different small-business people to write him checks to deposit back into his account.

I must say—negative cash or not—J has a lot of weight on his shoulders.

I call up Marshall and tell him to pick me up when they're all ready to go to the movies. I don't know what we're planing to see. I saw *Who's The Man?* with NeNe last week. I thought it was ridiculous, at best. I mean, oil in Harlem? Get real! And casting a million rappers just undermines the whole deal of being an actor or an actress. I guess this is the "Rap-exploitation Era."

I clean up to get ready for the movies. Then my phone rings.

"Hello."

"Come get me," NeNe demands.

"I can't."

"Why not?"

"I'm going to the movies with my friends tonight. I mean, we've been together this whole past week."

She sighs. "Look, I don't feel like arguin' anymore, okay." Now she sounds hurt. "I mean, my aunt been gettin' on my nerves as it is, an' I jus' wanted to be with you instead of hearin' her runnin' her damn mouth at me."

"What did you do?"

"I ain't do shit!" she says like I should know better than to accuse *her*. "She jus' been grouchy 'cause dis bamma-ass nigga *she* wit' don't treat her right, an' den she gon' get all in my face about what I *ain't* doin' right, man. Sick of her! She gettin' jus' like my mother."

"Well, what do you want me to do?"

"I want you ta come get me, Wes. Come on, man, I'll go to the movies wit'chall. I *need* to get out."

"We went out all last week, NeNe."

"SO! I mean, damn, man, I'm ya girl. Don't that mean somethin' to you? Come on, Wes. Come get me."

I sigh. "All right."

She gets excited. "Okay, I'm gettin' ready now. Like, how long it's gon' take you?"

"At least an hour and a half."

"An hour an' a half? Aw, you gots ta be crazy, you'n! I can't stay in here that damn long with her. Shit! I can catch the Metro for all that."

Well, catch it then, dammit! You driving me crazy! "Look, I have to wait for my friend to pick me up. Okay?"

"What happened to ya car?"

"I was in an accident earlier. I totaled it. So we'll have to ride with my friends tonight."

She gives a long sigh. "Oh my God!" She sucks her teeth. "Man, damn. How you do that?"

"This car hit me from the blind side; this guy was speeding while I was making a left turn."

"Where at?"

"On Florida Avenue."

She pauses. I figure it's better to lie to her about it than to tell her that I'm planning to sell it.

"Well, you got insurance, right? So you can get da money and buy another one. You can get a new Honda Civic like my girlfriend got. Them joints is like dat!"

Damn, now she sounds excited again! I wasn't even thinking about her jumping to conclusions like this. She thinks a lot quicker than I give her credit for.

"So what do you want me to do?" I ask, referring to picking her up again.

"Umm, pick me up from my girlfriend's house down'na street. You know the one, right?"

"Yeah, I know. The house with the green fence around their lawn."

"Yeah."

"Okay then. An hour and a half."

"And hurry up, too. Okay?"

"All right."

"Promise me."

"NeNe? Don't."

She sucks her teeth. "Dag, man, you ain't no fun sometimes, Joe. I mean, I still gotta work on loosenin' you up a li'l bit."

"Yeah, whatever." I hang up and smile to myself. I don't know why I like NeNe's ways more than I like Sybil's. It's weird, because Sybil is so much more thoughtful than NeNe. I guess NeNe's childish adventures keeps me on an exciting edge no matter how pissed off she makes me sometimes. I mean, you really need some type of spirited energy to keep a relationship going, you know? And I think that's what NeNe and I have right now.

I *know* the guys are not too happy about this. I can tell by the lack of conversation there is inside the car. But they *are* satisfied with my good news. And I briefed them on the lie I told NeNe about the car. So we're all planning to psych her out.

"We're very talkative t'day, aren't we?" she says sarcastically, sitting in the back seat between Walt and me.

Everyone chuckles.

"Yeah, you done messed up our guy talk," Walt says from her right. I'm sitting on her left and Derrick is in the passenger seat.

NeNe smiles. "It's a man thang. It's a mannn thang!" she says, imitating Martin Lawrence. She receives more chuckles from us.

"Yo, you should save some of that money and get a used car, Wes," Derrick says, starting it off.

"What?" NeNe responds radically. "No, we don't ride in *used* cars."

"Well, everybody can't afford a new car," Derrick argues.

"Wes can," she retorts, winking an eye at me.

"Why you say dat?" Marshall asks her from the wheel.

" 'Cause Wes got it like dat, Joe."

"You do, Wes?" Walt asks me over her head.

NeNe looks him in the face. "Shit! All he gotta do is pay wit' da insurance money. That's what insurance is for. I know. My sister been in like, three accidents."

Walt giggles. "She can't drive too good, hunh?"

We all laugh at it. But NeNe doesn't.

"That shit ain't funny! That's my damn sista!"

"He didn't mean it like that," I tell her.

"So?"

Walt shakes his head and looks out his window. We all sit quietly again as we head toward the Union Station parking lot. I guess my plan for the guys to help me talk NeNe out of buying a new car has hit rock bottom and drowned.

"So what are we planning to see?" I ask the group. We walk into Union Station and ride the escalators down to the bottom level where the theaters are.

"*Indecent Proposal*, shawdy!" NeNe answers. "That joint is gon' be like dat!"

"We saw that already," Marshall responds to her.

NeNe peers at him. "Well, I didn't, and y'all can go see what y'all wanna see. But that's what I wanna see." She grabs onto my left arm as we walk into the crowded lines past all the high-priced food stands. I haven't seen *Indecent Proposal* either. And I must say, it has a very contemporary plot.

Walt suddenly shields me and looks with big eyes. "Yo, go get in that other line," he says urgently.

I read him without verbal response and move quickly with NeNe's hand.

"Where we goin'?"

"In the other line," I tell her. I look in the direction of Walt alarmingly.

OH GOD! PLEASE HELP ME OUT OF THIS ONE! It's Candice!

Walt grabs onto both of her arms, trying to talk to her as I try to ease further into the crowd.

"What'chu doin'? We in line already," NeNe says, resisting my nervous pulls. But I think Candice has spotted me already anyway. She's heading this way now with Walt still trying to detain her. Marshall and Derrick are both staring helplessly. I guess everything happened a little too quickly for them.

"Ay, Wes, what's up?" Candice says to me. She's eying NeNe skeptically.

NeNe looks, leaning with her back to my chest and her hands reaching back for mine.

"Hi, Candice," is all that I can say. I feel like I'm about to hyperventilate.

Candice says demandingly, "Can I speak to you for a second?"

"Who you?" NeNe asks protectively, while not letting me go.

Candice X-rays her. "Look, I wasn't talkin' t' you, okay?" She's about three inches taller and twenty pounds heavier than NeNe.

NeNe shouts, "Well, BITCH, I'm talkin'na you!"

OH, PLEASE HELP ME, GOD! I pull NeNe back as I feel them ready to attack each other. Walt grabs Candice. And now there's drama inside Union Station with all the nosy instigators gathering.

"YO, WES, come on, man!" Marshall shouts, pushing through the crowd.

I halfway pick NeNe up and carry her as I tug her along with me.

"Get off me, Wes! I ain't afraid'a dat *bitch!*"

"Let her ass go then!" Candice yells back from Walt's arms.

"Yeah, let her go, you'n!" I hear somebody shout with giggles. "Let 'em get dat shit on!"

I pull NeNe through the crowd, forcefully, while Marshall rushes to the car in front of us.

Once we get outside, NeNe breaks my hold and walks ahead of me in anguish. Then she whirls around.

"So who da fuck was that, Wes?"

"A friend from school."

"Yeah, right!"

She faces me in her blue jeans and her red-and-white polka-dotted spring sweater. A black leather bag dangles carelessly from her right shoulder. More people are staring as they head to and from Union Station in the cool night breeze. I guess they picture this as a free screenplay.

I rush up to her and lead her back behind Marshall to the car. Derrick and Walt are still inside Union Station, hopefully holding back the fort until we can get out of here.

"Get off of me!" NeNe shouts. She breaks free and walks stubbornly by herself and hops in the front seat. She says to Marshall "Take me to my girlfriend's house. And I ain't got shit t' say to you, Wes!" she yells while slamming the door.

Marshall looks at her, but he doesn't say anything.

"Look, you're overreacting. She just wanted to speak to me," I plead.

"Overreactin' shit! I saw how she was lookin'. She ain't jus' no fuckin' friend! And I *said*, 'I ain't got shit t' say to you!'"

"Oh my God! I don't believe you," I continue pleading over the back seat. Marshall's already made it across the H Street bridge on our way to take her to her girlfriend's house off of Benning Road in Northeast. NeNe's friend lives about six houses down the street from her and her aunt.

I sit paralyzed as NeNe sticks to her words. She even jumps out and slams the door without a look back when we pull up in front of her girlfriend's house.

I lean my head into Marshall's back seat as we head back toward Union Station.

"So what now, Wes?" Marshall asks with a slight grin. I guess he can't help it.

I sigh. "Go home and cry into my pillow."

Marshall's cheeks rise for a fuller smile. "So you like her all that much, man? I mean, she pretty as shit—don't get me wrong—but she acts like a damn kid. You wanna girl like that for real?"

I chuckle. "You know what? To tell you the truth, I don't think I can help it now. I think I've gotten used to her."

Marshall just shakes his head, maintaining his silly grin.

Butterman

"Look, man, things are getting kind of rough right now and I'm down to my last four ounces, so it's simple economics to charge more for my last product. I mean, I could break these last four ounces down myself and sell them as eight-balls, halves and quarters and make more money than I could selling them to you as full-ass ounces. I mean, I gotta charge you more for my last shit, Ralph. It ain't nothin' personal, pal, it's jus' straight business."

I got my right arm wrapped around this white boy's shoulder out in Montgomery County. We're standing inside of his garage, where his father's sky-blue Corvette is parked beside Ralph's black 300 ZX.

Ralph shakes his blond, crew-cut head. His face is all pink and shit from trying to debate with me. He has two of his boys standing to the side, and I got Shank with me at the garage entrance, chilling with his .45 inside his belt. But I'm packing too now. I got this pretty-ass nickel-plated .32 inside *my* belt.

Ralph shakes his head. "I just don't know, man. I mean, I understand your situation and all, Butchy . . . but hell, man, fifteen hundred is a hell of a lot of money for an ounce."

I sigh. "Look, man, as soon as things cool down, then I can sell 'em to you for twelve hundred again. I mean, you gon' make your money back and I gotta make sure I make mine. So what you do is just tell your people that there's a drug price war going on because of the summertime rollin' around and all."

Ralph looks to his two boys to our right. These white niggas don't look too convinced. But I'm leaving with at least twenty-eight hundred for these two ounces. Shit! Maybe I should make the pitch now.

"Aw'ight, yo . . . gi'me twenty-eight for the two ounces and I'll cut you a break next time. Aw'ight?"

Ralph's dark-haired boy shakes his head. "Man, ounces are going for a straight grand everywhere where I've bought them."

I look to Ralph and frown. "Ay, Ralph, would you tell this guy. My shit is straight from New York, man. I got the raw cut!"

Ralph nods his head, agreeing with me. "Yeah, dude, his stuff is pretty legit."

His dark-haired boy hunches his shoulders. "All right then, if you say it's legit."

"Great! Hey, Charlie," Ralph says to his short brown-haired boy.

All three of these white boys are dressed like B-boys: extra large jeans, dance-hall shoes and cool, colorful sweatshirts. I met these white boys through Pervis out at the go-go in Maryland. Rare Essence was playing, and since everybody was calling me B, I just told these white boys that it stood for "Butchy." But it irritates me when they keep saying it.

Shank alerts himself while Charlie goes to get the money.

"What's up, man?" Ralph says to him.

Shank nods his head, standing with no expression like a hit-man is supposed to do.

Ralph takes out a cigarette and offers me one.

"Naw, man, I'on fuck around wit' no Camels or no Marlboros. Them joints is for you white boys."

Ralph shoves them at me anyway. "Naw, man, what's this shit about white or black? Go 'head, man, take one."

I laugh it off. "Naw, we only smoke Kools, Newports and sometimes Salems."

Ralph thinks for a minute as he drags and blows. His dark-haired boy lights up one too.

Ralph says, "You know, all them you just named have green labels. You think it's some kind of connection there?"

We all laugh. Even Shank is giggling. This white boy lunchin'.

Dark-haired boy says, "Ralph, you're bugged, man. We gotta get you checked out."

Charlie comes back with a shoe box. Shank straightens up and gets serious. Charlie gives it to me. I open it up and count the cake.

"Yup, it's all here." I make a move for the garage entrance toward my 3000. Shank covers me while Ralph tastes the blow off his finger.

He nods with a pink smile. "All right then, man. And remember you said you'd cut us a deal on the next one, right?"

I hop in my 3000 with Shank. "Yeah, man, I got'chu."

"Peace," Ralph's dark-haired boy says. He throws up his index and middle finger and spreads them.

"Aw'ight. I'll hit'chall back."

Shank frowns and shakes his head. I put the stick in reverse and back down the driveway.

"What's wrong, Shank? We jus' made a killin' off them dumb niggas."

"Hmm. White boy talkin' 'bout some peace. We'd have much peace if we kill them ma-fuckas. Much-ass peace."

"Ay, man, cut dat shit out. A whole lot of white people are cool. I mean, you startin'na sound racist. Us niggas ain't racist, are we?"

I start to laugh at my own joke. But I guess Shank doesn't get the humor because he ain't even smiling.

"Fuck them white boys, you'n! Fuck 'em all."

I look over to him. "Now, you mean'na tell me dat you ain't never been around no cool-ass white people?"

Shank looks back at me. "*You* prob'bly been. But white people don't treat us poor, jet-black niggas like they'a treat ya rich, light-bright ass."

I laugh at the shit. But he's only *half* right. "Yo, they'll just rather deal with me than with you, but they don't like neither one of us. And that's on'na real tip, Joe."

Shank smiles. "Yeah, so like I said, fuck 'em all."

We both chuckle as I jump on the beltway back to D.C. I'd rather have Shank with me than them other two cheesy-ass niggas I hired. Them niggas talk too much. They would have tried to get all cool with them white boys. I don't need to hang out with no white boys; I just want their easy-ass money. White people buy weight like a motherfucker!

I drive Shank down to our new meeting place off of Missouri Avenue and up from Emery Park. Steve, Otis and these two criminal niggas—Jerry and Boo—are all down here waiting for us, on time.

I pull up with Shank and hop out. "Yo, we got two ounces left to sell, and I'm gon' cut 'em down into twenty eight-balls for one-sixty apiece."

"One-sixty? That price is kind of high, ain't it?" this big-mouthed nigga Jerry asks me. I wanna tell you'n to stick his monster-looking ass to beating down and killing people and leave the damn business to me!

"That's only ten dollars more than we been sellin' 'em for. Niggas out here can stand it. They know our product is good. Our shit *keeps* customers, Joe!" Steve tells him.

"Yeah, good shit will keep these fiends comin', you'n. That's the sho' nuff!" Boo says with his crooked-ass grin. I mean, these two thug niggas look like they straight out the comic books. They're dressed all raggedy and shit. I'd hang out with Shank over them any-damn-day.

I look to see how smooth Shank looks in his blue Polo gear and Nikes. He's staring down the block as if he's bored. His black-ass skin is shining like he oiled it. For real! He a straight Big Daddy Kane-looking nigga, but shorter with a smoother face.

"Yo, Shank, you want me ta drop you off at Super Trak before I cut the shit up for these niggas, you'n?"

He nods and walks back to the car. "Let's roll."

These niggas are looking on like they're jealous of him. But they don't want him to catch them looking. Shank has them sharp-ass, penetrating eyes that can kill you from just looking at them.

"Aw'ight den, gang. I'll be back in sixty."

I hop in with Shank and roll to Fifth Street. It's the quickest way to get to Rhode Island. Then again, I could take North Capitol. So I make a left toward North Capitol instead.

I notice Shank been more quiet than usual lately. I wonder what's on his mind.

"Yo, what'chu thinkin' 'bout, man?"

He takes out his Trends of Culture tape from his jacket pocket and puts it inside my system, stopping the radio from playing this new TLC song, "Hat 2 Da Back." But he still doesn't answer me. That "Off & On" rap comes on. Shank just leans into my leather seat as if he's melting into the bass of this hype-ass song. I guess he's still thinking about this rap shit. But that ain't nothing new. He always has a slammin'-ass tape on him.

"Yo, man, Bink said you got skills on'na wheels, G. So what's the deal? Let me hear some rhymes on time."

This boy grins. I guess my attempt to rhyme to him sounded stupid. But fuck it! I got young'un smiling, right?

"I ain't really thinkin' 'bout shit but killin'nese Northeast niggas so we can stop lookin' like punks out here. I mean, 'nis punk shit ain't sittin' too well wit' my conscience. You know what I'm sayin'?"

I turn the volume down a bit so I can hear him clearly. "Yeah, I hear you. But we gon' get dem niggas when the time is right. They ain't really tried nothin' yet."

"That's because we been fuckin' hidin'!"

I don't say anything to that. I mean, I guess he got a point. But I don't want us to be no sitting target. And I still got money out here to make. So, you know, you have to do what you have to do sometimes to stay in business.

"Pride can get a man killed earlier than he really wants to die," I tell him. I didn't make that saying up or nothing. I'm just quoting what I heard Georgie say in his barbershop three years ago. Red was talking this same old tough-guy shit Shank talks, and Georgie was trying to school him.

"Some people are meant to die to set examples," Shank says back.

I chuckle. "Oh yeah? Well, like, damn near two hundred and fifty niggas set examples already in 1993, and it's jus' turnin' May an' shit."

Shank smiles. "Yeah, we try'na break last year's record."

I shake my head and say nothing. *Fuck it! I guess he's straight-up crazy!*

I cut up the cocaine and deliver it to my workers on Missouri Avenue. Then I jet back to the crib and call up Red's girl Keisha to see if he can have visiting hours again yet.

"Yay'ah, but I ain't goin'—" she says.

"Nobody asked you da go."

"—'cause I'm ti'ed a gettin' my hopes all up fa his ass and den—"

"Look, I just want Li'l Red when I go."

"—he fuck around an' disappoint me all'la time, shaw'. It's jus—"

"Would'ju shut da fuck up! I jus' want Li'l Red t'mar."

BLANG!

Damn! She hung up on me. I call her ass right back.

"DEN COME AN' GET 'IM DEN!" she shouts into the phone.

I shake my head and smile into my dresser mirror. *Keisha goin' crazy. For real!*

I got Little Red in the car with me heading down I-95 to see his pop in Lorton in Virginia. I didn't need to get a haircut this Thursday. I looked into the mirror like the Fonz this morning and said, "Fuck it!"

We go through all that identification bullshit before they lead us to the maximum security telephones. Damn! Red done fucked up on them visits where we could sit across the table with him. Now we have to look through this thick-ass glass window and talk through these telephones like they do in the movies.

"Yo, li'l man? Say 'what's up' to Papa," Red says to his son. I got my ear and Little Red's ear up to the receiver.

Little Red says, "Hi," shyly into the mouth piece. He's not even looking at Red.

"Yo, B, tell 'im t' look at me when I'm talkin' to 'im, man."

I try to get Little Red to look through the glass window, but he doesn't want to. Then he climbs down from the phone table and starts crying.

Red looks on like he's stone crazy. "Ay, what's wrong wit' my son, man? What the hell Keisha been sayin' to 'im?"

I shake my head and hold Little Red at my side. "Keisha givin' up, man. She losin' it."

Red nods. "That's what I wanted to talk to you about, B." I look into his hardened face. His hair been cut down so low that you can't tell the color. But he still looks like a reddish-brown Hulk. This nigga is huge like shit! I won't have to worry about nothing when he gets out. I mean, with Red *and* Shank . . . yo, that shit is gon' be the bomb!

"How much money you got?" Red asks me, snapping me out of my dreams.

"Almost a hundred Gs in'na bank, and like, fifty at da crib."

Red's eyes pop open as he cheers up. "Yo, dat a work! Now, listen up, B." He looks serious again with his nostrils flaring. "Leave dat street shit alone, man, and jus' lay low until I get out, 'cause crime don't pay."

I look at him confusingly. *I jus' know he ain't say what I think I heard.* I look at the phone like something is wrong with it.

Red frowns at me. "Yo, stop playin', you'n. I'm serious."

I don't say nothing. I'm hoping Red sees that I'm not trying to go for this craziness. I mean, every time things gets a little rough, niggas start running. Just like Wes did already. But I know Shank is still down with me. Joe will die fighting for his. Fuck this running away shit! I ain't stopping until I make a million. Then I'll probably want *ten* million.

Red says, "You hear me talkin' t' you, man?"

"Hunh?"

"The shit don't pay, B! I mean, you got money, so chill ya ass out and take a vacation or somethin' for a while until I get out'a hea."

I frown back at him. "It don't pay? How da hell you think I got paid, Joe? I mean, what da fuck are you talkin' about, Red? Them damn Muslims been gettin' to you back there or somethin, nigga?"

Red just stares at me. "Put my son back on'na phone."

I try to lift Little Red up, but he struggles against me and starts crying again. This shit ain't looking cool at all. Little Red's starting to act like a little spoiled girl out this joint.

Red is still staring at me when I look back at him. "Would you want your only son doin' some sissy shit like that to you?" I look into Red's serious-ass eyes. It damn near looks like he wants to cry with his son.

Damn! I'm gettin' butterflies in my stomach now. This visit ain't turnin' out the way I was thinkin'.

"Look, man, you gon' do what'chu gon' do. I'm out'a hea." Red gets up and walks to his left. The guards take him back and he disappears.

"Come on, man." I pull Little Red by his hand. He's still wiping tears from his eyes.

We head back up I-95 and listen to the radio. That Levert jam comes on, "Bring Back the Good Old Days." I guess Red is right. I mean, life was a whole lot simpler when we used to go to the go-go at Crystal Skate, the Panorama Room, Southern Coliseum, the Black Hole, the East Side. We'd book girls and just fist-fight them jealous niggas and shit. But now . . . niggas are fucking lunatics.

I get back to the crib and call up my girl. I'm keeping Little Red with me tonight. I got him in my living room playing that Sega game. I don't play it much myself, but I know he'll get a kick out of it.

Toya says, "Hey, baby. So you gon' pick me up from the airport at around four o'clock, right?"

"You can't come no earlier than that?"

"No, J, 'cause I have a lot of things to do before I leave Tuesday morning."

"Oh yeah?" I'm sitting here looking at a photo that me and Toya took last summer. "I miss you, girl."

"Awww, baby, I miss you too."

I smile. "What I tell you about that?"

"About what?"

"Makin' me sound like I'm your son or somethin'."

"What? Well, look, boo, if you don't like me talkin' sweet to you, then you gon' get tired of me this summer, 'cause I missed your curly-headed ass a lot."

My dick gets hard at hearing this shit. I wish she was home *tonight*.

"You think ya mom gon' get mad at you stayin' over here this summer?" I ask her.

She sucks her teeth. "I mean, J, I'm a grown-ass woman. I'm still gon' see my mom every chance I get. But like, we been goin' together for almost four years now. And my mom likes you."

I smile. "I hope she do."

"Yeah, but hey, baby, I'm about to run out with my girlfriends."

I snap to attention. "Where y'all goin'?"

"We goin' out, man! I mean, this my last week in Atlanta until August. And I'on know why you askin' *me* that. I need to be askin' *your* hot-ass where *you* goin'."

I laugh.

"Yeah, keep on laughing."

"I ain't goin' nowhere t'night. I got Li'l Red wit' me."

"You do? Awww, see how sweet you can be sometimes, boo."

"Yo, stop callin' me dat shit. I know this other guy name Boo. And dude ain't doin' too well upstairs, you know?"

She giggles. "Baby, you know how my mom got me doin'nat."

"Yeah, well, we gon' have to stop all that shit right here."

She laughs. "Okay, but I have to go. Love you."

"I love you too."

"I know you do, baby. But I love you more."

"No, you don't."

She chuckles. "Bye."

"Aw'ight."

I hang up and slide down onto my brown-carpeted floor with Little Red to play Sega Genesis in the living room. "How come you ain't look at your father t'day, man?" He hunches his shoulders. And fuck it! Life is rough sometimes like that. He'll grow out of it. Red ain't gon' be in jail forever. That nigga gon' be out in just eighteen months probably.

CHAPTER 10

Butterman

I'm speeding down Fourteenth Street Northwest to pick up my girl. I'm already running late and four o'clock ain't exactly the best time to be driving to the airport on a weekday with all this damn traffic downtown.

A taxi tries to cut out in front of me from my left. I move up and block his ass off.

"Hey, cin I get by, man?"

He looks like an angry Ethiopian and he has an accent. But fuck him!

"Naw, man, I'm in a hurry!"

He nods his head at the middle-aged white couple in his back seat. I guess he thinks they're more important than me. But his ass is wrong! My baby's coming home today! Nobody's more important than her.

I jump on 395 South, heading for Virginia, and turn right onto the National Airport exit. I think Toya said she's flying Delta. She has a cousin that works for one of them airlines. Dude pretty cool. But I keep forgetting if the shit is Delta or Continental.

I ride past a few pick-up spots and a million taxis and stop at Delta. I spot my girl immediately. And she don't look too happy. She's wearing off-white corduroy shorts and a matching knitted vest. Her gold is shining against her pretty, dark skin and her hair is pinned up in one of those high-ass French rolls. She's wearing gold loop earrings. She has the chiseled face of a model and she's shaped like that track star, Flo Jo, but without them *He-Man*–type muscles. I wouldn't like that shit.

I blow my horn. I jump out and lift up the trunk.

Toya walks over and starts throwing her suitcases in like she's trying to break them.

I stare at her like she's crazy. "What'chu doin'?"

She doesn't even look at me. "You should'a left earlier, 'cause you know damn well that I hate waiting at these airports."

I smile and grab some of her bags to put in my back seat. Toya filled my trunk up already!

"I tried, Toy, honest."

"Yeah, I bet you did." She hops in on the passenger seat and closes the door.

I slide in, close my door and drive off. I peep over at her; she's looking all gorgeous. She looks even sexier when she's pissed.

She stares straight ahead and says, "J?"

I'm licking my lips at her playfully. "What?"

"Could you stop staring at me, please. God! I mean, I got enough of that from all these damn skycaps try'na help me with my bags."

"Did'ju give your phone number t' any of 'em?" I ask her. I'm just joking with her.

"Yeah. He gon' pick me up later on tonight."

We both start laughing. Then Toya says, "Yup, I can tell we gon' have a hell of a summer, 'cause you pissin' me off already. And now I gotta live with you." She shakes her head with a smile. "Mmm, mmm, mmm. What I get myself into now?"

I suck my teeth and grin at her. "Girl, you crazy! You get breakfast in bed every day with me."

She can't help but smile at that shit! "Yeah, right," she says.

We roll back up to Fourteenth Street. An old, bummy white woman in dirty brown pants and a yellow T-shirt approaches cars from the middle of the road with a sign in her hands, begging for money.

I read the shit: PLEASE GIVE TO THE POOR AND HOMELESS

Yeah, right. She out her mind! Poor and homeless? She white!

Toya is watching her too. "Even white people got it bad sometimes," she comments.

I frown at her as I drive off past the green light. "You crazy! She prob'bly got rich-ass relatives that don't like her no more. She prob'bly married one of us when she was younger."

Toya grins at me. "Now, you know you ain't got no damn sense."

I'm smiling, saying nothing. All I'm thinking about is what we gon' do once we get back to the crib.

I lift myself up, loving her smooth, dark body with every stroke. And she's talking some good shit to me:

"I miss you, baby." She digs her nails into my hips. "Unnh, J! I missed you! I missed you!"

God damn! I can feel this nut in my fuckin' toes!

Toya is gripping me like shit! "Give everything to me,

baby. Oh, I feel you. Yes, J! YES!" She got one hand running wildly through my hair now. "UUUUW!"

I'm grabbing onto the edge of the bed, past Toya's head on my pillow. She's wrapping her flexible legs around mine while I come. And we sweating like hell in here!

Toya says breathlessly, "We gon' have ta take a long-ass shower, baby."

We're both on our backs and breathing like we just finished a marathon.

I smile. "Yeah, well, we gon' have ta chill for that shit, 'cause I'm tired den a ma-fucka."

She giggles. "You should be." Then she grabs onto my joint and starts to rub up and down on it.

I stop her and pull her hand away. "Yo, come on, don't do that. You try'na give me a heart attack in here?"

Toya just smiles.

We end up taking a shower together—after we go at it two more times. We dress and freshen up and brush our teeth and put deodorant on, and all that other shit before we head to Latoya's mom's crib in Suitland, Maryland.

I'm taking the beltway to Suitland. That white boy Snow's reggae song, "Informer" comes on the radio. Toya pumps the volume up.

"This the joint, baby! And I can't wait to go to the go-go. I was drivin' the chicks on my floor crazy with Rare Essence and Junk Yard. I was like, 'Y'all ain't hip? Well, I'm gon' have to get'chall up on this shit. This the D.C. shit, shawdy!' "

I just grin at her; she's in here making a clown out of herself, dancing around in my thirty-thousand-dollar ride. I guess she's happy as hell to be back home. I mean, she ain't been back here since Thanksgiving last year. I've been down to Spelman to see her seven times since then. But I don't know why people talking all that stuff about "Black Atlanta." I mean, it may be a whole lot of wealthy niggas moving down there and all, but it was boring like shit down there to me. Especially after hanging out in Brooklyn, New York. But I guess New York got enough niggas. So a lot of them want to get the hell away from there. I mean, it makes sense. New York is crazy anyway.

"Why you all quiet, J?" Toya asks me. She turns the radio back down for my answer.

"Man, I'm jus' thinkin' 'bout the difference between New York and Atlanta."

Toya frowns. "Oh, it's like night and day, baby. Night and day."

We get to her mom's house in Suitland. It takes me out how this neighborhood is all spread out and shit. It looks like the country in some parts of Suitland. Especially where Toya's mom lives. It reminds me of some parts of South Carolina where my peoples live.

We walk up the wooden patio steps. Toya opens her mom's new yellow-and-white screen door. She looks back at me and raises her brow. She takes a deep breath. "Well, here we go, J."

As soon as she opens the door with her key and we walk inside, her brown and round mother raises up from her black leather recliner; it sits in the living room in front of their 27-inch floor-model TV.

We all smile at each other and say "Hi." Two of Toya's girlfriends are here, and NeNe. I get nervous for a minute, thinking that NeNe's sister might be up in this joint. But I heard she married now, so I doubt it.

"Ha-a-a-ay y'all!" Toya squeals.

Time for me ta sit down and chill. You know damn well how women get when'ney ain't seen each other for a while.

It sounds like a circus in here; they're talking about how they missed each other and how dark Toya got and if she's been eating well and a whole bunch of other girl-talk. I watch television with a grin until NeNe grabs my hand and leads me outside and onto the wooden patio. I look down at her for an explanation.

NeNe's looking cute as hell out here with her sandy-brown self. She got on some hot pink lipstick and a matching skirt and earrings with a Rayon shirt that has touches of hot pink in it. She even got a new short-and-jazzy hairstyle. I'm ashamed of what I'm thinking right now.

"What?" I ask her.

She sucks her teeth and sighs. "Wes, that's what."

I smile, confusingly. "What about 'im?"

She throws her right hand on her hip. And this shit ain't doing me *no* damn good! I feel like jumping her bones out this joint!

"Why did I go to the movies at Union Station last week, J, and some ol' *bitch* gon' jump in my face over him, you'n? I was like, 'Oh, no! Let me find out Wes' ass been fuckin' around on me.' "

I try to hold in my smile, but I can't help it. I'm not really thinking about what she just said. I can easily get Wes out of that. But I'm still trippin' off the fact that I'm standing here on my girl's patio thinking about banging her little cousin. This shit is messed up. For real! I'm lunchin' like shit out this joint!

NeNe frowns at me. "That shit ain't funny, man."

"I know, I'm jus' lunchin' on it, that's all."

"Well, what is his problem, you'n? I mean, he think he *like dat* or somethin' now?"

I finally get rid of my smile so I can game NeNe back

up for Wes. "Naw, Wes ain't even about that, shaw'. For real. Knowin' you, you prob'bly went up there and ran ya mouth off before you even knew what was goin' on."

"That's right, you'n! I mean, how you gon' feel if some *bitch* jus' come up t' ya man?—I mean, some guy jus' come up t' Toya, shaw', talkin' 'bout some ol', 'Let me speak to you for a minute.' And oh my God! Then this bitch gon' look me in *my* face like *I'm* crazy!"

I'm smiling at her story now. That shit happened to me plenty of times in my whore days. For real! I had, like, three and four different girls stepping to me at once. But I bet Wes ain't know w*hat* the fuck to do! I just ignored them jealous girls when it happened to me. But the key is never to take no girl that you just banging someplace where your *real* girl or her girlfriends might spot you.

I ask NeNe, "What she look like?"

"Some ol' wanna-be-hip, light-skinned chick, you'n. Bamma-ass bitch."

I nod my head. I know who she's talking about now. She means that girl Candice from up U.D.C. But I ain't trying to screw Wes up no more. That nigga been good to me. He helped me to get my dough in the bank. And I got just the thing to say to NeNe to patch things back up for him.

I look into her dark eyes. "Now, see dat? That was his old girl I was tellin' you about when I first hooked'chall up. Now you den went all on a tangent when it wasn't even about that."

"Well, I ain't know who she was."

"Did you let Wes explain it to you?" If I'm right, she probably went crazy and didn't want to listen to nothing Wes had to say. I mean, all girls get like that when they catch you.

NeNe pauses and smiles up at me. "You know I didn't, you'n. I was mad like shit. I jus' told his boy t' ride me da *fuck* back home."

I got her now. All I have to do is tell Wes what to say.

I shake my head at her with a sly grin. "Mmm-hmm. See dat? Now you prob'bly got that boy all lonely an' shit now, over some *dumb* shit."

She laughs. "Aw, you'n, stop playin'. It ain't like we broke up or nothin'. I jus' cut his ass back for a while."

"You been takin' his phone calls?" That's the other thing that girls do when you fuck up. I mean, they don't even wanna hear your damn voice.

She smiles and giggles it off. "Hell naw, you'n! And Joe been callin' me like shit. I had my aunt tellin' 'im I wasn't there."

Now I have to get her emotions back into it. I grab her left hand with my right. "You still like 'im?"

She smiles and starts squirming like a kid. And yo, I'm pretty good at this.

"Yeah, man, you know I still like him." Now she all bashful.

"Aw'ight, well, what'chu do is talk to him when he calls, but you make him beg for a couple of days before you let him come see you."

"Aw, young'un, you want me ta play ya boy like a bamma. That's messed up." She's cracking up now.

I'm still holding her hand to let my plan sink in while she laughs. "No, I'm sayin', that's what Toya used to do to me—" *And she did, too.* "—and after that—" I lean over to whisper, "—we made love like fuckin' Martians was comin' and it was da end of the damn world."

NeNe breaks my hold and runs down the patio steps, cracking up. "Awww, Joe! Y'all niggas be lunchin' like shit, man!" Then she calms down and thinks about it. "But you know what? I'm gon' do that shit. Watch me."

We smile at each other and walk back inside the house. By now everybody has plates at the table except for me and NeNe. NeNe runs to the kitchen to get her a plate. I follow in behind her.

"I'm so tired, J. I just don't know what to do wit' my-self."

Me and my baby Toya are riding back home to our plush-ass Silver Spring apartment. My car clock reads 1:34. My baby been up since five o'clock this morning. Or yesterday morning now. No wonder she tired.

"Don't worry about it, girl. I'm gon' carry ya ass out the car, up on the elevator and t' da bedroom. Then I'm gon' take your clothes off and turn the ceiling fan on and put on some Whitney Houston."

"Whitney Houston? You mean some Intro, Shai or Silk or somebody. I'on listen to no Whitney Houston." She stops and stares at me with her head pressed back against the leather Mitsubishi bucket seat. "J, who you been listenin' to Whitney Houston with? You know I'on like no Whitney Houston."

Aw, SHIT! After all that game I ran to hook Wes back up, now my shit is in trouble.

"I like Whitney Houston," I tell my baby. But I do like Whitney a little bit. I'd *like* to fuck her.

Toya looks away from me and out her side window. "Mmm-hmm. You slippin', J. And I think I'll carry myself to bed and take my *own* clothes off." She looks at me again. "And you know what, J? If I get horny tonight, watch my ass go and take a private li'l shower."

I bust out laughing to play things off. Latrell is the one that likes Whitney Houston. But I can get out of this though. This shit ain't no big problem.

* * *

God damn! It's Friday and Toya ain't rolled over and spread them legs for me yet. I mean, she won't even jerk me off. This shit is killing me!

Then, she fucked around and got a job yesterday at Banana Republic. She don't start until next Monday. But I mean, how in the hell is my girl just gon' come home and get a job in two days? I just can't understand it. I mean, it's many niggas that need jobs. She could use my money. Toya don't need no job. She just walks out the house and catches buses around the city—she wouldn't let me drive her—filling out applications, and just gets a damn job like it's nothing.

Yo, I think it's a conspiracy going on now. These white men don't want us niggas to have jobs! I mean, he's working us the hell over.

I roll down to Missouri Avenue to talk to my crew. Bink finally ready to hook me up with that Virginia connection, but I think I'm gon' chill out for a bit like Red told me. Plus, I'm gonna have to hang out with my girl for these first couple of weekends anyway.

I hop out of my 3000. "What's up, what's up? So what'chall niggas think about my girl?" I rode past and stopped for a minute on Wednesday to show Toya off to these niggas, showing Steve what a real woman is supposed to look like. Then I drove Shank home to Super Trak again.

Toya said Shank was the coolest. Shit! Tell me something I didn't know. She said that I shouldn't even know the rest of these niggas. I played the shit off like they was just a bunch of boys on my tip. I'm just glad she ain't said nothing—yet—about me getting out of the business. She usually does. But I guess she's used to it by now.

"Oh, man, she was bad as shit from my view. But since she ain't get out da car, I'on know if she phat t' death or not in'na body," Jerry says first. This big, monster-looking nigga always the first to say anything. He reminds me of Biz Markie. But Jerry looks meaner than Biz. He got that wild-man, killer look with a high, raggedy-ass temple tape. Joe needs a comb.

"Yeah, ya girl is beautiful an' all'lat shit, B, but we got some bad-ass news for you, you'n " Steve says, looking gloomy.

I look at him in confusion. "Hell you talkin' 'bout?"

Steve looks to Boo, who's reading a newspaper, folded in half. "Give 'im the paper, man."

I take it from him.

"Read the story in the box," Steve tells me.

Otis is just standing to my left, kicking dirt around on the sidewalk.

I start to read it: THREE KILLED IN RIVAL GANG FIGHT

They got Rudy: *Rudolf Williams, 23, of Northwest.* And Kevy and shit! *Kevon Daniels, 16, of Northwest.* And some other young'un I don't know from back Northeast. I guess it's one of Rudy's cousins. But what the hell was Kevy doing with them niggas?

I look up with my heart racing for Kevy. "Why da hell was Kevy wit' 'em, man?" I ask Steve. I know Otis wouldn't answer me. And Jerry and Boo never met Kevy.

Steve shakes his head against the silence. "You cut 'im short, man. I guess Rudy caught up to 'im and told 'im he can get paid wit' dem. I mean, li'l niggas want cake too, Joe."

"Damn, man! I told Kevy to call me if he needed some fuckin' money, you'n! I told dat nigga dat shit!"

Nobody answers me. And when I look around I notice that my main man is missing. "Where Shank?"

Boo speaks up. "That nigga broke off like he was mad at the world. And like, at first, we was sittin' around talkin' about how it is in jail an' all, right. Then Shank jus' started buggin' out on niggas and broke out."

"What he say?"

Boo backs down and Jerry answers. "He was sayin' shit like, 'Y'all niggas is crazy! Real niggas don't die!' " They all start laughing as if they had been talking about it earlier. Jerry is shaking his head. "Yo, you'n, 'nat boy been listenin' t' NWA too long."

"All'lat rap shit," Steve says.

"Aw'ight, aw'ight, cut da bullshit," I tell them. "So what he do after that?"

Jerry fills me in. "Man, he walked up to Georgia Avenue, caught the 70 bus and rolled."

"Aw'ight, yo, y'all niggas stay together tonight in case something is up. Aw'ight? Steve got da beeper, right?"

"Yeah, I got it." Steve shows me the pager I got for him hanging on his pants pocket.

I move back to my car in a hurry. "Aw'ight, is er'rybody packed?" I ask them over my car hood.

"Yeah," Jerry says. He looks around at the rest of them. "You packin' ain't'chu, Otis?"

Otis looks startled. "Naw, man, I got my shit at da crib."

"Well, go da fuck home and get it den!" I holler at him. "And I want er'rybody dressed in black." I peel two hundreds and four fifty-dollar bills and throw them across my hood to Jerry. "I want er'rybody dressed in black. Even if y'all gotta go and buy some black shit."

"Aw'ight," Jerry says, counting the money with a smile.

I make a hard U-turn and head back up to Georgia Ave. Then I think better of that and head for Kennedy Street instead. Them Northeast niggas might ride up and down Georgia today, still trying to fuck with us.

But wait a minute! Rudy ain't with me no more, and

Kevy ain't either. Maybe this beef is off with us. I'm gon' page Max to see what time it is. He probably knows who these niggas are.

I jump out and beep Max and sit by a pay phone on Kennedy. This short, stocky guy named Cap walks up on me. I turn around on him about to reach for my .32. But damn! I didn't even bring it out of the house today. You can tell *I ain't* no killer. But fuck it, I'm a businessman anyway. *I* put this shit together!

"Yo, man, you can't be walkin' up on a nigga like that, you'n," I tell this nigga Cap. He lucky Shank ain't with me. I'd get Shank to pistol whip his ass for that dumb shit!

"Yo, ya boy Shank was 'round here wolfin' at the mouth last week, you'n. You should tell'lat nigga t' chill, Joe."

I look at Cap sternly. He should know better than to say some dumb shit to me like that. Shank will bust his ass up if I give him this message! But since I'm in Cap's turf by myself, I figure I have to play it off, real easy.

"Yeah, well, what it is is that we on'na move with this crew from back H Street and back Benning Road. So my whole crew is kinda jumpy right now, you know? He ain't mean it to be personal."

Cap nods his head. "Aw'ight, but chill'lat nigga out though, you'n. Chill'lat nigga."

"Aw'ight den," I tell him, trying to brush him away from the phone before Max calls back.

The phone rings right after Cap makes it around the corner.

"Yo, it's Max. Who beeped me?"

"Yo, it's B, man. I need to talk to you."

"Well, well. If it ain't Butter-bitch himself. I heard some niggas got'chu on the run now, Joe. What's up?"

"That's what I'm askin' *you*."

"You askin' me *what?*"

I watch a white-and-blue D.C. police cruiser drive by on Kennedy, heading toward North Capitol. "Who dese niggas is?"

"What? Aw, ma-fucka, I ain't forget that night you an' ya boy rode around hea try'na punk niggas, you'n. It jus' might be *my* crew that'a finish ya punkass."

"Yo, for real, you'n, the beef is off. I ain't even try'na get in no dumb shit, man. I mean, it's all about da money, G. It's all about da money."

"Yeah, you should'a thought about that shit before you started try'na play big boy."

"Yo, man—"

CLICK-CLICK! Damn! He hung the hell up on me!

Muthafucka! God damn! I'm sweatin' like shit!

Aw'ight, I'm cool. Shank said that shit was stupid when we carried Max and them! Now we might have two damn crews after us. But to hell if I'm gon' hook up with Rudy's cousins and them. I don't even know them niggas!

Okay. Okay. Okay. I'll beep Shank from another phone and figure out what we gonna do. I mean, Shank been ready to do these motherfuckers anyway. So I'll just buy us some Uzis, MAC-10s, Tech 9s or whatever, and get a lemon to run back Northeast and spray up every-fucking-thing!

I ride down to New Hampshire Ave, and use a pay phone to beep Shank. I wait for fifteen minutes but this nigga doesn't call me back.

God damn, Shank! Where da fuck you at, you'n?

Damn! You know what? I'm right across the street from where I got my first shot of ass from that pretty-ass girl Shaneeka. Shit! Bring back the good old days. But I think it's a little too late for that now. I done fucked up big-time! And it's worse when you selling weight, because rumors get around to a lot of greedy niggas that end up after your shit.

Damn, Red! . . . I might be ready t' die before you get out.

I got everything ready now: automatic assault weapons, extra shells from my boy Tee and a lemon from this used car lot. I just gave dude five hundred dollars under the table for this rusty blue Chevrolet instead of stealing one. He didn't record the shit, so he don't care. Now I'm just sitting in my living room waiting for it to get dark; it's almost seven now. I'm not doing no drive-by in the daytime. I'm planning to jump out right where these niggas live and spray every damn thing while they're out there chilling. The best time to hit niggas is on a Friday night before the clubs open.

"If they wanna fuck wit' me, then I'm gon' fuck wit' dem."

I turn around from the couch when I hear a key in my door. My girl walks in wearing all green today with shopping bags in her hands; her hair is done in a long bob. I just look away from her and back to the TV.

She walks into the bedroom wearing some black clog shoes. Now she's going into the bathroom. She comes back out and walks into the kitchen. I'm listening to her every step because I don't have nothing else to do. She ain't even giving me no pussy to calm my nerves down.

"What's wrong with you? I mean, you need some that damn bad?" She's standing over me now with orange juice in a tall, clear glass. I'm flipping this remote control through all these damn cable stations that don't have shit on that I wanna watch. So I turn back to BET videos.

"I ain't thinkin' 'bout that," I tell her.

She stares down at me anyway. "Well, what's wrong, baby?"

Damn! She looking good as hell in here. I pat my lap

for her to sit down. She does. Then she starts to run her hands under my shirt.

"I'm sorry about how I been treatin' you, baby. But you can't be slippin' and cuttin' up on me. And that was the first night I was here, too."

"Yeah, I'm sorry." I ain't even in the mood to game her. I'm just enjoying this shit while it lasts. I got things to do in a few.

She kisses me on my chin and starts to snuggle into my chest. "You want to, baby?"

"Why now?"

"Why not?"

I just smile. But this foreplay is feeling *good!*

Toya pushes me down with my back against the length of the couch. She climbs on top of me and unsnaps her bra. And fuck it! I know what time it is now.

Toya throws a towel across my naked chest. "Get'cha yellow ass out of bed and take a damn shower! Hurry up, J. Come on!"

Toya's in here running around like a squirrel. We went at it strong as shit; I'm tired as hell now.

"Look, Toya, I don't feel like goin' out tonight. Let's jus' order a pizza or somethin' and chill."

She stops what she's doing and looks down at me, stretched across my bed, as if I'm crazy. "You gots t' be out'cha damn mind, boy!"

"Oh, now I'm a boy?"

"If you talkin' that kind of shit you are." She runs through my closet and pulls out a royal blue silk outfit of mine. And it's wrinkled all the hell up. "Yeah, this outfit is like dat." She throws it on the bed, where it's still dry. "Here, wear this."

I frown at it. "Toya, now, that ain't even ironed."

"Well, get up and iron it then, dammit! Look, I'm not playin' with you, J. Now if you not gon' take me out, then let me know now so I can call up my girlfriends." She's looking serious as hell right now.

I get up from the bed wearily. Toya then pushes me into the bathroom.

"Stop acting like a damn kid! Now take ya ass a shower and come on!"

I smile at her and close the bathroom door. "You gon' be a rough-ass mom!" I holler out to her.

She laughs. "Shut up and come on!"

After we get dressed, we jump into my 3000 with nowhere to go yet but out. "So where we goin'?" I ask her.

She's putting lipstick on in my mirror. "Umm, Kilimanjaro's or something."

I look at my clock; it reads 10:37. It's dark. And . . . *I FUCKIN' FORGOT ABOUT MY PLAN! OH MY GOD!*

"Yo, we can't go to Kilimanjaro's tonight. Let's like, go to a club in Baltimore or somethin'," I tell my girl. I know I have to take her somewhere; she got me all dressed up, looking good and smelling good with her favorite cologne—Obsession For Men by Calvin Klein.

She looks at me evilly. "What? Look, J, I ain't come back home to go hanging out in no fuckin' Baltimore! What the hell is wrong with you?"

God damn! I done messed up again! Over some pussy! But hell; this my girl! This is Toya; she ain't just any shot of ass! This my future wife out this joint.

"Well, let's go out t' Maryland somewhere then," I tell her.

"Like where?"

"Umm, Classics or Oak Tree."

She nods her head. "Okay, that's cool." She leans back into the bucket seat.

"Aw'ight. But yo, I forgot to make a phone call," I tell her.

I pull the car over at a 7-Eleven and beep these niggas. The pay phone rings right back. They must've been right next to a phone somewhere.

"What's up?" Steve says.

I ask him, "Yo, how come y'all niggas ain't beep me earlier?"

"We was waitin' for you."

"What da fuck? I mean, y'all wanna do this or what?"

Steve hollers back at me, "Shit! How come you ain't call us earlier? It's ya plan!"

Yeah, he right. He right. It's my fault for getting some ass. "Aw'ight, yo. We gon' chill off that shit then 'til another day. But what I want y'all to do now is go park out at the Oak Tree at about two-thirty and wait until it closes. Then I want y'all t' like, walk through the crowds with ya pieces—but not with the Uzis. Aw'ight?"

"Aw'ight. But let me ask you a question, B. What da hell is we gon' do that for? I mean, do you know if these niggas are gon' be up there or somethin'?"

"Look, man, as long as I'm still payin' y'all, don't ask me no fuckin' questions! Now, just be up there!"

I slam the phone down and walk back to my thirty-thousand-dollar ride and my million-dollar girl.

"What was that all about?" she asks me.

"Nothin'. Let's roll."

The Oak Tree is slammin' like shit tonight! I'm sitting here drinking with my boy Spoon at the bar. This boy done cut all his dark curls off. I guess he been watching too many Onyx videos. I'd never cut off my hair. Toya wouldn't let me anyway.

"Yo, B?"

I take a sip of my rum and Coke. I'm only sipping this drink so I won't get drunk tonight. "What?" I ask Spoon.

"If I gave you a million dollars . . . would you let me fuck ya girl?"

I smile. "Fuck you and Robert Redford."

Spoon is watching my girl dancing by herself to our right, under the DJ booth on the dance stage. They're playing that "Whoomp! There It Is!" song. I laugh. Shank hates that song with a passion: "Them ma-fuckas should be lynched for makin' some wack-ass shit like that," he told me.

"What's so funny?" Spoon asks me.

"Nothin', man. I'm jus' trippin' off that *Indecent Proposal* flick," I lie to him.

Spoon smiles with glassy, drunken eyes. "Yeah, but it wasn't as good as I expected. I wanted to see dude bangin' 'er, you'n."

I take a strong look at Spoon's yellow ass. He's out here looking like one of my cousins, wearing black slacks and a Rayon shirt with his chest open like them Italians do in old disco movies: John Travolta and *Dance Fever*-type shit.

"Yeah, I forgot'cha ass was into that ol' kinky shit. Now stop starin' at my damn girl."

He laughs at me. "The darker the berry, the sweeter the juice for us yellow niggas, man. You know what time it is," he tells me with a grin. Spoon's fucked up already! I might have to drive Joe home tonight.

"Oh yeah? Well, stop sweatin' *my* berry and go find ya own, ma-fucka."

Spoon just laughs louder. Then he gets real quiet for a moment.

"Hi, Spoon."

A warm body leans up against my right shoulder. I flinch and see that it's my girl.

"Hi you doin', Toya?" Spoon says. He peeks at me and smiles. "We was jus' talkin' 'bout'chu."

Toya smirks at him and takes my hand, dragging me onto the dance floor. "You can't have me, Spoon. And nice haircut."

"Would you let me cut my hair like his?" I ask her with a grin.

She answers me without hesitation. "Of course not."

I laugh while she slips her hands around my waist on this crowded-ass dance floor. "So why you jus' tell him that his cut is nice?"

She smiles. "I was being sarcastic, J."

That slow Intro song comes on, the one that they re-made from Stevie Wonder's "Ribbon In The Sky." I look down at my girl and smile. "Yo, you told them to put this on?"

She smiles back at me. "What do you think?"

"Well, you know I'm too tall for this slow-draggin'."

"Shut up and bend ya knees then."

I chuckle. I look around while we dance. A lot of guys are taking peeks at me. But none of them look like they got no vendetta against me. People always looking at me: faggots and shit; jealous niggas; girls. And it's just be-cause I'm pretty. But I doubt if them Northeast niggas is thinking about me being at a party tonight. I'm probably after them more than they're after me now. I mean, I could probably ignore them and just go back to making money. But then again, if they punk me out, then cus-tomers that we're selling ounces to might start to take me for a sucker.

It looks like I have to do what I have to do. I'm not planning on being run out of my business. One hundred grand ain't gon' last forever. I have to keep my shit going.

My girl Toya is running her nails through the back of my hair and making my dick hard.

"What are you thinking about?" she asks me with her eyes sparkling from the disco lights.

"Makin' late-night love to you, baby."

She grins. "Just because we did somethin' earlier don't mean you gon' get it all the time."

I lean back and look deeper into her eyes. "So you tellin' me dat I'm on some kind of schedule or somethin'?"

She giggles. "You just might be."

I frown at her and shake my head. "Man, that shit is crazy."

We walk outside at the end of the party. The crowds are flowing out into the parking lot. I'm out here trying my hardest to get Toya back to the car and out of here as quickly as possible.

I spot Steve dressed in all black to my right. I look around and spot Boo further up in the crowd to my left. We nod at each other. But I don't see Otis nor Jerry out this joint.

If I could've had Shank, then I could have left these niggas the hell home and just took him with me. I been beeping young'un all night and day and he hasn't answered me. I bet he forgot his beeper or something. Shank ain't like the idea of having one anyway.

"Come on, let's get up out of here, Toya." I got my girl by her arm.

She pulls away from me. "Wait a minute, J. Let me holler at my girlfriend right quick."

"Ha-a-a-ay, Toy-Toy!" this tanned-skinned girl named Sharon screams. She's damn near tall as me and dressed in blue leather. They run up and hug each other like sisters.

I just sit here in the crowd and shake my head. I mean, girls always act like they have to go through all this extra drama-type shit when they see each other, like it's a ritual. I'm surprised they didn't see each other inside the party earlier. But it was kind of packed in there.

I move through the crowd to where Steve is. "Yo, where Otis an' Jerry?"

Steve looks past me in the direction of my girl. "Oh, dey like, headed over there somewhere."

BAP! BAP! BAP!

BOP! BOP!

BOW! BOW!

"OWWWWW!"

"SHIT!"

FUCK IS GOIN' ON? Niggas are running like elephants and zebras! I push my way through the crowd to get back to my girl. "TOY-YA!" I'm shoving guys and girls. "TOY-YA!"

I make it through and spot Sharon holding her side. I look down at it, seeing blood running through her leather outfit and into her hands. "OH SHIT! Where Toya at?"

Sharon bends over, screaming hoarsely, "Oh my God! Oh my God!"

I look past her, stop and look with my chest heaving and my heart pounding. *That ain't my girl right there; it's jus' some bitch dressed like her. It ain't my girl. IT'S NOT TOYA!*

I kneel down with my heart in my throat and turn her over.

"AHHHH, SHIT!"

I'M DREAMING, GOD! NOW MAKE ME WAKE DA HELL UP! PLE-E-EASE!

Tears are running out my eyes. All I'm hearing is wild screaming. All I see is blood all over my girl. I lean down to her head. "Oh, Toya. Baby."

I'M DREAMING—RIGHT? I'M FUCKIN' DREAMING! THIS SHIT AIN'T REAL! IT CAN'T BE!

I can feel my stomach turning and my dry-ass open mouth. It feels like I'm about to throw up. My hands are trembling over my girl's blood-soaked back. And my heart is burning inside my chest.

I can't hold it back. I CAN'T HOLD THIS SHIT BACK!

"TOY-YAAAAAAH!"

CHAPTER 11

Shank

*O*ff, *and, on. Trenda number two. Now, what'cha gonna do when, I, flow?*

Yeah, the Trends of Culture came off! Them motherfuckers went for theirs.

I'm out here on Eighteenth Street and Rhode Island Avenue Northeast, about to catch the E2 bus to meet these niggas up on Missouri Avenue in Northwest. I still ain't figured out what to do about this crazy motherfucker Rudy. But I made the right decision about not trying to cut Butterman short. He been on my dils-nick lately. He's been taking me everywhere with him, like I'm his new bitch of the week.

But oh, his girl is hy-y-y-ype as SHIT! She badder than a motherfucker. And she damn near black as me. I guess that nigga Butterman got a thing for jet-black niggas or something. I mean, his girl Toya is like, one of them dark-skinned, executive-looking bitches that people talk that "You look good for a dark-skinned girl" shit to. What? A black bitch can't look good or something? Cicely Tyson always looked good to me. She reminds me of my mother.

I think that's why my girl Carlette is so much on my dick too; her and Butterman just want to know what it feels like to be a "real-ass nigga" like Wes kept talking to me about. Both Butterman and Carlette are them half-breed-looking niggas. And the sun won't help them. They would probably get red and shit, like white people.

The E2 bus finally pulls up. I jump on, pay my dollar and walk to the back. Two older niggas are back there sitting in both of the corner seats and talking shit to one another.

"Aw, man, Riddick Bowe is fightin' nobodies. I mean, who da hell is a Jesse Ferguson?"

"Don't sleep, shorty. Ferguson almost knocked out Holyfield."

"Naw, that was a . . . Bert Cooper from Philly. And shit, dat dere was a damn fluke. But I'ma tell you what: Bowe needs t' fight that boah Lennox Lewis that kicked his ass in'na Olympics. See now, him an' Rock Newman are hidin' from'nat boah."

"Naw, he need'a fight Mike Tyson. That's who he need to fight."

"Hunh? Aw, man, 'nat damn prison done fucked Mike's head up, slim. I read in *Jet* magazine that Mike say he don't even think about fightin' no more. All he think about is prison bars and shit.

"Now, that's fucked up. 'Cause that damn girl done messed that man's life up. And she know damn well she wanted to give him some pussy that night. But what happened is that the shit ain't go down right. Mike jus' wanted some pussy, but that girl went up there expecting to get more than that."

"Mmm-hmm, yeah, 'cause they say she try'na sue him now."

"You goddamn right she try'na sue 'im! That girl knew who she was dealin' wit' when she went up in'nat hotel room. Shit! That damn girl said, 'This Mike Tyson. This nigga got some money, and I'm gon' go up here and give him some pussy.' And that shit ain't even right, man. It ain't *even* right."

Dude that just finished talking got one of those shaggy-ass beards. Other dude is clean-shaven. Both of them are brown and wearing T-shirts. But Shaggy-beard ain't finished talking yet. He looks about forty, and the other dude looks about thirty.

"What it is is that nigga mentality, man," Shaggy-beard says. I'm sitting here listening to these motherfuckers now. They're talking loud enough to make it easy. I'm sitting right up in front of them anyway.

"I mean, man, we da only race that bring each other down and degrade each other like we do. We'a say that word 'nigga' all day long, man; little kids sayin' it. And then we get mad when the white man says it.

"I mean, it's the same goddamn word. But then you get them brothers talkin' 'bout they done turned it into somethin' positive. You believe that, man? I mean, we done got so used to degrading one another, man, that now we wanna lie to each other about it and call it positive.

"You don't hear no white people callin' themselves honkeys or rednecks or no shit like that. Crackers. Naw. We da only race of people on earth that do it.

"That's why these young'uns are out here killin' each other t'day. They don't know who they are, where they come from or where they goin'. All they know is 'I don't like that nigga ova dere. I'm gon' shoot 'im.'

"I mean, these kids really hate one another, man. And some of 'em's parents ain't no damn betta. You tell a lady t'day, 'Ma'am, I think ya son is involved in some shit. And I'm just try'na let you know befo' he go and do something stupid.'

"And you know what these simple-minded-ass parents tell you t'day? 'Don't worry about my goddamn son! He ain't ya damn problem!'

"See dat? And it's that simple kind of shit that's bringin' the race down every damn day, man. Every damn day."

Other dude don't have nothing else to say. But Shaggy-beard still talking.

"An'ney won't do dat shit t' da white man. Talkin' 'bout how goddamn tough they are. But the white man make 'em into pussies when he gets to 'em."

Both of them get off the bus at the Fort Totten Metro station. Now they got me thinking. I got my pretty, wooden-handled .45 inside my belt now, and I did fuck up a white man. But for seventy fucking dollars when I'm getting paid a thousand a week to bust up niggas if I have to. I mean, no motherfucker gon' pay you to kill no white man! No fucking body!

Who you gonna shoot wit' dat, homie? And why does ya gat say, "Niggas only?"

That's that Lench Mob song. And then 2Pac says, *You love t' shoot a nigga but'cha scared t' pop a cop.*

Yeah. Them rappers talk that shit. But now it's this young dude in Texas about to get the death penalty for "poppin' a cop." I mean, niggas know what time it is when it comes to them fucking police officers, man. Especially white ones.

I read in that *News Dimensions* newspaper that Carlette reads, that this nigga named Terrence Johnson been in jail for like fifteen years for shooting these two white cops who were kicking his ass out in P.G. County when he was fifteen. That shit was back in 1978. They waited for you'n to turn sixteen so they could charge him as an adult. Now they keep denying his parole. And he a light-skinned pretty-boy with light-ass eyes like Butterman. I bet them faggots ripped his asshole to pieces in jail. I mean, that motherfucker was only sixteen! That's why niggas don't shoot cops. It ain't no damn mystery!

I walk up on these niggas chilling on Missouri Avenue, and guess what the hell they're talking about.

This big, bug-eyed nigga named Jerry that Butterman hired is talking: "Yeah, so if a nigga gon' die, Joe, he gon' die. I don't even see why ma-fuckas are afraid of death. I mean, you gon' go when you go, Joe. It's as simple as that. So I'm not all upset for killin' niggas. I figure they gon' die anyway, if not by my hands, then by another nigga's hands or a bitch wit' a knife, or even cancer out dis bitch."

Typical. These niggas are crazy! And here I am hangin' wit' dese losers.

They all quiet down when they see me in their midst.

"Yo, show 'im the paper, man," Steve says.

Otis gives me this folded newspaper. I read this shit inside the box: THREE KILLED IN RIVAL GANG FIGHT

Well, I guess I don't have to worry about Rudy no more. But damn he got some sixteen-year-old shot the fuck up too! See that shit? I did make the right decision, hunh? Then again, it's still gon' come a time when we gonna have to rumble with these Northeast niggas or somebody else. And I ain't even up for that shit no more; I'm having nightmares and all kinds of shit.

I've been faking Butterman out like I'm down though. I'm just waiting for him to ask me to kill somebody.

That's when I'm gon' sting him for some real-ass money. That five thousand dollars I got saved up ain't nothing compared to what Butterman is making. Rudy was right about that.

"So what'chu think, Shank?" this other nigga Boo asks me. Him and Jerry are both some bammas to me. I mean, Boo supposed to be in one of those halfway houses. They got all kinds of paperwork on these niggas. Me? I ain't never been caught for *shit!* Not even for Oak Hill Youth Center. And guess what? I'm gon' keep *my* sheet clean. These motherfuckers ain't a damn thing to me. Fuck these niggas! They just wasting their lives out here.

I give the paper back to Otis. "Fuck it, man. It ain't us."

"It might be us next if we don't get them first," Jerry says. "It's the law of the jungle, man."

Otis frowns at him. "What jungle? And we ain't no fuckin' gang; we jus' niggas out here try'na get money. This shit ain't no L.A."

I'm thinking, *Maybe this nigga Otis had the right idea all along.* I mean, not to be a pussy like him, but just not to get in no unsafe situations either. Hanging with these bammas will get me killed. You don't see Butterman all out with these motherfuckers. Butterman would rather hang out with some bitches, or Bink, or even Wes. Wes told me they went down to South Carolina for a birthday party. Now I know damn well that yellow-ass, *Richie-Rich*-type nigga wouldn't take any of these damn fools down there to see his family. I wouldn't want to go to no shit like that personally. Them light-bright niggas would've thought that I was a black Satan down that bitch.

Jerry shakes his head. "Otis, you's a *bitch,* man. I mean, when I was up in D.C. Jail, you'n, I jus' had to show ma-fuckas that I wasn't to be played with, that's all. So whether you gettin' money or not, you jus' gotta show niggas. In jail is the real deal, man. You ain't shit if you ain't been up yet."

Boo nods his head like he believes this shit. "Yeah, that's the sho' nuff, you'n. That's your real test in'nis game."

"And takin' a bullet if you have to, too," Jerry says. "I got hit in my arm once, and right here in my stomach." He lifts up his blue Champion shirt and shows us his shiny-ass skin that's healed over a bullet scar. "That shit went in and out, man. I jus' ran to the crib and wrapped the shit up and kept goin' at it."

Steve ain't saying anything. And I'm acting like I ain't paying no attention too.

Boo says, "Jail ain't all that bad, for real, Joe. I mean, at least you know, like, niggas ain't out there try'na kill you an' shit."

"You crazy, you'n!" Jerry yells at him. "Ma-fuckas gettin' killed like shit in D.C. Jail."

"Ain't that shit in Southeast?" Steve finally asks Jerry.

Jerry looks at him like he don't believe Steve just asked him that question. Then he smiles with this ugly-ass face of his. "You ain't never been ta jail, have you, Steve?"

"Fuck no!"

We all start laughing at the shit.

Jerry says, "That's how you become a man, Joe. I'm tellin' you."

I shake my head, frowning. *These niggas are out dey fuckin' minds! I mean, the more I listen t' dis crazy shit, the more sense I make.* Steve's not going for this jail-talk either.

Jerry looks to me. "Yo, Shank, I *know* you down, man. Now tell this boy, you'n. Real niggas die on the trigga like men, right? Like that part in that movie *Colors*."

He's talking about that scene where them two niggas face off and waste each other at the end.

I look Jerry in his bugged-out-ass eyes. All four of these motherfuckers are waiting for my answer like students. They really expect me to be crazy. And if I act crazy, I can fake all these suckers out for when I make my sting on Butterman.

"Ay, man, y'all muthafuckas are *crazy! Real* niggas don't die! We *multiply* out dis bitch! I'll kill all them niggas by my *fuckin'* self! I'on need shit but a MAC-10!" I grit at these niggas like I'm a straight-up lunatic. "Fuck this! I'm out'a here!"

I'm riding down Georgia Avenue on one of those double 70 buses, feeling good like shit. I know any day now Butterman gon' ask me to take somebody out. Then I'm gon' take the money and jet. I'm gonna hook up with my cousin Cal, head to New York and do whatever the hell we dream about. And fuck Butterman! He ain't gon' come after me. I read it in his eyes. He needs niggas like me just like the white man needs his army. In fact, he told me that shit when I first met his ass.

I got his stupid-ass runners believing I'm crazy now. I even got Butterman faked out. All I have to do now is wait it out.

"HEY, MR. BUS DRIVER! DROP ME OFF AT DA NEAREST LIQUOR STORE!" this wino yells. Dude is yelling from the back of the bus to the front of the bus. We up near that fire station on Georgia and New Hampshire.

Yo, I *have* to laugh at this shit. Niggas are crazy. But I'm not trying to be one, now. I feel like a "Black Man," like them Muslims talk about. I feel saved by JEE-ZUS! YES, LAWD!

I'm lunchin' like hell, I know. But I don't feel it no more, man. I feel free as a bird now. It's sunny outside.

Girls are starting to wear that sexy summertime gear. Muslims out here selling them *Final Call* newspapers with suits and bow-ties. I got a girl that's on my dick. I mean, Carlette loves me like shit! And I got rhyme skills to boot.

Yeah, fuck that going-to-jail-or-getting-shot-the-fuck-up shit. Me and Carlette gonna celebrate tonight. We gon' go see that *Indecent Proposal* flick all the way up in Wheaton, Maryland, somewhere, to get away from D.C. I already saw that movie, but Carlette's been asking me to go with her so she can see it. I mean, it's Friday anyway, time to get out.

"So how come you all energetic and smiling tonight?" Carlette asks me. I'm walking with her hand-in-hand to that Wheaton theater that got like eleven movies playing. We ate dinner at a seafood place earlier. I'm spending good money on Carlette tonight. She has that Shirley—I mean, Whitney Houston hairstyle, (because fuck white people), looking cute as hell. Niggas are up in here looking envious as hell.

"I got one of the finest-ass girls at the movies t'night," I tell her.

She's smiling like shit. I got her ass blushing.

"Unt-unh. What do you want from me, Nell?"

"What'chu talkin' 'bout?" My pager goes off for about the fifth time tonight.

Fuck Butterman and them bammas! I'm busy until tomorrow. Butterman wouldn't answer me if he was out with his damn girl! This her first Friday night back home from Spelman down in Atlanta. I know they're probably going out somewhere. So whatever you'n got to tell me can wait until tomorrow.

I got a life, too, muthafucka!

Carlette frowns. "God, who keeps pagin' you?"

"Yo, let me get'cha keys so I can put dis joint in ya car."

She gives them to me. I jog over to the car and throw my pager under the seat. I'm tired of the shit going off myself. I should have left this pager home anyway.

We head for the theater. I buy a big-ass bag of Gummy Bears inside. Carlette wraps her arms around me in the refreshments line. I look around while she hugs me. And yo, it's a bunch a girls in here—with boyfriends—starring at me and shit. I mean, I do look geared-up with my gold-and-white Tommy Hilfiger shirt, black Boss jeans and my all-white Nikes. But I think girls are staring just because I have Carlette with me. It fucks me up how girls be all on a nigga dick when he's with another pretty girl. Even ugly dudes.

"Would you sell ya wife for a million dollars?" Carlette whispers to me while the movie is playing.

I smile at her. "Hell yeah."

"Unt. No you didn't say that." She looks surprised, but she's still smiling.

"Yes I did," I whisper back to her, grinning.

"Unt-unh. So you would sell me, hunh?"

I look into her eyes and my heart feels like it jumped. "Yo, what'chu . . . What'chu try'na say?" I ask her. Damn! I had to strain to even get that shit out of my mouth.

She looks away from me and back to the screen. "Nothin'."

"So you wouldn't marry me, Darnell?" Carlette is drawing across my stomach again while we lay on my black satin bedsheets. It's about one-thirty in the morning—or at night—and we just finished "making love" earlier.

"You think I wouldn't?"

"I'm asking you."

I'm thinking about it. I guess I never really thought about marriage that much before. You know what I'm saying? I was just getting ass. And it ain't like I'm twenty-five or nothing. I don't even turn twenty until October 4. Carlette even older than me. She turned twenty-one in March.

I open my mouth to speak. "I prob'bly would, you know."

I guess I can't tell her yet that I'm gon' be breaking out to New York, and I might need her to drive me to Philly. She's even staying in D.C. to work and be close to me instead of going back home to Ohio this summer. But she says she has to do an internship down here anyway.

She doesn't respond to my answer. She just squeezes her body into mine, like she's trying to melt into my smooth black skin.

"Darnell?"

Aw, shit, I hate when she does this. Here comes another Joker's Wild. Watch!

"Hunh?"

"How come you never asked me to go with you?"

Oh. That wasn't that bad. "I ain't think you wanted no boyfriend."

"Why?"

"Because, you know, you a college girl and all."

She gets quiet on me. I guess my answer satisfies her.

"I had a boyfriend from back home when I first met you," she tells me.

"Oh yeah? Well, why you tellin' me dat now?

"I want to be honest with you. And I mean, I chose you over him."

Oh shit! You hear that shit? I'on know if I wanna hear no more of this. She might leave me for another ma-fucka too.

I can't help it. I have to ask her. "Would you do that same thing to me?"

"No."

"Why not?"

"I wasn't in love with him."

I smile. "So what'chu sayin'?"

She pauses. "Umm, no lie, Darnell, I thought about you all night when I first met you. I couldn't even sleep that night."

I chuckle. *Get da fuck out'a here!* I'm thinking. That shit sounds like game. "I only said a couple words to you."

"But it was the way you said it."

"What, rough and like—"

"Like you meant it," she says, cutting my words off.

I smile. "I did mean it."

"That's why I liked you." I shake my head and grin, just listening to her. "See, like, a lot of guys are sneaky and don't say what they mean. But you . . . I mean, you come right up front with it." She giggles and looks up into my face. "Even when you talk about . . . fuckin'."

I laugh like shit. But I need her to promise me a favor before we mess around and get too cozy in here. "Yo, umm, seriously, right. Would you do me a favor?"

"Anything."

I lean up and nod back and forth from my pillow. "Aw'ight. Well, I might need you to drive me to Philly one of these days."

She sucks her teeth and smiles, facing me. "Is that all?"

"But it might be jus', like, anytime in the day or night."

She doesn't say anything.

I look into her empty face. "So?"

"What?"

"Would'ju do it?"

She pauses again while I wait for her answer. This answer is important to me, because when I jet, I'm not trying to ride on no bus. At least not from down here. I'll just catch that New Jersey Transit line in Philly.

"Yeah," she finally tells me.

I squeeze her into me. "Beautiful."

"But why would you want me to do that?"

"I'd have to write you about it. Jus' trust me, okay? Like your pop says, 'Have some faith.' "

She kisses me and smiles. Then she lays her head back against my chest. "Okay. Only for you."

"Yo, where was you at last night, Shank?" Butterman is talking in a scratchy, drawn-out voice from his car. His eyes are bloodshot. He looks fucked up, like he was smoking and drinking all last night. We pull around on Fifteenth Street Northeast, up near Monroe. It's quiet back here; one of those grass-and-tree residential areas.

I'm wondering whether Butterman found out where I live. But I doubt it. Joe's too busy to be checking up on shit like that . . . I hope.

I look into his bloodshot eyes like I'm salty at him for even asking me. "Why?" I have to treat him as rough as I usually do. I can't have him getting suspicious. Smart niggas will do that when you start overacting. So I'm gon' just play this shit by ear.

"I was pagin' you, man. Me an' Steve, last night."

"An'?"

Butterman looks at me like *I'm* going crazy. "The fuck you mean, 'An', nigga? Where da hell was you at?"

I reach down into my belt and pull out my .45. You'n done pissed me off for real! "Yo, Joe, you don't talk t' me like you talk to them other niggas. I'll do ya ass right here. But I thought we was cooler than'nat."

Butterman just sits still in a white Polo shirt as if he's in a daze. He's not even looking at the gun in my hands. "My girl got shot last night, man."

I'm still playing it by ear. I ain't got nothing to say until he tells me the whole story. I'm just waiting for him.

"We was up at da Oak Tree last night, in Maryland . . . I had them niggas up there checkin' shit out in the parkin' lot in case I might have some problems."

He stops and shakes his head. "Stupid-ass Jerry wolfs off at the mouth to some guy he had beef with a while ago . . . Dude boy jumps out and starts poppin'. Jerry shoots him in the chest—so he told me—and then Otis fires on him too."

Otis? Get da hell out of here, I'm thinking. But I keep my cool and let you'n tell me the rest of the story.

"So once this nigga gets hit, he starts sprayin' bullets like a wild man. Muthafucka hit four people . . . My girl got hit in her spine. Bullet ricocheted and punctured a kidney . . . Dude in the ambulance said that she was prob'bly dead before she hit da ground."

That's fucked up! I really feel for this nigga now. Ain't that a bitch? But I'm still sitting quiet with my .45 in my hand.

This motherfucker starts laughing with tears running out of his eyes. "Yo, man. Like, I was plannin' to get them Northeast niggas last night, Joe. Fuck around and banged my girl and forgot about da shit. You know, pussy can do that to a nigga. But the deal is: them niggas wasn't there. I mean, I could'a been cool wit' my girl, man. Just me and her."

Yo, Joe is breaking the hell up now. His face is turning all pink. He's wiping his tears with the bottom part of his shirt. But I'm still cool. This might be my shot right here.

"And like, man, if you would'a been wit' me, Joe, it jus' would'a been me and you. Just like my boy Red used t' be. Just me and you, like that, Shank." He crosses his fingers to me.

Yo, I think he sniffed some blow last night now. He has that spaced-out-ass, crazy look about him. I can't even stand to look at him. But it might be time to make my pitch, while he's weak and not thinking straight.

I ask him, "So what'chu want me ta do?"

He rocks his head in circles like Stevie Wonder. I mean, this nigga lunchin' hard! "What da fuck *can* we do? We can't bring my girl back. We can't bring her back, Shank."

NOW! I look into his eyes like I'm ready to kill something. "See? If ya ass would'a took care of them niggas when'ney first tried that dumb shit on us that Saturday mornin', then things would'a been settled by now." *And I prob'bly would've been down to do the shit back den.* "But naw, you wanted to lay low, and all that did was make you fuckin' nervous. I mean, you had us runnin' around lookin' like bitches, man. I told'ju dat shit, you'n!" I pause and let him feel my words. I know he's ready to kill some motherfucking body! I mean, his girl got shot because of these niggas.

He's calming down now. He's getting himself back together. I guess I just had to snap him out of this *punk* shit! But he's still a punk. *Pretty muthafucka!*

"Mmm-hmm. And if we would've gotten them niggas by now, my girl would still be livin'," he says to me.

I can't let him go now. I got him! "So what'chu want, man? I'm ready ta smoke these niggas now," I tell him. I do feel mad. So it ain't like I'm faking. Toya was pretty as shit. And black like me.

Butterman looks at me. "When?"

"T'night, ma-fucka! No more waitin'. But yo, man. You tol' me, man." *HERE IT IS! LET'S PRAY FOR THIS SHIT!* I look into his eyes like I'm a mad man. "You tol' me you was gon' pay me *extra* when I killed. And I ain't no damn fool, you'n. I wanna be able t' say I had a motive *and* I got paid for it! You hear me?"

He looks straight back at me. This shit is as tense as you can get. But I can't back down now. THIS IS IT! DO OR DIE!

Butterman nods to me. "Money ain't no problem. I brought some with me. Look under your seat." I lean down and pull out a brown leather carrying bag. "It's ten grand in'nere. Go 'head and count it."

It's a fucking Uzi in this bitch with an extra cartridge, too! I look up at Butterman.

He forces a smile through his tortured-looking pink face. "I know you *been* ready ta fuck niggas up. So I figure I come strapped when I see you. I bought them joints yesterday."

I nod back at him and finish counting the money. He has it in hundreds, fifties and twenties. Each thousand is wrapped inside of rubber bands. But it's fifteen of them instead of ten. Maybe you'n is trying to test me.

My heart is racing like shit to pull this sting off. I feel like I have to say more to make it work. And I can start by lying to him with some punk-ass loyalty.

I look at him innocently. "Yo, it's more than ten grand here, you'n."

He smiles out the front window. "I just wanted to see somethin'."

"See what?"

He bites his bottom lip and looks into my face. "If you can count."

That's bullshit! We playin' a fuckin' game in here! I've seen this nigga outsmart ma-fuckas again and again.

I can't lie now. I'm nervous. But I'm not showing it. I can't. It's me against him. Brains against brains. Nigga against nigga. Light against dark.

"I figure your girl is worth more than fifteen Gs," I tell him. I'm gon' try another angle to get out of this hole. I got to. He's making it too motherfucking easy; that's how you mess up.

He nods his head. "Is you in it for the kill or for the money?"

"Fuck you talkin' 'bout?" I yell at his ass. "What da hell you in it for? What, am I supposed to do the shit because it's jus' some shit to do? Ya ass is makin' all'la money. Why can't you give me thirty grand to keep you in business, nigga? 'Cause see, I'm the only *real* nigga you got now. Them other stupid niggas gon' get'chu taken under. And I'm the only reason you was able to keep ya shit this long, Joe! Niggas wasn't afraid of you; they was afraid'a Shank!"

YES! I'm playin' it good. Now it's his move.

Butterman nods and rubs his clean-shaved chin. "What time we gon' do this shit?"

YES, MUTHAFUCKA!

"We wait until the sun goes down. Get them niggas when'ney don't expect it."

He smiles at me. "You must'a been readin' my mind."

Yeah, I jus' hope you ain't readin' mine. 'Cause the more time I give myself, the easier it is for me to get t' Philly with Carlette.

I set him up: "Aw'ight, yo. Drive me back t' da crib. I'm gon' call up some people I know from back Southeast. You round them other niggas up. And I'm gon' beep you back at like, seven-thirty."

He grins at me while he turns the key to ignition. "Where you live at?"

I smile at him to butter up my lie. "In Brookland Apartments in back of Super Trak. But maybe I can move out of that slummin'-ass crib now. Maybe I can move out to Maryland after we get dese niggas, Joe."

Butterman smiles and rides me to the dirty white

apartment complexes on Rhode Island Avenue, down the street from the Super Trak auto store.

I hop out with the bag of money and the Uzi in it. My .45 is back inside my belt. I turn back and stick my head through the window with all seriousness.

"Yo . . . don't'chu fuck around and try ta stop me t'night. 'Cause when I call these ma-fuckas from my old neighborhood, they ain't goin' out for kicks. And you bes' think about countin' some more money, too. 'Cause these niggas ain't for free."

"I got'chu. Everything is taken care of."

"Aw'ight. I'll beep you later." I turn around and eye some boys that really do live up in here. I run up into the building, playing the shit off like I know them. I figure Butterman ain't gon' wait around in the midst of this shit. All I have to do now is lay low and pay some of these niggas off to let me chill for a few minutes if I have to. I still got my .45 with me in case any of these boys want to squabble while I'm up in here. I might have pulled my sting off! I don't give a fuck about none of these niggas! I got fifteen thousand dollars and Butterman set up to think that I want more. I do. But I'll just have to settle with this cake so I can get the hell out of D.C. without becoming a fugitive for killing people in this crew bullshit. I mean, the way I see it, I wasn't really down with Butterman . . . I was just getting paid.

I'm back home packing my shit up like a crazy white woman in a horror movie. I'm about to get up out of this camp!

Fuck what'cha heard!

I'm throwing most of my best gear in a couple suitcases that I got from my mom. Most of this stuff I got ain't gon' make it though.

I walk into my living room and look around at my entertainment center with TV, stereo, equalizer, big speakers, a JVC VCR, and movies. Then I got this smooth black furniture, a Persian rug, posters on my walls. Damn! What can I do about all this stuff?

Fuck it! I'm taking all my tapes and as much of my shit as I can. I'm just gonna have to call Carlette and tell her to bring some of her suitcases. I'm gon' take my satin bed-sheets, all my sneakers and . . . Damn! Yo, a lot of all this stuff is just gonna have to get left. I mean, with the fifteen grand that I got from Butterman and my own five grand, that shit makes twenty thousand fucking dollars. Most of this stuff I bought was hot from Benny anyway. I can just buy better shit later on; that's all.

Yeah. That's what I can do. I'll leave Benny the key to this joint and let him and his boys rob it. I'll catch up to him and get the money another time.

I dial his number and he answers on the second ring. It's only about one o'clock, so I knew this nigga would be home. Benny's one of those strictly nighttime niggas.

"Yo, man, it's Shank."

"Who? Get da hell out'a here, shawdy. I thought ya ass was dead or somethin' by now. I mean, you ain't talked to me in like three months."

"Yeah, I'm try'na stay livin'. That's why I'm callin' ya ass up now."

"Oh yeah? Well, what'chu need a gun or somethin'?" He sounds real concerned and shit. But I got *five* guns now. And all the bullets for a street war.

I frown. "Naw, man. I'm 'bout t' break out. I was gon' let you have ya shit back. So what I'm gon' do, you'n, is leave this key somewhere and let you rob this shit. Then I'll jus' look ya ass up an' get a cut off it another time."

He laughs like shit. "What is this, an early Christmas present?"

"Whatever, black. Call it what'chu want."

I tell Benny where I'm hiding the key and call up Carlette.

Shit! She ain't even home. I *have* to leave a message this time.

"Carlette, this is Nell. I need you t'day, baby. This shit is code red. And bring like, two of your suitcases and drive over here as soon as you get this message. CODE RED, BABY! I'm in a hurry like a muthafucka, so hurry ya pretty ass up!"

I hang up and call up my Aunt Pam in Jersey, to talk to my cousin Cal.

"Darnell, honey, Calvin went to stay in New York this weekend. But he should be back by tomorrow night. He's made real good friends with some artists up there. And you know the Bruce family in New York that we Halls never really got along with?"

Damn! I don't really feel up to being all friendly right now. I'm ready to get the hell out of here. My nerves are running a mile a minute like the Six Million Dollar Man.

"Yeah," I answer her.

"Well, Cal's made good contact with a cousin Lewis from Queens. He's twenty-one, but his last name is Davis." She stops and laughs. "All these short last names we have. But he's still related to us."

Yeah, yeah, Aunt Pam. But I gotta go now. I mean, shit, my nerves are all fucked up!

"Aunt Pam, I got a 'mergency down here and I might need you to find me a temporary place to stay, up in Jersey."

My aunt gets quiet. She always thought I was good because I've never gotten locked up or nothing. But maybe she's thinking differently now.

"You know your cousin Peanut came down here talkin' about some guys were after him from Newark. He supposedly was hanging out with the wrong group of friends from East Orange, and they ended up having a feud or something. And you know that damn Ozzie went out here—just a week ago—and got himself arrested for trying ta stick up some white man in Atlantic City."

Fuck it! I ain't got time for this shit. I'm cutting her ass off.

"Aunt Pam, now you know I ain't never been in no trouble, but things are gettin' hot down here in D.C. too. And I'm trying to stay away from it. That's why I need ya help."

She sits on the phone, speechless. My heart is pumping like shit. I can't help it. This shit is hectic. My nerves are running in a million different directions. I feel like throwing the hell up, and I didn't even eat today!

She sighs. "Okay, boy, you know I always loved you."

WHEW! SHIT! "Thanks, Aunt Pam."

"Unh-hunh. So when you comin'?"

I know this won't sound good either, but it's the truth. "Tonight."

"Tonight?"

"Yeah."

She pauses again. "Okay. Lord help me."

I say my good-byes and all and hang up, excited like hell. All I have to do now is wait for Carlette to get over here and I'm off like a rocket.

I'M OUT'A THIS SHIT! THE STREETS AIN'T GETTIN' THIS BLACK NIGGA!

I calm down with as much of my stuff packed up as I can get without Carlette's bags to put some more shit in. I feel good as hell. I ain't felt this free in a long-ass time.

I take deep breaths and sit here watching this Saturday afternoon cowboy movie, waiting for Carlette. As soon as she gets here, I'm gonna call the phone people and have this line cut off.

Feet don't fail me now!

I'm laughing like shit, sitting here lunchin'. I'm about to get out and I'm never getting trapped in nothing like this again. NEVER! Life is too short for this dumb shit.

YO!

HUNH?

What da fuck are you doin', Shank? You punkin'na fuck out now, nigga, or what?

Naw, Joe, I'm just trying to live my life, man.

That's right! Fuck dat tough guy-shit, Nell. Life is more precious than'nat dumb ego shit. You smarter than'nat, Nell. You smarter than'nat.

Yeah, I know I am, you'n. You right. I know I am.

No da fuck you not. You goin' out like a bitch, nigga, runnin' from punk-ass Butterman. You should kill his ass and take the rest of his fuckin' money.

Yeah, that's right. Butterman do got more money. I mean, fifteen grand ain't nothing compared to what he's making.

Darnell Hall. Don't listen t' dat psychopathic bullshit. Fuck that! You'll make much more than Butterman with your hype-ass rhymes. All you need is to start makin' fat-ass tapes and get'cha name out there.

No bullshit, you'n! I got much skills.

And when you get to New York, wit'cha cool-ass cousin Cal, you gon' go for yours, right?

You damn right I am, Joe! I'm gon' get much damn props.

Come, on! I mean, get da fuck out'a here, nigga. It's a million muthafuckas travelin' all'la way up t' New York, every fuckin' year, jus' t' get their stupid-ass feelings hurt. And ya rhymes ain't no different from any other niggas'. That Mad Man shit already been done, Joe. So get off Redman's and Mr. Scarface's dick.

Yo, FUCK THAT, Nell! You still got skills, you'n. Write some other hype-ass rhymes. That gangster shit ain't the only thing you know. Remember what Wes told you? You would punk out if you didn't go for yours. And you don't back down t' nobody, right? So don't let nothin' stop you from goin' for yours, Joe! Do ya fuckin' thing!

That's right! That's right! THAT'S RIGHT! Yeah, fuck everybody that don't believe in me! Fuck all you punk-ass niggas! I'm getting the fuck out of here! And FUCK BUTTERMAN *AND* HIS BITCH! I mean, you know, if somebody shot Carlette, *I* would be the one who would want to kill them. But them Northeast niggas didn't even kill Butterman's girl. It seem like his girl was meant to die. That's his problem! I got in this shit for the money. Now I got some. So fuck everything else!

I jump up from my couch and pace back and forth, taking peeks out my peephole for Carlette. My VCR clock reads 3:39.

"Damn, Carlette! Come on, girl. Come the *hell* on!"

My cordless phone rings and scares the shit out of me. *Please be Carlette, God. This waitin' shit is killin' me.*

"Hello."

"Everything is ready, man. I'm gon' pick you up at Super Trak at like, six."

SHIT! It's Butterman. This muthafucka!

"Aw'ight, you'n." I ain't got nothing else to say to him. But I have to say *something* to let him think I'm still down. "Yo, this damn Uzi ain't no joke, you'n. We gon' get them niggas."

He says, "Yeah. Show 'em who dey fuckin' wit', right?"

"Damn straight. But aw'ight, yo, let me call these Southeast niggas back and tell them when to meet us."

"Cool. I'll see you later on then."

I hang up, thinking, *Where da fuck are you at, Carlette? Goddammit!* But I ain't ask Butterman about the money again. That was good. He's probably thinking he gon' get us to do it before he pays us. That's just the way I want it.

Little do that nigga know he gonna be waiting for a ghost at six o'clock. But where the hell is Carlette?

I walk back and forth through my house, all packed and ready to go. And you know what? I ain't talked to my mom in a long-ass time. Not even my little sister.

I call them up and my little sister answers the phone on the first ring: "Hello."

"Remember me?"

She giggles. "Nope, you'n. Who you?"

I laugh with her. "Yo, how you been?"

"Aw'ight."

"Any boys been try'na get'chu?"

She giggles again. "Unt-unh, Joe. Nobody mess wit' me like dat."

Good. "Well, do you 'member what'cha big brother looks like?" I'm just trying to pass the time. The clock says 4:23 and counting. And I won't feel as nervous if I keep talking to somebody.

My sister sucks her teeth, probably smiling like Carlette. Maybe she'll look for a jet-black nigga like me when she gets older, too, with her light-skinned ass.

"Yeah I 'member what'chu look like," she says with a smart mouth. "I mean, mom got'cha graduation picture all up on top of the TV. You can't even miss that joint when you walk in here, you'n. Dag."

WHAT? "Stop playin'. Mom got my graduation picture on'na TV?"

"Yeah, she do."

Get da hell out'a here! I mean, she didn't have my picture up like that when I left.

Now I'm nervous again at the shit I'm about to ask. "Umm . . . is she home?"

I can tell my sister's smiling. She's just like Carlette. "You wan' speak to her, don't'cha?"

I suck *my* teeth. "Shut up, girl, and get her on'na phone."

She laughs and screams in my ear, "MOM, somebody wants to speak to you!"

Goddamn! My heart feels hot like shit. This'll be the first time I said anything to my mom since she threw me out in October.

"Who is it, girl?" she asks my sister before she answers.

Damn! Sound like da same mean-ass Mom t' me.

She answers like she's irritated: "Hello?"

My chest is rising up and down for air, like somebody has a gun to my head. "Yo, what's up?"

She doesn't say anything. Then: "Where you at, boy?"

"In my apartment."

"How come you ain't called me 'til now?"

"I been busy."

"Mmm-hmm, busy gettin' in a bunch a damn trouble."

I shake my head, not believing this shit. She's still fucking evil!

"Yo, what'chu don't like me or somethin'?" My damn voice is cracking like a bitch. Maybe I am getting soft.

My mom doesn't answer me.

"I mean, all my life, Mom, all you did is talk shit and fuck wit' me."

"Who you think you talkin'—"

"I'm talkin'na you! I mean, you don't act like nobody's fuckin' mother, you'n! What da hell is wrong wit'—"

"I did the best I could, boy! Ya li'l ass was always fed and—"

"So da hell what? I ain't never felt like I was worth nothin'!"

"Well, well . . ." She's sniffing now as though she's crying. "You don't have no damn kids, boy."

My heart is beating uncontrollably. I feel real hot

around my chest. And my body is shaking like I'm about to have a damn seizure. All because of my damn mom. "How you know what I got? You never asked me shit. How da hell you know *shit* about me?"

Her voice is cracked too now. " 'Cause you my damn son, boy. You my *only* damn son."

Tears are starting to run out of my eyes while my chest heaves. I can't even stop the shit. Them motherfuckers just keep coming. I just sit on the phone in silence while they wet my face. Ain't no sense in trying to stop them. Fuck it. It ain't nobody here but me and my mom. And she can't even see me crying.

"Yo . . . why you got that Maya Angelou book?" I ask her. I still haven't figured that out.

"Your Aunt Pam gave it to me. She said it was a good book for me ta read."

"Did'ju ever read it?"

"Ain't never had time."

"Make time. I mean, 'cause, I don't know what all you been through in life, but I figure if Maya Angelou can go through all the things she did and end up being famous, then we all need to read that book."

My mom giggles, still sniffing. Her laugh is choked because of her tears. And this is the first-ass time she got me smiling in I don't know when.

"So when you comin'na see ya mother, boy?"

"Never," I tease her.

She gets quiet on me like she's taking it seriously. "You hate me that much?"

"Do you hate me?"

She pauses. "I ain't never hate you, boy."

"Yeah, well, I'll write you a letter, 'cause I'm goin' back to Jersey and then to New York to live. I ain't never wanna come to D.C. anyway."

"Hmm. I'm sorry 'bout that, boy. You know, love is a funny thing."

Yeah, she's talking about her love for that motherfucking Julius.

I hear a knock on my door. I walk over and peep out the peep hole. Carlette is standing out in the hallway with two, big light blue suitcases in her hands.

"Come on, Darnell, these things are heavy," she says through the door.

I wipe my eyes and face real good with my shirt before I let her in.

"Who's that?" my mom asks me.

I smile at Carlette while I answer. "Mom, she wants to marry me."

"She, who?"

"I'll tell you in'na letter. But I'm 'bout to break out now."

"Mmm-hmm. Whatever, boy," my mom says. I can tell she's smiling though.

I hang up and start grabbing my stuff. My VCR clock says 5:03.

I tell Carlette in a hurry, "Yo, let's get busy and get da hell out of here for Philly." *And yo, my mother likes me an' shit. She likes me!*

I'm too relaxed to say anything while me and Carlette ride up I-95 to Philadelphia. She's been kind of quiet herself. And this Sade *Love Deluxe* tape she has in is so damn smooth that it's not doing too good to spark any conversation. It just makes you want to lay back and chill.

I pick up the cassette cover and look to Carlette.

She smiles straight ahead, looking out into the busy traffic. We're doing about sixty-five.

"Don't even say it," she tells me.

I smile. "But you do."

"No. She looks like me."

I chuckle. "She like ten years older than ya ass."

"Well, as least I don't have any freckles like her."

I just smile at the shit as we get through Delaware and cruise into Philly.

I direct Carlette to Market Street. When we get to Eighth and Market in downtown Philadelphia, I get her to pull over so I can get all this stuff out. I got five bags, $19,500 dollars and five guns to sell once I get to Jersey. But I'll probably keep this wooden-handled .45. This gun is pretty like shit!

Once all my stuff is on the sidewalk, I hail a taxi. It only has to take me around the corner about five blocks to the Trailways/Greyhound station. But Carlette don't know.

She hugs me out in front of her car after me and this black taxi driver gets all my bags in. I'm wondering if Carlette can feel this .45 in my belt, under my hoodie, since she hugs me so tight. But if she did, she ain't saying nothing about it. And I changed my mind about giving her this .22 I got; it's too many guns out here for nothing already.

"So, you gon' call me so I can come up to visit you?" She don't look too excited while she asks me. I guess she feels like I'm leaving her or something and that I won't ever talk to her again.

I grab her gently by the neck. "If I hear about you being with another nigga, I'm gon' go crazy." I give her the envelope from inside my hoodie with five hundred dollars in it. Like they say, "It's the thought that counts," and she don't need no money as much as I need it.

She hugs me again and kisses my lips. She hops inside the car. I walk over to her driver side to look down at her.

She looks back up at me with stars in her eyes. I guess she really loves me.

I smile at her. "I do you, too," I tell her.

She smiles back. "Why can't you say the words?"

I look at her seriously. "I have to learn to. But it'll probably be you that I say it to."

She smiles even wider. "I hope so."

I nod my head and walk over to get inside this taxi before dude starts cussing me out or some shit.

I watch Carlette's blue Toyota ride past. I'm sitting here on my way back to Jersey after all these years, to stay. But I ain't staying that long. As soon as Cal graduates from high school next month, we're going to New York.

I pack up on a New Jersey Transit Line bus to Trenton. I had problems getting all of my bags on here, so I put some of my less-valuable-type shit inside them lockers for storage. I can just ride back down and pick it up tomorrow.

I lean back into the cushioned bus seats and chill. Like Ice Cube would say, "Today was a good day."

I'm smiling like a motherfucker. These other passengers probably think I'm crazy. But fuck them! Ain't none of them niggas just went through the shit I had to go through to get here today. So fuck them niggas. This my goddamn life.

Damn, though. I wish I had bought a magazine or something to read while I'm on here. Everybody's talking about Snoop Doggy Dogg. And that boy ain't even got his own hits out yet. That's some powerful shit to get all that damn press with no fucking album. I wish I could have my shit like that. But I got a whole lot of work to do before I get *that* big; if ever.

One things for sure though: like Maya Angelou, *I*

know why the caged bird sings too. Because his ass wants to fly. And the man ain't gon' get my damn wings. My ass gon' fly-y-y-y like a motherfucker.

'Cause I'm blacker than black, 'cause I'm black, y'all.

I'm on here trippin'. That's from that CB4 movie with Allen Payne rappin'.

But yo, I'm another brother that's browner than Bobby. I got the cool-ass styles that make the crowds mob me. I'm dressed to impress and never lookin' sloppy.

CHAPTER 12

Wes

I'm standing proudly in my red-and-gold cap and gown this Saturday afternoon of May 8, 1993, graduating from the University of the District of Columbia with a bachelor of arts degree in political science on this sunny but windy day. My mother is among the huge display of families and friends who have gathered inside of Dennard Plaza on the main campus. She arrived with three of her girlfriends and a few of their kids, holding me up as an example of a young black male role model. Now I look forward to taking the next stage and going on to graduate school in the field of education. Professor Cobbs said, "We still have a *few* good soldiers left." So then, let me go to war—an educational and image war, that is, and not any physical, gun war. And in the category of a war of integrity, us black men of this oppressed white world have been fighting to maintain our dignity since birth.

After the elaborate graduation ceremony has ended, I

step down from the crowd of happy graduates—mostly of African heritage, whether they be African-American, West Indian or Ethiopian—and join my mother and her friends.

My mother rushes to me from the crowd and squeezes me with a tight hug. "I'm so proud of you, boy." She steps back from me, happy-faced and wiping fresh tears. "God, this is one of the proudest days of my *life!*"

"Well, stop hoggin' him up and let's take some pictures with him," her tall, slender girlfriend Evelyn says.

"Oh," my mother responds. She whisks me around with her to face Evelyn's camera.

Evelyn takes several shots of us before I'm shoved and pulled and hugged like a rag doll to take pictures with everyone else.

"Don't damage my eyes with all these flashes," I tell them jokingly. "These contacts lenses are pretty fragile."

My mother looks at me sternly. "Oh, hush up, boy." Then she smiles. "You should've worn your glasses anyway, out here try'na be cute."

"Well, he is a wanted man now. I just wish he was old enough for me," Evelyn says to much laughter.

My mother playfully grabs me away from her. "You leave my son alone. I've already picked out a wife for him anyway, you old bat."

I shake my head with a grin. "Mom, Sybil and I are not getting married anytime soon." *And this reminds me that I'll eventually have to tell my mother about NeNe. But not yet.*

"If I've told you a thousand times, boy, I'll tell you again: that Sybil is a hell of a catch."

"What da hell took you so long, man? God!" Marshall asks me from behind his steering wheel. The guys and I are headed to the Classics nightclub in Maryland to celebrate. We all have on new outfits and whatnot, and

Marshall's afraid that a huge rush of college graduates will crowd up the club before we get there—since I took so long to get ready. Therefore, he's driving like *Mad Max: The Road Warrior.*

"His mom held his ass hostage, you'n. You know dat," Walt says laughingly. He's sitting in the back seat with me, and Derrick is up front with Marshall.

"Yeah, I had to break away from *my* peoples, too," Derrick says, grinning.

Walt sucks his teeth. "Look here, Joe: when I graduate, I'm gon' run off the stage and head straight for a hotel room and party for da whole damn weekend."

Marshall responds, "Yeah, *when* you graduate."

We all laugh before Walt can get out a rebuttal.

"Yeah, well, I'll be gettin' me some pussy on my graduation night, you'n." He looks to Marshall with a grin. "By da way, Marshall, when'na last time you had some ass?"

We all laugh again, including Marshall.

"Ask ya sister," he retorts.

"I did ask her. And she said she don't know you."

We laugh again as if we've paid for a Martin Lawrence concert.

We arrive at the crowded Classics parking lot area to find no spaces available.

"See what I mean," Marshall says to no one in particular.

"Fuck it, man. Park on'na side of the road like them other niggas did," Walt tells him, referring to the many cars we passed that were lined up on the road alongside the club.

Marshall wheels the car around to park illegally with the rest of the cars.

"They gon' all get tickets," Derrick says.

Walt sucks his teeth again. "Nigga, it's Saturday on

graduation night. Ain't no damn cops givin' no tickets out here, you'n. Da fuck wrong wit'chu?"

Derrick shakes his head while Marshall parks anyway. "You can listen to Walt if you want. But remember I told you," he says.

"Damn, yo! Look at the mane on'nat lion," Walt whispers to us. We all look ahead to a big-butt girl to the left of us, dressed in an off-white, form-fitting dress.

We giggle quietly.

"A 'mane' is the hair along or around an animal's neck. *Not* the beef around their ass. And it's usually found on the *male* gender," I comment to Walt with a smile. My academic humor receives a good laugh, too.

"Well, with humans—especially *black women*—their mane is their ass, Joe. Now shut da fuck up and keep bein' quiet."

We approach the front door, get searched down and pay our six dollars to enter the crowded dancehall and barroom.

Marshall turns and faces us as soon as we squeeze inside. The DJ is playing Lords of the Underground's "Chief Rocka." Stylishly dressed black women and men are dancing everywhere.

"See, I told y'all this shit was gon' be the hypest!" Marshall yells at us above the music.

Walt side-steps a dark brown sister, dressed in a peach-colored, two-piece skirt-and-jacket suit and takes a long stare at her behind.

"Yo, you'n, I'm 'bout ta buy *her* a drink," he tells us.

We chuckle at him as we slip our way in through the crowd. We're more like pushing and squeezing our way through. The small dance area in the middle of the room is already filled to capacity as well as the elevated stage against the back wall, so many couples are dancing around the chairs and tables that surround the dance floor. I mean, I hope a fire doesn't break out in here, because this place is fully stocked. We might as well be sardines.

"Damn, you'n! If you squeeze a bitch's ass in here, she won't know who did it," Walt says to Derrick.

"But why they gotta be bitches though?" Derrick questions him with a grin.

Walt frowns down at him from his taller frame and shakes his head. "See, I gotta stop hangin' wit'chall niggas, Joe. You know what da fuck I mean. Even bitches call each other bitches."

"But that don't make it right."

"Yeah, whatever, man."

After a while, we all get separated. Derrick and I end up together, just like always. We luck up and grab some seats alongside the bar, to the left of the dance-floor.

"You guys want anything?" a bald-headed brother working the bar asks us. He looks about forty, so I doubt if he has this bald-head fever that the New York hip-hop crowd has started.

"Yeah, let me get a Sex on the Beach," Derrick says.

We look at each other and smile.

"Sex on the Beach?" I ask him grinning.

Derrick is still smiling to himself. "You know, I figure that people talk about it so much that I thought I'd try one."

"Yeah, well, I know Walt's gonna be drunk. And if Marshall drinks too, then I might end up as the designated driver tonight."

"Aw, man, I won't get drunk off of one drink. I heard it's just sweet anyway."

I smirk at him. "We'll see."

The older, bald brother brings the drink as I turn to face the crowd.

"So what's up with you and NeNe?" Derrick asks me.

I bob my head to Da Youngstas' "Crewz Pop" as I answer. "We're talking again, but I haven't seen her yet. She acts like she's playing hard to get with me now."

Derrick grins while sipping his drink through a straw. "Yo, Marshall told me that Sybil been talking about you again."

I turn and look Derrick in his eyes. "Yeah, that's my mother's doing."

Derrick smiles so hard that he's forced to put his drink down. "Oh yeah? Well, what about you and Candice now? What's up with that?"

I smile, feeling like some kind of newfound mack daddy. "Man, I mean, I've just had a wild and dangerous last couple of months."

Derrick takes another sip of his drink through his uncontrollable smile. "Yeah, I'd say."

The DJ mixes in Dr. Dre and Snoop Doggy Dogg's "Nothin' But a G Thang." The crowd goes off, dancing up a storm! I even move out of my bar chair and find myself dancing.

The DJ mixes a fusion of hip-hop, reggae and D.C. gogo before later slowing it down with some new music from Big Bub—from Today—Silk, and the local boys from Howard University: Shai.

Before the night is over, I end up with two phone numbers. I mean, I haven't danced as much as I did tonight in my life! And I guess the women were a bit more generous tonight since many of them have recently graduated and have come back home to the D.C.–Maryland–Virginia area for the summer.

Marshall suddenly stops his car in front of my building. I lean back into the back seat, not anxious to get out yet.

"Come on, loverboy. It's time t' roll," Marshall implores.

Walt grins at me and tosses his big right hand on my shoulder from my left. "Yeah, this boy here had a stable of bitches t'night."

I glance up at Derrick to catch him shaking his head at Walt's insistence upon using the word "bitch."

"What we gon' do with him, Wes?" he asks me.

"Y'all gon' leave me da fuck alone about that shit, that's what," Walt says, beating me to a response.

I answer Derrick with a smile. "I don't know, man. It's a whole lot of things in the black community that need to be worked on."

"Oh yeah? Well, I ain't one of 'em," Walt interjects, crossing his arms across his chest defiantly.

I struggle out of Marshall's car and wobble my tired head toward my six-story building's entrance.

"You comin' over to watch the NBA playoffs t'mar?" Marshall asks me.

"I don't know why y'all sweatin' the Knicks. I mean, y'all know it's gonna be Jordan all the way," Walt says with much confidence.

"We'll see," Derrick chokes in.

I look back inside the car to Marshall, from my building's sidewalk area. "Yeah, I'll see you guys tomorrow."

I get inside my tiny apartment, make it to the bed and fall out on my face. I grab the phone from off of my night-stand and check my C&P answer mail to see if NeNe has called me while I was out all day and night. I have a few messages of congratulations but nothing from NeNe. Well, I did tell her that I'd be out all day, so it's cool. I guess.

I wish I could have invited her to the graduation. Then again, Sybil and her family were there and my mother forced me to take pictures with her and everything before we left the campus. And then with the feud between NeNe and Candice and . . . Well, you get the picture. It would have been just a big mess to invite NeNe. It's a good thing she told me that graduations are too long and boring for her anyway.

I called NeNe this Sunday morning and she wasn't in. I'm beginning to wonder now where she's been. Compared to most hip guys like J, I guess you could say that I'm pressed. But he's *pressed* about *his* girl. He's not all that debonair when it comes to Latoya. So I guess even the players can be tamed by the right woman.

It's almost twelve o'clock. The first NBA final will probably start before I reach Marshall's house in Northwest. He's already told all of us that he's not going to pick us up today after having to drive late last night. And tonight we're planning on going to the Ritz for college night. The Ritz's all four floors are expected to be filled to capacity.

I catch the 80 bus, transfer at the Fort Totten Metro station, and catch the 64 bus to Northwest. It's always pretty quiet on the buses on Sunday mornings. Usually there are a few church folk on the bus. Me? I've never been too much into religion. I guess you could call me a worldly guy. But I do believe in God. Or at least some force of order and creation that connects the universe to this thing called life.

Many of the bus stops are advertising Mario Van Peebles' movie, *Posse,* about black cowboys. *Dragon: The Bruce Lee Story* is being advertised as well.

The 64 bus lets me off on Eleventh Street, right down from Marshall's house on Thirteenth. And he lives too close to Candice's place for comfort, right down the street and around the corner to be exact.

Before I reach my destination, the older brother sitting

in a side seat to my right shakes his head at me while holding a paper in his hands.

"They still out here killin' one another," he says. "Babies against babies."

I hop off the bus and ponder his rhetorical comment.

What the hell can we do about it?

I shake the thoughts of D.C.'s homicide rate from my mind. Last time I heard it was nearly two hundred. But again, *What the hell can we do about it?* Kids today will shoot you even when they *know* they're wrong.

I knock on the door and walk into Marshall's basement apartment after he opens it. Walt is laid out in his usual space on the two-person couch inside of the living room. He's stretched out and still asleep in some sweatpants and a T-shirt.

I look to Marshall for an explanation. "What, he spent the night?"

Marshall stretches out on the long couch where Derrick and I usually sit. "What does it look like?" he throws back at me with a grin.

I just smile and take a seat in the one-person chair to the left.

"So what'chu gon' do about a car now?" Marshall asks me.

I sold the Acura Integra for nine thousand dollars and put the money in my bank account along with the other four thousand I had saved from working for Butterman. But once I get to grad school, in a year, that money is going to vanish. I'll need a good job, scholarship grants, loans and my mother's help for grad school.

Where there is a will, there is a way, I'm thinking.

"If I can't stand to be without one, I'll buy a used car," I tell Marshall.

"Do ya mom know you ain't had no job for three months?"

I frown at him. "Are you crazy? Hell no!"

"Well, how you gon' just up and buy a car?"

I shake my head and think about it. "I guess I can't buy a car then, can I?"

Marshall chuckles and kicks his feet up on the arm of his couch. He's wearing gray shorts, a white T-shirt, and no socks. "Yo, you gon' have to start makin' up some good lies or somethin', man. 'Cause you know you can't hide that money from her forever."

"Well, how do other illegal guys hide *their* money?"

"They don't. Most of the time their parents just look the other way. And a lot of times they don't have any money to begin with, so their parents are happy to see it, you know?"

"Well, what about us struggling good boys, who need money so we can set up households, start up a business and provide for *our* families? Or even go to graduate school like I'm about to do? I mean, how come there's so little money for us? And after all that college loan stuff, we end up twenty and thirty thousand dollars in debt."

Marshall shrugs. "That's the way it goes, man. I mean, you know that, Wes. You sound like you in here talkin' jus' t' be talkin'."

"You know damn well that's how America works, you'n. And all them drug dealers eventually end up dead, in jail or strung out on that shit themselves. I mean, it sounds like, to me, you been hangin' out wit' dat Butterman and he done messed ya thinkin' up. What happened to the Wes that I used to know: the Wes that would make the whole world make sense in one damn paragraph?"

Marshall lets his question hang in the air like a hot-air balloon. I guess he has a point. J's fatalistic train of thought has weakened me. I guess I *have* lost my bearing on what my goal is and what strategy to follow as a young black man in America.

"And that girl NeNe is comin' from the same fast streets, man," Marshall adds. "Girls like her never mature enough to stay with a guy like you. I mean, yeah, she was able to hang in the beginnin' when you first met her, and then when you got a car and some money. But can she hang for the long walk up that lonely road called sacrifice? 'Cause you know, man, what my father always told me about women: If a woman is not willing to sacrifice for where you two eventually want to get to, then she ain't worth the shoes she walkin' in."

I smile. "Hmm. That sounds like a good one."

"Yeah. I'm tellin' you, man. Ain't no glorious, romantic relationships without no struggles in *this* life, Joe. That shit is for the movies. Everything in *real* life takes time."

I nod my head, still smiling. "I guess like they say, good things—"

"—come to those who wait," Marshall says, finishing the famous cliche used by us "regular guys" in America. I guess now is the time to shake off the elusive hold that the fast lanes have secured on me.

By four o'clock, all of us are alive and watching the second NBA playoff game.

Walt says enthusiastically, "Damn! Barkley strong like shit, Joe! That nigga throwin' niggas."

I look to Derrick, who's still bewildered about what to do with our friend Walt.

"Oh yeah, Wes? What's up wit' Farrakhan, man?" Marshall asks me out of the blue. He's back in his favorite spot on the floor, directly in front of his television.

"What? What about him?" I ask, confused.

Walt sucks his teeth. "Ma-fucka playin'na violin and flutes and shit now," he answers and frowns. He shakes his head in disgust. "White man even got Farrakhan goin' soft, you'n. That's fucked up!"

"Wait a minute. That's just the image the media is trying to portray. Because I read that Farrakhan ain't changed his views on nothin'," Derricks rebuts.

I nod my head, agreeing with Derrick. "I know. Farrakhan plays the violin, and now every medium in America wants to showcase it."

"Well, he better not fuck around and do no ballet or no shit. 'Cause they'a really have his militant, hate-the-devil ass then."

We all laugh loudly. Walt has about as much sense as a peanut.

Derrick looks to me and opens his right hand toward Walt. "This is black America, Wes. How can we fight against brothers like him?"

Walt just laughs at it. "You can give me a fat-assed woman, some corn chips and a forty-ounce, nigga. And I'll be cool."

Marshall shakes his head from the floor. "You know who he reminds me of?"

"Who?" I ask him.

"Sweet-Dick Willie from *Do The Right Thing.*"

We all start laughing.

"Yeah, but Robin Harris tells it like it is, man. That's why niggas liked him," Walt comments.

Marshall says, "I wonder how famous he would have been if he didn't die."

"Yeah, 'cause niggas still on his dick now, you'n." Walt nods with a big baby-faced grin. "Yeah, you can call me Sweet-Dick Willie. That shit's aw'ight wit' me."

After the game and the news, Marshall turns to MTV and Walt immediately starts to trip off of Beavis and Butthead.

"Huh-huh, huh-huh, huh-huh. You guys suck. Huh-huh, huh-huh, huh-huh. They don't get no ass. Huh-huh, huh-huh, huh-huh. Yeah. They're jerk-offs."

We all laugh hilariously.

Marshall looks to Derrick. "I mean, you gotta have a guy like him around, man. This nigga was born to lunch, Joe."

Derrick shakes his head, still grinning himself. "Anyway, I got two interviews comin' up next week. But one of them is in Baltimore."

"So you might be relocating?" I ask him curiously.

"Yeah, nigga! That's what people do when they get good jobs," Walt yells at me.

"What about you, Walt?" Derrick challenges.

"Oh, I'm thinkin' 'bout hookin' up wit' dem D.C. Service Corps niggas."

Marshall nods. "Yeah, I've seen them. Don't they all wear blue jackets?"

"Yeah."

"I've seen them before too. But what exactly do they do?" I ask Walt.

Walt gives me a puzzled smiled. "Oh, I'on really know yet, you'n."

We die laughing for about the twentieth time at Walt's craziness. He's a true comic case. You have to love this guy!

Derrick asks another question through his laughter. "How you gon' go and get a job and you don't even know what they do?"

"Look here, you'n: if them ma-fuckas is gettin' paid, I'on care what they do."

"See that? Walt's the kind of nigga that white people love to put in movies. And the whole goddamn world'll think we're all like him," Marshall says jokingly.

"Well, that's better than showin' them a nigga like you, jerkin' off in the bathroom," Walt snaps back.

"How do they perceive us in other countries, Wes? I mean, you were in Germany and all," Derrick asks me seriously.

"Well, the things they often have to go by are news reports, movies, TV shows, magazines, books and music. I mean, it's not like they can sit in here and hear black people having the type of conversations and doing the things that we do. They basically have a showbiz and a crime-and-poverty image of us."

"Oh, so like, a black middle class doesn't exist to them?" Derrick asks, trying his hardest to grasp it.

"Yeah, something like that. But remember, we *did* have *The Cosby Show* and *The Jeffersons* for them to watch."

"Did you *do* any German girls when you were over there?" Marshall asks me.

I look at Marshall humorously. "Marshall? How long have we known each other?"

"Since we went to Banneker together," he answers. Then he grimaces: "What was that, thirteen, fourteen?"

"And did I live in Germany then?"

"Naw."

"So, I mean, do you think I was sexing girls when I was a kid?"

Marshall laughs at himself. "Oh, my bad. I wasn't even thinkin'."

Walt shakes his head at him. "Y-u-u-u, big dummy!"

We just can't seem to stop laughing at Walt's hilarious antics. He's now imitating Redd Foxx from the *Sanford & Son* show. But I'm sitting here starting to think about NeNe again. I haven't spoken to her since Wednesday afternoon.

I sneak on the phone in Marshall's kitchen while the guys are still bugging out and dial my C&P telephone mail service.

NeNe has finally called. But not with any good news that I can tell through her whiny, stop-and-go, distraught speech.

"Man, umm, my cousin Toya . . . You'n, she umm, was out wit' . . . And . . ."

Hell, I can't understand this! I hang up on my phone mail service and call her aunt's house.

"You ain't callin' that bamma-ass young'un is you, Wes?" Walt walks into the kitchen asking me.

I turn the phone away from him as it rings.

"He better not. I already told that boy she ain't worth it," I hear Marshall yelling from the living room.

"Hello," NeNe answers with a cracked voice.

I shove Walt away from me.

He walks out of the kitchen shaking his head at me. "Yeah, she done put da whip appeal on his ass, you'n. Like a ma-fucka!"

I stretch the phone cord away from the living room entrance and deep into the kitchen, toward Marshall's untidy sink.

"What's goin' on?" I ask NeNe.

She sniffs before she answers me. "My cousin got shot, man. She umm, was out wit' Butterman and got hit in her back."

Okay, okay, okay. This shit is terrible! But what can I do?

"Well, is she in the hospital or what?" I whisper. Lord knows I don't want the guys to hear any of this. I'd get a bunch of "I told you so."

NeNe gets hysterical. "In'na fuckin' hospital? She *dead*, you'n! My fuckin' cousin is dead!"

SHIT! I don't need this at all. Not at all!

"So where is J?"

"I'on fuckin' know, you'n." NeNe whines this out in the painful drawl that people have when they're extremely upset. "I mean, his ass ain't call us back when we kept pagin' him yesterday. And, umm, I think they went and did somethin' crazy."

No, Shank! DAMN! It won't change shit, man! It won't change a damn thing!

"So, so, you want me to be there for you or what?" I ask her nervously, stuttering.

"Yeah, man. I need'ju, Wes. I need'ju like shit. I can't even think right."

"I'm coming, now. Okay?"

She sniffs and answers, "Okay."

I hang up the phone. I walk back out of the kitchen, past the guys and head to Marshall's basement apartment entranceway.

Derrick looks at me as if I've lost it. "Where you goin', Wes? We got the Ritz tonight."

"I'll be back," I tell him, quickly opening the door.

I hear Walt through the closed door when I reach the outside, "That boy ain't comin' back, Joe! You know exactly where he goin'!"

I run down to Eleventh Street to see if a 64 bus is coming. Since it's Sunday, I know that the buses are going to be running slow.

No 64 bus is in sight, so I jog down to U Street to catch the Cardozo Metro. I jump on the Yellow Line and ride it to Chinatown at Seventh Street, where I transfer to the Blue Line toward Addison Road.

I'm thinking about nothing but Toya, J, Shank, NeNe and the terrible street violence of this nation's capital city. I see no people, just images and colors as my mind races to my destination before I can actually get there. I can't bring NeNe's cousin back. Where the hell is J? And I'm hoping Shank hasn't finally killed someone.

God, I like him! We need more of his kind of bravery on our side and not on the devil's side.

I get off the Blue Line Metro at the Minnesota Avenue stop and run back to Benning Road Northeast, toward NeNe's aunt's house.

Before I reach her short street along this dark, commercial area on Benning Road, I see groups of young black men, standing, profiling, and looking. And now I'm suddenly cautious. I've always been in a car when I've come to pick NeNe up or see her. I would pass these same tough faces again and again without actually having to be near them like I am now. It's Sunday, the weather is warm, it's past eight-thirty and the sun has already set.

I eye a few of them to my right and a few of them leaning on cars to my left. Up the street toward NeNe's block are more of them. I feel guilty that I suspect them. But how would you feel in this situation when you never really had to pass through this type of shit? I mean, I've always been where these kind of brothers are not. And when I was with Shank, Steve, Otis and Rudy, I knew that they were on *my* side.

I slow down my walk and try to take it easy as I notice even more guys standing inside of an alleyway to my left, behind a corner store. Maybe it would be a good idea to speak and keep going as if everything is cool. I mean, why am I acting paranoid?

"Hi y'all doin'?" I ask a few of them, breaking my English. But when I look into their skeptical brown faces only a couple of them even hint at a response.

Out of nervousness, I find myself being driven inside of the corner store.

"Who da fuck is he?" I hear one of them ask as I enter with a racing heart.

The store has a stench of old, stale food. One thick-built Korean man is out walking the floor between two tightly-packed aisles of groceries, candies, cookies and bags of chips and pretzels. Alongside the left wall are Coca-Cola freezers, packing sodas, juices, milk and alcohol.

I grab a Tropicana orange juice from the freezer and a

bag of fifty-cent corn chips from the front. The thickly-built Korean man on the floor nods to me with a slight smile. I approach the elevated cash register situated behind a bullet-proof glass and put two dollars on the rotating counter for the middle-aged Korean woman.

"One fifty-nine," she says, bagging my food and returning my change.

I pocket the forty-one cents and grab my bag from the rotating bullet-proof counter. I glance out the door to see if I can spot where these brothers are before I walk back out. Before I reach the door, a young sister appears to be shoved inside the store, giggling.

"Stop, nigga! You play too damn much!" she hollers out of the open door to one of them.

I get by her, hoping that her distraction will allow me to get around this last corner and up the street without them paying me any mind. My heart starts to thump as I receive a sudden silence from four black males, all dressed in dark, undescribable clothing. The only thing I would be able to say is, "They were all dressed in dark jeans and dark sweatshirts"—which many of these youths dress in today. I'd sound like a paranoid white man.

"Yo, you'n, you got a couple dollars on you?" one of them asks me.

Oh God! Why me? WHY ME? I keep walking as if I didn't hear it.

"Fuck you can't hear or somethin', Joe?"

I turn and face him. He's slightly shorter than me and slightly browner, with a black bandanna tied around his head, dressed in clothing that can camouflage him in the tinted darkness. But it's only dark in this particular spot. I see more light up the street from us. And the cars riding down Benning Road give me a sense of security that this brother's not going to do anything stupid. *He's not that crazy,* I'm hoping.

"Naw, man, I'm just trying to get to my girl's house," I tell him apologetically. Which is absurd! Why should *I* apologize? And now my jumping, burning heart and nerves have me answering questions not even asked. He didn't ask me where I was going anyway.

"What? Joe, I'on give a fuck who you know around here. You got some money or what?"

I look past him at the other three guys, hoping that they don't file in line to back him. Not to mention several more of them from around the opposite corner. I feel like I'm in a war zone. My mission is to make it to the end of this block and then scramble up the street to NeNe's aunt's.

I slowly take out my wallet from my back blue jean pocket.

Don't give him anything! Make your stand against this craziness! NOW!

NO! Give him what he wants and secure your life. You're only one man, Wes. Remember that.

That's right. I have a whole lot of living to do yet. I'm going to grad school next year.

I hold my bag in my left arm and open up my wallet to hand him two dollars. He looks down at it and back into my face as if I'm being unreasonable.

"Muthafucka, if you don't give me ya money, I'll silence ya life right here!" He draws inside his pants and pulls out a gun. Over his shoulder I can see the others starting to walk toward us. I don't know if they're going to help me or him. But I don't have time to wait and find out!

I chop down on his arm holding the gun as hard and as fast as I can with my free right hand. It's a move my father taught me when I was eight and living in Germany. He taught it to me to disarm a stick or a knife. But it works with guns too.

The gun flies from this brother's hand as he jerks to grab his right arm. "SHIT, NIGGA! Yo, fuck him up, you'n! Fuck this nigga up!"

I drop the orange juice and corn chip bag from my arm and run for my life with my wallet still in my left hand.

"WE GOT ONE!" I hear them yell as I break around the corner and reach the bottom of NeNe's aunt's block.

I'm not foolish enough to run straight like in *Boyz in the Hood*. NeNe's aunt lives on the left side of the street that I'm already on; however, safety tells me to zig-zag in and out of these parked cars and holler for help.

"HELLLLLP! HELLLLLP!"

BOP! BOP!

Glass flies from car windows as I continue running.

BAP! BAP!

BOP! BOP!

OH SHIT! I'M HIT! NO-O-O!

I'm still running and heading for NeNe's aunt's, hollering, "HELLLLLP! HELLLLLP!"

I can't feel my right arm!

OH, GOD! MY CHEST IS BURNING! PLEASE, GOD! NO-O-O! LET ME LIVE!

"What da hell is goin' on out here!" I hear a deep, booming voice yell.

"Call'la cops. They just shot that boy!" another voice hollers.

I slam into NeNe's aunt's screen door and fall through it. NeNe opens it up with large eyes.

"OOOOOW! OH MY GOD!"

"Get him inside," a male voice says, lifting me up from behind.

Then a feminine voice: "We called the cops already. Just lay him out on the floor."

"WESSS! DON'T DIE ON ME, MAN! DON'T DIE!"

I can feel my chest rising frantically. "Huff, huff, huff."

AIR! AIR! BREATHE! BREATHE!

I see NeNe's teared face over me. "No, no, NO-O-O-O! WES, BABY, DON'T CLOSE YOUR EYES! DON'T CLOSE YA FUCKIN' EYES!"

The feminine voice: "Calm down. All we can do is wait for the police."

The deep, male voice: "Goddamn shame! Young'uns ain't got no damn sense."

My chest is caving in! My head feels light! I'm shaking. I'm losing it! I'M LOSING IT!

Oh, God! I'm sorry, Mom! I'M SORRY! I LOVE YOU! MOOOOOOM!

Epilogue

Butterman AKA Jeffrey Kirkland, Jr.

Twenty-four people were killed in Washington during one week in June. The homicide rate was up to like, 232.

It's August now. I'm chilling down in Hampton, Virginia, hiding out until shit calms down in D.C. I got a slammin'-ass beach-front apartment with a balcony. Only cost me $725 a month. But I have to pay the utilities.

That nigga Shank cut me a short and got me for fifteen grand! It's my own fault though. I started to trust that nigga too much. He wasn't my real friend or no shit. I guess now I'll just hustle here and there and wait for my boy Red to get out of Lorton in like, a year or two, you know? I still got eighty Gs in the bank for us.

Wes ended up getting shot in the shoulder right on NeNe's aunt's block off Benning Road Northeast—the same day that I jetted out. Boy thought he was dead, but he had just lost a lot of blood and he fucked around and fainted.

Wes is cool. He ain't deserve that shit; niggas are just getting too crazy out here. I heard he's going to grad school next year now. I wish him nothing but luck. *Nothing* but luck!

Me? Just let me say this: I fucked around and waited for Shank's ass that Saturday up at Super Trak, and that nigga never came. We checked that Brookland Apartments building where I let him off. Them boys acted like they never even heard of Shank. Then Jerry and them were like, "Fuck him! Let's roll."

We rolled down to Max and then set up around H Street Northeast, and hopped out with all our guns and shit. But something told me to chill by the car for a few.

As soon as Max and his boys came out from around the back, he was yelling, "Yo, we ain't do that dumb shit, Joe! What's up wit' all dis? I was jus' bullshittin' wit'chu." He was talking about killing Rudy and Kevy in that shoot-out with them Benning Road niggas.

I mean, I knew Max and them ain't do that shit. I just wanted to find out exactly who we were up against, you know? But stupid-ass Jerry shot at him anyway before I could even say shit.

All I heard was: *BOP! BOP! BOP!* Niggas separated on both sides and started breaking every which way. Max had, like, eight of his boys against us.

Steve broke back to the car with me. "Let's get da fuck out'a here, you'n! That nigga Jerry out his damn mind."

Yo, he ain't even have to tell me twice!

As soon as we started to roll, I thought about picking the rest of them niggas up; they were trapped in all them gunshots like some kind of old-fashioned cowboy movie. Then a police cruiser whipped around the corner from the left.

That shit ran right past me and Steve like they didn't know we were in it. Then we heard more sirens coming when we made it around that first corner. So I rolled the lemon back over to Northwest on Florida Avenue, where me and Steve left it and jumped out to break around his crib down in the Shaw area, behind Howard University.

Next day, I packed up my shit, jumped in my 3000 and rolled. Word was out that them niggas found out where I lived, so I was out before the sun came up.

Steve told me Otis and Boo both got shot at and arrested with like, four of Max's niggas. Max was shot dead, taking three bullets in his chest. Jerry almost escaped, trying to run and jump on a 92 bus at Eighth and H Streets. But Max's trigger-man, who Shank had punked out with that handshake shit when we rolled around there that time, ran Jerry down. He shot him in broad daylight in front of like thirty witnesses out on that busy-ass intersection. And do you know that you'n ran around in an alley and the cops never caught him? Ain't that some shit? Anyway, Jerry took one to the chest and one to the head. All this shit was in the newspapers. I guess he died like a real-ass nigga, hunh?

That makes me think of this new dumb-joke I made up. Because see, I ain't the one to sit around and wait to get snagged by no cops and sent to jail, or shot the hell up or no shit. Bink wouldn't have stayed around either. But that nigga Bink too damn cool to end up in some dumb shit like I'm in now anyway.

Well, here it goes: This dumb nigga robbed a bank for ten million dollars and got away with it. Then he hooked up his boys, his family, gave to charity, and lived like he was about to die of AIDS in a year, buying up everything he could get his hands on.

After a while, the jealous niggas that didn't get paid started to dime on him, helping the feds to track down all the loose money.

And when the FBI finally caught up to his ass, one

white investigator laughed and said, "Shit, man, with all that damn money *you* got away with, you could'a been living in fucking Australia by now! I mean, I just don't get it. Why did you choose to stay in the same dirty neighborhood?"

Dude looked up at him, hand-cuffed to a chair with droopy-ass eyes, and said, "Well, ta tell ya da honest t' God truth, Mr. Officer. I, ahh, didn't think I was allowed to leave da country. And I's afraid'a wo'da."

I shake my head and smile . . . "Dumb muthafucka."

And what? I mean, I can't bring Latoya the fuck back! *I'm* still living . . . and, you know, I'm trying to move on with my life. But for real though . . . I'm lonely like shit. I don't feel nothing but emptiness. Then I saw that *Poetic Justice* movie last week, and that shit ain't do me *no* damn good! So I guess in the long run, Red was right: "Crime don't pay." And I still ain't really speaking to my family. That's fucked up! Ain't it?

But on the real tip, money ain't shit when nobody loves you. Wes was right too: I don't know what love is. But how can a nigga love in this fucked-up-ass world they got us living in?

Dirty money leads to dirty living every time. So I guess I'm a pig now . . . that don't fly straight. *Scarface.* 1983.

Wes AKA Raymond West

I am a very lucky man. It's Monday, November 22, 1993. And I'm still living.

When I got shot in May, the bullet went into my right shoulder and lodged inside the bone and muscle fiber under my right arm. The doctors said that they could actually allow it to stay there without it doing any harm, but my mother insisted that they take it out.

I was told she screamed, "Are you crazy! I don't want no damn bullet sitting inside my son's body! What the hell kind of doctors are you?"

I laughed when I was told about it. But I was unconscious when it happened.

My mother went on to curse NeNe out in English, Spanish *and* German! She didn't want her "ten *miles* in radius to my son!"

I didn't at all agree with this. But I wasn't exactly in any position to argue, was I? The only thing my mother knew was that her only child had gotten himself shot while trying to visit "some loose floozy" that he had gotten himself somehow mixed up with.

Of course, NeNe didn't take this lying down. I was told that a big mess ensued inside D.C.'s General Hospital hallway over who could and who could not visit Raymond West, "during his recovery or *ever!*" my mother had argued.

It took three months for me to gain full recovery of the proper use of my right arm. I then ended up receiving a population statistics research job in Virginia where I can actually use some of the things that I studied in political science. I did well on my GRE Exam and Professor Cobbs secured me a scholarship to help out with financing grad school next year—along with the money I still haven't told my mother about. He also allowed me to talk to the Southeast youth who participated in his program this past summer.

It seems they were all excited about asking me how I knocked a gun away from a guy, and how I felt when I got myself shot. I guess these events have now validated me as one who *knows* how it is—which is crazy! However, I don't think they would have listened to me quite so pointedly had I not knocked away a gun, kept my wallet, gotten myself shot at and lived to tell about it.

They did catch two of the guys suspected of assaulting and shooting me that night, but on some other charges.

Newspapers and TV crews wanted a story, but my mother ran *them* away as well. All they were concerned about was running some gang- or street-related crime-buster story anyway. The white media doesn't give a damn about young black men like me! How about interviewing guys like me before we get shot or killed?

The big news today is that the government voted against having D.C. become the nation's fifty-first state by a congressional vote of 277 to 153. D.C. Congress-woman Eleanor Holmes Norton is now beefing up the fight, speaking about how unfair "taxation without representation" is to the District.

A month earlier, Mayor Sharon Pratt Kelly had actually asked President Bill Clinton if she could deploy the National Guard to control crime-infested areas inside the District. Not only did Clinton turn her down, but D.C. police officers were pretty pissed off, saying that she had earlier cut police budgets and lessened the police population in the District.

In the hip-hop world, Tupac Shakur is in constant trouble, Snoop Doggy Dogg is set to release his album *Doggy Style* this week—with a trial coming up for the alleged murder of a man in California at the end of this month—and the media looks as if it's launching a full-fledged war against "gangster lyrics," claiming that it instigates a lot of the crime, sex, drug use and black-on-black murder.

On the more positive side though, I've just finished reading *Essence* magazine's special November issue on black men in which they interviewed Arsenio Hall and Speech from Arrested Development. Queen Latifah has an awesome song in "U.N.I.T.Y". Tupac's "Keep Ya Head Up" now looks hypocritical for Tupac after being charged in New York city for supposedly sodomizing a 20-year-old woman along with a group of friends. Two weeks before that he was arrested for shooting two police officers in Atlanta. But he hasn't been proven guilty in either case yet, so let me hold my thoughts on it.

Anyhow, several other songs are being made against violence like "Gangsta Lean" and "Put Down The Guns."

Speaking about rap music, I wonder what Shank is up to. I sure hope he hasn't gotten himself killed or arrested. Walt told me that J ran from the District for his life. I've heard nothing about Shank, so I guess he's somewhere in hiding too.

Me? Well, my mother kind of forced me to move back in with her until I decide what grad school I want to go to next fall. She's been hinting at Howard to keep me near. I mean, I feel like some kind of Mommy's boy! But what can I really say to her after getting myself shot and almost killed? She wants to know every damn place I go now and demands a phone number! She actually calls to check up on me too!

"I can't let you get away from me, honey. You *are* my only son," she constantly tells me now.

By the way, Howard's football team went 11-0 this year and will be playing in the Division I playoffs for a bowl game next week. Isn't that something!

As far as NeNe and my love life is concerned: I've been talking on and off with Sybil. But NeNe can't have this number, and she doesn't want to talk to me when I call her now anyway. I guess it was kind of embarrassing for even *her* to go up against my red-headed mother over her only son.

I just wish NeNe the best now. I hope that she's able to find another guy like me and stay on course toward a proper family home. I mean, God knows how so many young black women like her are ending up pregnant with no spouse. Then again, NeNe was always pretty conscious of protection against pregnancy. I *can* give her that credit.

As far as crime and the D.C. streets . . . I mean, what do you want me to do? Walt and Marshall and I still hang out, and Derrick received that job in Baltimore which only allows him to visit with us every other weekend. And all we can do is continue to live while staying away from problem areas.

I believe American society is rapidly approaching chaos that can't be stopped by laying blame on hip-hop culture, guns or the black family. The white supremacist culture of America and the world has to take the bulk of the responsibility. You can't expect black people to continue to live within conditions of fluctuating poverty forever without them going crazy. Something's going to have to be done to uplift the spirit and morale of the American poor, and it can't be done with words. America must find some capital to eventually shell out and begin to reverse this wheel of destruction.

All I, Raymond West, can do is live, marry and raise proper children who will do their best to live right and call out against injustice. Like the concerned citizens who scared away those guys and called the police for me when I got shot that night, more people are going to have to stand up against not only crime, but unemployment, foreign-trade policy and all the other gimmicks employed to keep the poor poor. And if more people were able to keep their thoughts and actions positive, we could change a lot of things. But then again, conscious people have been saying this since the beginning of time.

In a nutshell, the elder brother Tony was right: We black Americans are gonna have to accept responsibility for what we become and how we react to situations in our community, not "the man."

I know, I know, I'm starting to preach to you, right? Well, guess what? I'm planning to teach and continue to do the best that I can do to get involved in bringing about a reversal of the dire situation in our community. Now, what are you planning to do?

Shank AKA Darnell Hall

It's 1994. four hundred and sixty-seven were killed in D.C. in '93, fifteen more than last year. My mom told me a white cop was one of the last to die when he got shot in the face on Fourteenth street around my old neighborhood in Southeast.

I've been in New York now since last summer with my cousin Cal. Me and Mom write each other and talk on the phone now. Well, I do more writing and she does more phone calling. She keeps me up on the D.C. news and shit, like when their water system was fucked up for three days. And when like, twelve D.C. cops were arrested for some crooked-ass shit that they were doing on the streets.

Yeah, me and my cousin Cal been hanging out in New York with a whole crew of cool artist-type niggas since last July. We even ended up getting jobs with this movie company when this white man heard us arguing about that movie *Menace II Society* in this popular deli restaurant in Manhattan. I mean, you'd be surprised how many people in New York are trying to get paid.

Anyway, I was saying to Cal that that *Menace II Society* shit wasn't going to change anything. But my cousin was saying that they showed "the real," and how niggas don't be thinking. Yeah, whatever.

Then this hip, happy-faced white man introduced himself and asked us if we would like to read and review movie scripts, you know, to give his company the young black male point of view on film. It was just me and Cal that day, and I let Cal do the talking because I still don't really fuck with white people like that. You know what I'm saying? Them motherfuckers have to prove peace to me. And then some!

Anyway, they pay us pretty good. I've been reading a lot and getting a whole lot of ideas from that shit to use in my raps. Plus, I see that Morgan Freeman finally got some balls by directing that Arsenio Hall movie, *Bopha*, about a South African family. Danny Glover played this father who wanted his son to join the police force even though his son was a revolutionary.

That shit was kind of good. White people are some motherfuckers though, ain't they? But right now I'm waiting for that Harlem movie, *Sugar Hill*, to come out. Dude that played the lead singer in *The Five Heartbeats*, Michael Wright, stars in it with Wesley Snipes. And *Surviving The Game*, starring Ice T—Ernest Dickerson's second movie after directing *Juice*—is coming out. And when Al Pacino's *Carlito's Way* came out up here, a lot of Puerto Ricans were excited. It was all right, too. But I don't know why they ain't use a real Latino. And why did he have to have a white woman as his girl? That's the type of questions me and Cal ask in our reports after we read the scripts. But of course they did it for the money; that's white people for you.

Me and Cal living all right! We got shit going on from our two-bedroom apartment in Queens. Then we meet up with the rest of the crew and ride to the parties and clubs and shit, like, thirty niggas deep sometimes. But we not into that tough-crew shit. I mean, I was about to fuck this nigga up in Harlem (Uptown) last week. Hopps was talking more shit than I could take from one nigga.

But my crew chilled that shit out. Squashed it, you know. We don't roll to get into no fights and shit. And like I always knew: a lot of times if you hang out with niggas that ain't right, your shit ends up not being right.

I wrote a song about that tough-type shit. But I don't glorify it like them west-coast rappers do. It's called "Lucky # 7."

Here's a little flavor bite. All right, bust this:

> *Yo, let me tell you the nitty gritty about America's capital city. A lot of brothers are living shitty. But up in G-Town them white folks is all high siddity.*
> *They like to print us on front pages. Shouting, 'Look at these criminals! Shouldn't we keep them in steel cages?'*
> *And many brothers ain't givin' a fuck. Living life, day by day on their luck, hoping they don't get bucked.*
> *But then I rolled a fuckin' seven. And like Griff said, I was a nigga headed for heaven.*
> *Now people say I smile more often. I guess so, my brother, I'm not a zombie in no coffin.*
> *Now later this year, I'm turning 21. I'm not a gangsta no more, and I'm no longer on the fuckin' run.*

I got *mad* skills now! Motherfuckers in New York are on it because I had an advantage when I first came up here. Niggas thought that I wouldn't have skills because I was from D.C. They were—at first—saying shit like, "Aw, hopps, D.C. niggas is *mad* fake. Them niggas be bitin' like fish to worms, G. You ain't got no skills, nigga. Get off da mike!"

Then I ripped shit on them like:

"I think it's 'bout that time, for Cool-ass Nell t' take front stage. So I can just jam what I slammed on my rhyme page, last night. Now watch as I blow and the crowds get hyped and ripe to my rhyme flow. But I don't rap all fast, 'cause I'm not Flash. My rhymes will stun, like a Funkadelic Bop Gun.

"I'm not out here to twist up my tongue or grime with wack styles. Or try to raise my voice and scream and holler with weak rhymes. Grab them suckers up by the collars for wastin' dollars. Because they only making record piles—that get smashed and trashed.

"Now I got cash that I stash with a status that's legal. I'm hittin' harder than Philly's Eagles. So don't fuck with me, brother! Choose another . . . My style is lethal."

Niggas went off! They were all on my dils-nick calling me L'il Rakim. I mean, a lot of these motherfuckers up here are trying to be so damn original that you don't really know what the hell they're saying. Then their delivery and timing be all messed up. But my shit is in there! And no more gangsta lyrics for me. Fuck that shit!

Like Big Daddy Kane said, *"Why should I settle for gangsta contrast/when I rap about gettin' some ass?"*

That's my nigga. He kicked it like: *"To prove that I'm a gansta only brings me trouble, but to prove that I'm a lover . . ."*

Yeah, that's the way I feel too now. But I don't really fuck around with these New York stunts. And believe me, these stunts up here are a trip! Girls are rough as shit up here. I don't know whether to talk to them or punch them in the mouth for talking shit with them fucked-up-ass attitudes. I guess if I was a New York nigga I'd know better how to deal with these biddies.

Anyway, I'm still talking to my baby Carlette. It's official now. She's my girl. She comes up here twice a month and stays for a weekend. Then Cal talks that silly shit: "Yo, this ain't no *School Daze*, nigga." But they like each other. I even wrote a song about my baby.

Oh, you want another flavor bite, hunh? It's called "Lady Love":

Some brothers are known to be hard as hell. Like this one named Nell, who was only headed for jail. But then her soft hand touched his chest. She kissed his cheek, and then laid his mind to rest. And on his lonely nights of stress, Lady's strong love was Nell's only and best request.
But then he was asked to pass her test.
She asked Nell to grant just one wish . . . Lady Love wanted his care like a gold-fish.

Yeah! That's some old, smooth groove-type shit for the ladies. Get like a mellow-ass track to hook it up right.

I still got twelve thousand dollars of that money I stung from Butterman in D.C. I got the shit in the bank now, too. Me and Cal bought some equipment to practice sampling, looping and hooking up beats and shit. Niggas we roll with have some shit too: turntables, drum machines and lots of old records. Plus, Cal been doing artwork on flyers and shit like that that niggas are paying good-ass money for.

I'm gon' have much, much, much flavor in '94! But I'm not ready for no contract yet. I mean, labels been asking me, but I got time and money *and* a job, so I ain't in no hurry. You know what I'm saying? I'm trying to make sure I got a good manager and a lawyer to get the most out of my contract. Plus, I wanna experiment with some more music and perfect my lyrical skills so the money can roll in right when I do blow up.

And as far as the criminal zone? As long as the white man owns this country and don't let niggas get a piece of the pie, they gon' keep killing and robbing and illin'. You can't expect *everybody* to be able to turn positive. I mean, I've always liked music and movies. I don't know what these other niggas out here are into. But as long as they can see other people getting paid, you can't expect them to just to sit around being poor and shit.

And as far as a lot of these niggas making violent raps, well, I'm trying to get away from that. I'm not gon' use that Mad Man rhyme. I'm looking more at perfecting my skills and talking about a range of different subjects. That Mad Man shit was kind of cartoonish anyway.

Right now the best new shit out in New York—to me—is Akinyele, once he stops that "utta, utta, utta" shit and just rhyme. Then you got Erick Sermon. The Tribe. Pudgee Tha Fat Bastard. The Soul. The School. Queen. Lyte. KRS-1 Man . . . and just a whole bunch of underground shit: Black Moon. Top Quality. Nasty Nas. Rumpletilskinz. Jeru The Damaja and the motherfucking Wu Tang Clan and that young'un Shyheim!

Without rap music, I think it would be a whole lot more crazy shit going on. So fuck all that bullshit the media is talking about! Them broadcasters just looking for a scapegoat to America's problems. I mean, Farrakhan got the *Torchlight* already. But you know, the white man damn sure ain't gon' listen to him. So, everything is everything.

All I can say is just go for yours like I did. But remember, I ain't never been to jail, I graduated from high school, I believe in myself, and besides all that crazy shit I used to do, I ain't never killed another nigga. Or I guess I should say, another black man caught up and confused in the struggle. Because that's what "niggas" are, caught up in it.

Now that's *the real*. Peace! And I'm out!

A Note From The Urban Griot

Everything worthwhile in life takes time and persistence. There is no such place as "easy street" no matter what you hear or what you see. So get over it.

However, I take exception to a particular view expressed within the text of *Capital City*. That is: I believe crime does pay. It pays with prison time, paranoia, your peace of mind, the lives of friends and family members, and eventually your *own* life. But I chose to tell a story of three survivors because I want us *all* to survive.

Fortunately, I didn't have the big-time friends within the drug trade to offer me cars, fast money, and sexy women. Honestly, like many other young black males in America, it would have been extremely hard for me to turn those offers down. But with the *lack* of those offers, I got a chance to maintain my freedom from a self-destructive lifestyle.

Sure, there are still many things that I would like to have, many places I would like to go, and many things that I would like to do. But sacrifice is a reality and a stage that we *all* have to go through in life in order to gain success.

Right now, I would love to have a multi-million-dollar film deal from a major studio. But since the people with the money and the connections have yet to step my way, I'm still pushing for it. But it's cool, because I'm a hustler, and life is the *big* hustle.

So this is *my* sacrifice to get me where I'm going. And recognize the game from a schooled old head: become skilled in something valuable, develop new ideas in it, con someone for the finance, and be prepared to starve while you flip and fry up the money. Because "easy street" ain't nothing but an uncooked pan of runny eggs on a broken stove. It won't fry.

The Urban Griot Series:

College Boy
Capital City
Cold Blooded

Future titles:

One Crazy Night
The Season
Room 517